ADVENT DARKNESS

THE SWORD OF DRAGONS
BOOK 4

Jon Wasik

For Natalie

A dear friend whose sense of humor is as dirty as mine,

And whose undying support has encouraged me for as long as we've known each other.

Also by Jon Wasik

The Sword of Dragons *(Reading Order)*
1. *Rise of the Forgotten*
1.5. *The Orc War Campaigns*
2. *Burning Skies*
3. *Secrets of the Cronal*
4. *Advent Darkness*

Chronicles of the Sentinels Trilogy
1. *Legacy*
2. *Retribution*
3. *Champions*

Project Sirius
1. *The Awakening*
2. *The Alpha Expedition*

CONTENTS

ACKNOWLEDGMENTS

Thank you to my wonderful Starshine, Beck Wasik, for believing in me every step of the way, and helping me through revision after revision, cover designs, layouts, and everything in between!

Thank you to my sister Tanya for never doubting I'd make it as a writer.

Thank you Wayne Adams for toughing it through the first round of beta reading. Thank you to Chloe for making such incredible maps!

Thank you to all of my social media followers, you all rock! Especially for putting up with someone who fails at social media as completely as I do.

And as always, thank you to the Welts family, especially Nick and Natalie for listening to all my ideas, for beta reading, and for cheering me on!

SWORD OF DRAGONS CHARACTER REFRESHER

Cardin Kataar – The Keeper of the Sword of Dragons, Cardin has been custodian of the powers and knowledge granted by the Sword for a year and a half. Most recently, he was crowned Prince of Tal, a position of power he desperately wishes to give up, but knows that he cannot while his father remains unconscious.

Kailar Adanna – Previously a Warrior in the Devor Guild, Kailar was dismissed after killing hundreds of innocent, mind-controlled civilians at the Battle of the Wizards' Guild. However, the up-and-coming leader of Devor saw great potential in Kailar and decided to appoint her as personal advisor.

Letan Velethar – A Lieutenant in the Devor Warriors. He remains a steadfast member of the Guild, and a former lover of Kailar's.

Sira Reinar – While still a Warrior and a Lieutenant in the Tal Guild, Sira has been placed on indefinite leave due to the unusual circumstances of sharing her mind and body with the soul of an unborn Star Dragon.

Reis Kalind – A non-magical Warrior, Reis has struggled to prove himself against Mages all of his life. However, when given the chance to hold the Sword of Dragons and gain power of his own, he refused, citing that it would not resolve the overall problem of the marginalized non-magic people of Halarite.

Anila Kovin – One of the Covenant's most trusted guardians, but with the Covenant gone, Anila now spends her days guarding the Cronal deep in the ancient dwarven city beneath Archanon.

Dalin – Once a Wizard, Dalin left the Guild when its new leader ordered him to disobey a promise made to the former Grand Master, Valkere. Now he acts as a personal advisor to Cardin, and struggles to adapt to his new life as a civilian.

Elaria – A gifted explorer, Elaria is a Dareann Elf who keeps finding herself drawn into the struggles of Halarite. She was last seen escorting the dwarf Gilrin back to Darea after the shattering discovery made in the ancient dwarven city. She sympathizes with the dwarves.

Gilrin – A dwarf of the Dareann College of Serelik, and unusual in that he is not of the servant class, he accompanied Elaria and Baenil to Halarite to explore the dwarven city. When he learned that ancient Dareann Elves were responsible for taking away dwarven magic, he threatened civil war.

Baenil – A member of the Dareann College of Serelik, Baenil is an archeologist who was caught exploring the catacombs beneath Archanon and was forced by the Covenant to help them uncover ancient secrets. He helped uncover the truth about what the Dareann Elves did to the dwarves.

King Eirdin Beredis – He was the former King of Tal, the most beloved ruler in centuries. In a rather nefarious plot, he was murdered by a wraith posing as one of the Six Gods.

Prince Idrill Beredis – He was largely responsible for his father's murder, but met a fate worse than death when the wraith consumed his soul in order to occupy his body.f

Wizard King Sal'fe – Ruler of Falind, Sal'fe has used the unique power of the Staff of Aliz to bring wealth to Falind, and has thus vastly improved its infrastructure and defenses. However, his true motives are unknown, and he has turned combative towards the Allied Council ever since Cardin was crowned Prince of Tal.

Queen Sechel Leian – Ruler of the eastern kingdom of Erien, Queen Leian now rules from the northern city of Lassil, after her capitol of Maradin was flooded by a tsunami, and then further devastated in the fight against the undead.

Grand Master Wizard Valkere – Former leader of the Wizards'

Guild, Valkere was killed holding off Nuuldan while the rest of the Wizards fled the former other-worldly Guild Hall.

Grand Master Wizard Syrn – Newly appointed ruler of the Wizards, Master Syrn is far more conservative than Valkere was, and has pulled most of the Wizards back into the Guild. She has taken on the role of Speaker in the Allied Council.

Nuuldan – The first Dark Dragon, formerly a Star Dragon, Nuuldan was long-thought dead until he fell from the stars and landed on Halarite. He has spent the intervening months seeking out methods to regain his power base.

Endri – A green-colored Star Dragon, Endri has been a mentor and companion to Cardin for nearly a year. When Cardin was crowned prince and could no longer spend adequate time training, Endri left to learn more about Nuuldan's actions and movements.

Amaya Kenla – Formerly a Tal Warrior, Amaya was imprisoned by Prince Beredis for refusing to follow an order to kill a bandit camp full of families. After King Beredis recovered, he pardoned her and her companions, and inducted them into the Guardians of Tal, a special unit of soldiers who answer directly to the King, and have the power to speak in his name. Her team played a pivotal role in ending the Orc War Campaigns. Her whereabouts since the end of the war are unknown…

General Arkad – A giant even amongst orcs, Arkad commanded the orcs on their home world, and then commanded them during the first months of the Orc War Campaigns. He was gravely wounded on the field of battle, and then was never again seen, presumed killed in action.

Tana – Shaman of the surviving orcs, she has lived on Halarite for nearly two years. After gathering as many orcs as she could, she led them deep into the Wastelands to hide from the humans. Her long-term goal is to one day stand united with the humans against the army that invaded her home world.

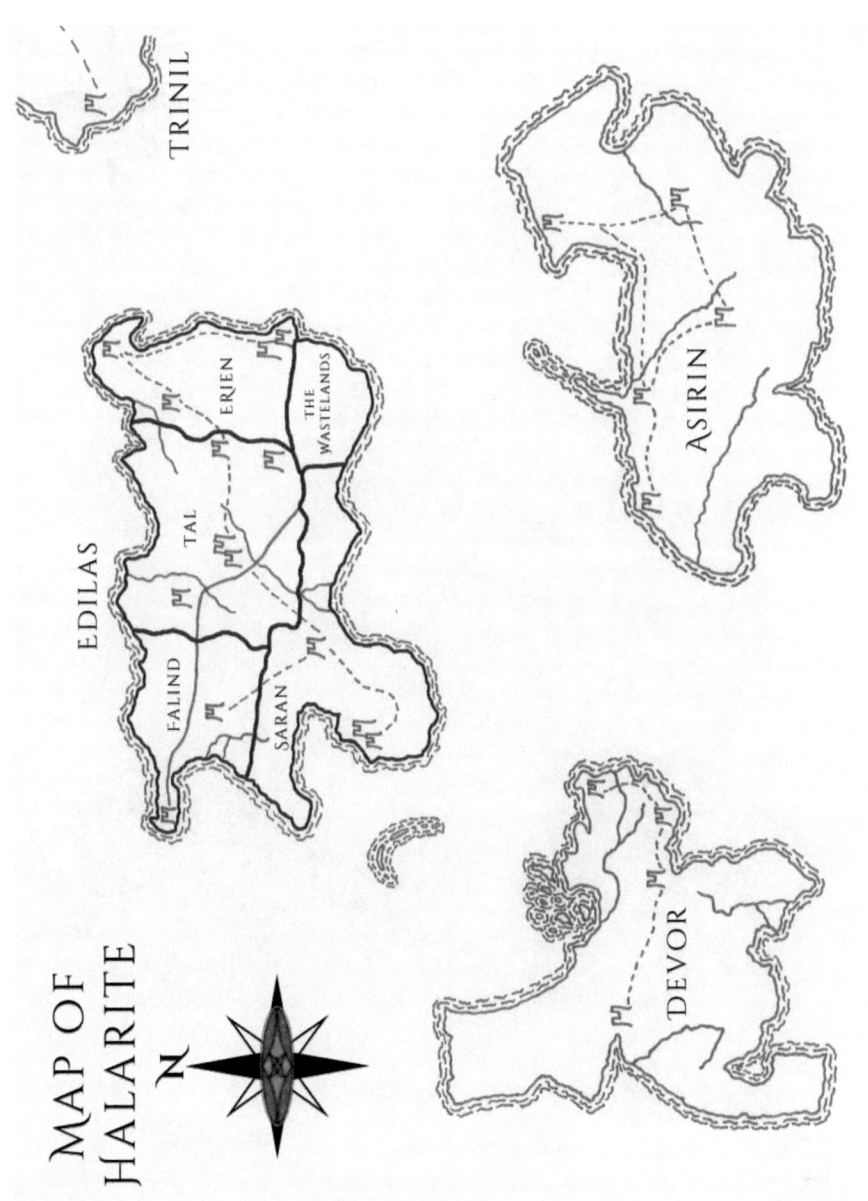

MAP OF HALARITE

N

TRINIL

EDILAS

FALIND

TAL

ERIEN

THE WASTELANDS

SARAN

ASIRIN

DEVOR

EDILAS

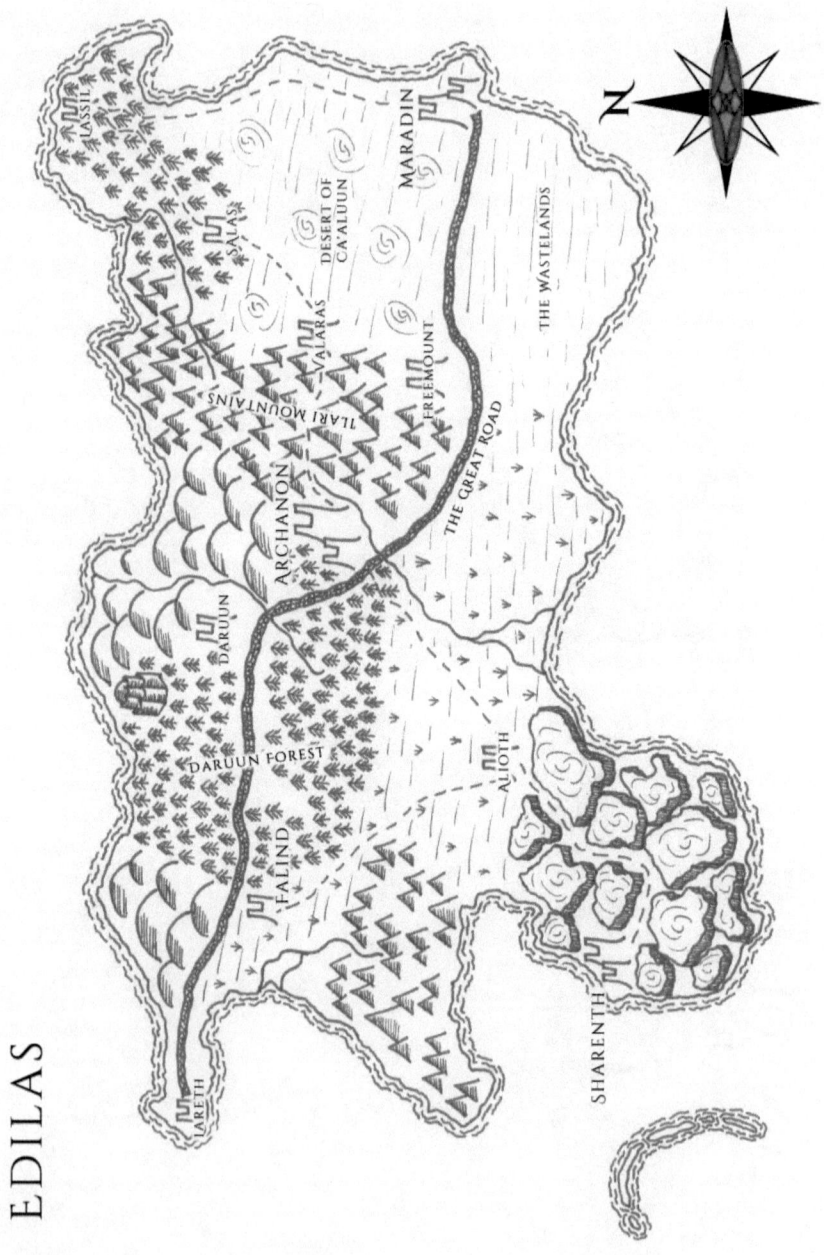

DEVOR

CRYSTAL BAY

CRYSTALLINE PEAKS

CRYSTALLINE FOREST

AGRIAT ISLANDS

BARRIER MOUNTAINS

TIERAN PORT

CORLAS

NEOLAS

EDINGARD

CENTRAL PLAINS

FROZEN PEAKS

PLAINS OF GLASS

N

ADVENT DARKNESS

They do not invade, they occupy;
When they arrive, you lost long ago...

A reckoning was at hand.

Unfortunately, it was *her* reckoning.

The warrior whose armor was segmented plate steel, darkened almost-black as part of its forging and enchantment process, marched through the corridors of the capitol building of her empire. Extendable armor-claws flinched in their sheaths as she, the warrior who had failed to secure the crystal on the Star Dragon home world, held her head high and squared her shoulders back, passing beside stone-black pillars and through a navy-blue stone corridor.

Weeks had passed since her failure on Stella, against a village of *monks*, against a Wizard and a *human* woman who fought ferociously, but whose power was pitiful compared to the warrior's. Weeks in which she might just have thought, hoped, even dreamt that she would escape punishment.

Until the summons arrived by way of messenger, who sneered at her with contempt as he hand-delivered the orders.

Never-the-less, she would not cower, she would not waver. After all, she was the last of her house. The only survivor from a family that had once ruled her world for millennia. She did not cower before her conqueror then, and she certainly would not now.

I am Aezara Tanlen, she thought. *Daughter of the last true Emperor.*

The vast double-doors ahead of her were already wide-open, a foreboding welcome to the court. The doors were pitch-black, a stark contrast against the navy-blue walls, but matched by the equally-black pillars and mirror-marble black floor. The throne room, as she entered with her head held high and her shoulders squared, was likewise-colored, but had the addition of multiple great black banners hanging from the ceiling, bearing the blue sigil of House Zelnir, the ever-watchful eye.

It was said that the eye embroidered into the banners was enchanted, and anywhere they resided, the Emperor could see. Today, the Eye of Sageth Zelnir would watch her punishment, of that she had no doubt.

Striding across a golden carpet, Aezara ascended the first flight of stairs towards the throne, and then knelt upon the landing before it and bowed her head. Three thousand years ago, such an act would have been uncomfortable in plate armor, but now, trapped as she was within, she was accustomed to it.

"My Lord," she spoke, her voice raspy through the steel helmet.

Sageth sat upon his throne, which was a black, enchanted chair carved directly from the natural stone of their world. Artificial ley lines, which were etched into the throne and flowed down into the carved and polished stone beneath, glowed white, while the Emperor's pale, sky-blue hands rested upon them. His eyes flared fire-orange as he stared down at her, an imposing figure. Long, black hair was pulled back into an elaborate, looping ponytail, and his violet robes hung tight against his well-built frame.

Even thousands of years old, Sageth was an imposing and daunting figure to most, a vision that the people could rally behind.

When he spoke, his voice echoed with a tone that he always imbued within his speech, giving him a supernatural, menacing tone. "Aezara." A pause. "Take that helmet off."

With his permission given, enchantments released their hold, and at her mental command, the helmet automatically separated into multiple pieces and peeled away like an onion, revealing beneath a blue-white, translucent face. The segments of her helmet lay flat against her pauldron and cuirass, allowing long, unkempt sea-green hair room to breathe.

For the diminished look she might have had, one thing was never conquered by her Emperor – the fire in her eyes, flaring bright-orange as she opened her eyes and stared at the cloth boots of her conqueror. "You summoned me, My Lord."

The Emperor's vizier, a scrawny man at seven feet tall, appeared at Sageth's side, handing him a black stone tablet, enchanted so that he could use a stone to either swipe through existing writings upon it, or to write his own words. Gazing upon the tablet, the Emperor's impassive face read for a moment. "You have failed in your mission."

Aezara clenched her jaw. "I have, My Lord."

He looked upon her then. "You have not failed in two and a half thousand years."

She knew punishment was coming, but she tried to judge how severe it would be by the sound of his voice. He was calm, cool, collected, and one might have thought that she might be spared the worst. Unfortunately, she had seen him spend three days executing a rival with that same demeanor, and so she feared that it did not bode well for her.

"I give my most sincere apologies, My Lord," she spoke with all reverence. Her eyes darted to the tablet, then back at Sageth's feet. "If you wish, I can describe beyond my report the events of the battle."

The battle where she had been sent to retrieve a mysterious, powerful crystal on Stella, guarded by a being she had only known as Naerala. A being, as it turned out, who was a Star Dragon in a humanoid guise.

She held her breath, waiting for the pain. The armor she was cursed to wear would no doubt become the instrument of her torture, as it had so often throughout the millennia. Any moment, and it would begin…

"There is no need," he spoke at length. "Much has been brought to my attention since then. Our…" The Emperor hesitated, glancing over his shoulder, towards a vast array of curtains behind him that separated the throne room from a balcony overlooking their capitol city. "*Ally*," he said the word with some distaste, "neglected to tell us what the crystal actually was."

Aezara had heard little news of Stella since her hasty retreat. "May I inquire what it was, Lord?"

Sageth looked down upon her contemptuously. "A Star Dragon chrysalis."

She almost literally jolted from surprise. "A dragon egg, My Lord?"

"Yes," he nodded. "The spirit of which now resides within the human woman you fought."

Her eyes furtively glanced back and forth as she considered the implications, and the pieces connected all at once. "Our ally wished to infect the chrysalis before birth," she said, still keeping her eyes downcast. "He wished a dragon to be born of dark magic."

With a thoughtful nod, Sageth released his grip upon the armrests of his throne, the white glow of the ley lines dying almost instantly, and he pressed his fingers together. "Yes. It might have been an interesting event to bear witness to."

It might have brought about a horrible darkness, too. Aezara knew that whatever reason the Dark Dragon, Nuuldan, had wanted the crystal for, it would not bode well for the Universe. Now she was glad that she had failed her mission.

"I do not believe it coincidence," the Emperor spoke, and she felt her jaw clench. Did he know her thoughts? "Yet another powerful magical convergence upon Halarite and one of its denizens." No, he didn't know. His thoughts dwelt elsewhere. Perhaps she might come out of this unpunished after all.

Tearing her mind away from her selfish desire to avoid pain, Aezara thought of his statement. The world of Halarite, populated by humans who, until recently, thought themselves alone in the Universe, had indeed found itself at the center of many vitally important occurrences, past and present.

As if following her thoughts, the Emperor began to recount all that they were aware of. "Five thousand years ago, a world was destroyed, the refugees of which fled to Halarite." *The Necromancers of Vestuul,* she inwardly nodded. "Remnants of that world bearing the unconscious body of our new ally has crashed down upon Halarite. Three thousand years ago, after the Sword of Dragons was forged, it was given to the Wizards to hide upon Halarite. Then, one of their Wizards found the orc world and used his powers to subvert thousands of them to his will and seize control of Halarite." *The Wizard Klaralin.* "He failed to hold power, only for us to stumble upon his wretched, loathing self when we invaded the orc homeworld. Allowing us to use him as our first instrument of subversion upon Halarite, planting the seeds that are already growing to fruition. Disaster fell upon them when the remnants of Vestuul crashed. And now…"

He paused and leaned forward, gazing down upon Aezara. "Now their most powerful kingdom lies in the ruins of civil unrest and near-destruction by a wraith."

More shocking news. Aezara had yet to hear of this incident. She had been too busy preparing for the invasion of Darea.

For the first time that visit, she gazed up into the burning eyes of her conqueror. "A wraith?"

"One of their own making," he nodded. "And he helped reveal the presence of a powerful artifact of dwarven and elvish design that lies beneath Archanon."

Her mind raced with the implications. All of these incredible things, all centered around Halarite.

Only one other world that they knew of had ever seen such a confluence before. Their own world. Their home.

"You believe another Conduit is on Halarite," she exclaimed in awe.

His otherwise stoic face cracked the barest hint of a smile. "Yes. It is the only explanation."

Barely conscious of her actions, she glanced behind her, down the corridor she had entered from. Beyond which lay the true source of the Darksteel Army's power.

The Conduit.

Sageth stood up and circumnavigated his throne, and with a wave of his hand, the curtains drew apart, revealing the vast expanse of the capitol city. Reddish-yellow light spilled in from their sun, a sickly color that she would never grow accustomed to. Clasping his hands behind him, Sageth gazed out upon that city. Upon a dying world.

"Our need for a new Conduit grows greater every day, Aezara," he spoke louder. "If one is indeed on Halarite, we must conquer them now."

Startled, she stood up without realizing what she was doing. "My Lord, we are not ready. Our troops have already committed to the Darea campaign, we cannot stop now…"

"Do not lecture me, child!" His wrath came full-blown, and her suit of armor, touching every inch of her body, sent searing, agonizing pain into every nerve ending. Aezara collapsed to the ground, her breath catching in surprise from immeasurable pain.

In an instant, or perhaps after a year, the pain ended, and her vision, swimming as it was, returned to her. Sageth stood over her now, his right hand slowly rejoining the other behind his back.

With her body complaining at every inch of movement, she returned to her kneeling position. That was the punishment she had expected. Except that Sageth had waited until she no longer expected it. He no doubt drew great pleasure from toying with his victims that way…

"Our forces have grown sufficiently by now," Sageth spoke, his quiet resolve returned. "The invasion of Darea will continue. Keep our naval forces fully committed. Use any ground and air forces that we can spare for Halarite. Assemble them, train them, brief them. Gather whatever intelligence you require. Before the year is out, I want Halarite under our rule, so that we may begin our search for the Conduit in earnest. Do you understand me?"

She blinked away the remnants of tears and pain and pressed her forehead to his boots. "Yes, My Lord. I will take charge."

"And take that human general with you," Sageth said as an afterthought while he returned to his throne. "This will tell us whether our efforts with him have been successful."

"Yes, My Lord," she repeated, carefully guarding her thoughts.

Resuming his seated position, the Emperor rested his hands upon his throne, the ley lines thrumming to life and reverberating against her soul. She took that as a dismissal, and immediately bowed out of the throne room. Once through the doors, she turned away from him, and composed herself.

Once she could stand straight again, she marched away, while hiding her thoughts from her face.

Another Conduit. It would begin all over again. A sickening emptiness grew in her stomach, but as she passed multiple imperial guards, she kept her face as stoic as she could. She could not let them, or any of Sageth's eyes, see her break.

Eventually she found her way out of the great corridors of the capitol and stepped out into the air. Aezara wished she could say fresh air, but it hadn't been fresh in centuries. She stared out at the vista, beyond the gleaming skyscrapers of an overly wealthy population, to the deadlands beyond. The haze of a reddish dust storm slammed against the city's weather shield, lighting up the sky in a cascade.

Her world was dying.

The question was, what would she do? If another Conduit was

found, would she let it happen all over again?
Could she watch another world die?

Chapter 1

THE NEW GENERAL

Prince Cardin Kataar.

Even three months later, it sounded strange in his head. Never in his life could Cardin have guessed that he would be Prince of Tal, or royalty of any kind.

Yet there he sat, on the raised throne in Archanon Castle with a silver crown atop his brow, his growing almost-black hair helping it fit snugly, and wearing black and silver courtly robes. *What I wouldn't give for a simple pair of trousers and a tunic,* he thought to himself, feeling itchy and overly hot, buried as he was beneath layers of cloth in the warmth of Edilas's summer.

The throne room was a long hall, serving as a mead hall in ages past, but now adorned with great statues of former rulers that stood taller than the throne, reaching almost fifteen feet high and gazing down upon all who visited. A marble floor was broken up by a long, red carpet that stretched from the foot of the steps of the throne all the way to the double entrance doors.

Standing upon that carpet, staring up at Cardin indignantly, was the newest Warrior General, a man named Ackaron Vellar. Voted into his position only yesterday by the remaining Warrior Commanders, Ackaron was a tall, broad man, with perfectly-cut sandy-brown hair and deep brown eyes. Cardin had hoped for a better choice. Or at least, a man who was less like the now-disgraced General Idann Kale.

Not a day didn't go by that Cardin didn't begrudge his own new position as Prince. Today was possibly the worst of them all.

"The Warriors simply will no longer accept letters of mark from the throne," Ackaron stated smugly, his hands planted on his hips. Cardin, seated ten feet up from Ackaron, tried desperately not to roll his eyes. For three months, he'd wondered why the Tal throne was sat upon such a high pedestal, but now he thought he understood — from up here, any subject's attempt to appear intimidating merely looked ridiculous.

Governor Maral, Archanon's longest-standing governor, stood at the base of the stairs and glared at Ackaron. "As we have already informed the Warriors," she spoke, her wizened voice sharp and clear, "We are undergoing a substantial reorganization of all financial matters in the kingdom to overcome the shortcomings that Prince Kataar inherited. You will be paid in due time."

Refusing to look at Maral, Ackaron's eyes remained fixed on Cardin. "With all due respect, you have had three months to resolve the situation! We no longer trust the throne to honor its dues."

The rumbling of anger was already growing within Cardin's chest, a rushing sensation that sparked his blue eyes. "That is not for you to determine," Cardin retorted harshly. "Nor is it my intention to further discuss our reserves with you. You have a duty to the people of Tal…"

"I have a duty to my Warriors," Ackaron interrupted.

"You dare interrupt your Prince?!" Maral scolded, aghast. She flashed warning eyes at Cardin, and he recognized the danger, too. Ackaron, unlike Idann, was bold.

"Merely because I am tired of the rhetoric," Ackaron replied, still refusing to meet Maral's eyes. The longer he did so, the more convinced that Cardin was of his arrogance. "We have been fed the same line for three months, ever since the truth about the castle's empty coffers was made public."

That had been a calculated move on Idrill Beredis's part to usurp the throne from his father, Eirdin. It had worked, too. Combined with the magical influence of a possessed Covenant member, it had incensed the farmers and other peasantry of Archanon to riot, and created the distraction necessary for the Prince and the possessed Pevrin to murder Eirdin.

Throwing Tal into further turmoil. And now Cardin was left to clean up the mess...

"We either get paid in gold," Ackaron stated boldly, his eyes narrowed at Cardin with a heavy brow, "Or we simply stop providing our services."

That was a worrisome threat, and Cardin raced to think of a way to convince Ackaron not to follow through. The Warriors held most of the greatest fighters of Tal, trained since childhood to protect the kingdom and its people from all threats, internal and external. The timing couldn't be worse, what with tensions on the rise with Falind again due to Cardin's appointment as Prince of Tal.

More than that, Cardin finally had a name for an external threat, one which he had been warned about by an orc shaman last winter, and one which he had personally encountered during an attack against the spiritual villagers of Stella three months ago.

The Darksteel Army.

He had only one thought, one hope of keeping the Warriors on-task. "You would leave the innocents of the kingdom defenseless?" He asked the question in an accusing tone, intent on using guilt to persuade the new General.

"Our services are not free of charge," Ackaron immediately replied, still smug.

Cardin's mind raced, and his very next thought was, *What would King Beredis do?*

He knew the answer immediately. Eirdin Beredis would have stood up, spoken loudly with that deep, commanding tone he had, and forced Ackaron to see reason. He had had a presence unlike any other, and could inspire the most selfish person to stand up for others.

But Cardin was not Eirdin Beredis. He did not have a commanding presence or tone of voice. He had only words, and lately, even his inspiring words often failed to make people see reason.

Never-the-less, he had to try. So he looked to the Warrior code, which he knew all too well, since he had once trained to become a

Warrior himself, long ago.

"It is your duty to protect the innocent," he began, forcing as much confidence and volume into his voice as he could, allowing the ire he felt to give his voice a distinct edge. "The Warrior code demands that you-"

"Do not quote the code to me," Ackaron interrupted disdainfully.

"DO NOT INTERRUPT ME AGAIN," Cardin roared. He had leapt to his feet and glowered down upon the General. Ackaron didn't even flinch, which surprised Cardin considering he felt his own powers flex. The Sword of Dragons was strapped to his back in an enchanted scabbard, the throne having been replaced with one without armrests to allow Cardin to keep the Sword on his person at all times. He felt it vibrate in its sheath, his powers incidentally rushing into it.

With clenched fists, Cardin let that power remain welled up within him. Some of the royal guards in the throne room stirred, their hands grasping their longswords, indicating which of them were Mages. They stood one each between the statues, usually a silent but intimidating reminder to visitors that the royalty was protected. But Cardin needed no protection, not with the growing powers that the Sword of Dragons had taught him over the past year.

Seething, Cardin almost wanted Ackaron to say something else. However, despite the defiance in his dark eyes, the general did as commanded and kept his mouth shut.

"I don't care what you think of my past," Cardin began. "I don't care if you resent me for refusing Guild induction. Who I am *today* is what matters, and whether you like it or not, I am Prince of Tal and ruler in my father's stead."

Cardin noticed the twitch at the corner of Ackaron's eyes. In a sort of last will and testament, King Eirdin Beredis had left a sealed letter behind declaring Draegus Kataar King, should Eirdin die before publicly announcing a successor. Unfortunately, Cardin's father remained on the edge of death, a soulless shell being cared for at the Wizards' Guild in the north. However, despite how many people respected and honored his father, the Warriors resented him almost as much as they resented Cardin, for Draegus had left the Guild at the request of Eirdin some seven years ago, to serve as the King's personal guard Captain.

"You may consider this a direct order from your Prince," Cardin continued. "You will continue to provide protection for the citizens of Tal. You will continue to provide border security in light of Falind's recent threats. And you will work with the Commanders to devise a strategy to thwart an invasion. The throne will continue to give you letters of mark until such time as we can repay you. Regarding said payment, it *will* be made in due course. Do you understand the orders I have given you?"

Ackaron's mouth opened to speak, but he paused and narrowed his eyes. Cardin felt the familiar rushing sensation from anticipating conflict, his fight-or-flight instincts taking hold when they had no place. It had become a constant battle for him since he had been named Prince.

After another moment, Ackaron began asking, "Your *Majesty,* how can my Warriors provide protection when-"

"I asked you a question, General," Cardin interrupted.

"When they are starving?" Ackaron continued, his voice rising close to a shout. "Without payment, how can we be expected to buy food?"

"The letters of mark can be traded," Cardin stated, flustered.

"Farmers and merchants aren't accepting your letters of mark!"

Cardin stopped short. That was news to him. "As of when?"

"As of last week," Ackaron stated, surprise at Cardin's ignorance apparent upon his face, his voice lowered to a normal speaking level again. "I would have thought you would know," he looked pointedly at Maral. She looked as baffled and surprised as Cardin.

The rage and anger within Cardin was gone, deadened by the knowledge that things had degraded further than he realized. "Which merchants," Maral asked. "Where?"

"All of them, all across Tal," Ackaron replied. "I assume the Merchants' Guild and Farmers' Guild voted to reject the letters."

Cardin exchanged shocked expressions with Maral. Drawing in a breath, he nodded. "Alright, I'll look into this. You have my word."

Ackaron looked ready to reject Cardin's word, but then stopped short of a reply. After thinking further, he nodded. "Thank you, Your Majesty." Surprisingly, Ackaron bowed.

"You are dismissed, General," Cardin said with a nod.

Rising from his bow, Ackaron turned on his heel and marched out. Cardin forced the power welled up within him and the Sword of Dragons to dispel, and the royal guards released their grips on their weapons, allowing their black and silver tabards, bearing a mountain with swords crossed in front of it, to display proudly to Ackaron as he marched out of the main doors.

Cardin descended the steps, and said to Maral, "I want representatives of the Merchants' and Farmers' Guilds in here at once."

"But, Your Majesty," Maral sputtered.

"No buts," he shook his head, stopping on the bottom-most step. "They need to answer for this."

"Yes, Majesty," Maral nodded, "However I feel it is my duty to remind you that you are due at the Allied Council after mid-day. Your meal is being prepared as we speak, and then you must depart for the Wizards' Guild at once."

Cardin opened his mouth to retort, but stopped, and then clenched his fists. There was so much that needed to be done in Tal, but given the increasing tensions in the Allied Council, he couldn't afford to miss a meeting.

Letting out an exasperated sigh, he nodded. "Right. Dammit. In that case, summon them for my return tonight." His stomach grumbled suddenly. "For after dinner," he added with a grimace. He had skipped too many meals in the past three months, but that also meant he would once again have no time to wind down before bed. Assuming he could actually sleep tonight, for a change.

"I shall have Steward Kai send runners at once," Maral bowed.

"Thank you," he smiled wearily at her. "Please have Dalin meet me for lunch, too. I need to bring him up-to-date on what we just learned before we travel."

"Yes, Majesty," she bowed again. "And I believe Mistress Reinar wishes to join you for lunch."

Cardin smiled, warmth blossoming within his chest again. "That would be wonderful."

He and Sira almost never had time together these days. She was on leave from the Warriors' Guild due to the passenger currently sharing her body, the spirit of a dragon released from its chrysalis long before it was ready. Sira's body protected it, and it had likewise healed grave wounds for her when its chrysalis was broken.

Looking at Maral pointedly, he said, "Don't forget to eat something as well, Governor."

She returned his weary smile. "Of course, Your Majesty."

He knew what that placating statement meant. She was going to skip mid-day meal again to see to the affairs that Cardin could not. Stirrings of guilt twisted in his stomach, but the truth was that without Maral's insistence on going above and beyond, the kingdom would have fallen into complete disarray. Cardin simply didn't have the time to handle everything.

To say that he was in over his head was the understatement of the year.

Chapter 2

DECLARATION

Who knew that entirely new governments could form in only three months?

Kailar Adanna certainly never expected things to move so quickly. Not on Devor, a colonial continent that had endured over fifty years of cowering before a thriving criminal underground. An underground that she had largely helped dismantle through her service to the local Warriors' Guild.

Except, there were pockets of the underground still intact, pockets she had not been able to root out yet due to her new commitments as advisor to the newly forming government. Which was why today, of all days, her lifelong commitment to the ways of the Warriors would be essential.

Today, the Devor Imperium became official. If anyone was going to strike against the government, it would be here, now.

Brushing a black lock of hair out of her pale face, Kailar stood off to one side in the Tieran City Hall, a wooden structure built in the earliest days of the new colony and, therefore, quite simple. It was composed of two rooms, the front antechamber and the meeting room, separated by a set of ironwood doors with an elaborately carved moulding surrounding it.

The meeting room, where twelve members of the city council once met, now sat representatives from every major city on Devor, which was to say three mayors and their assistant mayors, and two councilors from the remnants of Tieran's city council, chief of whom was Councilwoman Reyla Aurin, who sat at the far end of the table, her back against newly-installed broad windows looking out upon the bay.

Crowded into the opposite side of the room, and streaming out into the antechamber, were many of the city's most influential, come to witness a truly historic occasion.

Kailar scanned that crowd for any malicious looks, any nervous-looking citizens who didn't belong. Of course, there were at least two dozen crammed into the room, and they kept milling and shifting about anxiously, everyone excited for today's event.

There was a time when she could have sensed a threat through magic moments before the danger presented itself. But there had also been a time when she had been connected to star magic. The Star Dragons had put an end to that. Thanks to her brief ownership of the Sword of Dragons, she now had the ability to use dark magic. The trouble was, dark magic and star magic didn't mingle. She couldn't sense when someone gathered power for a strike, except maybe the barest hint of shifting energy, a press against the void of her dark powers, and that was something she couldn't rely upon.

So she had to rely on her otherwise normal five senses.

Across the table from where she stood, two Warriors likewise provided guard. The first was Commander Kent Querlin, a dark-skinned man with dark eyes and short black hair. After today, he would become General of the Imperial Army. Next to him stood Lieutenant Letan Velethar, a pale man with bright red hair and a beard to match, and blazing blue eyes that studiously avoided meeting Kailar's gaze.

She felt a rush when she glanced at him, but pushed her feelings aside and looked back to the crowd. Now was not the time.

The scraping of a wooden chair, and Councilwoman Reyla stood up and cleared her throat. The assembly grew silent, and despite her paranoia, Kailar even spared a moment to watch the councilwoman. Despite the occasion, and her future role in the new Imperium, Reyla still wore rather simple clothes, if still appropriate for the occasion – a sky-blue blouse and flowing burgundy skirt, matching the new colors of the Imperium. Her black hair was pulled into a neat ponytail, with only a couple streaks of silver here and there, belying her relative youth, and her strong jaw clenched ever so slightly, while her amber eyes surveyed the room.

"Good morning, everyone," Reyla spoke softly. Kailar marveled at the affect Reyla had, speaking with such confidence that no matter how quietly she spoke, she commanded the attention of everyone in the room. Her voice was even, measured, and carefully calculated, as Kailar had discerned over the past few months, to ensure no one's attention strayed. "Today we find ourselves at the threshold of something wondrous and new, a bold step into a future that none could have ever dreamt of before. For the first time in ten thousand years, Halarite shall give birth to a new nation.

"None can deny the struggles we have endured, particularly of late. None can deny that one of many reasons for our declaration today is because we have been left to fend for ourselves, abandoned by those who would reap the benefits of our continued servitude, while bearing none of the responsibilities owed to us." Kailar marveled at Reyla's lack of anger. Instead, the councilwoman spoke with an enduring resolve. "However, what we do today is not an act of anger nor of defiance. Rather it is an act of solidarity. An act of faith, in each other and in our future together. We have endured together even when we thought that there was nothing to unite us. Yet as my advisor reminded me only a few short months ago," Reyla's eyes fell upon Kailar, "we have always been united. One land, one people, undivided by the politics and old wounds of the four kingdoms of Edilas. Our struggle and strife in a common land has united us."

With a careful, controlled motion, Reyla reached down and picked up a golden quill, provided by a goldsmith in town for this very occasion. "Today, this quill, and the declaration we sign, marks the beginning of a new future, one which we shall step into together."

Reyla bent down, dipping the quill into an ink well, before she carefully began to sign a large piece of parchment with the very declaration of unity she had spoken of.

Kailar turned her attention back to the crowd, knowing that if anyone would strike, it would be during the signing, when all eyes were to be on that single golden quill. If they waited until after the signing, it would be too late for them to stop the formation of the new government.

There was movement in the crowd, a jostled parting of heads. Someone was pushing through from the back. She reached underneath her black cloak and grasped the handles of two darksteel daggers, the two she had commandeered from a would-be assassin only a few months ago. The Warriors had taken back the weapons they had issued her, but these were rightfully hers for defeating that assassin.

There were a few words of protest from the crowd, as whomever drew nearer increased their pace. Kailar carefully drew the daggers and pushed outward with her powers, creating a void within that filled with dark energy, and she further channeled that power into the blades, setting them humming quietly.

Suddenly a man in rags burst forth, his face stubbly, his hair a mussy mess. "Stop," he shouted. All eyes turned to him, as Reyla paused in her signing.

Letan and Kent drew swords and moved to intercept him, but instantly Kailar knew something was wrong. If your intent was to assassinate the delegates, you don't announce your arrival. Not unless you wanted to draw everyone's attention to you. Away from somewhere else.

Away from the new windows.

Kailar snapped her head towards the windows, and saw three men outside shoving the onlookers aside while drawing scimitars. They were the true assassins!

There was no way she could intercept them herself. Even if she launched an attack upon one, it would leave the other two free. So she did the only thing she could think of. "Look out," she shouted, and dove onto the table to close the distance just enough to project a dark magic shield ahead of her, just barely past Reyla.

The instant she had done so, glass shattered as three blasts of arcane magic lanced through the window and slammed into Kailar's shield, flashing a purple-white flare of light. The pressure on her mind was minimal, and that meant they were nothing more than Mages, and not the much more powerful assassins from Falind.

Seeing that they had already failed, and that Kailar was now protecting the representatives, the trio turned tail and ran. Kailar allowed her shield to drop and looked back at the disheveled distraction, his wails of terror and failure muffled as Kent and Letan wrestled him to the ground.

Looking back, Kailar saw that Reyla had ducked, but now peeked over the table at Kailar, their eyes locking for a moment. Kailar hesitated just a heartbeat, and then she scrambled to her feet on top of the table, almost bumping her head on an iron chandelier. "I'm going after them," she declared, and bounded over Reyla's head and landed just inside of the window, her boots crunching glass.

The window hadn't completely shattered, so she let out a pulse of dark energy from her daggers, just enough to break what was left of the windows, and then she leapt through, catching her cloak on shards and shredding it.

The crowd surrounding the city hall had parted to allow the assassins to flee, and that gave Kailar a clear view of them as they headed for the harbor. It figured, as she had only ever known sailors to use scimitars on Halarite. Pumping dark magic into her leg muscles to give her unnatural strength and speed, she charged into a headlong run after them, while replenishing the magic in her daggers.

By the time she caught up to them, they had already barreled around a turn onto a pier and were bolting towards a moored ship, which Kailar noticed was already casting off. They had planned and timed this so that they could escape to sea and not answer for their crimes.

She roared, "Cowards!" and leapt high, her excess strength allowing her to close the remaining distance and to plunge her daggers into the middle one's back, a middle-aged man that was likely the brains of the operation. They tumbled onto the salted wood of the pier, but the others kept running.

Through time and experimentation, Kailar had found that the darksteel daggers were nothing like normal enchanted weapons. Whatever enchantments they held, she could not utilize due to their nature, but the material of the blades themselves, and the gems in the pommels, very much like a Wizard's focusing gem, provided ample magic charge, more-so than even a Warrior's longsword. Yet for all of her testing, never before had she been so incensed. When she swung her blades from her chest outward and released all of the magic pent-up within them, the blast waves not only tore through the fleeing assassins' shields and through their bodies, flinging them violently through the air, but her blasts crashed into the stern of the ship and shattered the windows of the captain's quarters, twisting wood and lurching the ship to port.

The blast waves had also nudged the ship forward, moving it faster out of port while still more sails were dropped to catch the wind. Kailar gawked at the damage she had wrought. It had been the most powerful attack she had yet unleashed with dark magic. Almost as powerful as the blasts she had unleashed upon Cardin at the Battle for Archanon.

One of the two assassins' bodies slapped against a post and splashed into the ocean, while the other tumbled to a stop near the end of the pier, and she stared in utter shock at the state of it all. Even from halfway down the pier, she could see that she had snapped his spine, as he was folded backwards in a completely unnatural position, and she knew that his belly had to have torn from such a forceful bending.

It was terrible.

It was wonderful.

It was terrifying.

She looked down upon the man she had stabbed in the back, and noticed for the first time that he still squirmed, coughing uncontrollably. Standing, she shoved him over onto his back, careful not to cut him again, but blood flowed from his mouth, and she knew that she had pierced his lungs. He would be dead in minutes, and she was still uncertain of her ability to heal others.

That left the ship. Despite the damage, the name was clear upon it, *Pranid*, and she started at that. She recognized it. The same ship that had tried to smuggle Egil away a few months ago. Through forced cooperation, they made the captain give up Egil, in exchange for letting him leave port.

Now she regretted letting the captain go.

Could she portal aboard it? Kailar had never tried to create a portal on a moving vessel before. How did it work? Could it work?

The clomping of boots upon the pier distracted her, and she saw Warriors rushing to her aid, as unneeded as they were. They could not reach the ship, and Devor had no navy to chase after them.

Part of her considered trying to make a portal in the air ahead of the ship and trying to time a jump through to land on the deck, but if she didn't time it just right, it could go very wrong. What happened if something passed through the exit portal just as she arrived? Would it impale her? Or worse?

As the Warriors drew up next to her and stopped, panting, she lowered her daggers and sighed. This time, she would have to admit defeat.

But one thing was for sure – the Devor Imperium would need to commission a navy as quickly as possible.

And security would need to be tightened.

That would be her next advice to Reyla. After all, assuming the signing of the declaration proceeded despite the attempt on her life, Reyla was slated, by unanimous decision of the other mayors, to be the first Empress of Devor.

Chapter 3

STRANGE REFLECTIONS

A stranger stared back at Sira Reinar through the mirror.

Amethyst-hued eyes gazed back, flicking about her face, looking at all of the familiar features, trying desperately to feel reassured that only her eyes looked different. She still had a light speckling of freckles, made darker by spending her days outside walking around Archanon, around the castle grounds, exploring a city she had visited too many times in the past year and a half, yet had never truly known until now. Her hair and eyebrows were platinum-blonde, stark white against her freckled and tan skin.

Yet for as familiar as her face was, she felt strangely disconnected from it. She knew why, of course, but even after living in her new reality throughout summer, she still couldn't get used to it. A part of her still felt lost, confused, and that part grew with each passing day, rather than shrank.

Her eyes wandered down her body, naked in hers and Cardin's quarters in Archanon castle, much larger than their previous guest quarters, now that Cardin was Prince. Her body was as fit as ever, as that was one part of her daily regiment she would never give up, exercising to ensure she remained a fit Warrior, despite the indefinite leave she had been granted. Yet at the sides of her tummy, bright violet markings edged into view. The tips of claws on her left, a tip of a tail on the right.

Turning around, straining her neck to see, she stared at the violet markings upon her skin, imprinted like a tattoo, but given by no needle. No, in fact, she had suffered far worse pain than the needle of a tattoo artist to receive this marking.

For the image of a small, violet dragon was set on her back. The image of what the dragon might have looked like, had it been allowed to gestate within its crystalline chrysalis for another few decades.

Now, thanks to an attack upon the village in Stella by the Darksteel Army, that dragon's soul shared her body. *More* than just her body, they shared a deeper bond, a link between souls and minds, distinct yet ever-present with each other.

As she stared at the detailed lines of the tattoo, she heard the dragon's spirit, Raida, speak with Sira's voice in her mind, *"That's a fine looking body."*

Sira didn't know whether to laugh or smirk. Raida certainly had a sense of humor more akin to Reis's than Sira's, and she wondered where the young dragon had learned it from. She had joined with Sira with an already-developed personality, though it seemed to evolve freely.

Are you talking about mine or yours? Sira thought.

"Yes," Raida replied. A warmth coursed throughout Sira that she equated to Raida smiling, and despite her previous line of thought, Sira couldn't help but smile. *"Ah, excellent, I had hoped to make you feel better! Some of the villagers used to use humor to make each other feel better."*

Raising a curious eyebrow and facing the mirror fully again, Sira asked, *Is that where your personality came from?*

Not waiting for Raida to reply, she turned to the bed, which was mostly a tumbled mess since she hadn't left the room yet this morning, and so castle servants hadn't been there to make it up yet. Set on the foot of the bed were her chosen clothes for the day, a pair of black trousers, a stark-white shirt, and a pale-tan tunic laced up the front. It wasn't the nicest set of clothes she could have worn for today's Allied Council meeting, but since she would once again be relegated to sitting behind the Tal table as a guest rather than a participant, she really didn't care anymore.

While she dressed, Raida replied, *"I believe so. I wasn't fully conscious during my entire time in Stella, but towards the end, I started to spend as much effort as I could observing the villagers. Some of their personalities might have worn off on me."*

She had her trousers on now and was stuffing the white shirt into them when she paused and looked up at nothing in particular so that she could ask, *Just like your personality is wearing off on me?*

Raida didn't reply at first, and Sira somehow knew the dragon spirit was thinking carefully about her next words. *"Perhaps."*

Sira nodded, and finished tucking her shirt in. While pulling the tunic on and then lashing a light-colored leather belt around it, she could feel Raida's spirit rumbling within. Either that or Sira was just hungry, and since she hadn't eaten breakfast, that was just as likely. Still, she felt guilty for her accusatory question, and thought, *I'm sorry, Raida. I guess I'm just having a bad morning.*

"It's okay, food will change that." Raida's tone changed to a more up-beat one. *"Hey, can we try bacon again?"*

Sira laughed, and set to pulling on a pair of leather boots, leaning her backside against the bedframe as she did so. *I'll ask if they can make up a special order. We usually only eat bacon for breakfast.*

"Well that's silly," Raida remarked. *"Something that yummy? You should eat it with every meal!"*

Laughing again, Sira finished buckling up her boots, and then headed out into the castle, passing by a pair of patient servants waiting for her to leave the room. She had memorized the castle layout by now, and walked without really paying attention from the north wing into the back of the castle, where a large dining hall was sat with multiple chandeliers hanging from the ceiling and numerous windows were set at the back, looking out into the castle gardens and the guards' training grounds beyond that.

A grimace drew across Sira's face when she saw that Cardin was already well into his lunch meal, along with Dalin and Jeric Ferel, an upper-city nobleman, and the man King Beredis had entrusted with his succession orders. They were in deep conversation, though to Cardin's credit, as soon as Sira walked in, he looked up and gave her a full smile. "Good morning, sleepy-head," he called to her. She smiled as well and crossed to the head table where they sat. Dalin and Jeric knew enough to leave a seat next to Cardin for her, and she sat down with her back facing the windows. From her left, another castle servant immediately came to her and set down dishes and silverware.

"Good morning, Miss," the servant, a young woman with dark hair, pale skin, and blue eyes said. "We have a lovely stew for lunch, if you'd like, and fresh-baked bread." No sooner had she said that than did the door to the kitchen open to allow another servant out, running food to someone else somewhere in the castle, and the smell of the stew and bread wafted over to Sira, setting her stomach growling harder than a cat's purr.

"Oh that sounds lovely," Sira smiled. Raida's presence flared for a second, reminding Sira to add, "Any chance for some bacon?"

Cardin and the others glanced at her curiously, but the servant merely chuckled. "We'll get some frying up right away, Miss," she said, and walked back to the kitchen.

It was so strange. To have such a large room, to live in such a large place, to have mirrors and servants. All of it had made Sira uncomfortable at first, but now she wondered if she could go back to living under her parents' roof in Daruun ever again.

For that matter, whenever she decided to return to the Warriors, what would she do? Would she go back to Daruun, away from Cardin? Would she ask to transfer to Archanon?

She glanced at Cardin, but after he finished another spoonful of his own stew, he cleared his throat and told her, "So, I, um, have some interesting news I was just relaying to these two."

He motioned to Dalin, a former member of the Wizards' Guild who, despite being an exile now, still wore his customary blue robes everywhere. She often begged him to let her change out his wardrobe, but he insisted he needed his robes, specifically for the handful of runes he had embroidered into them. Since they had met Dalin, his hair had turned greyer, but considering he was over two hundred years old, the fact that he looked as young or younger than Cardin and Sira, who were only in their early thirties, it was still an impressive feat.

And then Cardin motioned to Jeric, a sharp-looking man with a horseshoe ring of white hair around a bald head, a matching white goatee, and blazing blue eyes.

"The new Warrior general is threatening to withdraw all support until the throne can pay him in gold," Cardin explained.

Sira wasn't sure she heard Cardin right. But once the words registered, her stomach dropped, along with her jaw. "He what?!" Her voice had gone up an octave in shock.

With a grimace, Cardin nodded, but he didn't quite look her in the eye as he continued, "He claims the Merchants' and Farmers' Guilds are no longer accepting letters of debt."

Her eyes bulged out in further surprise. "I can't...I don't believe it. What...why? Why would they do that?"

"We were just discussing that," Jeric said impatiently, "before you arrived."

She flashed him an annoyed look. Raida echoed her thoughts, *"Pompous ass."*

It took every bit of self-control in Sira not to laugh. Immediately after, however, she felt guilty. Jeric had every right to be annoyed at her. For that matter, she was annoyed with herself. *I've been staying in bed later and later,* she thought. Not sleeping, but thinking, and talking with Raida. Trying to find a defined edge where Raida ended and Sira began.

A horrifying well of sadness opened up inside of her, consuming her once again, just as it had that morning. Would this ever end? Would she ever feel okay again?

The servant set a bowl of stew on her plate, followed by fresh, soft bread that looked like it might just melt in Sira's mouth. Raida purred, or at least that's how Sira equated the strange sensation within her thoughts whenever Raida was excited and happy.

Distracted from her self-reverie, Sira dug into her food while only half-listening to the conversation between Cardin, Jeric, and Dalin. Jeric suspected that the city and, for that matter, all of Tal was still bristling over the lies that their former beloved King had told. The castle coffers had been near-empty ever since the King had been ill and his brat of a son enacted new laws, effectively spending all of the kingdom's gold reserves on selfish pursuits. That had been before Kailar had found the Sword of Dragons.

Once the Wizards healed the King, he tried to undo all of his son's mistakes, but between the war against Kailar and Klaralin, the subsequent campaigns against the orcs in the Wastelands, and then the cataclysmic meteorite storm and Necromancer invasion, Tal Kingdom's reserves were never replenished. Especially not with Sal'fe charging an arm and a leg to heal or resurrect fallen Warriors and soldiers during all of that.

Tal had taken a beating over the past year and a half.

And there were kingdoms worse off than Tal, even after the First

Demon, Degrin, had devastated Tal by killing the King and his son. *And taking away Cardin's father,* she thought, flashing eyes at Cardin while he listened to Jeric and Dalin debate the finer points.

Governor Maral suddenly appeared at the entrance to the dining hall. "Your Majesty," she called. *I'll never get used to Cardin being called that…* "It is time."

Sira cursed inwardly, and sucked in two big spoonfuls of stew before she stood up along with Cardin, Jeric, and Dalin.

"But what about my bacon?" Raida asked plaintively.

No sooner had she asked that than did the kitchen door swing open, and the servant came out carrying a small plate of fresh-cooked bacon. Sira snagged a handful as they passed by, thanking the servant, and then she followed Cardin and the others out.

They stopped by their quarters so that Sira could retrieve her sword, which she lashed onto her belt, and then they headed towards the edge of the city.

The days would soon arrive when the various royalties of Edilas would no longer need a personal Wizard to ferry them to the new Allied Council chamber, but that day had not yet arrived. Outside of the southeast gate of Archanon, an archway was still under construction, along with a matching archway at the Wizards' Guild, soon forming a permanent two-way portal between the two locations. Similar portals were being constructed at Falind's capitol city, bearing the same name as the kingdom, as well as at Erien's current capitol of Lassil, Maradin still being unoccupied after the skies had burned.

Thinking of Maradin, Sira grimaced. It was one of two cities that were essentially erased in recent years. And while parts of Maradin remained and could be rebuilt, they had discovered two difficulties that would make it almost impossible. First was that the wounds in magic caused by the deaths of the crystalline beings known as Navitas were still dangerous, and any who strayed too close were drained of life. The city was surrounded by almost a dozen of those wounds. Second was that Maradin's main source of drinking water, underground wells, were tainted by seawater and dead bodies after the tsunami, making it impossible for any population to survive there.

"You're really in a down mood today, aren't you?" Raida asked.

Guilt and embarrassment swelled inside of Sira. She hung back from the rest of the group, catching only bits of discussion between the trio. As they left the castle, they were joined by several royal guards, resplendent in their ceremonial armor and black-and-silver tabards. Not that Cardin needed protection, but it was traditional to have an escort whenever they left the castle. Something else Sira was having trouble getting used to.

Sorry, she thought to Raida. *I just…I'm sorry.*

"You have nothing to be sorry about," Raida encouraged. *"This would be difficult for anyone, I think. But hey, at least it's me you're stuck with, and not someone with a less charming personality."*

A smile crept across her face. *How do you keep doing that?*

"What?"

Making me smile.

"Well, I know you have your heart set on being sad today, but I like how it feels when I make you smile." She blinked her eyes, and felt them go wide. Raida added, *"You know how you can feel it when I smile? I can feel when you smile."*

She hadn't thought of that before, but Sira realized that it made sense that emotions would be a two-way street, not just feeling them, but enjoying the good ones. It suddenly occurred to her that likewise Raida would not like feeling depressed, and that the dragonsoul was probably getting the full brunt of it when Sira felt overwhelmed by it.

After several minutes of walking along behind Cardin and the others, they emerged outside of the western gate, the hot summer sun blazing down upon them. The sweet smell of mountain flowers caressed her nose, and she drew in the scent and allowed it to calm her.

Cardin, on the other hand, sneezed, and she barely contained a snicker. "Uh, damn allergies," Cardin complained. They stopped outside of the gate, and Cardin and Dalin looked to one another. He asked the Wizard, "Care to do the honors, or shall I?"

Dalin, whose original staff was lost to the Necromancers last winter, had a new staff, created for him by a mystical force on Stella, though it had almost cost him his life. Coupled with a special stone at the top of it, Dalin's powers had noticeably improved with the staff, and he appeared to relish any chance to use it.

Planting his staff on the ground, Sira felt a pulse of power ahead of the assembled troupe, and a moment later, a wide blue-white wall of light appeared, a portal that no doubt led to the plaza in front of the Grand Wizard Hall at their newly rebuilt complex.

Still bracketed by troops, Cardin led the group through the portal, and to the other side, far to the north, but still technically within Tal's borders.

It was surprisingly warmer up north than in Archanon today, and Sira almost immediately felt her brow begin to sweat. Usually it was the other way around, and she grimaced at that. *I'm glad I didn't wear more layers.*

Ahead of her was the increasingly familiar sight of the Grand Hall, a stone and marble structure with countless columns and doors wide and tall enough to permit a Star Dragon to enter, if one were to ever visit. *Then again, if Astaria was any indication, some dragons would be far too big to fit inside of that hall.*

She felt a pang of guilt at her memory of the great red dragon from Stella, the only living "First One," according to Endri. Raida was technically Astaria's child, or would have been.

The grounds of the Wizard complex looked a lot better than they had three months ago, when Sira, Cardin and Dalin had returned from Stella. Back then, the Wizards had just endured an attack by Degrin, a half-ascended being, known as a wraith, that had used all of his powers on Halarite to assault the Guild complex and obtain the last Cronal piece.

Gods above, I hope we don't have to endure any more disasters or calamities.

All of the scorched grounds in and around the complex had been restored to their green, grassy state thanks to the influence of the Wizards, and the entire complex was now surrounded by defensive stone pillars that could create a shield around and, unlike Archanon, *above* the complex, thus protecting from future meteorite storms, if one should ever occur again. Additionally, she'd learned that the pillars could be used by Wizards, or even Mages for that matter, if it became necessary, to direct and unleash elemental attacks from giant crystals set at the top.

The rest of the complex was spread out in a wide campus of multiple buildings, the Wizards taking full advantage of living on open land now, instead of the created realm of their old, destroyed Guild complex.

Once the troupe was clear of the portal and Dalin came through last, allowing it to close, a single Wizard Acolyte, Alabran if she remembered his name right, stepped forward to greet them. He wore burgundy robes with black trim, and wielded a dark-oak staff with a ruby at the top.

"Greetings, Prince Kataar," he bowed. "Welcome back."

Cardin returned the bow, and Sira stepped up next to him, no longer willing to allow herself to be relegated to the back. She also bowed to Alabran. "Thank you," Cardin said. "How's my father?"

"I am told his status is unchanged," Alabran grimaced. "No worse," he said a little brighter, "but also no better."

Sira grasped Cardin's hand, and he clenched it. He was getting better at hiding his emotions when having to perform as Prince, but she knew that deep down, he was still hurting over his father's condition.

"Thank you," he said curtly, barely a waver in his voice.

"I believe you know the way," Alabran faux-smiled and motioned to their left.

Indeed they did. Allied Council meetings were held generally three days a week now, and the new meeting hall at the Wizards' Guild had been completed and been in use for a month.

With Alabran walking just ahead and beside Cardin, the troupe set off towards the Council building. While not nearly as tall as the Grand Hall, the Council building was necessarily large, meant to not only contain the meeting room, but also space for royal entourages from each kingdom to rest during the meetings. It also included a full kitchen to serve meals for the longer council meetings, of which there were far too many for her tastes. Several peasants from every kingdom had been hired by the Wizards to work that kitchen and to serve the Wizards in general, but when Sira had first learned of that, it had made her curious as to how the Wizards had served themselves and cleaned up after themselves back in their old Guild complex. Had they used magic, or had they been forced to 'demean' themselves and actually perform such menial tasks?

"I still don't know if I like them," Raida thought. *"I mean, Dalin is a fine fellow and all, but he left the Guild, right?"*

Grand Master Valkere was a good Wizard, Sira reminded Raida, even though the former Grand Master had died before Raida's time with Sira. *And I know that Dalin was fond of his former mentor Aenar.*

"True. I suppose there's no such thing as a universally bad or good group of people, is there?"

No, there's not, she agreed.

Like everything else in the Guild complex, the structure was made of stone and marble, including the reflective blue-white marble floor, broken only by a plum rug that led from the entrance in the antechamber to the meeting hall entrance.

They all stopped a moment just inside of the antechamber, and Cardin addressed their guards, "You're dismissed until further notice."

The soldiers all snapped to attention and saluted Cardin, and then neatly and uniformly filed away and into their customary waiting room.

With that, Sira, Cardin, Dalin, Jeric, and Alabran passed through the finely-crafted, elaborate aspen doors, with gold and silver foil inlaid into swirling patterns. Inside, the new meeting room was hexagonal, and much better than the old war room they had been using in Archanon, allowing not only for a little more space in general, but more guest seats behind each member's table. The ceiling was also higher, and in the center there was a steel-framed glass dome, allowing ample natural light in.

She felt Cardin's hand tighten again, and his shoulders bunched up, rising closer to his ears. She gently rubbed his back, even if he couldn't feel it through his many layers, kissed him on the cheek, and then sat down on one of the chairs against the wall behind the Tal table, which was the first table on the right when they entered.

Unlike the tables in Archanon, these were finely-crafted marble or granite tables, or rather they had probably been conjured that way by master Wizards, and each table was a different color to match the kingdom they served. Tal's was black with flecks of silver, while to the right of that was the Wizards' Guild's table, which was a light-blue, almost-white granite table. The newest Grand Master, Syrn, sat in her plum-colored robes, her aging face creased with wrinkles and a shock of silver hair pulled back into a tight bun. Next to her sat two more Wizards, though Sira didn't know who they were.

To the right of the Wizards was the table designated for the Covenant of the Order of the Ages, made of a deep red table-top and midnight-black legs. That table had remained vacant in the wake of the revelations three months ago. The Covenant had lied to the people of Halarite for ten thousand years, claiming their knowledge came from sacred texts called the Cronal. The Cronal, it turned out, was a set of four enchanted items that allowed the Covenant members to travel to an astral plain known as the Great Library. *That* was where they had gained their knowledge. In the wake of their deaths, the clerics of the Order had yet to elect new Covenant members, and it was debatable whether they ever would, or whether the clerics would simply take on the role of spiritual leaders.

Further along was Erien's table, made of a deep-blue lapis lazuli stone. Queen Sechel Leian, a middle-aged, tall woman with dark hair and tan skin, sat in the center of that table, her white crown gleaming in the noon-day sun filtering down from the skylight. Sira noticed that Queen Leian watched Cardin carefully as he sat down, and she wondered what their closest allied kingdom's leader was thinking about him.

Next was another table that usually was unoccupied during these meetings, that of Saran kingdom. Saran's capitol of Sharenth had been completely destroyed by the Dark Dragon Nuuldan, and since the entire royal family had been killed in the process, no successor had been chosen, even now. The table was composed of a dark golden-colored stone with flecks of black in it.

Today, that table was occupied. The Warrior Commander that had stepped up to defend Saran against the necromancers, a broad, strong man named Asil, sat by himself at the table. This drew Cardin's attention as well, and he and Jeric conversed in hurried whispers. Asil commanded the Warriors of Alioth, the largest surviving city of Saran, but had only assumed the role of General in all but name.

Completing the circle of tables was Falind's, whose table was made of jade. Sitting behind it was the only Wizard King of Halarite, Sal'fe. An exile, like Dalin, he had tricked Cardin into giving him the Staff of Aliz, which had the power to grant, or take away, life, and heal practically any physical wound. The Wizard King wore deep green robes with bronze trim, and his fabled staff leaned against the table next to him. He had a neatly-trimmed gray beard and equally neatly-trimmed hair.

Once upon a time, it was King Beredis who was lead speaker of the Allied Council. Since his murder, Master Syrn had taken on the role, and she stood up to address the Council.

"Members of the Allied Council," she began, her voice strong for a woman that had to be over three thousand years old. "Let us call to order. Though we have much to discuss, as we always do, I have been asked to immediately yield the floor to Commander Asil for an important announcement regarding Saran Kingdom." She nodded to

Asil, and said, "Commander, the floor is yours."

Sira sat up straight, keenly interested in what news he had. Did Saran finally select a new ruler?

Asil stood up, shifting uncomfortably as he did so. He was definitely not accustomed to public speaking.

"Thank you, Grand Master," he nodded. "As you all know from the past, I am a man of few words. So I will get to the point." He glanced at Sal'fe, and said, "Yesterday, the Commanders of the Saran Warriors concluded negotiations and signed a new declaration with Falind Kingdom. As of yesterday, our lands, our people, shall now fall under King Sal'fe's rulership."

Sira was nearly deafened by the outburst from the Council.

Chapter 4

DIVISIVE UNITY

Amongst the deafening uproar, Cardin was the only one to remain silent, his thoughts racing through possible implications about the pronouncement. Queen Leian and her General, Zilan, both stood up and protested. Master Syrn was quiet, but the two Wizards sitting beside her immediately began conversing animatedly. And all around the guest seats, people either shouted outrage or whispered to one another.

But Cardin leveled his eyes on Sal'fe. Sal'fe didn't meet his gaze, but instead appeared to revel in the ruckus caused by Asil's proclamation. This was an unusual and unexpected play by the Wizard King.

Something was wrong.

Cardin stood up slowly, which finally drew Sal'fe's attention to him, but for whatever reason, he refused to actually look Cardin in the eye. Turning to Syrn, Cardin caught her eye, and nodded. Though he definitely didn't connect to her the way he had Valkere, in this instance their cause was united, and she nodded and stood up herself. Using magic to enhance her voice, she bellowed, "Silence!"

Her booming voice echoed in the marble and granite-laden room, and it actually hurt Cardin's ears. She very effectively brought the room to order.

Motioning to Cardin, she asked in a more normal volume, "You have a question, Keeper?"

His jaw clenched at her use of his title of Keeper of the Sword. There had been considerable outrage, not too dissimilar to now, over his appointment as Prince of Tal. Everyone had been united against him in stating that he could not be a voting member of the Council since, by their original agreement, he fell under the unified orders of the Council. They therefore declared his appointment as Prince impossible. He had stoutly reminded everyone that matters of succession were internal, and could not be influenced by the Council, as per the original articles set out in the first three months of the existence of the Alliance. Arguments ensued, and he had lost a lot of support that day, but ultimately retained both his rule as Prince and his seat on the Council.

It might all bite him, and the rest of the council, in the proverbial backside today.

"With respect, Wizard King," Cardin turned to Sal'fe, "in the past, your…" He paused, realizing that he should choose his words with extreme care. "Your *focus* has always been on the wellbeing of Falind. Your votes have always reflected as much. It seems strangely out of character for you to suddenly take such a vested interest in another country."

Cardin's eyes darted to Commander Asil. He had a question for the commander as well, but he had to be patient and allow one question to be answered at a time. Sal'fe regarded Cardin coolly, but still didn't look him directly in the eyes. That, too, was unusual for Sal'fe.

After a moment's consideration, Sal'fe stood up and addressed the assembly. "My interest has always been the well-being and safety of Falind, and has been for millennia. When it serves my people, that interest extends to the rest of Edilas, since allowing the rest of Edilas to fall into chaos would represent a threat to Falind." Sal'fe nodded to Asil, and continued, "Saran has been leaderless for nearly six months, and has endured increasing unrest not unlike what has happened to Tal in recent months." Cardin felt the burn of embarrassment. "I decided that it was time to do something about it, and have been in negotiations with Asil and the other Saran Commanders for the past month."

Before Cardin could voice his concern or outrage, Syrn beat him to it, "You negotiated an international treaty involving another member of the Council without including the rest of the Council!" It wasn't a question, it was an accusation. While Cardin had only had a chance to overview the articles of the Alliance, he was fairly certain that Sal'fe had, at the very least, violated the spirit of the articles, if not flat-out violated the articles to the letter.

"The Council has lost most of its voting members, Grand Master," Sal'fe lifted his chin. "And Saran itself was slipping closer and closer to civil war over succession rights. Sides were being declared, and armed conflict was inevitable."

"Is this true," Cardin asked Asil.

Unlike Sal'fe, Asil looked Cardin directly in the eyes. "It is, sir. Even amongst the Warriors, there was talk of uniting behind one would-be ruler or another, and the arguments were becoming..." He paused and glanced at the rest of the Council. "Passionate."

Silence fell upon the chamber, eerie and almost deafening against the prior bursts of outrage. Civil wars were not unheard of on Edilas, the last one taking place, if briefly, in Tal when the Beredis line overthrew a tyrannical ruler and seized the throne for themselves centuries ago. Civil wars were usually messy affairs, on more than one level.

And despite Cardin's suspicions about Sal'fe's motives, Saran finally having some leadership wasn't exactly a horrible turn of events.

"Very well," Cardin nodded. "However as I'm sure you'll agree," he nodded towards Sal'fe, "Even with Saran swelling your ranks, you still may only have one vote on the Council."

Sal'fe opened his mouth to reply, but Syrn interrupted, "You cannot be serious! You support this action, Keeper?"

It took all of Cardin's self-control not to contract his hands into fists, and he quickly reigned in his frustration. Looking to the Grand Master Wizard, he nodded stoutly. "I do."

Queen Leian, surprisingly, sided with Syrn. "This represents a fundamental shift in the political power structure of the entire continent," she said while standing up, graceful as ever. "There has *always* been four kingdoms."

"Not always," Sal'fe pointed out. "Whatever faults the Covenant had, the history recorded by the Order of the Ages was accurate. We started as a single kingdom, and divided when Tal became far too great to manage itself."

"That was ten thousand years ago," Leian retorted, her hands balled into fists.

"And what has adhering to that structure given us?" Sal'fe demanded, his face screwing up into a frown. "Countless Lesser Wars. Death and destruction. Stagnation in our culture and technology. Sometimes reversing progress, as noted by the existence of proper plumbing in Archanon and *nowhere else*." He shook his head resolutely. "The time for stagnation, for adhering to tradition for tradition's sake, is at an end. We must begin to look towards making a brighter future for all of our people."

"What do you think this Council is about?" Syrn asked. It occurred to Cardin that the four representatives of the Council now all stood and faced off against one another, which was a new record. Usually the meetings didn't devolve into shouting matches and standoffs until at least an hour into them.

"In the spirit of cooperation," Leian added, her voice taking on that annoying haughty tone when she quoted law or boasted about her kingdom, "and according to the letter of our articles, international relations between the kingdoms must be openly discussed during Allied Council sessions."

"This is not a treaty," Sal'fe slammed his fist on the table. "Saran ceased to be a voting member of the council following the death of all of its political leadership. You speak of the articles as if they mattered to a kingdom that no longer benefited from those articles, who no longer had a say in how they were enforced. I offered them what the rest of you would not!"

"Representation on the Council," Cardin interrupted the others before they could retort. "Along with protection."

Sal'fe again refused to look into Cardin's eye. But it was Asil who replied, "Precisely. And a leader behind whom the constituent parties could rally behind."

Cardin nodded, and a second later, another thought behind Sal'fe's ability to assume rulership over Saran occurred to him. "And unlike Tal ten thousand years ago, the breadth of both of your kingdoms is no longer too difficult to rule over. Not when you and dozens of your people can create their own portals." He spoke specifically of the assassins that Sal'fe had trained, Mages whose powers now exceeded a normal Mage, to include the ability to open portals on their own.

"Precisely," Sal'fe nodded.

Silence engulfed the chambers once again, but this time it only lasted seconds. "You planned this from the beginning," Leian accused with a near-whisper.

Sal'fe's right eyebrow arched upwards. "No. However I was prepared to take advantage of such an eventuality."

All at once, Cardin realized that Sal'fe had been playing a much longer-term game than any of the other kingdoms. Maybe it was because he was a Wizard and had thousands of years to plot and scheme. And yet, in less than a year and a half, he had elevated Falind to a whole new level on the field. According to reports that Cardin had read shortly after being made Prince, new defenses had been erected in the Falind capitol city, along with other infrastructure improvements. Based on Sal'fe's specific words only moments ago, Cardin suspected he was also building a water and sewer system for the city, and if he was doing that, what other improvements was he making?

Every time Cardin thought he understood Sal'fe and his motives, he found himself having to re-evaluate the exiled Wizard. Now that he was Prince of Tal, it made him more uncomfortable than ever.

Yet Sal'fe had done precisely what Cardin thought Halarite needed now more than ever.

He had created unity.

At least, between Falind and Saran.

Cardin looked to Syrn. "May I address the Council further?"

She eyed him suspiciously, but then nodded. "Very well."

Stepping out from behind the Tal table, Cardin walked into the center of the room, a position he was much more accustomed to speaking from due to his past interactions with the Allied Council. He felt much more in his element there, and he decided that if he was to be labeled as 'Keeper of the Sword' rather than 'Prince of Tal,' then he would take advantage of that mindset.

Pausing in the middle, he turned slowly in a circle to look at each of the three remaining members, all of whom still stood. Remembering lessons in patience, he waited, until one by one, they each realized that he had the floor, and so they each sat down to give him their full attention.

Once the three were settled, he began, "This past winter, we learned of a greater threat to Halarite than any of us previously realized. An outside threat. Many on the Council thought it untrue, particularly because we first learned of it from an orc shaman who had waged war against us. Yet now, after my friends and I," he looked pointedly at Sira in the back of the room, who smiled encouragingly at him, "fought a small contingent of them on Stella, I believe the existence of the Darksteel Army is true. I also believe that they have targeted us."

"You have already said much of this," Syrn stated impatiently. Cardin really missed Valkere...

"Yes I have," he nodded to her. "And to be frank, it still boggles me that the existence of a proven threat has become a political issue, rather than a rallying issue. We should be united against this foe, if for no other reason than the fact that they would rather us be divided. Why else cause so much chaos and destruction? Why else arm the orcs with their darksteel weapons and armor?"

"We handily defeated that army," Leian reminded him, "precisely *because* the four kingdoms, along with the Wizards' Guild, united against them. The opposite of what they wanted."

"Indeed," he replied, turning his attention to her. "And I don't know if us uniting was part of their plans or not, though I doubt it. Yet for that unity, here we stand now, each kingdom having endured a devastating blow at some point or another, and only one of us having more than recovered from that blow," he looked pointedly at Sal'fe, who continued to keep his eyes away from Cardin's.

Ticking fingers on his hands, he said, "Falind was the first to feel it when Kailar assassinated their king. Then Tal endured the assault by Klaralin and his orc army, and if the Star Dragons had not intervened, we may very well have lost against such a powerful Wizard. Then Erien suffered the loss of their capitol to both a natural disaster and an invasion by the Necromancers of Vestuul. That same natural disaster brought forth a new nemesis, who subsequently wiped out the Saran capitol and its entire leadership. That same nemesis later killed numerous Wizards, including the former Grand Master. And to top it all off, Tal's King, and perhaps the person most passionate about this Alliance, was murdered by his son and a wraith."

He shook his head, and added, "All of this in less than two years.

And while some of this could not possibly have been brought on by the Darksteel Army, such as the meteorite storm and the initial return of Nuuldan, most of it can be traced back to one source."

It was Syrn who spoke Cardin's conclusion out loud, "Klaralin."

"Exactly," he stated triumphantly. "And given that Klaralin provided darkened steel to the orcs, I am beyond certain that he was in league with the Darksteel Army. He also was the one who pointed Kailar to the Sword of Dragons, and while that ensured the Star Dragons would come to our aid, it also further involved us in the larger Universe, ensuring that, for instance, the elves and the dwarves of Darea came to Halarite. Given the beliefs of the Order of the Ages, that was sure to cause further unrest, culminating in the wraith manipulating the people of Tal into an uprising long enough for him to kill King Beredis and enthrall countless citizens."

Cardin remained silent after that, allowing the others to process all that he had said. Ever since Cardin, Sira and Dalin had returned to Halarite from Stella, these facts had weighed heavily on him, and the more he thought about it all, the more it terrified him. It seemed so big, so overwhelming, that he thought it impossible for Halarite to stand up against the coming storm.

But now that he had said it all out loud, now that he had told the Council, he immediately felt lighter. He wasn't alone in the fight anymore.

Queen Leian conversed with her General in silent whispers, while Syrn consulted the other Master Wizards accompanying her. Sal'fe, on the other hand, merely stared thoughtfully at his hands, his face unusually telling of the various emotions and thoughts going through his head, changing from suspicion to concern to realization and back again. Usually the Wizard King was much more stoic.

Leian was the first to speak up again, after several protracted minutes of side discussions. "I cannot currently find fault in your assessment, Prince Kataar." He noted her use of his royal status rather than Keeper title. Did that mean she was beginning to support him over Syrn? "However it begs the question of what we can possibly do to combat this?"

"For starters," he replied, "work together, as we already have been for the past year and a half."

"That is a difficult proposition," Syrn scowled, "When one of our members refuses to."

"And that," Cardin turned to her, "is the exact opposite of what we need right now. Don't misunderstand, I strongly believe that King Sal'fe should have clued us all in to his intentions and actions. However, if we allow ourselves to divide over this now, we will only further serve to ripen ourselves for our enemies."

"It is not quite so simple," Leian pointed out cautiously. "To allow his usurpation to go unanswered invites further independent, counter-productive action."

So much for her supporting Cardin's position. Would he ever get used to the complexities of politics? Would they ever *not* annoy him?

"Be that as it may," he conceded, "I believe that just as we did against Klaralin, we can do the unexpected, the unanticipated, and unite further, despite our grievances. Whether or not he was right to hide it from us, Sal'fe has done precisely what was needed. Saran can now organize and be uplifted again, and be far more prepared to stand against the Darksteel Army than they would have if left to fall to civil war. Make no mistake," he held up a finger, forestalling any interruptions, "while I believe Saran's military will be a boon, I'm talking about more than just military strength. I'm talking about crops. Food. Water. I'm talking about each kingdom's ability to endure sieges and long-term warfare, our ability to absorb the economic impact." Which, admittedly, Cardin was completely unprepared for. Economics was not something he knew much about, and his advisors, particularly Jeric, were instrumental in teaching him the finer points.

"And it would seem that more than just Saran needs to recover in that regard," Syrn jabbed. Cardin felt warmth in his cheeks.

"Indeed," he nodded without looking at her.

After a short pause, Queen Leian asked, "Just how long do you believe we have before this Darksteel Army invades?"

He shook his head. "I cannot begin to guess, other than to say it is likely to be soon. But if we're lucky, we still have a few years."

By the gods, he hoped so. If the Darksteel Army invaded now, they could practically steamroll right over Halarite's defenses.

No one would be safe.

Chapter 5

THE NEW IMPERIUM

Returning to city hall, Kailar was relieved to find everyone was okay. Letan and Kent had stayed behind to guard the assembled mayors and Reyla, having dispatched the other Warriors to Kailar's aid. The crowd had been forced out of the building and away from it, and a line of Warriors surrounded the building defensively.

"They got away," she remarked morosely. "Well, not the assassins," she corrected. "They're definitely dead, but their ship got away." She looked specifically at Letan. "It was the *Pranid*."

Letan's eyes sank, realization and regret softening his features.

Kent asked, "That was the ship Egil tried to escape on, wasn't it?"

Kailar nodded. "The same."

Reyla looked to the other mayors with a grimace. "A ship, you say?" she asked Kailar. "I'd be willing to bet it is sailing east."

Kailar frowned and nodded. "Yeah, I watched it go for a while. How'd you know that?" She had expected it to sail north, for Edilas.

Now Reyla's eyes hovered on Kent, before turning back to Kailar. "These are rumors only, however it seems as though the criminal underground remains strong on Asirin." Kailar recognized the name as the colonized continent east of Devor, some three to four weeks to the east, depending on the wind and the ship. "And they took in all of those who fled from Devor."

"Which means," the mayor from Neolas, a plump, wealthy man with an apparent love for vibrant green clothes, said, "they're working together to stop the Imperium."

Reyla pressed her lips into a thin line. "It appears so."

The mayor from Edingard stepped forward now, her dark face resolute, brown eyes sharp with defiance. "Well then, what are we waiting for?" She picked up the golden quill still on the table and dipped it in the ink well. "Let's make it official, and to hell with Asirin."

No one objected, and after the Edingard mayor finished signing, the Neolas mayor stepped forward and added his loopy signature. Then the mayor from the refugee settlement near the Plains of Glass, where most of the Corlas survivors called home, added his signature.

Finally, Reyla stepped up to the head of the table, and completed her signature. Officially ratifying the formation of the first new government on Halarite in millennia.

"It is done," Reyla nodded.

And then, one by one, the mayors bowed deeply before Reyla, followed quickly by Kent and Letan. "Your Imperial Majesty," the Neolas mayor groveled. "It is a supreme honor to finally be able to call you as such."

Kailar should have felt joy. She should have felt *something* positive. Three long months of work had boiled down to this. Really even longer than that. Yet something in her stomach blocked all feelings of happiness and excitement.

Maybe it was because they weren't bowing before *her*. Hadn't she already made peace with that? She was still Reyla's closest advisor, even if she felt sour about not having heard the rumors regarding Asirin before today.

"Please rise, my friends," Reyla said with a smile. "And thank you all for everything. I suppose my prepared speech for the masses is not necessary at this time, so I will get right down to business." She motioned to the chairs, and everyone took their seats, with Reyla at the head of the table with the declaration, Kailar to her left, and Kent to her right.

Once everyone was settled in, Reyla began, "As promised and agreed to, all actions previously discussed shall be undertaken. Mayors will retain positions of powers, henceforth known as Lords, and their influence will reign beyond the borders of their cities."

There was no need to tell the new Lords this. Reyla, as Empress, would rule Tieran Port and the lands on the north side of the peninsula up to the Barrier Mountains, including the Agriat Islands. The Lord of Edingard would take the south part of the peninsula. The Lord of Neolas had ownership of a far greater land area, but much of that land had less value than on the peninsula due to a lack of resources. And should the area around Corlas become safe again, that Lord's rulership would extend up to and including Corlas and the crystal mines. The Crystalline Peaks and Crystalline Forest would be left alone, to continue to be tended to by the Navitas. If contact was ever established with them again, Reyla would seek a treaty with them, to ensure they remained amicable neighbors.

Reyla turned to Kent. "Kent Querlin, you are hereby appointed General of the Imperial Army, and are to carry out the conversion of the Warriors to the army at once." That act was first suggested by Kailar early in the discussions surrounding the new Imperium. The Warriors were ripe for corruption, relying on negotiable payment and being able to be swayed by anyone for the right sum of money. Imperial soldiers might also be susceptible to bribes, but if Kent followed Kailar's advice, he could reduce the likelihood of that happening.

However, the involvement of the Pranid had Kailar thinking, and since she had grown accustomed to having her opinions heard, she cleared her throat.

Reyla smiled, and gave her a knowing look as if she had expected Kailar to have a thought. "You have another suggestion?"

She nodded, glanced at Letan, and then avoided his eyes. "I think we should do more than just reorganize into a standing army. The Pranid makes it clear, if we're to deal with any external threats, it'll likely come from the sea."

Kent raised his eyebrows. "That is no small order. Our only shipwrights make fishing trolleys and small dinghies. We do not, in fact, own as a nation any vessels capable of long-distance travel, let alone warfare. All ships currently utilizing our docks are either civilian-owned or owned by one of the Allied kingdoms."

A grim look drew across Reyla's face. "And it'll take months, even years to construct new shipyards, let alone new ships. Leaving us vulnerable."

There was an obvious solution, and Kailar very nearly spoke up, but then hesitated and decided to back down. It was too extreme, too radical. She glanced at Letan, knowing he would never approve.

She must have outwardly shown her desire, for Reyla looked at her once again and insisted, "Speak your mind, Kailar."

Still hesitant, she looked down and studied the table, the declaration, the golden quill. But she couldn't avoid it. It was the only chance they had, she felt. "We should identify which ships belong to civilians and conscript them."

For as small as the gathering was, it was amazing how loud a general murmur of surprised conversation could be. Everyone tried to talk over one another, but a sharp look from Reyla was enough to silence them. She considered Kailar's suggestion for a moment, and then nodded grimly. "Unfortunately even combining our resources, we don't have much in the way of gold to offer civilian captains yet, but we can at least promise them *some* payment, and food. Our farms weathered the meteorite storm quite well, the winter harvest was bountiful, and our spring looks like it may be a good one." She nodded and smiled at Kailar. "An excellent suggestion."

Kailar felt her cheeks warm with a smile, and she glanced at Kent and Letan. Both looked rather concerned by this turn of events.

However, when Reyla addressed them, they gave her their full attention. "General, see to it. Offer all civilian captains the opportunity to join our ranks willingly, knowing that one way or another, we'll take care of them and ensure they can provide for their families." Reyla paused. "Better yet, Kailar," Reyla turned to her, "arrange a meeting with the captains, I shall address them myself and make the offer."

With a curt nod, Kailar replied, "As you wish. If I may make another suggestion in this regard?"

Reyla raised a patient eyebrow. "Of course."

"We should commission all weaponsmiths on Devor to begin forging new one-handed swords for Mages to utilize during sea combat. Ships are close quarters and any boarding activities or defenses will be severely hindered by longswords."

"Excellent idea," Reyla beamed. "General, see to it, and begin regular training regiments with whatever small weapons are available now. We need our Mages to be able to hit distant targets with their magic, *and* be able to fight in tight spaces."

"Uh, yes, Empress," Kent nodded. "As you wish."

Curiosity crossed Reyla's face. "Is something wrong, General?"

"Uh, no, Empress," he shook his head quickly. "Not at all."

Narrowed eyes stared back at him. "General, I prefer my top advisors to be open with their thoughts and opinions. Speak your mind, and do not dally about it."

Shocked by her forwardness, Kent hesitated further, exchanging furtive glances with Letan, who had his eyes fixed on Kailar now. She hadn't noticed it before, but he stared hard at her, and because she still couldn't look him in the eye, she wasn't sure what he was thinking. Was he suspicious of her motives?

"To be frank," Kent started, hesitant, "I fear if we try to force anyone into military service, which I feel we will be required to do when we conscript their ships, it may create a rather low reputation for the Imperium from the outset."

"Oh?" Reyla looked at him curiously. "May I ask whose opinion might be affected?"

"Well, the people of Devor," he said blatantly, his hands restlessly fidgeting on the table. Kailar understood why he was so nervous. For all of his distaste of former Mayor Evern, Kent was like Letan, he preferred following the letter of the law, and as of today, Reyla's word was law. To question her decisions was tantamount to insurrection, as far as he was probably concerned.

"I see," Reyla nodded. "In that case, I shall present the offer to them with the utmost care and precision. However, make no mistake, these early days will require many sacrifices and considerable dedication and hard work. We will all need to step up, or our fledgling nation will flounder, leaving us open not just to the predations of the criminals of Asirin, but also of the kingdoms of Edilas. Once we present our declaration of independence to them, some or all of them may try to forcibly take our lands back."

It was a risk, to be sure, but Kailar and Reyla had already agreed that it was unlikely. Especially if they presented Devor's move as beneficial to Edilas. Never-the-less, more than anyone else, Kailar didn't trust Sal'fe, and she feared that he would make a move against Devor independent of the others.

Hopefully Kailar was wrong.

Looking to the new Lords, Reyla nodded. "Do you all require travel accommodations back to your holds, or will you be our guests tonight?"

The three Lords requested Kailar take them back, and she nodded. It was one of her more boring duties, but she had agreed to it. As the only person on all of Devor capable of making portals, her abilities made her essential to quick communications.

"Very well. Once you return to your holds, please spread the order to all weaponsmiths to create molds for new seafaring weapons. Beyond that, for the moment, please administer your new lands as you see fit. Good day, everyone," she added while standing up. A broad smile drew across her face. "And welcome to the first day of a new age."

Chapter 6

UNEXPECTED PROPOSAL

The recovery ward in the Wizards' Complex was something of a new concept for the Wizards. After Cardin's father Draegus had fallen prey to the wraith in the dwarven city beneath Archanon, they had rushed him to the Wizards' Guild, hoping someone knew how to heal him.

Back then, a lifetime of three months ago, the relatively new ward was overfull of wounded Wizards and civilians from Tal alike, thralls of the wraith snapped out of it when Cardin had defeated it.

For the Wizards, injuries had been rare in their self-created pocket universe, and those injuries were usually from magical accidents by the young. Now back on Halarite, the need for the recovery ward was greater than ever.

Unfortunately, there was nothing the Wizards could do for Draegus. His body lived, but his spirit was absent. That duality seemed impossible, since as far as the Wizards knew, no one's body could survive without their spirit.

Now, three months later, when Cardin, Sira and Dalin entered, the ward was empty except for his father and a single Wizard tending to him. Multiple beds, each adorned with a white comforter embroidered with gold runes, lined the walls of the ward, and like the rest of the new Guild complex, the granite walls were interspersed by plentiful windows, allowing the evening sunlight to cast glowing shafts of light into the room.

It felt warm and inviting. The perfect place for someone to recover.

Approaching his father's bed, Cardin nodded to the attending Wizard as she stood up from a chair. It was Master Wizard Sana, a grey Wizard whose specialties included healing wards and enchantments. They were her comforters all throughout the ward, one of which had healed Cardin upon his first visit to the Wizards' Guild over a year ago.

"Prince Kataar," she nodded curtly to him. She was always a woman of few words and even less patience for disturbances in her ward.

"Master Sana," he nodded back. Looking to Draegus, his ghostly-white face unmoving, his hair turned stark white, Cardin asked, "How is he?"

"The same as ever," she replied wearily. "But you may, of course, sit with him for a while."

"Thank you," he gave her a weak smile, his stomach sinking as his eyes searched his father's face for any sign of life. No matter what anyone said, he blamed himself for letting his father take the fall. It should have been him. If it hadn't been for dark magic, it *would* have been Cardin. Yet as Sira reminded him every time, if it wasn't for dark magic, the wraith would have won. Drawing in a breath, he looked again to Sana and added, "We won't be long, I promise."

Showing no emotion beyond an apparent perpetual annoyance, Sana nodded and left the ward, her ash staff clacking on the reflective marble floor as she went. Cardin sat in the chair that Sana had previously occupied and stared at Draegus for a moment. Sira came around behind him and rested her hands reassuringly on his shoulders. She knew why he was here, as did Dalin. Cardin would put his hand on his father's head, and try to connect with him, try to find his soul.

He'd repeated the exercise at every opportunity, hoping that somehow, the Sword of Dragons would intuitively give him the ability to bring Draegus back from the brink. He failed every time, but he couldn't give up. More times than Cardin could count, the Sword had come through for him when he needed it the most.

Never before today had his need been greater.

Cardin lifted his hand up, even though it felt heavy, and reached over, hovering over his father's forehead. "Alright, Father," he spoke softly. "Let's try this ag-"

The clacking of footsteps upon the marble floor interrupted him. Reluctantly looking away from Draegus, Cardin was surprised to see Queen Leian entering the ward, and even more surprising, she was unaccompanied by any members of her guard.

"Prince Kataar," she spoke softly, as if afraid she might wake Draegus from a restful sleep. Glancing at Sira and Dalin, she asked, "Might I have a word with you in private?"

Frustration rushed into his chest, and he wanted to tell her that no, she could not, not now. This was his first chance in over a week to see his father. Unfortunately, diplomacy was important, as Jeric reminded him daily. Grimacing, he craned his neck to look up at Sira and nodded.

Giving him an encouraging smile, she rubbed his shoulders for a second and said, "We'll go get something to eat and bring it back for you."

Then, nodding to Dalin, she led the exiled Wizard from the ward, leaving Leian to speak with Cardin.

Stepping cautiously into the room, she nodded towards Draegus. "Has there been any change?"

"No," he replied, his face drooping as he again looked to his father. Then he remembered that he was addressing a fellow royal, and so he stood up and gave her a slight bow. "What can I do for you, Queen Leian?"

She stopped just short of passing the foot of Draegus's bed, a strange expression upon her face. Immediately Cardin was on his guard as he searched her sea-blue eyes for a sign of her intentions. Usually the Council members returned to their kingdoms after a Council session, with the occasional exception of Cardin. Why had she decided to speak to him now, alone and outside of official channels?

"You spoke well in Council today," she began, the confidence he was accustomed to hearing in her voice as strong as ever. "Your points were well thought out, and quite compelling." As an afterthought, she smiled and added, "As they always are. I confess I am always taken with your ability to infuse so much passion into your words, yet remain logical and thoughtful."

Feeling his cheeks warm, Cardin fidgeted with his hands, suddenly remembering the Royal Ball in Maradin, when she had tried to make him open up to her. Was that her intention now? Did she intend to ask him for some secret about Tal?

I really don't want to think of Leian as an opponent to verbally spar with…

Unsure what to say, he simply replied, "Um, thanks."

Leian attempted a warm smile. "You spoke truth when you said King Beredis was more passionate than any of us about seeing the Alliance succeed, but I believe you are a most worthy successor."

Now he was being compared, in a positive light, to Eirdin Beredis? There was no other way to describe it, he blushed. Yet no sooner had that happened than did he suddenly feel a greater surge of suspicion. She had never been one to give idle compliments, and he knew she was trying to garner his favor. But to what end?

Already annoyed about losing time with Draegus, and completely unsure what to do with his suddenly fidgety hands, he folded his arms. "While I appreciate your compliments, I can't imagine that's why you're really here."

A brief flash of anger burned in her eyes, but it quickly cooled. Suddenly Leian threw her head back in a high-pitched, amused laugh. "Oh my dear Prince Kataar, you never cease to amuse me. Even in Maradin, you were never one to mince words. For one who is so skilled in giving impassioned speeches, that is quite an oddity."

Again that night flashed through his head. Was this somehow a bizarre continuation of their verbal sparring? "I'm complicated that way," he stated simply. "But unlike in Maradin, we stand now on equal footing, don't we? So is there really a need to dance around whatever subject you've come to speak to me about?"

Grinning widely at him, and taking another step closer to him, she replied, "Ah, but you do not see that because we are equals, the need is ever greater." A brief thoughtful look overcame her eyes, and she nodded. "I concede, however, that because of my intent, perhaps we can be more truthful with one another. I do believe we are a perfect match, you and I."

Cardin's heart stopped for just a split second, as did all thoughts.

He blinked.

Blinked again.

Had she really just said what he thought she said?

"Um." Another silent pause. "E-excuse me?"

Her grin failed just a little bit. "You do not see it?"

"I, uh," he involuntarily took a step back, but she stepped with him. Suddenly the three feet between them was most certainly not enough space. A rushing sensation coursed through his chest, and fight or flight instincts screamed at him to flee.

"Our kingdoms have always enjoyed a long, healthy peace between one another," she continued. "Trade thrives, and we have always come to one another's aid. And as you have repeatedly told the rest of the Council, unity is needed if we are to survive. Falind and Saran have joined to become one, so it is only logical that Erien and Tal join."

"I mean, we already are fast allies," he quickly replied, stepping backwards again, unfolding his arms and waving his hands defensively in front of him. "You said it yourself."

"But this would formally unify our kingdoms," she pointed out. Looking to his father as she passed his head, she nodded to him and added, "Besides which, I know that you would rather someone else rule Tal." She looked at him pointedly. "You would much rather be here, with your father, or out in the field looking for a cure. If we were to marry, I could rule our kingdoms as one, and you would be free to do whatever you felt is needed."

The more she talked, the less he heard. All he could do was think of reasons to get her to leave or to drop the topic. "What about Sira? I love her."

"I know you do," she nodded. "This would be a political marriage, dear Cardin." That was the first time she had ever addressed him like that, and it almost made him jump out of his skin. It sounded and felt wrong. "I have no qualms about you keeping a mistress."

Suddenly red-hot rage overcame reason and fear. "She's not a mistress! She deserves a hell of a lot better treatment than that!"

"Oh?" Leian quirked an eyebrow upwards. "Do you intend to marry her?"

"I, yes," he sputtered, "I mean, if she wants to someday, but that's not the point!"

Her patience was apparently wearing thin, and she met his anger with her own, her face twisting down into one of rage. "This is politics, *not* romance. You are a member of royalty now, and sacrifices are a part of your life." *Gods, do I know that,* he thought. "I would happily marry your father if he were awake, but he is not, and he is not likely to, either."

Something snapped inside of Cardin. He stopped backing up so suddenly that it startled Leian into stopping as well. Next thing he knew, his finger was planted against her collarbone. "Don't you *dare* talk about my father that way!" His shout echoed against the granite walls, amplifying his rage. "Don't you dare speak of him as if he's a commodity you wished you could have acquired! He's a person, an individual, someone with feelings and hopes and dreams, and right now it's all he can do just to hang on!" She backed away from him, breaking contact with his finger, but he kept it pointed at her accusingly. "That's the problem with you royal types, you think people are your pawns to do with as you please, but we're not! And I'm sick of it, sick of all of the political maneuvering, the shell games, the smoke and mirrors, I'm done with it all!"

"Peace, Keeper," she shook her head, holding her hands up defensively. "I did not mean to imply that your father was not-"

"Don't make it worse by lying about it," he interrupted. "You said exactly what you meant."

Leian gaped at Cardin. Countless emotions played across her face, ranging from fear to outrage, and as he took a moment to try to calm himself and collect his thoughts, he lowered his accusatory finger and stared into her eyes. His rage died as the weight of his words sank in.

In one moment of outrage, he had just jeopardized an alliance thousands of years old. He knew he should have apologized, but he couldn't. Everything he'd said, he felt justified in saying. There was even a hint of smugness in his chest, feeling like he'd finally had the chance to say what so many commoners had wanted to say.

After taking an inordinate amount of time to collect herself, Queen Leian finally nodded. "Well. I suppose there is nothing more to say between us."

His eyebrows involuntarily rose up, but he bit back the reply he wanted to say and thought it instead – *we're not lovers having a spat. Get the hell out of here.*

Giving him the barest bow, she said, "Good evening, Keeper," and then she spun on her heel and stalked out, her boot heels clicking on the marble floor rather loudly in the sudden silence.

The rushing energy in Cardin still coursed through his veins, and he knew he wouldn't be any help to his father now. A mixture of outrage over her words and fear over his words made his mind run rampant, and focusing on anything now would just be impossible.

Since Sira and Dalin hadn't returned yet, he let out a deep sigh and sat down next to his father, intent on waiting in silence.

Of course, he never got what he wanted these days. Moments after Leian walked out, another figure appeared in the doorway. Part of him didn't want to look there, he wanted to ignore whomever it was. However, the woman cleared her throat and said in a strong voice, "Begging your pardon, My Lord."

Grinding teeth, he looked up to find one of his guards, wearing her ceremonial steel plate and chain armor and a black tabard with the kingdom's symbol in silver, a mountain guarded by crossed swords. Her hair was equally black, neatly kept in a ponytail, and her face, well-tanned, projected strength. He recognized her only as a member of the guard today, but he had not yet gotten to know each and every one of the royal guard, so he didn't know her name. He did note, however, the Lieutenant rank insignia on her brooch, holding her cloak on.

Sighing his frustration, he nodded. "Yes, Lieutenant?"

Taking that as a cue to enter, she stepped in, her gait confident. His eyes flashed to her waist and he suddenly took a greater interest in her – she had a custom Warrior's sword on her right hip rather than a standard-issued guard's sword.

Stopping a good ten feet away, she bowed deeply to him. Feeling awkward sitting while she did so, he stood up and nodded. When she stood up again, she looked at him with striking electric blue eyes. Those eyes darted towards Draegus, and he saw a brief flicker of a pained expression. Looking directly into Cardin's eyes, she said, "My name is Amaya Kenla." He wasn't sure how she did it so fast, but in a flash, her left bracer was off, and she pulled up the sleeve of her tunic, revealing a brand similar to the kingdom's logo, but different in that instead of a mountain, the swords crossed in front of a crown. "I am...I *was* one of King Beredis's Guardians." A second later, and the sleeve was down, and she was expertly lashing the bracer back on, something she clearly was accustomed to doing frequently.

This mildly surprised him. He had learned about the Guardians shortly after becoming Prince, a select group of royal guards that had the full confidence of the King, and were authorized to speak in his name when on missions. His father had commanded them, which meant he and King Beredis, and possibly Prince Beredis, had been the only ones in Tal who knew who all of the Guardians were. So far, only two other Guardians had come forward to identify themselves to Cardin.

"I have some important information to pass on to you," she continued. "About a village of orcs in the Wastelands and their shaman."

Cardin's blood turned to ice. *Another shaman?!* This was dire news, indeed. The ever-familiar weight on his shoulders mounted, and he slowly sat back down in the chair. His face must have shown his feelings, for Amaya's eyes grew wide and she shook her head rapidly, "Oh, no, no, it's not like that, Sire."

A frown drew down his face. "It's not like what?"

"I'm not here to give you bad news. In fact, quite the opposite."

An orc shaman was good news? Was it news of the shaman's death? He motioned to one of the chairs next to another bed and said, "Well, then, please have a seat and tell me what you need to."

She grinned at his invitation, an unexpected expression like that of someone who had just been proven right about something. Pulling the chair up, but sitting a respectable six or seven feet away, she sat with perfect posture and considered her words for a moment.

"It's a bit of a story, to give you the full picture," she stated, "But I'll sum it up as best as I can. I became a Guardian right at the beginning of the Orc War. Actually my whole team was inducted. We were once Warriors," she patted her sword pommel, "but were arrested and disbanded from the Guild when we failed to live up to Prince Beredis's...well, one of his laws."

Cardin couldn't help but grin. "I have some idea of what that's like." When the King had fallen ill, likely from the Prince poisoning him, the Prince had taken the opportunity to enact multiple restrictive laws that resulted in countless people becoming imprisoned. Now that Cardin was learning more and more about how economics worked, he suspected that the Prince had done so in order to charge as many people as he could extra money for the release of those imprisoned under the new laws, to help fund his wasteful expenditures.

"Once the King released us," she continued, "he inducted us into the Guardians, and we were sent on a lot of missions throughout the war. Including a mission to defeat General Arkad."

A shudder crawled down Cardin's spine. General Arkad. After Klaralin's defeat, Arkad had appeared to lead the orc army on a renewed invasion of Tal. He was a giant hulking orc, easily a head above the already tall orcs, and he was likewise much stronger, and his intelligence seemed to almost equal human levels.

Cardin had faced off against Arkad twice. The first time, the General had utterly humiliated Cardin with near-instant defeat, and it was only because of Dalin's interference that the General was forced to retreat. The second time had been in the Wastelands, the day before the Great Storm swept up from the south. Arkad had been much more interested in retreating already, and so after only a brief skirmish with Cardin, the General had used his enchanted axe to set the forest ablaze, cutting Cardin and the rest of the Allied Army off from pursuing them.

Narrowing his eyes at Amaya, he said, "Rumors abounded after my last fight with Arkad that he was dead, and we never saw him again after that night. Were you the one to finish him off?"

"No." She paused. "In fact, I helped him and his people escape."

He gaped at her, trying to process what she had just said. But before he could stop her, she launched into the tail of meeting a second orc shaman, named Tana, contesting the shaman that had backed the invasion. Tana apparently wanted peace with humans, but knew that the bad blood between orcs and humans was far too strong to even conceive of approaching the Allies, so she took all of the orcs she could influence further into the Wastelands, to hide and wait out the war, and prepare for the day when they might stand side-by-side with humans against the enemy that had invaded their home world.

"The Darksteel Army," Cardin whispered, the connections falling into place in his head. "The shaman I defeated first warned me about them, if not in name, and told me they would come for us eventually."

Amaya nodded. "Tana had foreseen the invasion of their world, but was forced to flee before it happened due to a corrupt leader that had marked her for death. She fled to Halarite, and began to uplift a tribe of orcs. You should see them, Sire, they wear tailored clothing and speak much like Arkad speaks, with perfect grammar. They're not the savages we thought them to be." A doubtful look came over his face before he could stop it. "It's true! I've seen it for myself, and they're getting better."

He was about to voice his doubts fully, but then stopped when he realized the implications of her words. "You've seen them again?"

She nodded and glanced at Draegus. There was a definite pain and a look of regret in her eyes every time she looked at his father. "Just after the Battle for Maradin," she began, "King Beredis recognized that Halarite was extremely weakened. He believed that the attack by the necromancers, and by that Dark Dragon, was evidence that everything you feared was true, and that Halarite faced invasion. He remembered what I'd told him about the orc shaman and her visions of humanity and orcs standing side by side on the battlefield. So he tasked my team to find Tana and her people again."

Cardin's mind reeled. King Beredis had *wanted* to ally with the orcs. The same people who had invaded Tal and the other kingdoms over and over again, who had helped Klaralin's second bid for power. Cardin had fought countless orcs. They were evil, soulless creatures, they always had been.

Except, this Amaya Kenla didn't believe so. And she had convinced King Beredis of as much.

Narrowing his eyes at her, he asked, "I take it you found them."

"Only two weeks ago, yes," she nodded. "And just last week, I returned. I…" Her voice caught, and he noticed for the first time the redness in her eyes. The building moisture. She had cried recently, and might be ready to do so again. She looked at Draegus, and her perfect posture was lost as she slouched forward and covered her face a moment. Then, she wiped her face and looked at him. "I wasn't here when Degrin killed the King." Her voice shook. "I wasn't here for Captain Kataar when he…he needed…" She drew in a deep breath to steady herself. "I failed my duty as a Guardian."

A well of emotion built up in Cardin's chest, cinching his throat for a moment. Gulping it down, he shook his head. "No you didn't. You were away on orders. You were performing your duty, Lieutenant, not failing."

She smiled weakly, but he could see that his words had not assuaged her guilt. "In any case, knowing what the Prince was like, but not knowing what you were like, and not knowing how you would react to news about a living orc shaman, I decided to observe, to see what kind of a ruler you were. I didn't want to risk the safety of the orcs, since they very well could be the last of their species."

He quirked an eyebrow at her regarding that assertion. "You think their entire world was wiped out?"

"I don't know," she shook her head. "None of the orcs alive on Halarite today saw what happened after the invasion finished. Did the dark army slaughter them all? Why do they invade? It seems like no one knows what the Darksteel Army does after it invades a world."

Cardin nodded with a grimace. "Yeah. I wish…that is, I hope we don't have to find out. But I'm afraid we will someday."

Drawing in a breath and wiping away some of the moisture with her gloved hands, she sat up straight again. "In any case, time is running out. The shaman said she would move her people if I didn't return quickly, out of fear that their location was compromised by someone intending them harm. Tana wishes to meet with…well, with you. The leader of Tal."

The grimace on his face drew further down. Another meeting. Another task on his shoulders. Part of him balked at the idea of a peaceful meeting with orcs.

But, having seen how the orcs fight, he knew that if they could, in fact, stand against the Darksteel Army with the Allies, it could very well be worth the effort.

He also couldn't ignore the fact that King Beredis had sought the orcs out of his own volition, not to destroy them, but to talk. The least he could do was follow through, and see where it led.

"Alright," he nodded. "But I can't tonight. I've already arranged an important meeting that I can't put off back in Archanon." He paused, trying to remember what was already on the agenda tomorrow. As always, there was a lot, and depending on how his meeting went with the merchants and farmers tonight, he would need to meet with the Warriors' Guild again.

But this was important. "Tomorrow morning," he nodded, just as Sira and Dalin appeared in the door.

"What is tomorrow morning," Dalin asked, startling Amaya. She bolted up from her chair and looked towards the new arrivals.

Cardin suppressed a chuckle at her surprise, and then waved his friends in. He saw them carrying trays of food and smelled fresh-cooked sausages, and his stomach growled angrily. He could fill them in while they ate. "You'd better all sit down. There's a lot to tell you."

More than just orcs, he realized, glancing into Sira's eyes uneasily. How would she react to Queen Leian's proposal?

Chapter 7

DARK ENVOY

BANG! BANG! BANG!

Kailar stirred, mumbling something about a dream of sailing ships flying through the sky. Had the banging been from the ships crashing into a wall of light? The blankets thrown over her were warm, and she could have stayed there for an age. The cold chill of a winter night in Tieran bit at her, the moisture in the air making it feel even colder.

BANG! BANG! BANG!

She started again, but not nearly as badly, and realized someone was at her bedroom door. Though still bleary-eyed, enough energy surged through her veins to make her leap from bed, pulling one of the daggers from its sheath beneath her pillow.

"Who's there?" she demanded.

There was a distinct pause. "It's me," Letan's voice called out hesitantly. Kailar felt a rushing sensation, her face warming against the cold. It was the last person she expected. Having been disbanded from the Warriors' Guild, but not having nearly enough money to purchase or even have a new home built for herself, she stayed in the Inn at Water's Edge these days, almost for free thanks to her favor with the inn's proprietor, Alric.

When she didn't say anything back, he added, "The Empress requires your presence immediately."

The edge in his voice snapped her out of reverie. He wasn't there for a midnight swoon or out of a desire to talk, but for business. Something was up, and based on the fact that absolutely no sunlight was visible from behind her room's drapes, it was urgent.

Rushing to the door, she pulled it open to stare at him with wide, worried eyes. His blazing red hair was a mess, and his blue eyes flickered in the light from the candle he held on a small tray in his right hand. He'd thrown on a white tunic and black trousers in a rush, his sword lashed onto a belt visible beneath a heavy cloak. Whatever was going on had happened fast, and he was as unprepared as she felt.

"What's going on?" she asked after recovering from being lost in his eyes.

"A small group of armed soldiers appeared through a portal on the city's edge," he replied. "They've asked to speak to our leaders. Empress Reyla wants you there when she first meets whomever they are."

He hadn't even finished explaining and she was already throwing her trousers on over her sleeping tunic, not caring to change into something nicer or more appropriate. While she finished pulling them on and her belt after that, Kailar's mind raced with possibilities. They came in portals, but armored, so not Wizards. She also thought it unlikely to be Sal'fe's assassins, since they usually wore stealthy clothes rather than armor, but she also realized that if they decided to give up on stealth, it would make sense for them to wear armor.

Was that who it was? Had Sal'fe sent them to demand that the Imperium surrender Kailar? The Allies didn't even know yet about the Imperium, so perhaps that was why they had asked for the city's leader, not the Empire's.

After tying her belt on, she lashed her two dagger sheaths on as well, placing the one she had pulled into its place after the fact. Turning, she found Letan staring at her absently, his eyes only vaguely focusing on her. She paused, but then motioned with her hands. "Well come on, show me the way."

Snapping out of his thoughts, Letan turned, said, "Right," and headed out of the inn. Kailar grabbed her black cloak on her way out the door and wrapped it around her shoulders, clasping it with a simple silver brooch. They descended to the first floor, and then rushed out the door of the empty dining area and into the dark streets of Tieran. The cold instantly bit at her face, and her first exhalation of breath puffed a cold cloud into the night air, flickering in torchlight from the streets. There were precious few everlasting torches on Devor, but Tieran, being the biggest and oldest city, had the most.

Letan quickly led her northwest, until they came across a contingent of Warriors, including General Querlin, surrounding Empress Reyla, standing in front of city hall. The Empress had taken a little more time to make herself look presentable, but as usual, that meant rather simple and unassuming clothes, while her hair was pulled back into a neat ponytail.

"Kailar," she said with relief. "Has the Lieutenant brought you up to speed?"

"I think so," she nodded, not bothering to look at Letan. "An armed group demanding to speak to you?"

Reyla nodded. "Whomever they are, they have remained on the edge of the city rather than violate the city borders. No names were given."

Pressing her achingly-cold hands against her dagger pommels, while inwardly wishing she had thrown more clothes on, especially gloves, Kailar said, "Well let's not keep them waiting any longer, then. I've got your back."

"As do your soldiers," the General added quickly. The Warriors had not yet been officially reformed into Imperial soldiers, but that conversion would take place hastily in the coming week, especially if a new threat had found its way to Devor.

With Letan next to him, General Querlin led the troupe west, while Kailar walked in stride next to Reyla. The city streets were understandably deserted, and Kailar looked up to search for the moons. None were above or to the west, and she remembered that both were rising only just before sunset right now, and so had already set. She glanced back to see barely a sliver of the larger moon peaking up over the distant ocean horizon.

If there were assassins in black waiting in the shadows around them, the lack of ambient light meant that the General and his soldiers might be completely unaware. They could be surrounded, walking into an ambush.

Her grip on the daggers tightened. It took all her self-control not to draw them.

Within minutes, they approached the edge of town, and Kailar strained to look around Kent and Letan to see what dangers awaited them.

It was not at all what she expected.

The first surprises were the overly-large, heavily armored beings bracketing the visitors. Not overly large like very tall humans, but altogether a different species. They had to be at least eight feet tall, maybe taller. More terrifying was how they blended into the darkness due to the darkened nature of their armor, their faces concealed by helmets with a T-shaped opening. The only illumination on them was apparently cast by balls of soft-glowing blue-white lights hovering in the hands of two of their companions.

Those companions were considerably shorter than the eight-footers, but still at least as tall as Kailar. Their armor was also made more of chainmail than plate, but like their taller companions, it too was darkened steel. They wore plate helmets as well, but more of their faces were exposed, revealing pale-blue skin that reflected brighter than anything else. The magical lights hovering in their hands made their faces ghostly-white.

Standing in the middle of the visitors, bracketed by the ghostly apparitions, stood a man in black and navy-blue robes, his white hair slicked back. He stood at six and a half feet, his face was gaunt and pointed, and the golden ears were pointed like an elf's. The man also had the arrogant look of a politician who thought he was a god's gift to the Universe.

This wasn't a delegation from one of the kingdoms, that much was clear. Nor were they visitors from the Dareann elves.

As General Querlin brought the Devor troupe to a halt with fifty feet to spare, Kailar started when she fully grasped what was going on. A delegation composed of at least three different species stood before them, three species that she had never met or even heard of.

Glancing around for any signs of a trap, she was relieved to find that the visitors had been watched closely by at least a dozen Warriors, all fully armed and armored, and likely the entirety of the night watch.

Yet, as she glanced furtively at the towering brutes and the light orbs of the ghost faces, she was afraid that the soldiers of the

Imperium were outclassed. If it came to blows, Devor might depend almost entirely upon Kailar's dark magic.

Her knuckles hurt from how tight her grip on her daggers were.

Reyla looked to Kailar, her face flickering in torchlight. "Stay by my side, please." And then she stepped forward, with Kailar keeping pace. Reyla gently pressed against Kent's shoulder, and he and Letan parted for the Empress.

They didn't stray very far ahead of their protectors, and Reyla set herself in a strong posture. The five entities in front of them were all taller than her, yet she showed no fear or cowardice before them, and Kailar was impressed with her new Empress.

"Greetings," Reyla called to the others, her voice commanding and steady. "I am Empress Reyla Aurin of the Devor Imperium." She did not bow, didn't even nod. She had taken to her new role of Empress well.

The gold-faced, pointy-eared man in the middle bowed deeply, flourishing his arms out as he did, before he rose back up and smiled. Even in the pale-blue light of the magic orbs, Kailar saw that his eyes were a sort of burnt-yellow color. "Greetings," he replied, his voice high and airy, a mist of haughtiness curling around every word he spoke. "I am Ambassador Xavien of the Darksteel Empire. I come before you in peace."

Something about his voice and his attitude made Kailar doubt his peaceful intentions, but her eyes flashed again towards the giant brutes, and their armor. There was something awfully familiar about their armor that set her on edge.

Somewhere in the distance, a duzai wolf howled into the night air, drawing the attention of both of the brutes who turned just enough for her to see their weapons secured to their backs, and that brought her memory to the fore front.

They bore great battle axes, the heads cast in the same darkened steel as their armor. She had seen identical weapons once before.

Klaralin's orcs.

She searched for weapons on the ghost-faced pair, seeking to confirm her suspicions, but they bore none. Instead, she noticed that they wore plate-metal gauntlets, with violet-colored gems embedded on the backs of their hands. They were pure casters, she thought, but unlike Wizards, their gauntlets and the gems embedded in them were their focusing implements, possibly enchanted to give them specific powers.

And the Ambassador had no discernible weapon, but that didn't mean anything. He was possibly the most dangerous of all.

Glancing towards the stars above them, Xavien said, "I apologize for the late hour of our arrival. We should have perhaps confirmed that it was day before arriving."

Reyla gave a curt nod, and spoke across the distance, "If you have travelled from afar, it is no wonder that you did not know better. Apology accepted. Now I must ask in earnestness, why have you come all this way?"

Kailar looked at Reyla curiously, but tried to keep any expressions from her face, while simultaneously fighting the urge to shiver. Her cloak was woefully inadequate for how cold it was, and her ears began to ache.

"It is a matter requiring lengthy discussion," Xavien gave a painfully-fake smile. "However to summarize, the Darksteel Empire has designs and intentions for this world, which I believe you call Halarite, but we do not wish to trounce upon your sovereign territory. In fact the opposite is true, as we wish to ally ourselves with you."

Though she may have tried to hide it, Kailar saw Reyla's shoulders tense, and she couldn't help but feel a sudden tension as well. That was a bold opening statement by Xavien. There was perhaps a veiled threat in his words, too.

Reyla did not look to Kailar, but she knew the Empress was immediately suspicious by the sound of her voice when she asked, "Ally with us to what end?"

Xavien looked perplexed. "Why, to ensure peaceful cooperation. To avoid bloodshed. Perhaps even, if you should find the benefits of sufficient value, membership within our empire."

That was unexpected. It was also somewhat unsavory, though Kailar couldn't quite point to why. Something felt off about this whole exchange, and she hoped Reyla felt it too.

Perhaps to be diplomatic, Reyla asked, "Tell me, what possible benefit could there come from such a membership?"

"Protection," was Xavien's automatic response, as if he had anticipated such a question.

When he didn't elaborate, Reyla asked, "Protection from what?"

The smile that crossed Xavien's face could have been described as wicked, even if it was meant to be placating. "Everything. Rival countries, rival worlds. We have armies to spare, and countless navies that we could bring to Halarite to defend your borders and shores." Reyla's head snapped back at that, especially considering the conversation they had had only hours ago about building a navy.

Kailar had succeeded in gathering as many privateer captains as she could earlier in the day, but most had been resistant to throwing in their lot with Reyla. Nevertheless, Reyla had convinced most of them with promises of freedom and money, and a chance to bring their families, and their crews' families, to Devor to ensure the Alliance would not harass them for joining Devor's navy.

The last few captains had required more persuasive methods involving more than a few threats of force, particularly from Kailar.

The fact remained that Devor's military power, especially on the sea, was woefully inadequate. The promise of a navy to protect their shores might very well entice Reyla, and that worried Kailar. She didn't like or trust Xavien, and the fact that the weapons that the giant brutes possessed looked like the ones Klaralin had provided the orcs made her infinitely more suspicious.

Still, there was no way she could voice such concerns just now. She would have to be patient.

After considering Xavien's words, Reyla drew in a breath and nodded. "As you have come here under a banner of peace, and since it is very cold, I would like to welcome you to our capitol city as guests, and propose that we talk further indoors."

Xavien's smile was arrogant, and had the look of a man who felt like he had just hooked a particularly large fish. "I agree."

He felt himself a hunter. Kailar feared that Devor was his prey.

Chapter 8

PARTING WAYS

Everything was wrong.

Sira gaped around at what she knew to be the throne room in Archanon, but nothing was the way it should have been. The slate-gray stone walls were stark-white, and the statues were gone, replaced by rows and rows of long wooden benches painted white. Even the stairs and platform for the throne were gone, replaced by a dais with a stone archway. She was surrounded by countless people, many of whom she didn't recognize.

To her right sat Dalin, who stared up at the dais with misty eyes. Sira frowned at him, and tried to ask him what was going on, but her voice wouldn't work.

"Does he always cry at weddings," a woman's voice asked from her left.

Sira wheeled around and stared, slack-jawed, at Kailar. Her hair was done up in mirrored-braids, like how Elaria used to do her hair when they first met the elf. Stranger still, Kailar wore lighter colors and, aside from the bemused look she gave Dalin, seemed strangely pleasant.

Wait, did she say wedding?

Sira looked up at the dais, and her heart stopped for a beat.

Waiting under the arch were both Cardin and Reis, both wearing finely-tailored clothes. In fact, they wore the same clothes they had worn at the Royal Ball in Maradin. Cardin wore a fine silk white shirt underneath a burgundy tunic with black trim, along with black silk trousers and fine leather boots. Reis likewise wore a white shirt, but his was underneath a copper-colored tunic, with the top button undone, along with brown trousers and boots, and a strange flatcap tilted to one side atop his head.

Dread welled into the bottom of her stomach. Who was getting married? Cardin or Reis?

A portal suddenly opened near the back of the dais, and Grand Master Wizard Syrn appeared through it, calling the assembly to her attention. She smiled, which in and of itself was a disconcerting sight, and pointed down the aisle towards the double-doors behind everyone.

Sira turned, and her heart sank. Queen Leian, wearing the same navy-blue dress from the Royal Ball, stood at the entrance, beaming sunlight filtering through the window above her and casting her in a glow.

Jerking awake, Sira's eyes shot open and she drew in a sharp breath.

Back in their room in Archanon castle. No queens in sight, no Kailar.

Just her, the faint glow of dying embers in the fireplace, and Cardin beside her, sleeping hard after another long day, and undisturbed by Sira's dream.

What...the hellfire?

She shook herself and shuddered, before extracting herself from the four-poster bed, pushing past royal-blue curtains and into their room. Her feet screamed at her when they touched the cold stone floor, so she bounced across it until she found the nearest rug. It wasn't warm by any means, but it was a lot better than stone.

Outside the windows, darkness reigned but for a handful of everlasting torches illuminating the gardens. She walked over to the window, having to bounce across another section of bare stone floor, before sinking into the couch set against the window, and stared. She could just see the pre-dawn glow growing in the east from her vantage.

"That has to be the strangest dream you've experienced yet," Raida

remarked in Sira's own voice. *"At least, since you and I joined."*

With a dark, gloomy grimace, Sira sighed and drew her knees up to rest her chin upon. *I think it may be the strangest dream I've ever endured.*

"Does it mean anything?" Raida inquired. *"Does it mean what you told Cardin yesterday was a lie?"*

Her stomach cinched at Raida's words. Did it? When Cardin had told her about Queen Leian's proposal, the manner in which he'd told her made her confident that he never intended to go through with it, and that he would adamantly continue to turn the queen down.

She wasn't worried, and she had told him as much. But if it was a lie, was it to Cardin, or was it to herself?

That thought alone sent a fuming rage into her chest. *I shouldn't care,* she thought.

"What do you mean?"

I mean this sort of thing never mattered to me before. Her hands contracted into fists, the muscles on her forearms bulging. *Especially before last year, I never cared what Cardin did with his life.*

A welling internal silence followed. Out in the hall, she heard muffled clanging and bangs, and knew that castle servants were already busy getting the castle ready for the coming day. But all she could do now was think inwardly and realize that she had just lied to herself again.

"Didn't you?"

Clenching her eyes shut, she let out an annoyed sigh. *Okay, maybe I did. But my point is, I decided over ten years ago that I was going to focus on myself. That I was going to be my own person. My career, my life was going to be what mattered to me, and I was going to rise in the ranks of the Guild. Cardin made his choice, our plans for our lives together vanished, and I decided not to look back.*

And now here she was, despairing over a dream in which Cardin married someone else. All while she struggled to come to terms with her new reality, her new shared existence with another entity.

As much as she loved having Raida in her thoughts, as much as she loved getting to know a Star Dragon's soul, the fact was that she was losing herself to it. Maybe all of this, her despair and jealousy over Leian, was further proof of that.

Never had she been one to pine over lost loves before.

Unless that was a lie, too.

Her emotions were out of control. She was losing herself, and instead of being able to lean on Cardin, as he had leaned on her so often over the past year, he was too busy.

Prince Cardin Kataar. The thought fueled her rage, not because she was jealous of his power, but because she needed him more than ever, and *that* thought enraged her like nothing else.

Sira screamed inside her head, *I shouldn't need anyone!*

Drawing her arms up and burying her eyes in them, she let out a silent scream, her breath airily escaping her throat. If Cardin hadn't been in the room with her, she would have let it out full-volume. But no, she was stuck in there, trapped with him, in the castle, away from the life she knew and loved and trapped with a...

Her silent scream died. Guilt welled up inside. Was it her guilt or Raida's?

"I'm so sorry," Raida intoned, her voice remorseful. *"I didn't mean to entrap you, I..."*

Don't be sorry, dearest, she shook her head rapidly, the remorse for her thoughts overwhelming her. *It's not your fault. It's no one's fault. Or it's mine, it's all mine.*

Tears streaked down her face, and she buried her eyes in her arms again. *It's all my fault.*

"No, Sira, it is not your fault. It never was." Warmth coursed into her core, physical and emotional, fighting back the chill of the night. *"Stop hating yourself for things outside of your control."*

We control our own lives, she replied, sniffling. *There's no one else to blame.*

"And why must someone be assigned blame? You've taught me that life happens, and that no matter what, we can never control everything. You're doing the best you can." The giddy feeling that she associated with Raida smiling coursed into her. *"I'm in this with you, remember? So we'll get through everything together."*

The deep well of darkness within her soul eased back a bit, the shining light of Raida illuminating the way. Sira smiled and nodded, and then wiped the tears from her face. *Together.*

"Tell me what you need?"

Sira drew in a deep breath, and then looked towards the bed. She couldn't see Cardin through the drapes surrounding the four-poster, but the growing light from outside at least let her see the bed frame.

Cardin was the love of her life. Of that she had no doubt. But she still needed to be her own person. She still needed to find her own way.

Maybe I should go on my own adventure, she thought. *Without Cardin. Just you and I, Raida. Give us time alone. We could hike into the mountains, maybe.*

"What about the meeting with the orc shaman today?" Raida asked. *"I've never seen the Wastelands or an orc before."*

Smiling and chuckling audibly, Sira nodded. *After that, we can go.*

A knock at the door startled her out of her thoughts, and she choked back the last of her tears. Cardin groaned out a complaint, but a second series of knocks answered him back.

That would be the castle steward knocking. It was time to get the day started, especially since they would be setting out early.

Another groan escaped Cardin and she could hear him turning over, but then his groan paused midway. "Sira?"

She couldn't help but grin, and called out, "I'm over here."

More shuffling followed, and then the drapes on her side of the bed parted to let his head stick out. Bleary-eyed, he peered out at her and asked, "What's going on?"

Her chest tingled at the thought of telling him about her dream, so she just shook her head. "Nothing, I just couldn't sleep and didn't want to wake you."

"Oh," he said, which then promptly turned into a giant yawn. She felt one creep up in her, too, and let it loose, just as the door opened to allow the steward, Kai, in. She was a severe woman who often wore plain, if tidy clothes, and she seemed to do a well-enough job managing the house.

"Good morning, My Lord," she stopped inside the door and bowed. "I apologize, but you asked to be awoken at dawn."

Sira glanced outside to find that the sun hadn't appeared to rise yet, but then remembered that there were mountains to the east, blocking the first rays of the sun a little longer.

"Yes, of course," Cardin sighed, and then let out another yawn, before he pulled himself out from the drapes of the bed.

Kai called out into the hallway, and a pair of servants rushed in to help Cardin get ready for the day. Sira scowled at that, somehow hating the idea of other people doing for her what she could do herself, but Cardin had wearily stopped protesting after his fifth day as Prince, and let the servants do their jobs.

Then again, she thought, *I don't mind them cooking breakfast for me.*

While the servants bustled about getting Cardin out of his night gown and into traveling clothes for the trip ahead, Sira busied herself doing the same, while Kai left the servants to attend their prince. Several minutes later, they walked out to the dining room and sat in their usual places at the main table. Dalin joined them only minutes later, while the savory scents of cooking pork and eggs wafted out of the kitchen.

As much as she was looking forward to a hike in the mountains, she would miss breakfast in the castle more than anything. Well, the food part, anyway, not the part where Cardin always had to talk about politics or something similar through meals.

Dalin and Cardin began discussing their meeting last night with the Merchants' Guild and Farmers' Guild, a meeting that Sira had decided to skip.

"If we can't get the bandit raids on outlying farms and inns under control," Cardin said through a sigh, "they're going to continue to refuse to work."

"Not to mention their claim of monsters attacking anyone near the mountains," Dalin nodded. "I have been giving that claim some thought, and I have a disturbing theory."

Cardin and Sira looked at him curiously. Just then, servants came forth with plates of their breakfast. *"Yes!"* Raida exclaimed. *"Bacon! Oh, and is that steak, too?"*

As the servants set plates before them, Dalin continued. "When Reis and the others activated the beacon in the dwarven city, they drove the kiklar out. Since then, the guards down there have reported several large rodents wandering the streets in growing numbers. Perhaps the kiklar, deprived of their usual food source, are finding ways out of the caves beneath Archanon into the foothills."

Sira grimaced at that thought. She had never seen a kiklar first-hand, but she had seen their webs when they fought Zairel a few months ago. A shiver ran down her spine at the thought of giant spiders.

A grimace drew down Cardin's face. "Gods, I hadn't thought of that. But yeah, I think you might be right. Honestly I'd dismissed their claims of monsters as them being overly demanding for protection, but..."

"But if it is the kiklar," Dalin nodded. "We need to find a way to help protect them."

"Which means increased patrols," Cardin nodded.

Just then, Governor Maral arrived and found her customary seat to enjoy breakfast. "Good morning, My Lords, My Lady."

Everyone mumbled a 'good morning' back. Cardin looked at Sira with narrowed eyes, but then an idea appeared to spark in his head. "Governor, once you've eaten, can you send a message to Daruun asking to have Reis report here?"

Sira eyed him curiously, but Maral simply nodded, and then looked at Dalin. "Might I send the messenger by way of portal before you depart today, Dalin?"

"Of course," he nodded.

"What are you thinking?" Sira asked, before finally diving into her breakfast, much to Raida's delight.

A smile stretched across his face. "I've been thinking about how I need a new Captain of the Guard, and I think there was more than a little wisdom in King Beredis's move having my father, who was at the time a Warrior, become captain. Not only did he bring experience, but he was able to advise the King on matters concerning the Warriors."

Another pang of jealousy wrenched at her gut. She knew the Warriors, too. But she tried to cool those pangs by chomping heartily down on a piece of steak. The fact was, she was on indefinite leave from the Guild, but she strongly desired to return, once she felt ready. She had only just made the rank of lieutenant before her adventure on Stella, and that was a significant step forward in her career as a Warrior. She had no desire to give that up now.

She also recalled how Reis was miffed at his own lack of promotion, and that he desired to bring about a greater change throughout the kingdom regarding the disparity between magic users and non-magic users. As Captain of the Guard and advisor to the Prince, he would be perfectly placed for such goals.

Grudgingly, Sira admitted it was a stroke of genius on Cardin's part. If Reis accepted, however, it would mean she wouldn't have her friend in the Guild anymore. She would feel even more isolated from others.

At least I'll have Raida...

If Raida could purr, she would have just then, but instead settled for infusing warmth into Sira's soul.

The others continued to chat about the state of the kingdom, but Sira found her thoughts turning inward again, wishing she could contribute in some meaningful way, and also wishing that things could go back to how they were before Cardin's coronation.

Ten years of mundane and three months of dealing with 'Prince Cardin' sandwiched a year of considerable time spent together with Cardin, Reis, and Dalin. For all of the terrible things going on in the world through those years, at least they had had each other, and she was able to actively contribute to making the future better.

The group finished breakfast, and Maral spoke with Kai to send a servant to Daruun through one of Dalin's portals. They agreed to meet the servant outside of the western gate shortly, and then together, Sira and Cardin headed back to their room so that they could gather what they needed. Sira quickly packed a small travel backpack, just in case. Their goal was to only spend the morning with the orcs, knowing that Cardin would need to return to Archanon quickly to continue dealing with the Warriors' Guild, and other matters of the kingdom.

Out of habit more than anything, Sira threw on a light cloak, even though she knew it was oppressively hot in the Wastelands during this time of year. She wore light leather armor as well, and strapped her white-dyed sword onto her left hip. With the pack pinning her cloak against her back, and thus keeping her shoulders clear, she was ready. Cardin didn't change into armor, he remained in a fine white silk tunic and black trousers, with the Sword of Dragons strapped to his back, and nothing more.

No one in the castle knew where Cardin was going besides Sira and Dalin, only that he was meeting with an official from another power. The deception was necessary, he insisted, because if the other kingdoms got word of the orcs before they knew the full story, they might mobilize a second invasion of the Wastelands, and no one could afford that sort of action just now, not if they were to prepare for a potential Darksteel invasion.

When they were both ready, they looked to one another across the bedroom, and Cardin smiled. Sira tried to smile back, but something faltered in her, and the smile felt forced.

Everything is different now, she thought.

Cardin's smile drew down just a little, but when he opened his mouth to talk, Sira felt a spark of energy press up against her soul. She turned west, towards the front of the castle, at the same time that Cardin did.

"A portal in the city," he frowned. That frown quickly blossomed into a giant grin. "It's Endri!"

Despite her apprehension, Sira's stomach leapt in excitement, and the two of them ran out of the bedroom, meeting up with Dalin in the hallway, who likewise had felt the portal, and then ran for the front. By the time they reached the double-doors leading outside, the Star Dragon had landed in the courtyard beside a fountain.

The sun gleamed off of Endri's verdant scales as he towered before them, eclipsing all neighboring structures in height, including the castle. He gazed down upon them with pin-point emerald starlight for eyes, watching as they gathered before him.

"Greetings, Cardin," Endri spoke through thought, his voice soft and deep like a man full of patience and understanding.

"It's great to see you!" Cardin exclaimed as he stepped closer and rested a welcoming hand on the dragon's forearm. "I didn't know when we'd see you next."

The last time they had seen the emerald dragon was shortly after defeating the wraith. He had checked in with Cardin after reporting their adventure on Stella to the rest of the Star Dragons, and intended to continue Cardin's training with the Sword. However, due to Cardin's coronation, he had no time to spare for training. Finally, after several days of pestering Cardin, Endri decided he would search for more clues to how the Dark Dragon Nuuldan had known about the conjured realm that the Wizards used to occupy before returning to Halarite, and he disappeared into a portal more than two months ago.

Acknowledging the others with Cardin, Endri looked at them and said, *"Sira, Dalin. I am pleased to see you again, as well."*

A grin stretched across Sira's face as she stared into his beautiful star-eyes, while Raida's soul seemed to purr. "Hi, Endri."

Cardin hesitated and backed away from Endri. "I am sorry, my friend, but I still am not in a good position to continue our training." The Star Dragon drew his head down lower so that they didn't have to crane their necks as much. "We were just about to leave for an important meeting, and after that..." Cardin's voice trailed off and he looked helplessly at Sira.

"That is unfortunate," Endri replied, his face contorting into a surprisingly good imitation of human despondence. *"However, I have not come to train you. Rather, I have found a potential lead on the identity of whomever is helping Nuuldan."* Cardin gaped at the dragon in surprise. *"Unfortunately, it is a bit of an awkward situation, and I could use your help to find a particular person and ask them questions."*

Sira frowned and asked, "Here on Halarite?"

Endri's snout weaved back and forth in a negative. *"No, on another world."* There was hesitation in his voice, and it made Sira instantly suspicious. *"It is one of many worlds that acts as a hub of trade and cultural exchange, and so is host to people from hundreds of species at any given time."*

"Incredible," Sira said before realizing she was speaking out loud. "I didn't know such places existed."

Raida felt giddy inside. *"Can we go there? I want to see!"*

"The problem," Endri continued, *"Is that Star Dragons are still rare and would stand out on such a world. Or at least, within the marketplace. In order to find the person who has the information required, I would need a human to enter the marketplace and find them, and either question the person themselves, or bring them out of the market to speak with me."*

Even before he spoke, Sira knew exactly what Cardin's response would be. "I...I am so sorry, Endri, but I can't help you right now. There's just too much going on in Tal, things are too chaotic right now. If I left on such a quest with you," he paused and drew in a breath, held it, and exhaled, his shoulders slumping. "I would be beyond negligent of my duties. This really is the worst time."

Something in her screamed about that, and for once it wasn't Raida. This was important, at least as important as meeting with orcs and brokering peace, at *least* as important as negotiating with the various guilds. Perhaps more-so.

Endri's features drooped and he hung his head. *"I trust no one but you three with such a task. Can you truly not spare even a day or two?"*

Letting out an exasperated sigh and flipping his arms up in frustration, Cardin replied, "I really can't, Endri, surely you unders-"

"I'll go," Sira interrupted.

Cardin stopped cold and wheeled on her, horror in his eyes, while Dalin and Endri stared at her. "What?"

She felt her stomach rush, but pressed on, "I'll go."

"But," Cardin shook his head. "Sira, I..."

Shaking her head, she said, "It's perfect, Cardin. I'm not needed here, I can't go back to the Warriors yet, but I'm going stir crazy just sitting around watching you play politics."

His face turned shades of pink, and she immediately felt the clutch of guilt in her chest. That was the wrong phrase to use. When he didn't reply at first, she drew closer to him and wrapped her hands behind his neck to force him to look at her. "Hey. I need to contribute, okay? And this is important." She glanced up at Endri and asked him, "Would that be acceptable?"

The Star Dragon looked hesitant, his star-eyes darting between Cardin and Sira, but eventually he nodded once, his snout dipping down and up several inches. *I believe so, yes.*

It wasn't the vote of confidence she wanted, but it was good enough. Sira looked again at Cardin and gave him her best fake smile. "See? I'll do this, you go do what you have to do, and we'll meet somewhere in the middle, having both accomplished wonders."

Wow, even I don't believe that line, Raida remarked.

Quiet, you, Sira admonished.

But she could tell that even Cardin didn't quite believe it. "Sira," he shook his head, "I need you here. I know you feel like you've done nothing these past few months, but your presence has kept me sane. It's kept me-"

Something flared in her, a remnant of her tumultuous thoughts this morning, and she interrupted him, "What about *my* sanity?" Immediately she felt embarrassed, and she looked down and away, breaking her hold on Cardin and turning away from him. "What about my needs, Cardin? I *need* this. I need to *do* something, alright? So just let me go."

Her word choice was questionable, and she mentally bashed herself for it. *Don't let me go as in we're through,* she thought. *Please don't think that's what I meant, it really wasn't.*

When Cardin didn't reply, she slowly turned her head to look into his eyes. She saw the hurt and fear in them. She knew her words had made him think exactly what she hoped he hadn't. "I'll be back," she corrected. "I promise."

He forced down a gulp and nodded. "Alright. If you wish to go, I won't stop you."

His word choice was precise. He won't stop her, even though he technically could, as her sovereign. Her appreciation grew ten-fold when he chose not to exercise that power over her.

"Thank you," she smiled weakly. She started to say something else, something neither had said to each other in over ten years, something she was afraid of. But she stopped herself, *because* of that fear.

Drawing in a breath, she instead nodded to Endri. "Alright. I already have some provisions," she patted her backpack, "so I'm ready to go. What do we do?"

Endri stooped down low, as if prostrating himself before a ruler or religious icon, and he stretched his right front paw out. *"Climb on to my back,"* he instructed. *"Place your legs just behind the wing joint and hold onto the spine in front of you."*

A rushing sensation coursed through her, and a wide-eyed smile overcame her face. "Seriously?"

"Hey," Cardin complained. "How come you never let me ride?"

Endri raised an eyebrow. Or maybe he arched both up, Sira couldn't tell from her current point of view. *"If you wish to come along now, you may."*

Cardin clamped his mouth shut, any further protest of jealousy instantly killed.

Carefully, Sira stepped forward and stood at the front of the Star Dragon's paw. Massive black claws jutted out from his digits, and his emerald scales looked hard as rock, while the paw itself was half as tall as Sira. She reached out and gently placed a hand on his paw, and was unsurprised to find that the scales had almost no give to them, and they were indeed stone-hard, yet surprisingly his 'skin' was exceedingly warm.

"You will not hurt me, I promise," Endri encouraged.

Smiling, she walked past the paw, and then hefted herself up his forearm, and awkwardly climbed further up, grasping at what little give he had in his scales, which was next to none. Once she was high enough, she grasped one of his dark-green spines and used it to heave herself up higher. Endri drew in a breath, his rib-cage expanding and the sound of rushing air surprising her.

Finally, she was atop the dragon and she eased down, her toes behind the wing joint as the dragon had requested. She clutched the spine ahead of her – it was smooth and hard, and unlike his scales, it gave off no heat. She was thankful that it was a late-summer day. She was also surprised by the lack of any smell – she had expected such a massive creature to have *some* kind of scent, but there was nothing. Was that normal?

When Endri moved, it startled and jostled her, and she gripped the spine tighter. If she wasn't extremely careful, she was afraid she would get bumped up and forward and impale herself on it. Hopefully Endri knew how to move with a rider.

She beamed down at Cardin and Dalin, and despite her fears, the rushing excitement of such a wonderful new experience made her exclaim, "This is amazing!"

Despite his fears, Cardin managed to smile for her. Then he turned serious again. "Be safe, okay?" he called up.

"I will," she gleefully called down. "I promise! Now go, do your thing and make the world a safer place!" Patting Endri's side, she said more quietly, "Let's go."

"As you wish," he replied.

Endri drew down then, like a snake coiling up for a strike, and then leapt up into the air, leaving Sira's stomach on the ground below while pressing her hard against his back. "Wooooooh!"

His wings whipped out in a rush of wind, and then she felt his muscles surge beneath her as his wings pumped hard, suddenly pushing her backwards as they propelled forward and higher into the sky. Her grasp on the spine became a death grip, and it was all she could do to hang on.

"I'll watch over her," she heard Endri assure Cardin. *"You have my word."*

And then, while they were still above the city, a wall of blue-white light appeared before them, and Endri sped them through to another world.

Chapter 9

RETURN TO THE WASTELANDS

Cardin watched with his heart thudding in his chest as Sira, astride Endri, soared into the sky. Just as they launched upwards, a shadow crossed over his, and he glanced back to find Amaya emerging from the castle, accompanied by a Wizard who wore forest-green robes with golden trim and held a pinewood staff in her hand.

The Wizard appeared young and was perhaps Dalin's age, although Cardin couldn't be certain. Amaya, on the other hand, wore clothes intended for travel in the heat of the Wastelands, a pair of tan trousers and a white tunic, along with an olive-green cloak made of a light material that fluttered easily in the wind. Her only armament was her Guild sword strapped to her right hip.

The familiar burst of magic from a particularly powerful portal tore his gaze back up to the sky, and he watched as Endri and Sira disappeared through a wall of light, which winked out of existence moments later.

She was gone. A pang in his chest forced him to draw in a sharp breath, and he felt an emptiness overcome him.

Why did it scare him now more than ever? Was it because she was going after the most dangerous single enemy they knew of? Or was it more than that?

The answer came to him almost immediately. It was his father's condition, the fear of losing his last family member that he knew of. It had driven home the fact that life was precious and fragile, or rather brought that fact boiling back to the surface of his thoughts, just like when his mother had died.

Cardin was afraid of losing anyone else.

Drawing in another breath for courage, he turned back to Amaya and her companion and nodded. "Lieutenant."

She bowed deeply, "Your Majesty." Was Cardin ever going to get used to being called that? "May I present to you the Wizard Nia."

The green-robed Wizard bowed lightly. "Greetings, Prince Kataar." Her mannerism was simple and to the point, and he immediately had the impression that Nia wasn't as outgoing as Cardin or Reis was. Yet when she rose from her light bow, there was the slightest smile raising the edges of her mouth. Her light brown hair was short, cut just above the nape of her neck, and her deep brown eyes belied the kind of intelligence and wisdom that came with living for centuries.

Motioning beside him, Cardin said, "This is Dalin, one of my chief advisors."

Dalin nodded, his face hard as he acknowledged Nia. Cardin wondered whether there would be an issue between Dalin and Nia, given Dalin's exile from the Wizards' Guild. He had left the Guild in protest of Grand Master Syrn's orders countermanding the former Grand Master's wishes that Dalin remain at Cardin's side, and Cardin was forever grateful for his friend's sacrifice.

An awkward silence had fallen amongst the four of them, so Amaya cleared her throat to break it and said, "Nia has been on special assignment from the Guild to accompany my unit over the last year, ever since the Orc War." A warm grin drew across Amaya's face as she looked appreciatively upon Nia. "She has been a steadfast companion, and one whom I absolutely trust."

Nia's previously emotionless eyes displayed a sudden warmth, the tiny hint of her smile suddenly growing to much more.

Raising an eyebrow, Cardin said, "To be honest, I'm surprised Master Syrn has allowed the arrangement to continue."

Their smiles disappeared, and they both looked to Cardin hesitantly. "Well," Amaya started. "Technically speaking, her assignment is still incomplete, so…"

"I have not yet checked in with the Guild," Nia stated, her voice soft but direct. "I do not intend to until I am no longer needed by the Guardians, as per the wording of my original orders."

Cardin's eyes opened wide. "I see." He looked to Dalin, who at first looked just as surprised, but his expression quickly changed to a mischievous grin.

"Well then at least you will not be faced with the decision I was," Dalin stated.

"Quite," Nia mirrored his grin.

The tension was gone, and Cardin knew now that the four of them would get along just fine. "In that case," he turned and motioned towards the western gate, "shall we?"

As the four of them made for the gate, two of the castle guards outside suddenly stepped forward, and Cardin, having anticipated their actions, held up a hand. "Stay here," he ordered them. "I won't be needing a guard detail today."

The soldiers looked uneasy at his orders, but they didn't object, and returned to their posts bracketing the entrance to the castle.

Walking quickly, the troupe headed for the gate with the rising sun at their backs. Cardin's earlier apprehension about Sira's absence returned, but as they left the Castle District and marched along the main road towards the western gate, his uneasiness turned towards the coming meeting. The last time he had faced an orc, it had been the other shaman, whose name he couldn't remember. She was the one who had warned him of an unstoppable army invading entire worlds. Now that the threat of the Darksteel Army loomed over them, he couldn't believe that it was coincidence that another orc shaman asked to speak to him.

Yet this new shaman, Tana, never served Klaralin, according to Amaya. The other shaman claimed that she attacked Cardin out of loyalty for her fallen master. Did this mean that Tana would not? Shamans were notoriously more intelligent than their subservient orcs, so perhaps a real dialogue could be opened between them. And if there were indeed more orcs in the Wastelands, maybe she could exercise the kind of control over them needed to ensure another war didn't break out between them and the Alliance.

The kindling of hope warmed his chest. If he did this right, they could all come out on top.

When they passed through the gates, they found a castle

messenger waiting for them, a young girl who held a sealed note in it. "Sire," she bowed before him. "I have the note addressed to Reis Kalind of the Warriors ready to go."

Cardin nodded, and then looked to Dalin. "Would you be kind enough to create a portal to Daruun for her?"

Dalin narrowed his eyes at Cardin for a second, and then he shook his head. "I am afraid I will not." Cardin gaped wide-eyed at him. "You need to practice your magic, Cardin."

Drawing in a breath to rebuke Dalin, his words caught in his throat, and then he laughed. "You're right, of course," he sighed. It was an opportunity to flex his magical muscles, and considering he had only ever conjured a handful of portals in his life, it was important to keep practicing whenever he could.

Without grasping the Sword, he instead closed his eyes for a brief moment and focused magic through his body. The flow accelerated, creating a rushing sensation within, until it felt ready, and he projected it ahead of him, beyond where the castle servant stood. His focus faltered for only one moment, but once he corrected it, a spark of light flashed before them, and a familiar blue-white shaft opened.

Looking to the servant, he nodded, "There you go. Be sure to ask the Wizard assigned to Daruun to send you and Reis back as soon as possible."

"Yes, Milord," she bowed again, and then dashed through the portal. He waited for two counts after she passed through, and then released his hold on the magic, allowing it to dispel back into the world and the portal to collapse.

"Well done," Dalin nodded appraisingly. "You overcame your mistake almost instantly."

"I learned from the best," he beamed at Dalin. "But I don't know where we're going next," he looked to Amaya and Nia purposefully.

Amaya nodded, and then looked at Nia, who stepped forward and planted her staff in the grass. The jade stone embedded at the top of her staff flashed green, and a second later, another blue-white portal opened exactly where Cardin's had been a second ago.

This was it. For all he knew, the next couple of hours could spell the victory or defeat of the Allies in the future. Everything might hang in the balance.

"I should go first," Amaya stated, "in case there are orcs on the other side."

Cardin motioned her on, and she stepped through the portal confidently. Dalin glanced at Cardin and then likewise preceded him. Glancing at Nia, whose green robes fluttered in the artificial wind caused by the portal, he stepped past her and walked through the portal.

As always, it was like walking through a door from one room to another, but he was instantly blasted by heat and humidity. For the first time since the war, he found himself standing in the Wastelands of Edilas, far to the south of Tal.

They stood in an open field of dead or dying grasses knee-high. The sky was clear, and the sun was much higher from the horizon, indicating that they had traveled further east as well as south. To his left was more open field, but to his right, far into the distance, it looked like the land abruptly ended. When Nia stepped through the portal and it closed behind her, it grew quiet enough that he thought he could hear the sound of crashing waves. Were they down by the southern coast?

Ahead, maybe a thousand feet before them, was their destination – an orc village.

No, village wasn't the right word. 'Village' implied something small with relatively few people. The encampment – no that wasn't right either – the *city* of tents and yurts before them sprawled far into the distance, with tiny spires of white smoke rising into the air from countless small cooking fires.

Taking in the vista, he quickly realized that it wasn't just tents, but other structures had been erected as well, using a combination of wood and animal bones covered in leathers and weaved cloth. Rooftops of structures that weren't tents were covered with thatched grasses.

And there were orcs everywhere. He always thought that they looked unnatural. Tall, lanky creatures that easily were a half a foot taller than Cardin on average, orc males had pale, mottled skin, and were utterly hairless.

In the past, the orcs he had encountered wore poorly fashioned leather armor or rags of clothes taken off of human victims. The only exception had been Klaralin's orcs, who had donned darkened-steel plate and chainmail armor.

These orcs were nothing like that. Every orc on the edge of their settlement drew closer and stared curiously at them, wearing finely-tailored tunics and trousers. Some even wore sandals, while others were barefoot. Not a single one of them roared or attacked them, they simply stared curiously and patiently.

Amaya started to walk towards the village, a smile on her face, but then she stopped short and glanced back at Cardin and Dalin. "Perhaps we should wait," she decided, and came back.

However, that decision was abandoned when, much to Cardin's surprise, two human men emerged from the growing crowd of orcs. They wore clothes, not armor, but one man carried what Cardin recognized as a standard-issue longsword in a sheath on his belt, while the other had a pair of daggers sheathed on his belt.

"Elic, Peren!" Amaya called and rushed towards them.

"Amaya," one of the men called out. "I was starting to worry, it's been over a week!"

"I know," she said when she met up with him. It looked like they wanted to embrace one another, but they settled for handshakes. Cardin guessed the man who spoke was Elic, whom he sensed was a Mage, and was well-built for combat with defined muscles pushing out against his tunic. The other man likewise was strong, but stood a head taller than Elic and had black rather than brown hair, and his height gave him the overall appearance of a lithe person.

Cardin stepped forward, wary of the gathering orc crowd but interested to find out who these men were. "I know, I know, I'm sorry," Amaya nodded. Her joy at seeing them vanished, however, as Cardin came up beside her and her two companions noticed him.

Elic's eyes grew wide in surprise. "The Keeper of the Sword!"

Something constricted in Cardin's chest, and he nodded. "Hello," he said awkwardly. It just occurred to him that if these men were part of Amaya's Guardian unit, they had been in the Wastelands for six months. Which meant they didn't know what had happened in the spring.

"Elic, something's happened," Amaya started. "We…" She paused and looked at Cardin, before meeting Elic's eyes. "A lot has happened, and I don't think there's any way I can soften the blow. King Beredis was murdered."

Both Elic and Peren grew pale, despite their well-defined tans. They looked to one another, and Elic in particular staggered backwards. "Wha…what?"

Cardin wanted to say something, but he knew that this was something Amaya had to tell them, so he stood by patiently as she filled them in. Halfway through her story, three more humans joined them, two women and a man, each wearing plain clothes but sporting different kinds of weapons. Amaya started over to quickly fill them in, ending with, "The King had left behind sealed orders dictating who would become the next King, and as it turns out, Captain Kataar was to be King."

Amaya's five Guardians gaped at Cardin. Elic asked, "Does that mean...?"

Nodding, Amaya confirmed, "The Keeper of the Sword is now Prince of Tal."

All at once, Amaya's five Guardians dropped to one knee and bowed their heads. "Forgive me, My Lord," Elic spoke for the others. Cardin had the growing sense that Elic was Amaya's second-in-command. "I did not realize and did not show you the proper respect."

Cardin's face flushed against the heat of the Wastelands. He drew in a breath, noting absently that it didn't stink down south nearly as bad as it did by the marshlands up north, and he said, "Please, stand. There's no need to bow before me. Especially not as Guardians."

Elic smiled and stood, the others following suite. "Thank you, My Lord. I have heard plenty of stories about you from those who fought side by side in the Orc War, and I must say that it is an honor to meet you."

Blushing yet again, Cardin smiled and glanced at Dalin, who merely rolled his eyes at Cardin, but still grinned.

Amaya explained to Elic and the others, "I spent the last week observing the Prince to ensure he would not break the trust of the orcs. From the sounds of it, however, our timing in finding the orcs probably couldn't be better."

"Indeed," a raspy voice called from the orc settlement. The group of Guardians turned as one and parted, revealing that two distinct orcs had emerged from the crowd. Cardin tensed at the sight of them, particularly the larger one. Standing well over a foot taller than the other orcs, he recognized General Arkad, former leader of the orc invasion forces in Tal. Though he did not wear armor, Arkad looked every bit as terrifying as Cardin remembered, perhaps even more-so now that he sported multiple scars upon his face, including his right eye, which had apparently been wounded so badly that the General had lost the use of it. He didn't wear a patch over it, as a human might, but that made the mangled visage of his eye ever-more disturbing.

The other orc was considerably shorter than all other orcs, which Cardin understood was normal for orc shamans. Like all of the other orcs, she wore finely-tailored clothes, though she chose a skirt instead of trousers. He wondered for a moment if they had tailored their clothes to emulate human styles, or if their style was born from their own home world.

This was the moment. *First impressions,* he thought. This was when everything would either turn for or against them all. Who would make the first move?

I will.

Stepping forward once, he bowed deeply at the waist. "Good morning," he said. Standing up, he added, "I am Prince Kataar of Tal."

The woman bowed in kind. "And I am Tana, First Shaman of the orcs. This is General Arkad."

Cardin glanced at the giant general, who merely nodded gruffly and spoke in his deep, rumbling voice, "We've met."

Did Arkad hate him? Did he hold a grudge? For that matter, did Cardin? He felt no small amount of anger as he remembered the Warriors that Arkad had slaughtered at the Relkin Mining Camp. Anger turned to rage when he remembered the rest of the war, and of meeting the General in the Wastelands one more time before the General had used his enchanted weapon to set the forest ablaze. Many Warriors had burned to death in that blaze, or suffocated in the smoke, before the great storm doused the flames.

There was no denying that Cardin *wanted* to hate the General. Desperately.

But that wasn't why he was here. He reminded himself that there was far more at stake. So he opted to compliment the General instead. "You were a worthy adversary," he nodded his fake appreciation.

Arkad merely grunted.

Tana smacked him in the stomach, and he started. "Yes," Arkad replied. "Our battles were certainly…memorable."

Cardin supposed that was the closest he was going to get to a compliment.

Then, remembering his manners, he motioned beside him and said, "This is Dalin, one of my chief advisors."

"Another Wizard," Tana nodded appraisingly. "You are most welcome."

"Thank you," Dalin bowed. "However I should tell you that I am not a member of the Wizards' Guild."

Tana's eyebrows rose up curiously, a strange sight since she had no actual hair on her brow. "I see. In any case, if you will follow me," she motioned towards the center of their settlement. "I think we have much to discuss."

Cardin nodded while avoiding Arkad's stare. "Yes, we do…"

Chapter 10

OPENING DIALOGUE

With a full contingent of soldiers surrounding them, Kailar walked with her Empress and Xavien towards the city council chambers. The hint of predawn had grown in the minutes since they met the Darksteel representatives, and as they walked east into town, it lit up their faces.

Xavien walked side-by-side with Reyla, which relegated Kailar to walk to Reyla's right, and Letan and Kent to walk beside her, while Xavien's delegation walked to the left. With the sun still not quite risen, most citizens in Tieran were asleep, but a few sleepy, curious gawkers stared out of their windows at the passing entourage.

Kailar kept her senses turned outward, ready for an attack at any moment. The soldiers of Devor were distracted, eyes turned on Reyla and the curious arrivals, so she took it upon herself to look for any signs that this was a prelude to an ambush. Her hands icily gripped her daggers, and she could count each and every heartbeat thudding in her chest.

But the moment never came. No one attacked, and before long, they arrived at the double doors into the wooden council chambers.

The entourage had walked eerily silently, so when Reyla spoke, it startled Kailar. "Our Imperium is very newly formed, and I am afraid we have yet to build a proper capitol building," she explained to Xavien. "However, for the time being, the former city council chambers should suffice."

Smiling through his teeth, Xavien replied, "Indeed, this will do quite nicely."

Reyla turned, "Kailar, would you be so kind as to inspect the interior and start a fire?"

Somehow that request burned at Kailar. Not only did she not wish to leave her empress's side, she felt indignant about being relegated to a servant's task. A second later, she dismissed that notion, and realized that Reyla was more concerned about a second assassination attempt.

Bowing lightly, Kailar replied, "At once, Empress," and stepped ahead of the group purposefully. She glanced sidelong at Letan, trying to catch his blue eyes in the glint of torch light, but he was focused entirely upon the new arrivals. Was he as suspicious of them as Kailar was?

Grabbing an everlasting torch off of a mount next to the entrance, she opened the ironwood doors with a creek, and peered into the antechamber. Aside from a reception desk, it was empty. Crossing the antechamber in long strides, she quickly opened up the second set of double-doors, and nearly jumped out of her skin when a loud ruffling noise met her and an ocean breeze blew her hair back.

Calming her racing heart, she reminded herself that the windows looking out upon the bay had been smashed only yesterday, and heavy curtains had been hastily strewn up until the glass could be replaced.

The sconces holding candles on the walls had been given fresh candles, so she set about lighting them with the eternal flame of the everlasting torch, before she then set the torch on the stone mantle of the fireplace next to the doors and arranged a few logs into the freshly-cleaned fireplace. *At least the servants are efficient and attentive,* she thought as she admired the fact that not a single trace of ash or coals was left behind from yesterday's fire.

Once the logs were prepared, she moved to pick up the torch to use it to set them alight, but then paused. That would take time, without kindling, and she had another idea.

Kneeling again, she pulled out a single dagger, and pointed the tip of the blade into the heart of the arranged logs. Creating the increasingly familiar void within, her body charged with magic, and that magic easily flowed into her dagger, before she shaped and molded it.

Focusing her will, fueled by the anxiety she felt towards the new arrivals, the power within the blade sparked and bucked, anxious for escape, and when she felt warmth coming from it, she released that power. It streamed out as a burst of blue flames, almost instantly lighting the logs. She forced more power into her blades, and tried to hone that power as best as she could and keep it flowing.

Satisfied that the logs were properly hot, she cut the stream, and the blue flames died out, replaced by the softer orange light of regular fire.

Grinning, Kailar grabbed the torch, looked around the chamber one last time, and then went back out into the antechamber to finish lighting the sconces out there. Finally, she went outside, replacing the everlasting torch in its place, and nodded.

Looking specifically into Reyla's eyes, she said, "The chambers are prepared, Empress."

With the slightest quirk of her lips, Reyla acknowledged Kailar's double-meaning, and then led the delegation inside.

Once in the antechamber, Reyla again turned to Xavien. "Are your companions part of your negotiating team, or protectors only?"

"Ah, yes," Xavien's burnt-orange eyes darted to his entourage. "They are largely a protective escort. I take it this is an antechamber?" Reyla nodded. "Then they may remain here."

The four guards snapped to attention, and separated into the four corners of the room, where they took up positions staring into the center of the room.

"General," Reyla turned to Kent, "you and Lieutenant Velethar please remain here as well. Ambassador Xavien, would you permit my chief adviser Kailar to accompany us in these talks?"

A sense of relief washed over Kailar upon Reyla's words – she had begun to fear she would be asked to remain behind as well.

"Of course," Xavien nodded.

Reyla nodded to Kailar, and she moved to precede them into the chambers. A flash of sudden motion startled her, and instinctively Kailar drew her daggers as one of the lithe, chainmailed visitors suddenly blocked her, his hand held out to halt Kailar.

Pulsing dark magic into her daggers, they set to humming, and the sound of drawn swords rang through the antechamber.

"Stop," the ghost-like man commanded, his voice somehow modulated to sound like three octaves at once. "No weapons will be permitted while we are absent from Ambassador Xavien's side."

Heart pounding, fingers tingling, Kailar was prepared to defend herself. Movement from the corner of her eye told her a sword-wielding person had come up next to her, but she didn't dare tear her eyes away from the ghost.

It took a few moments for the ghost's words to register in her mind, and she frowned, lowering the daggers ever so slightly. The ghost still hadn't drawn a weapon, but his gauntlets were definitely enchanted, the violet gems inset into them glowing brightly.

Ready to object, Kailar paused, and realized that she, too, didn't necessarily need weapons to defend herself or her empress.

"Kailar," Reyla's commanding tone called out.

Lowering the daggers further, Kailar turned, and started for a second when she realized that it was Letan who had rushed to her side, ready to defend her.

When Kailar met Reyla's eyes, the empress commanded, "Leave your daggers with the Lieutenant."

Her grip tightened, but she nodded, knowing that if she wanted to be a part of this first meeting, she would have to do as asked.

With a barely-hidden sigh, Kailar sheathed her blades, and set to work unlashing them from her belt. Finally, she turned to Letan, met his blazing blue eyes, and saw the look – fear. Caution. Suspicion.

He didn't trust the newcomers either.

Widening her eyes for a brief second, she then blinked twice in rapid succession, her assuring him that she shared his suspicions, and she would do all that she could to watch out for Reyla. Letan sheathed his sword and accepted the daggers.

When Kailar turned back to the doors into the chamber, the ghost was already gone, having silently moved back to his position in the back right corner, the lights of his gauntlets doused.

With the moment passed, Kailar strode into the antechamber then, and stepped to one side to await the others. Side-by-side, Reyla and Xavien walked in, and Kailar made a show of closing the double-doors, looking again into Letan's eyes until the doors closed.

Another frigid ocean breeze blew in, so instead of going to the backside of the room, Reyla motioned to the chairs closest to the fire.

Xavien graciously took the one whose back was to the fire, and Reyla sat opposite of him rather than take up the head chair. Kailar took a moment to tend to the fire and throw another log on before she sat down to Reyla's right.

"Well, then," Reyla smiled plaintively. "Let me be the first to officially welcome you to our humble little world of Halarite."

Something in Xavien's smile was off, and Kailar narrowed her eyes at him. He replied, "Thank you."

Asking the same question burning in Kailar's mind, Reyla asked, "Have others from your empire journeyed to our world before?"

"Of course," Xavien acknowledged, startling Kailar. Her surprise must have shown on her face, because Xavien looked pointedly at her and added, "I would not have known where to come had we not sent scouts ahead to locate places of power upon your world. It is better than having ambassadors wander the wildernesses of new worlds aimlessly."

Kailar had to admit that it was a good point, but then she remembered her first encounter with someone from another world. "I am surprised that you came here," she said, "rather than seek the most powerful person on our world."

Suddenly she realized that she had spoken out of turn, and looked apologetically at Reyla. Reyla acted as if this were perfectly natural, and showed no hint of the impropriety Kailar had just shown. She was an adviser only, not a negotiator, not a leader. Reyla should be the one to ask questions or make points. Cueing in on Reyla's attitude, she looked back to Xavien, and waited patiently for him to respond.

"You refer to the one known as the Keeper of the Sword, I believe," Xavien acknowledged. "Prince Cardin Kataar of Tal, is it?"

Kailar's eyes widened. Not about Cardin's recent coronation, that news had already reached Devor. No, she was shocked at how much Xavien knew about Tal and Cardin.

"It would seem you know much about our world," Reyla pointed out.

"Indeed," Xavien nodded. "I confess that it is our usual procedure to learn as much as possible about a new world before sending official representatives to it. And to fully answer your previous question," he looked again at Kailar, "we chose Devor because we acknowledge already that the kingdoms of Edilas are less likely to welcome us cordially, thanks largely to the prevalent religion there."

Kailar's eyes narrowed, but she held her remark back. Reyla, thankfully, said it for her, "The Order of the Ages is prevalent on Devor as well, even if there are fewer representatives here."

"Indeed," Xavien said. *He says that a lot,* Kailar thought. "However we assessed that due to the fervent independence felt by the citizens of Devor, and the lack of Covenant members on this land, you would be far more accepting of off-worlders than Edilas. Indeed, the common folk of Edilas have shown a propensity of violence towards what they deem to be outsiders."

Unable to hold back, Kailar said, "You know an *awful* lot about what goes on here."

"As I said," Xavien smiled, "we ensure we know as much as possible. Our Empire is currently composed of members from over thirty worlds, and we have been to far more worlds, met far more species than that. We have become quite skilled in these matters."

Somehow that statement sent a chill down Kailar's spine.

"Yes," Reyla frowned. "You mentioned the perks of membership including protection, such as naval protection."

Turning his attention back to Reyla, his smile grew ever-larger. "Indeed, that is but a taste of what we can offer, should you choose membership. You have pointed out that your Imperium is very newly formed, which I take it to mean that your standing army and naval force is rather lacking."

Of course he would know that, Kailar thought, gritting her teeth.

"We are stronger than many might think," Reyla evaded tactfully. There was no hint of indignation in her voice, only a casual statement of fact, even if it was a stretch of the truth. "However, I would say that additional protection would not go amiss. Tell me, do you offer such protection for non-members in any capacity?"

More and more, warning bells went off in Kailar's head, and she wanted to scream for Reyla to stop. They were revealing too much about themselves, even indirectly.

Then again, as she looked upon Xavien, saw the cold, calculating soul behind his smile, she suspected that he already knew exactly how ineffective their defenses were at the moment. He knew they were vulnerable.

His arrival now, the morning after the Imperium became official, the morning after an assassination attempt, it wasn't a coincidence. Maybe Kailar was being paranoid, but paranoia had kept her alive for a long time, and she wasn't about to stop listening to her instincts now.

"I am certain that we could make arrangements," Xavien pleasantly said. "However, if you will permit me, I would like to lay out for you the benefits of becoming a part of our great empire."

Reyla smiled patiently, but more and more, Kailar felt like this was a trap of some kind. Not the kind she could fight with magic and daggers, either.

"By all means," Reyla replied. "Tell us all about the Darksteel Empire."

Chapter 11

THE DEADLANDS

The wall of light of Endri's portal passed over Sira, and they traveled from the warmth of a summer morning to the scorching heat of a new world.

The sky before them was cloudless and blue, revealing the first unusual and breathtaking feature of the third world Sira had ever visited outside of Halarite – a blue and white giant arc bowed across the sky, with defined lines and apparent gaps between colors.

Blurring motion in her peripheral, and Sira gaped around as Endri swooped them around a terrifyingly tall, sheer-faced red mountain. And that was when she realized that Endri had brought them into the middle of a mountain range that put the Ilari range east of Archanon to shame. The monolithic peaks stretched up to dizzying heights, many of which were so steep that she couldn't imagine anyone climbing them free-hand even on the best of days. Anywhere the slopes weren't too steep, the stark, dark red was broken by the deep green of trees, grasses, and other flora, and as the humidity pressed against her, Sira realized that they were in a jungle environment, not too dissimilar to the shores of Port Hope, save for the mountains.

"This is exhilarating!" Raida declared.

And as the strangeness, the grandness, and the terror she had felt for a brief moment subsided, Sira found herself agreeing. A new world, vastly different from Stella or the Celestial Spires, and she was the first human from Halarite to ever see them.

Eyes turning upwards again, she gaped at the pearlescent arc that stretched from horizon to horizon, and shouted above the whipping wind, "What is that in the sky?"

Endri's head tilted up a moment, and his bemused voice echoed in her mind, *That is what is called a planetary ring. Not unlike what surrounds some of the worlds orbiting Halarite's star.*

With widening eyes, Sira felt her jaw fall open. Decades ago, astronomers on Halarite had created telescopes, similar to the ones sailors used but more powerful, that could see the strange 'moving stars' in their sky more clearly, identifying them as actual distant worlds like Halarite. And at least two of the ones near Halarite had large rings encircling them.

"That's incredible!" she shouted. "It's beautiful!"

"Yes it is," Endri agreed, but Sira noted a timbre in his voice that hinted at sadness.

When the emerald dragon didn't speak further, she leaned forward, conscious of the spine she gripped to steady herself, and asked, "What is it? What's wrong?"

Endri's head tilted upward again, and the sound of a sigh echoed through her thoughts. *"I was not yet born when the rings of this world formed, but I know the story of how they came to be. It is…unpleasant."* Tilting his head to one side so that one eye could look back at her, she swore the dragon grinned at her. *"However, knowing you humans, and you in particular, I know that you will ask repeatedly until I tell you the story. Especially knowing what we are about to see."*

She frowned at the dragon's last words, but then jolted when she realized just how low they had soared. The tops of the jungle trees raced by Endri's paws, a few feet, maybe even just a few inches away. Ahead, she saw an unusually low, tree-covered mountain, and they were headed right for it.

Wide-eyed, she backed up, willing Endri to turn, or fly higher, or *something,* but instead the dragon changed the pitch of his wings, and they slowed dramatically, pitching her forward against the spine. Just when she thought they were going to hit the mountain, the dragon warned, *"Hang on!"* and began to pump his wings, slowing them even more-so and nearly throwing her off. At the last moment, a clearing appeared beneath them, and Endri roughly set them down in it, the ground thundering in protest, echoing the jolt in Sira's body.

"There we go," Endri said confidently. *"Not a bad landing, considering I had to ensure you did not fall off."*

The sudden quiet after hearing nothing but howling wind seemed deafening, until the sounds of the jungle began to press in all around them. Some grinding, scratching bug noise took up a chorus in every direction, and then what she guessed were multiple birds cawed out. Or maybe not birds, she truly couldn't be sure what made the noise.

Endri's massive paws were partially occluded by tall ferns reaching up to his knuckles, so there was no telling what was beneath. Still, after the jarring landing, Sira was ready to get back down onto her own two feet. She started to adjust and prepared to slide down, but Endri looked back at her curiously. *"It might be faster if you stay on my back while we walk around the mountain."*

She blinked at him and frowned. Glancing first at the mountains, and then at the jungle all around them, at the tree branches that were right at the height she sat atop Endri, Sira shook her head. "Thanks, but I think it'll be safer to walk." Something howled from behind them, and she craned her neck backwards. "Uh, maybe."

With a soft mental chuckle, echoed by a strange rumbling from his throat, Endri assured her, *"Nothing will attack you while you are with me."*

She nodded and looked intently at the ground. Endri slowly lowered down as much as possible, stretching out his left leg so that she could clamber down it. As she worked carefully and slowly, using some of his elbow spines as foot and hand holds, she asked, "If there's still more distance to go, why land here?"

Hopping the last five feet down, she shuddered when she discovered the ground was soft, and the ferns were waist-high. She hoped nothing on the jungle floor would crawl up her trousers.

"As I said on Halarite," Endri replied, *"If anyone knew of my presence, it might cause a stir amongst those in the bazaar, and the person we need to talk to might flee. Especially if they fear a Dark Dragon."*

Sira nodded up at him, taking a moment to gaze into his star-like eyes and feeling lost for a moment.

Breaking herself out of the gaze, she looked around and asked, "Alright, then where do we go?"

"I will walk you to the edge of the jungle," Endri replied, and began to walk towards the left of the mountain. *"Then you will need to walk the*

remaining few miles through the Deadlands."

Sira felt a pang of fear. "Uh, Deadlands?" She stayed rooted to the spot for a moment, but when Endri didn't stop walking and pushed his way into the jungle, she ran after him. "Hey, what are the Deadlands?"

Endri kept his snout pointed ahead and weaved in between trees effortlessly. Sira, on the other hand, immediately began to trip over roots and vines, and had to very carefully weave her way through the jungle to keep up.

"*The Deadlands and the planetary rings are, unfortunately, related,*" Endri began after a moment. As they trudged on, he explained, "*Long, long ago, a powerful man ruled over this entire world. By powerful, I mean he was capable of great magic. However, when a rival world challenged his authority and threatened him with invasion, he decided that rather than send his armies to meet the invaders, he would frighten them off with a terrible show of power.*"

Endri looked up for a moment, through the dense canopy of the jungle towards the rings above. "*This world once had a single moon. So the man met the general of the invaders and told the general that if they did not leave at once, he would bring the moon down to crush them all. When the general scoffed and called the man's bluff, the man raised his hands into the air, and summoned as much power as he could. Moments later, he pulled. The moon drew closer to this world. And closer. Until the ground trembled.*

"*The general was terrified, able to see the moon come closer every second, and he ordered his armies to retreat, calling the ruler a madman for dooming his own world. The ruler stopped, but the damage was done — so much power had been required, that he had directly drained the life of everything around him for miles, killing the jungle, killing the* soil." Sira almost lost her footing, she was so lost in Endri's story. She couldn't imagine the kind of power necessary to do what Endri had described, and wondered if even Star Dragons could ever summon so much power.

"*In the end,*" Endri spoke solemnly, "*the plants did not just wither and die, they turned to ash and were whisked away on the wind. The soil was left without any means to grow life again. And the moon,*" he again looked up for a brief moment, "*was too close to this world, and broke apart. Over the course of thousands of years, it disintegrated and surrounded this world, becoming a planetary ring.*"

The trio walked on in silence after that, with not even Raida able to conjure up a remark over what they had learned. Finally, after an age, Sira said, "That's terrible. And terrifying."

"Indeed," Endri replied.

Thinking about the emerald dragon's tale, she frowned, and asked, "But, I thought magic was derived from the stars. How did this ruler drain the life of everything around him rather than directly from the star?"

"All life is a conduit for the energy of the stars," Endri explained. *"And some are able to draw in and conduct energy more efficiently than others naturally, while others, while* conscious *beings, can improve their ability to conduct magical energies through meditation and reflection, by improving their mental, emotional, and psychological state. The man I spoke of had gained knowledge of incredible power, and of how to force other life to act as his conduit, without ever learning to become a better conduit himself. He orchestrated his magic by forcing other life to cast it for him or with him, and since plant, animal, insect, all other life around him wasn't able to draw in power from the stars like you or I can, it drained them. Only the soldiers of the invaders were left untouched, and that only because they knew how to shield themselves from such magic."*

With a mournful nod, Sira let out a shuddering sigh. It was proof that she, along with everyone on Halarite, still knew very little about how the Universe worked. *And it seems as though there are many terrifying secrets left to uncover.*

Warmth washed through her soul, and she recognized Raida's attempts to sooth her. Sira smiled at that, and wished she could actually hold her newest, greatest companion. Instead, she wrapped her arms around her own torso and held on tight.

Endri brought them to a sudden stop, and she looked up from the jungle floor then to find that they had rounded the mountain and reached the edge of the trees.

At first, she paused next to Endri, but then, swallowing away her fear, she proceeded forward, and brought herself to the very defined edge of the jungle.

It was dreadful to behold. The green jungle floor, the ferns, the trees, it all just *stopped.* Leaving behind a red, hard, crusty soil, and an endless, hill-less expanse, as far as the eye could see. A feeling of absolute wrongness crept up into her soul, and it sent shivers and goosebumps all along her body. Within her, Raida stirred uncomfortably, her soul suddenly restless, wanting to run, hide, just plain get away from the wretched land before them.

Except, it wasn't totally lifeless. Several miles ahead, hazy in the dusty air, were several metal spires jutting out of the ground, and tethered to most of them was something wholly unexpected above the dead, bone-dry lands.

Ships. Actual naval ships, except that they floated on the air, and instead of sails on masts, they were suspended from massive semispherical objects above them, lashed down onto the ships by nets of rope.

"What…are those?" she asked.

"Those are known as airships," Endri replied. *"A more advanced form of craft than your naval ships, to be sure, and capable of covering great distances over land in short timeframes."*

"I'll bet," she murmured. The airships were all different sizes, but were pretty much the same general shape – a standard ship shape, a bloated bladder above them, and strange-looking blades around center pistons on the backsides, with the largest ship having some on the front.

Except for one. One ship was different from all of the others, and it hovered on the far left, moored to one of the spires. It had no giant bladder tethered above it, but rather it had those strange blades-on-piston things above it, whirling rapidly, somehow keeping the ship aloft.

"Think we could go for a ride on one of them?" Raida asked.

With a grin, Sira shook her head. *I doubt it.*

Disappointment flowed through Sira. *"Oh…"*

Hey, we just flew on the back of a dragon, Sira reminded her companion. *Don't you think that's better?*

"How can we know until we try?"

Pausing mid-thought, Sira nodded. *Good point.*

"Your companion speaks truth," Endri startled her from her thoughts. Wide-eyed, she turned and gaped at the dragon, eclipsed in the shadows of the jungle, with star-like eyes blazing out at her.

"You…you can hear Raida?"

"Indeed I can," Endri nodded. *"She has been projecting her thoughts outward rather than focusing them on you."*

"I didn't know that," Raida said, her voice betraying how shaken she was. *"I thought only Sira could hear me."*

"You must learn to focus your thoughts. In time, you may even be able to project your voice into others who are not dragonkin."

"You, uh, can't hear my thoughts, though, right?" Sira asked cautiously.

With an amused voice, Endri replied, *"No, I cannot. Your inner secrets are safe."*

"Good," she nodded. *No offense, Raida, but having one entity privy to my inner most thoughts is enough.*

"No offense taken."

Endri quirked his head to one side, but otherwise remained still.

Sira turned again to the Deadlands and drew in a deep breath. "So, uh…what or who am I looking for?"

"The person's name is Kemila of Gevron," Endri supplied. *"All I know is that this person commands one of those airships, and that rumor has spread that they fled here, to the Teledin Bazaar, after witnessing a Dark Dragon unleash its power. The rumors did not say who the Dark Dragon attacked."*

Frowning, Sira asked, "You keep saying 'them.' Any idea as to a gender or species for Kemila?"

"Unfortunately, no. The rumors that I learned did not say what species they are, and different people told me different genders."

"Fantastic," Sira grimaced. "So I'm going to be looking for a needle in a haystack." Another frown drew down her face. "I see the spires, but… where's the bazaar?"

"Directly ahead of you," Endri said. *"Do you see the wisps of smoke coming from the ground around the docking spires?"*

Sira's eyes wandered down, but through the haze of the blowing red sand, it was difficult to see anything else, even the base of the spires. "No, actually."

"Either way, follow the setting sun."

Startled, she gaped up at the sky, at the reddened, hazy sun ahead and slightly left of her current direction. When they'd left Archanon, it was early morning. Would she ever get used to differing times and lengths of days when travelling to other worlds?

A dizzying mixture of fear and excitement coursed through her veins, and she drew in a deep, shuddering breath.

"I am with you, Sira," Raida assured her. *"Fear not."*

She smiled, and immediately felt a little braver.

Raising her chin up, she stepped out into the Deadlands, and headed straight for the sun.

Chapter 12

APPEASEMENT

Following initial introductions, Cardin, Dalin, and Amaya were led into the village, towards one of the newly-constructed buildings in the center of the city. The gathered orcs dispersed upon a word from Tana, and the city largely went on with its business. Succulent smells wafted throughout as meals were prepared. Leatherworkers tanned hides. Butchers carved up fresh kills, though Cardin didn't dare discern what it was the orcs hunted in the Wastelands.

Most interesting of all was when they came across new buildings under construction. The combination of planks of wood, bone from large creatures, and large hides should have looked archaic, but their craftsmanship was incredible, and the houses, if that's what they were, looked distinct but well-built. Bones were not simply thrown together, they were sanded and shaped and fitted perfectly and served as frames. As such, the frames weren't perfectly flat, and every building sported a curvature to their design, with the roofs being particularly small.

Eying the rib bones used in one house's construction, he suspected he knew what creature might have produced such a large rib cage. "Do you still use Qrishag as domesticated animals?" he asked.

Tana gave him a fanged grin. "Indeed we do, Prince Kataar. They are a versatile and adaptable species, and are well-suited to innumerable tasks, including plowing fields, hauling heavy loads..."

The shaman broke off, but Arkad finished for her, "And in times of need, they are excellent heavy mounts for war."

Cardin shuddered, remembering that fact all too well.

Farms. Tana had mentioned farms. They hadn't seen them on the edge, but surely there were farms surrounding the city. Frowning, he asked, "How do your farms, and your buildings for that matter, survive against the annual Great Storm?"

Tana looked around the city with a grimace. "We have not yet lived in this location long enough to stand up to one with our current practices. However, the Great Storm is not all that different from the monsoons on our homeworld. We have methods of protecting tilled soil from flooding and erosion."

Surprised, Cardin gaped at the shaman. "That's incredible. Heavy rains have wiped out entire fields on Halarite."

Nodding patiently, Tana said, "We know. And before you ask, yes, we are willing to share our knowledge at some point. But trust must be earned, and an exchange of knowledge is preferable to simply giving up our valuable secrets."

It made sense, and Cardin actually felt excited at the prospect. Maybe, just maybe, the four kingdoms and the orcs had a lot to offer each other. Maybe they could reconcile.

Maybe they could stand together against an otherwise insurmountable enemy.

They came upon a building, constructed similarly to all the other ones with qrishag rib cages framing what was essentially a longhouse, and they ducked through a heavy leather curtain. Cardin was further surprised, having expected the longhouse to have been built on bare ground, but the orcs had laid down a wooden foundation, the footwear of visitors and locals alike clomping upon the planks.

I need to stop underestimating them, he thought.

Inside, a stone fireplace had been built in the exact center of the room, though a fire did not burn at the moment. Given how hot the Wastelands were this time of year, he was grateful for that. A long, crafted table, the top made of stained wood and the legs made of lathed bone, was set on one side of the fireplace, and that was where Tana led them. She and Arkad stood behind two chairs on one side and motioned to the four on the other.

Cardin stood directly across from Tana, and Dalin next to him, while Amaya sat further still. The other Guardians and Nia waited outside. When Tana and Arkad finally sat, Cardin and his delegation followed suit. Pausing after sitting, Cardin stared across the table at Tana, whose head and neck were the only parts of her body that were visible. She was easily the shortest person present, and he had to remind himself that she was the spiritual leader of a civilization of orcs. He had to take her seriously if he wanted anything meaningful to come from today.

"Now, then," Tana folded her hands under her chin and looked meaningfully at Cardin. "Do you know why I have asked you here?"

Raising an eyebrow, Cardin glanced down the table at Amaya before he nodded at the shaman. "Amaya says you wished to speak to me. She mentioned visions you have had in the past."

"Of standing side-by-side with humans on the field of battle, yes," Tana nodded.

"Battle against what?" Cardin asked, even though he was sure he knew the answer.

Staring at him with cool, red eyes, Tana drew in a deep breath, and then very slowly said, "The Darksteel Army."

Cold chills prickled along his spine, and Cardin shifted uncomfortably in his chair. It was exactly what he feared.

"They're coming here, aren't they?" he asked.

"I believe so." Tana glanced at Arkad, and said, "Our world fell to them recently. While I was not there when it happened, the General was."

Cardin's eyes leveled on Arkad, and for the first time, their gazes met and held. Arkad's grizzled, gnarled face was still disturbing, but Cardin forced himself to hold the gaze as he asked in a quiet voice, "How bad? What can we expect?"

The General held his stare as he spoke, "They will come in overwhelming force. In the fields outside of your cities and villages, all over your world, they will emerge from massive portals. Foot soldiers, cavalry, archers, spell casters, and war machines. They will surround each and every city in minutes, and will press in before you know what hit you. Only our largest cities with the greatest standing armies held against them for more than a day. Our capitol fell in weeks."

The giant of an orc drew in a deep, airy breath, and sighed heavily, his eye dipping downward. "We held to the last. Our shaman ran early, taking half of our remaining forces with her when Klaralin offered her sanctuary if she would agree to serve him."

A rushing sensation passed along Cardin's fingertips, and he clenched his hands into fists. "Klaralin…" Tana and Arkad both looked at him and nodded solemnly. Looking at the shaman, he asked, "How did you resist his pendant?"

"He did not know of my existence," Tana replied. "I was exiled from my world before the invasion, and I fled to Halarite where I led a single village."

"Tana was meant to be the next leader of our world," Arkad explained. "When the ruling shaman learned of this, she ordered Tana's execution. I…" He hesitated and glanced sidelong at Tana. "I did not know it back then. I was loyal to my shaman, but I was loyal to my people as well. It is complicated, but in recent years, I have served three shamans, Tana being the last. She is our best hope for a future."

Narrowing his eyes, Cardin asked Arkad the same question he'd asked Tana, "How'd you resist Klaralin?"

"I was not present on Halarite when he regained his pendant," Arkad explained. "I was still on our home world resisting the Darksteel Army. By the time I fled, using a potion the previous shaman had given me, Klaralin was already defeated. My men and I arrived as the Archanon invaders fled into the Wastelands. The shaman and I rallied them. She gave me leftover armor that Klaralin had somehow brought with him. At the time, all I could think of…" The general trailed off, as if something had caught in his throat.

Leveling his one-eyed gaze upon Cardin, he said, "Our ancestors fought and died by way of an enraged state. I have heard some call it 'berserker,' but it can cloud our judgment. I was still riding such a state when I arrived, and the shaman took advantage of that, using her mystical influence to goad me into doing her will without thinking. I did not notice the armor Klaralin had provided us was exactly like the Darksteel Army's. I didn't care. After losing everything, all I cared about was *winning*." His head hung low, and he shook it slowly. "Seeing how my brothers and sisters were treated by humans for over three thousand years, I thought your people barbarians. I slaughtered your people. I slaughtered innocent children." His eye darted towards Amaya for a brief second, and then looked at Cardin unwavering. "I am truly sorry for the atrocities I committed."

Cardin stared back blankly, his mouth hanging open ever so slightly. This was truly a day of firsts, and he didn't know how to reply. How could he?

In truth, he wanted to hate Arkad. The General had led his troops on a raid against the Relka Mining Camp, killing innocent people, *children*. He had led a raid upon Valaras, leveling the surrounding farms, killing families. He had led an assault upon Archanon, breaching the waterways and attacking houses and shops in the Blue District.

Arkad *should* feel guilty, and Cardin had every right to hate him. In his gut, he knew that he could never, ever forgive the general.

But Arkad was one...*man*. Not a thing, a man.

Looking at Tana, and then staring around at the well-built longhouse, Cardin acknowledged that Amaya was right. The orcs were no more barbarians than humans were.

Plus, King Beredis had wanted this. Wanted this meeting, this alliance.

Because he knew what was coming. Just like Cardin did.

Looking away from the general he detested, the Prince of Tal stared at Tana, focused his thoughts on her rather than the man he hated.

"My people hate orcs," he said. "And I imagine there are plenty of orcs who hate humans."

Her jaw tightened, and she nodded curtly. "Very much so," she said quietly.

"So how do we bridge the gap between us? How do we find common ground upon which to build a military alliance?"

Tilting her head to one side, Tana replied, "We begin by acknowledging a common enemy. Halarite is our home now, and we wish to protect it as much as you do." Her voice shook when she added, "We have nowhere else to go."

Cardin nodded. "Alright, I'll grant you that. Only yesterday, I convinced the rest of the Alliance that the Darksteel Army might be coming here sooner rather than later. Hopefully not for years, but still relatively...soon..." Cardin trailed off as Tana shook her head. "What?"

"We do not have years," she said, inducing a cold chill into Cardin's heart. "I fear we have weeks at best."

His extremities felt numb, and his vision darkened at the edges as the reality of her claim set in.

Weeks.

They could never recover enough in weeks to stand against a worldwide invasion force.

Tal alone needed at least a year to overcome their economic issues, that was what the governor and his advisers insisted. And Erien was almost as bad off. Their armies were devastated.

All except for Falind's. Even they weren't well-off enough to stand against the Darksteel Army, not if Arkad's description of the invasion of the orc world was accurate.

Looking to Dalin, who stared back at him with intense worry in his eyes, Cardin's jaw hung wide open.

His Wizard friend asked of Tana, "How do you know this?"

"A new vision," she said darkly, as Cardin turned back to her. "And Arkad and I have consulted about both my vision and our observations from our world before the invasion."

"Our cities were thrown into chaos years before the invasion," Arkad explained. "At the time, we could not see it, but as political upheavals and famine and other disasters struck, we now see the patterns that someone had manipulated us for a long, long time. Weakening us. Infighting reduced our armies, battered our defenses, wore our citizens down, eroded trust in our government."

Cardin blanched. It was exactly what he'd feared, what he'd suspected. "The same thing has happened here."

"Precisely," Tana nodded. "Only your situation has been made worse by forces outside of the control of a third party."

"The meteor shower," Amaya reasoned. "Nuuldan."

"The wraith," Dalin added.

"Halarite is ripe for picking," Tana said. "The Darksteel Army comes. We have little time to negotiate a peace."

With a dry mouth and heavy heart, Cardin nodded. "So it would seem." His mind vacillated between being blank and running rampant with thoughts of how to defend against such an overwhelming force.

The four kingdoms could never hope to stand against the Darksteel Army. It would be a long shot if they had years to prepare, let alone now, with weeks, or even days left.

Looking at Tana, then Arkad, he realized even the orcs wouldn't give them much of an advantage.

But it was better than nothing.

It was a start.

With a grim expression, he said, "Alright. Let's start with what would appease you and your fellow orcs."

Chapter 13

PRETENSE OF PEACE

As dawn crawled slowly on into late morning, Kailar and Reyla listened intently to the representative of the Darksteel Empire. They learned of vast armies spread across dozens of worlds, of immeasurable riches shared amongst all members, of power beyond imagination.

All it required was submission to the Empire. To name one's sovereignty as 'in the name of the Darksteel Empire,' to fly their flags above the Imperium's.

Maybe some would consider it a small price to pay.

Kailar didn't think it was.

When Xavien finally completed his well-rehearsed, long-winded speech, Kailar and Reyla sat silently, contemplating all that the ambassador had just told them. It was impossible for Kailar to discern what Reyla was thinking, but she hoped her empress wasn't considering capitulating to them.

It was too good to be true.

Just like the Sword of Dragons had been.

Just like Kailar's supposed ally, the master manipulator that turned out to be Klaralin, had been.

She knew, deep down in her gut, that Xavien was manipulating them.

It was Reyla who spoke up first, as propriety would dictate. "This is all quite a revelation, Ambassador," she began, speaking in measured beats, slow and methodical. "If I may ask, where do you see this meeting going from here?"

Xavien looked only mildly surprised by Reyla's question, and Kailar almost let a smile crease the corners of her mouth. It was a calculated response from Reyla, entirely non-committal and keeping the initiative on Xavien's side. It gave Reyla an opportunity to gain more information before proceeding. *Knowledge is power,* Kailar thought approvingly.

After recovering remarkably fast, Xavien replied, "I am authorized to begin immediate negotiations with you, Empress," Xavien replied, folding his hands on top of each other. "Your Imperium may join us as soon as this evening, at which point we will be happy to begin integration efforts."

Raising her eyebrows a fraction of an inch, Reyla said, "That is rather fast, do you not think so?"

There was the slightest bit of movement in Xavien that caught Kailar's attention. A flinch, subtle and mostly hidden beneath his stately clothes. "Perhaps," he acceded. "I would imagine that there is more you wish to know?"

"Naturally," Reyla replied plainly. "For starters, you offer much with this 'membership' as you called it. However, I cannot help but wonder what we would be required to give up in return? Surely your army, for instance, has only grown so large through acquiring recruits from member governments."

"Naturally," Xavien repeated Reyla's word. "The Darksteel Army would provide all protection for you, there would be no need for you to have your own standing army. We would absorb your existing troops into our ranks."

Kailar's stomach turned at that fact. It made sense, but it still didn't sit well with her. She suddenly imagined General Querlin or Letan donning the darkened-steel armor, wielding enchanted darkened-steel weapons, and marching amongst the giant brutes in the antechamber.

On another world.

Far from Halarite.

Far from Devor.

Leaving them all at the mercy of the Darksteel Empire's whims.

"I am not sure I can accept that requirement," Reyla replied, much to Kailar's relief. Xavien drew in a breath to respond, but Reyla held a hand up, and said, "However, your offer is also not one to be dismissed lightly. Additionally, when we first met this morning, you spoke of other options that did not require full membership. An exchange, for instance. Warships for some other good or service."

"Ah," Xavien replied lamentingly, shaking his head. "You see, any military aid we provide could only be repaid in kind. That is how we trade as a rule, I'm afraid. Military for military. Crop for another crop. Service for another service. As you might imagine, currency between non-member worlds is worthless, so bartering is necessary. Surely you understand."

Reyla nodded thoughtfully, but the uneasiness in Kailar's gut grew stronger. Xavien was maneuvering them, she was sure of it. Kailar's mind raced with questions, seeking one appropriate to the moment, wanting to try to catch Xavien in a lie, or force him to admit something.

At length, the Empress said, "I am afraid that we cannot negotiate so quickly, not when we are but a fledgling power ourselves and have much to build. I understand," she held up a hand again, forestalling Xavien's next words, "that you can help us build rapidly and efficiently. However, I am unsure that I would wish to give up so much to attain such rapid progress. I am not saying I am *not* willing, however you must understand that it is a decision I cannot make in a matter of hours."

Xavien tilted his head to one side, as if nodding, and replied, "I understand your caution and diligence, and it is admirable. However, I must urge you to consider the matter quickly."

Kailar frowned, and without thinking first, she asked, "Why?"

Her muscles tensed, and she glanced at Reyla, but the Empress did not rebuke her.

Xavien considered her question for a second, but the answer came to Kailar before he could speak, and since Reyla hadn't rebuked her just now, Kailar pressed on. "Because of your plans for Halarite? The ones you spoke of when we first met?"

A hint of a smile crossed Xavien's face as his burnt-yellow eyes gazed into Kailar's. "Well, to put it succinctly, yes."

"What might those plans be?" Reyla asked.

At that, the ambassador visibly hesitated. "I am afraid that I am not at liberty to discuss that with you."

Arching a curious eyebrow upwards, Reyla replied, "That seems somewhat inappropriate. You say you have plans for our entire world, but are unwilling to share it with us despite your quest for our membership in your empire?"

There was a slight shift in Xavien's attitude, as a colder tone fell over his voice. As with everything Kailar had observed with him, it was subtle, but it was definitely there. "As a steadfast rule, I am not permitted to speak about military matters with those outside of the Empire. Should you wish to join us-"

"So your plans involve military action," Kailar interrupted triumphantly.

Xavien's face contorted, ever so faintly, and the ice in his voice grew colder. "Yes."

"Curious," Reyla frowned. "Why offer us overtures of peace and membership, then? Under normal circumstances, I would not admit this to an outsider, but it is plain for all to see – we are far weaker than the four kingdoms of Edilas, a much easier target."

Narrowing his eyes, Xavien replied, "Again, I cannot tell you details involving such matters, aside from the reasons I have already mentioned. What I can tell you is that my leadership has decided to pursue peaceful relations with your new Imperium. All shall be revealed to you, if you would only join us."

"What if we don't?" Kailar asked. "What will your leaders do then?"

The barest hint of a grin flickered at the edge of perception on Xavien's face. "I cannot say."

Was that a subtle threat? Kailar narrowed her eyes at him.

"If I may, Empress," Xavien said to Reyla, "Your subordinate is rather...*in*subordinate."

Kailar's face warmed at that, and she felt the boiling of indignation growing in her stomach. However, Reyla replied, "Her question was valid, and I always encourage my advisers to speak their mind."

"I see," Xavien narrowed his eyes again, and looked sourly towards Kailar. She wanted so very much to punch the smugness off of his mug at that very moment.

Reyla steepled her fingers in front of her lips and looked down at the tabletop thoughtfully. Kailar wanted to urge Reyla to tell Xavien to go to whatever hell he believed in, but she knew that wouldn't be advisable, especially considering Xavien's subtle threat.

In fact, they weren't exactly in the best negotiating position. And that maddening grin ever-so-slightly tugging on Xavien's cheek told her that he knew as much.

"I know you wish for an answer sooner rather than later," Reyla finally said, looking Xavien directly in the eyes. "However I must take some time to consider this. I *am* willing to quickly move towards a peace treaty, at the very least."

A flash of contempt appeared in Xavien's eyes, but he recovered quickly. "Very well," he nodded. "Shall we call in a scribe to draft such a treaty?"

"Not today," Reyla corrected, lowering her hands. "Tomorrow. That will give me time to discuss the matter with the Lords of Devor and ensure their interests are represented in the treaty."

Narrowing his eyes, Xavien paused for several seconds before he nodded. "Very well. I shall return tomorrow." He scooted his chair back and stood up, and Reyla and Kailar took that as a cue to follow suit. "Empress Reyla, on behalf of the Darksteel Empire, I thank you for your time and consideration in this matter. I look forward to continued negotiations."

"As do I," Reyla half-bowed. "Thank you, Ambassador."

Kailar took that as her cue, and she walked over to the doors to the antechamber and opened them up. Kent and Letan were still outside waiting patiently in the center of the chamber, while Xavien's guards remained stoic in their corners.

Stepping aside, Kailar watched as Reyla and Xavien walked out side-by-side. Looking to Kent, Reyla said, "General, please escort the ambassador and his entourage to where they arrived, and then return here at once."

Kent snapped to attention, and then said, "Ambassador, if you will follow me."

Xavien snapped his fingers, and the four guards immediately left their corners and fell into formation around him. Then, without another word, he and his troupe followed Kent out, leaving Kailar, Letan, and Reyla alone in the antechamber.

Kailar opened her mouth to speak, but Reyla's hand shot up, palm open, to stop her. The empress's eyes were on the outside doors, keenly watching as Xavien's entourage walked further and further away.

Looking first to Kailar and then Letan, Reyla said, "Come," and led them back into the council chambers. "Close the doors," she ordered, and Kailar complied.

The trio then gathered around the fireplace and warmed themselves. Letan handed Kailar's daggers back over to her, and she gratefully lashed them back onto her belt.

A haunted look had fallen upon Reyla's face, her hands stretched out towards the warmth, her eyes reflecting the flickering firelight. Kailar waited patiently, wondering what Reyla's next words would be, but no one spoke. Whether by her stopping hand towards Kailar or the look on her face, Letan knew not to talk, either.

Finally, one of the doors opened, permitting Kent to enter. After closing the door, he joined them by the fire, with the four of them standing in a semicircle around it.

With narrowed eyes, Kent said, "I take it by the look in your eyes, the meeting did not go well."

Reyla sighed contemplatively, her eyes lowering for a moment. "It was unexpected. Xavien is a master at his craft."

"He's good," Kailar agreed. "But at least we caught him flat-footed once, when we forced him to admit plans for military action on Halarite."

"That was not a victory," Reyla's hollow gaze fell upon Kailar. "That was not a mistake on Xavien's part."

Faltering in her triumph, Kailar frowned. "It wasn't?"

"It was part of his intimidation efforts," she replied. "He wanted us to know that their armies are set to attack. That joining their empire would be the only way to save us from the same fate that the kingdoms now face."

Kailar clamped her mouth shut. She had been so certain that they had tricked the ambassador into revealing that information. It seemed Kailar was the one who had been fooled, and the burn of embarrassment warmed her cheeks.

"Is that what they wanted?" Kent asked quietly. A scowl drew down his face. "I suppose I shall have to work faster to organize our army."

Reyla's eyes narrowed, and she looked closely at her General. "Perhaps that is wise, however I am afraid that we would be outmatched."

Flashes of the orcs under Klaralin's control passed through Kailar's mind, and she grimaced. "Unfortunately I think you're right. And I think this is a lot bigger than any of us know." She told them about her theory, about the armor and weapons the orcs used, and how it was almost identical to what Xavien's brutes wore.

Pressing her lips into a thin line, Reyla nodded. "I've read reports from the Allied Council. The orc shaman that the Keeper of the Sword killed at the end of the Orc War claimed an invasion force large enough to invade their entire world had forced her to flee to Halarite, and that the same force might have already set its eyes upon Halarite. Perhaps this is that force."

A horrifying sense of dread opened up a giant, gaping hole of darkness in Kailar's stomach. She folded her arms in front of her stomach and pressed, willing the feeling to go away. "I think it's a good bet," she murmured. But then the growing despair gave way to something else.

Curiosity.

"Why did they do this?" she asked quietly. The others looked to her, and her eyes darted back and forth amongst them. "Why the overtures of peace, of us joining them? Why did Xavien agree to even just a simple peace treaty?"

Kent furrowed his brow. "Perhaps their army is not so large as to be able to invade all of Tal. Perhaps they wish to be able to concentrate their forces upon Edilas to ensure a swift victory."

"Maybe," Letan nodded. "I mean, Archanon alone will be a tough nut for them to crack, between its city shield and the Keeper of the Sword." Kailar tried not to let herself feel indignant about Cardin's possession of the Sword.

Tried and failed.

"He's not *that* much of a game changer," she grumbled.

Letan looked at her, eyes hardened. "Considering what I saw you do..."

Closing her eyes, Kailar nodded, as flashes of the untold hundreds she'd killed in sweeping waves of her dark magic ran through her memory. She didn't say anything, didn't admit that Letan might be right.

"Nevertheless," Reyla said, turning back to stare into the fire. "I believe there must be more to this. Kailar is correct that Xavien was all too anxious to get us to agree to anything approaching peace between us and the Darksteel Empire. I believe this tells us two things. First, that their assault upon Halarite is coming sooner rather than later. Second, there is something unique and important in the Imperium, something they either want or don't want."

"Something they fear," Kailar blurted out. "Something they don't want involved in the defense of Halarite."

"Maybe that something is you," Kent said to Kailar.

She nodded thoughtfully, wondering if that could be true, but then stopped and frowned. "If that were true, would they not want the same with the...I mean, with Cardin Kataar and Tal?"

"Maybe they've already sent a delegation there," Letan suggested.

"But what of the Allies?" Reyla asked. "Peace with Tal would be impossible in the current political climate of Edilas without making peace with the other kingdoms as well. An attack upon any of the other kingdoms would force Tal to respond, according to the articles of the Alliance."

"So that doesn't make sense," Kailar shook her head. "If they don't fear Cardin enough to make peace with him, they don't fear me enough to make peace with Devor."

"Maybe it isn't fear at all, then," Letan suggested. "Maybe they want something we have."

"If they weren't afraid of something," Kailar countered, "and they just wanted something, they have the strength to take it from us."

Kent nodded. "I agree. Fear seems more likely. But what could possibly make them afraid of us? What does Devor have that no one else does?"

The idea struck her, and at the same time, she and Letan looked to one another wide-eyed. "The Navitas," she said.

Reyla's eyes widened. "The crystalline beings in the west?"

Kailar nodded. "Yeah. That is the only thing that I can think of on Devor that could make the Darksteel Empire nervous."

Furrowing her brow, Reyla asked, "Why, though? If they invaded only the Imperium and left the Navitas alone, the Navitas would have no reason to go to war with them."

It was a good point, and Kailar chewed the inside of her cheek nervously as she thought about it, a habit she had recently picked up. "I don't know, then. But the Navitas have to be the answer. There has to be something about them. Maybe..." She hesitated, and looked at Letan. "Maybe I should go pay them a visit."

There was a shift in his eyes, a sudden look of worry. Or maybe she imagined it. But she wondered if he still cared, despite how much he apparently detested her now.

Rubbing his face, Kent said, "Well, scouts reported two weeks ago that the glow from the Crystalline Peaks has continued to recede, but it is not known if it is truly safe to approach them or not."

"It's a big risk," Reyla agreed. "I cannot allow you to endanger yourself on such an endeavor."

"Do we have a choice?" Kailar asked. "We need information if we want to have any hope of getting an advantage in future negotiations."

"I agree," Reyla replied, "However I simply cannot risk you. We can send a messenger or a scout, perhaps."

"I don't think that'll work," Letan replied, his eyes breaking from Kailar's to address his Empress. "The Navitas know Kailar, they know me. They don't know anyone else."

"And," Kailar quickly interjected, "it would be riskier to send Letan. Without a connection to star magic, I'm likelier to be able to withstand a discharge from the peaks."

"What if you don't withstand one?" Reyla planted her hands on her hips. "You are the only person in the Imperium who can create portals, Kailar. You also have incredible power that could be put to use defending us from the Darksteel Army. I cannot allow it."

"But…"

"No," she cut her hand through the air, as if slicing off her retort. "End of story. We shall find another way to inquire with the Navitas, or else gain the knowledge we seek another way."

There is no other way, she thought grudgingly, teeth grinding against one another.

"Now, I need you to gather the Lords immediately," Reyla commanded. "Bring them here at once."

Kailar's instinct was to say no, to mouth off. The rebellious part that had spent over a decade in the wilderness, fending for herself.

Instead, she bowed low, said, "Yes, Empress," and stalked out of the room.

She knew she was right, and she knew she had to talk to the Navitas. But maybe that would be something she would do in her own time.

After she brought the Lords to Tieran.

Chapter 14

THE TELEDÎN BAZAAR

Sira's first clue that she approached civilization was footprints, hoofprints, and wagon trails in the dirt. It was only a scattering of them at first, but they were a dead giveaway in the lifeless soil.

And then the smell assaulted her.

Spices. Flowers. Searing meat. Smoke.

It started as a faint odor, but grew in leaps and bounds with each step, until it became a veritable siege upon her senses.

Worst of all was the smell of sewage. Of human and other waste. It loomed over the other scents, intermingled, and soured everything, including her stomach. The stench mixed with the growing heat almost made her dry-heave.

"Dear stars, what is that?!" Raida whined, and Sira had the strange urge to paw at her own nose.

Not knowing how to reply, Sira trudged on. Smoke rose ahead, seemingly from the ground surrounding the docking spires, yet no hint of other structures or people milling about presented themselves. *So where are the footprints leading to?* she wondered, staring down at the growing number of impressions.

It was only a few minutes later that Sira finally had her answer, when she came across the first crack in the dead, dry ground.

Like dirt that had endured a rainstorm and then quickly dried, leaving a craggy, spider web-like pattern of fissures in the ground. Except these cracks were over a hundred feet wide, and almost forty feet deep. When she came to the edge of one such crack, she had her first view of the Teledin Bazaar, spread out into the fissures of the Deadlands.

Sira's first impression was a sea of people. So. Many. *People!* Milling about, wandering from vendor to vendor, talking, singing, yelling, bellowing, and every manner of communication she could think of. From her vantage, they looked like giant swarms of ants, and distinguishing one entity from another was near impossible.

The main buildings of the bazaar were built directly into the walls of the cracks, taking advantage of the natural cover from the scorching sun. Given how hot it was, even now that the sun raced for the horizon to rest for the night, Sira could understand the importance of such a decision. There were two levels, with a haphazardly-built walkway lining both sides so that stores were built one atop the other, two full levels of shopping and inns and taverns and who knew what else. Signs, colorful draperies, and tapestries adorned the entrances to many of the shops, and people streamed in and out of their wide and tall doors like a flowing stream.

In the middle of the bazaar's grounds, especially where the cracks widened the most, were tarps and tents and awnings, allowing for even more shops, and shoppers to peruse them and seek refuge from the blaze above. The only exceptions were where the towering docking spires rose up, whose bases occupied the center of the 'squares' they were built within. Made of steel or some other hardened metal, the interlacing latticework towers reached a good three hundred feet up, with stairs circling upwards around them, service ladders inside, and at least one crane-like device on each to hoist goods and supplies up and down to the ships.

The Teledin Bazaar made the Archanon Market District look tame.

"Now that is a sight," Sira breathed, drinking in the vision before her. Everything was cast in a red hue now that the sun had drawn closer to the horizon, and several of the merchants began the tedious task of lighting up their respective areas.

Sira's eyes wandered along the edge she stood upon, and only a couple hundred feet to her right, she saw one of several artificial ramps built up the edge of the crack to the surface. A caravan of camel-like creatures were being led up it and onto the Deadlands. She had only seen a few camels, back in her brief visit to Maradin, but these creatures were larger, grey in color, and sported what she swore looked like long, curling moustaches.

"I get the feeling that today will be a day of many firsts for us," Raida excitedly quipped.

I get the feeling you're right, Sira nodded, smiling despite the uneasiness in her stomach. She was armed, true, but she was literally walking into a completely unknown situation. Her Warrior training told her to be wary of everyone and everything, but glancing back down into the bazaar, she feared that would be impossible, or at the very least overwhelming and exhausting.

Worse, as the camel driver trudged past her, she overheard the alien being mutter something to the camels in a completely unknown language, no doubt urging them on.

How could she find this Kemila of Gevron if she couldn't ask anyone for directions? *I don't suppose you're able to help me understand the languages we'll encounter.*

Surprisingly, Raida replied, *"Possibly. More than half of the residents of Stella had translation pendants on at all times, so I am familiar with how the magic feels."*

Sira's spirits lightened at that, and she looked back towards the ramp just as a group of four people trudged up it. Given how hot the Deadlands felt now, she imagined travelling during the night was probably the best way to go, and that meant more would be coming.

As even more visitors started their ascent on the ramp, she reasoned she should get down now, before she had to fight a flood of outgoing parties. Steeling herself, Sira marched towards the ramp, and after pushing past two ten-foot-tall wolf-like humanoids, she clomped down the metal ramp. More groups were trudging up, and she had to squeeze by near the outer railing, hanging precariously twenty feet up over the edge, to ensure she wasn't trampled.

Finally, when she reached the bottom, she slipped off to the side and tried to breathe deep, only for something to wisp into her nose and set her on a sneezing fit.

"Oof," a gruff, deep voice said. "You mus'be new."

Between sneezes, Sira searched for the source, only to find that she had squeezed right by a burly looking, seven-foot-tall person in her haste to get off of the ramp. Person was a somewhat loose description, since he had the head of a bull, and beneath his tarnished plate armor, she saw that his entire body was covered in brown fur. A pair of pearly-white horns, one of which was missing a good inch of the tip, adorned his head, and he stared down at her over his long, brown snout.

"Um," she said intelligently before another fit of sneezes wracked her body.

"Take it easy, little..." The bull trailed off and furrowed his brows. "Pardon me, I almost 'sumed gender. Miss? Sir? Other?"

Blinking tears from her eyes and rubbing furiously at her nose, Sira stared up at the man, and noticed for the first time a brooch clasping a cloak over his shoulders that held a symbol of a sword and axe crossing over one another.

"Might be a local law officer," Raida remarked.

Sira agreed, but then frowned. *Wait, I can understand him. Are you already translating for me?*

"No," Raida replied. *"But I think I sense the magic of a translation pendant."*

That made sense.

"You okay?" the bull asked, touching the brooch. "Can y'understand me?"

Sira nodded, "Yes! Sorry, just-" Another sneeze interrupted her, and her body ached with the force of it. "Ugh. I'm sorry," she said through a stuffy nose.

"No worries," the bull replied. "Welcome to Teledin Bazaar, where every food, incense, and seasoning in the known 'Verse can be found. You'll get used t'it if you stick 'round long enough."

"Thanks," Sira tried to smile through puffy, teary eyes. "Um. Miss. You asked earlier."

"Ah," the bull's lips pulled back in his equivalent of a smile, flashing square, flat teeth. "As I suspec'. Not many humans h'v'been 'round here lately, so I'm a bit outta practice, see?"

Sira gaped around, now that she was at eye level with the Bazaar. Beings of every shape and size imaginable and unimaginable stalked by, most of them on two legs, though at least one intelligent-looking being on four legs trundled up the ramp past the bull.

"M'name's not easily translated by this here pendant," the bull tapped his brooch, "but y'can call me Chetrin, or jus' Chetre if y'like.

'Chey-truh' is how it's pronounced, see?"

Sira nodded, stifled another sneeze, and replied, "Nice to meet you, Chetre."

"Don't b'fooled by my pleasant demeanor and all, miss," the bull nodded. "I'm part've the security 'round here, and if ya don' follow the rules, you'll be on my bad side, see?"

"I do not want to be on his bad side," Raida said with a shudder.

"I understand," Sira nodded.

"See'n how this you're firs' time in Teledin, lemme explain some of the basic rules t'ya." Chetre clomped a little ways past the ramp and clamped his hand down on a rather large wooden sign with alien text written into it. "D'ya read Basic?" Sira shook her head. "Thought not. Well for starters, there's lotso folk 'round here, crowdin', especially during the day, sticking to the shade like beetles to dung. So's no magic except for translatin'. Defense is the 'ception, if you're attacked. Lots of security like me is about, but that don't mean we can keep eyes on everything. Oh, and, uh," Chetre nodded down at her hips. "Best keep tight grips on coin and weapons. There's slippery fingers all abouts here, see?"

With a grim nod, Sira replied, "Not surprising. We have our fair share of pickpockets where I come from."

"Well, they be tricky here, 'cause ya never known what species might try, and they've got some tricks up their sleeves, or scales, or fins, or whatever." Chetre moved his hand down the sign, pointing along as he spoke. "Also, absolutely no portals within the bazaar. None, y'hear? It's too crowded, someone's liable to get hurt accidental."

Looking back out at the crowd, ranging from ten-foot-tall behemoths to two-foot-tall beings. Anyone could get caught in the wrong way around a portal, especially since portals were often invisible from behind. Sira wondered, with her stomach turning inside itself, what would happen if someone walked the wrong way into a portal.

"Understandable," she said after swallowing back bile.

"Oh, and I skipped a part," the bull's finger moved back up a line. "Light is another 'ception to magic. No flames, y'hear? Heatless light if y'need light."

Sira frowned, and looked around, knowing that she'd seen vendors light up the fronts of their stores. How were they doing it if they weren't using fire, magic or otherwise?

The closest storefront, a good fifty feet beyond the bottom of the ramp, was barely visible between milling people, but she caught glimpses of what looked like a glowing tube. Not fire. The blue-white glow reminded her of the glowpanels from the dwarven city beneath Archanon.

"Alright," she agreed, and hoped there was enough light in the market that she wouldn't have to worry. Flameless light wasn't a power she had learned to cast herself.

"Finally, this here's an interplanetary market," Chetre's finger moved to the bottom block of text. "Lot's o' cultures, some more easily 'fended than others. Rule of hoof 'round here is don' be 'fended. If someone insults your customs and beliefs, don' take 'fense to it, just move along. If some 'un gets all 'fended 'bout your actions, they're lookin' for trouble. Find one of us," he pointed at his brooch, "or otherwise defend yourself." Looking her up and down, one side of his face irked upwards. "Y'look like y'can defend yourself, so I'm not too worried 'boutcha."

All in all, his speech patterns, even translated, were a little awkward to follow, but Sira got the gist of the rules. All pretty basic, considering how complex it must be to police such a diverse bazaar.

"Alright, sir," she nodded to Chetre. "Thank you for your time, and-"

Chetre's nostrils flared once, twice, sniffing loudly, and then his ears twitched. A second later, his head snapped towards the middle of the market. "Hey!" he bellowed, and clomped off heavily towards the sounds of shouting.

"I guess that concludes orientation," Raida said, mildly amused.

With a grin, Sira sighed and looked around.

Where exactly are we supposed to start?

"Well it's an airship captain we're looking for, right?" Raida asked. Sira nodded. *"Head for the nearest spire."*

With a smile stretching across her face, Sira thought, *Good idea,* and looked skyward. The nearest spire had one of the larger ships with a giant bladder floating above it, and if she had to guess, was one bazaar 'square' away.

Drawing in a bracing breath, and then sneezing, Sira forced back mucus and dry heaving, and headed towards the spire. A long queue of people had lined up and were slowly trudging up the ramp, so she followed along towards the end of the line, not quite brave enough to try to push in between groups. However, she soon realized the futility of that notion, as the line grew ever-longer and curled around the center of the square.

Sighing, she looked up at one woman, red-skinned with a pair of tiny horns poking through black hair, lizard-like eyes, and what Sira swore were leathery wings tucked behind her shoulder blades, and said, "Excuse me, may I pass through?"

The woman blinked at her once, and then blinked *sideways* at her, a different set of eyelids, translucent and somewhat disturbing. She hissed at Sira, said something in a language she didn't understand, and looked back up.

Uh, Raida? Any chance on that translation magic?

"I'll try," Raida replied. Sira felt the press of magic inside of her chest, right on her collarbone, that sent a rushing sensation through her torso. A second later, Raida said, *"Try again."*

"Excuse me," Sira stepped along as the line jerked forward. The red-skinned woman blinked twice at her. "May I pass in front of you?"

"Get to the back of the line like everyone else," the woman scowled, and proceeded to ignore Sira.

"That's not what I mean-"

"You heard her!" a yellow-skinned man behind the woman growled. He was only half the height of the woman, and Sira for that matter, but he made up for it with pure muscle. "Back of the line, wench."

Fear was replaced by anger, indignation, and Sira glared at the stout man. She debated saying something else, but instead decided to shove between the man and the woman, gruffly. "Oye!" the man protested.

"I beg your pardon!" the woman screeched.

Once on the other side, however, Sira merely turned towards them, gave a mock salute, and headed for the spire, shaking her head. "Asses," she grumbled.

With that obstacle out of the way, she next had to fight a constant stream of shoppers heading towards the ramp, made worse when she exited the square and headed into a narrower part of the cracked ground. However, the further she got, and the darker it grew, the easier it became, with fewer and fewer people.

By the time she made it to the square with the spire, the crowd was noticeably thinner. A pair of men, who looked very much like elves, guarded the base of the stairs winding up the steel spire, and she decided they must be crew members.

Marching towards them with purpose, she thought, *Raida, you ready for more translation?*

"The spell will last until I dispel it," Raida affirmed.

The elves, both a good foot taller than her, turned as she approached, and exchanged frowns with one another. Before she drew too close, both men thrust out open-palmed hands, and the one on Sira's right ordered, "Stop right there, human."

She would have anyway, but she came to a jerking halt when the other man placed his hand firmly around the hilt of a sword. They meant business.

"This is a royal Albatar ship," the man on the right stated. "Move along."

Sira cleared her throat, and began, "I'm looking for an airship captain by the name of-"

"I said move it!" the man growled, reaching for his sword as well. Every muscle in Sira's body tensed, and she likewise reached for her white-dyed longsword.

The moment she touched it, however, the others immediately drew their weapons, whose blades gleamed golden in the firelight. The blades immediately set to humming, and she felt the press of magic flowing into them.

"Woh, woh, hold it!" she backed away, but didn't dare take her hand off her sword. "I'm not here to fight!"

"Then turn around and leave the square, now," the first man ordered. "You've no business here."

Suddenly Sira was wondering if coming here was a mistake. She'd already aggravated a pair of locals and now some royal guards. *What next?*

"Hey, you three!" a booming voice echoed in the square. Sira turned towards the source, and watched as what she swore was a humanoid *bear* squeezed out of one of the buildings lining the square. His eyes flared bright orange, and he lumbered towards the spire base.

"You had to ask," Raida remarked dryly.

The two royal guards had entered aggressive combat stances,

127

obviously ready to attack Sira, and perhaps would have. But the moment they saw the bear-like man trouncing towards them, his silver chainmail armor in stark contrast with his brown fur and clinking noisily, they eased out of their stances.

As the newcomer drew closer, Sira eyed the brooch on his pauldron, and realized he was another bazaar guard. She relaxed, but then realized with a start that he was barreling down on her, not the royal guards.

"What's the meaning of this?" he demanded, his glowing orange eyes flaring before fading to a subtle shade of copper.

"This *human* tried to get aboard the ship," the only one of the elves with a tongue sneered.

"That's a lie," she defended, backing away as the bear-man loomed over her. "I was trying to ask them a question!"

"And then she put her hand on her weapon," the elf added.

"Only after you did!" she peered around the behemoth and glared accusingly at the elves.

"They're guarding a royal ship," the bear growled. "They're allowed to defend against interlopers." He took a step closer to her, and though he didn't draw a weapon to intimidate her, he didn't need to.

Feeling a touch of indignation despite her base human fears screaming at her to run, she frowned up at the bear's eyes and said, "And just how the hells was I supposed to know that?"

The bear pointed a claw at a wooden sign next to the stairs. "It's written plain as the dirt beneath your feet," he grumbled, and stepped closer to her until only a foot was left between them. One of her feet, not his.

"Well I can't read that," she grumbled, "so instead of being so defensive..."

The bear's hand lanced out faster than she could see, and seized her left shoulder painfully. "Ignorance is not an excuse to break our laws."

She didn't mean to, she *really* didn't, but the moment the monster-of-a-man wrenched her shoulder, she and Raida pulsed out a defensive magic that shoved the guard back, yanking her arm free.

The guard sneered. Copper eyes pulsed bright.

And he drew his battle axe from behind his back.

"We should run," Raida intoned.

The guard drew back and swung down. Sira darted left, using a magic shield to deflect the axe from otherwise cleaving her arm off. And then she did exactly what Raida screamed at her to do.

"Run!"

Chapter 15

THE CHASE

"I told you coming here was a bad idea," Raida intoned while Sira scrambled out of the square.

"You did no such thing!" Sira shouted, half-bouncing off of a cart as she skirted around a couple of slow-walking...*creatures.*

"No, I didn't, but I should have," Raida replied.

A roar, an actual *roar* boomed behind her, and though she didn't dare look back, she heard the booming thumps of heavy footprints, the bear-like guard no doubt giving chase.

When it was too late to change course, Sira realized with a start that she had ducked down a different alley, rather than head back for the one she had come from. Her spirits sank at that, realizing that the only possible guard who might at least *listen* to her was back near the ramp.

Ducking, dodging, running — Sira did it all. And finally, when she was at least halfway down the alley, she looked back.

And felt the color drain from her face.

Three other bears had joined the first, and they barreled over and past everyone and everything Sira had dodged around.

So she ran faster. Past elves, over dwarves and other Halfling-like creatures, under barrel-like arms of ten-foot-tall men and women and other. Her progress through the alley was marked by smells, and the ever-narrowing of the walls, until the shops pressed in on either side, squeezing people as they passed through.

The positive side? The bears couldn't run abreast of each other anymore and had to go single-file, making them at least a little less terrifying when Sira glanced back at them.

And then, finally, when she thought even *she* couldn't squeeze between the shops, she burst out into another square, with another spire reaching into the sky. Looking back at her pursuit, she saw the lead bear trying to squeeze out of the narrow alley.

This square was a lot more crowded than the royally guarded one, and the spire was surrounded by double-layered shops in the bazaar walls. A particularly dense throng of people, gathered around a group of entertainers playing on drums and shouting and hooting, caught her attention, and she wove her way into the crowd, never stopping and only slowing as much as she had to.

Sira barely heard the bears roar again, the pounding drums and off-key singing covering her escape, and the spectators hardly paid her attention, except to grumble at her when she bumped into one or very nearly barreled over a dwarf.

"Sorry," she called over her shoulder, and then finally passed through to the other side of the gathered spectators. To her left and just behind her was the stairs up the spire, and she arched her neck to look up. Hovering above her was the unusual ship she had spotted before descending into the Bazaar – not suspended by a massive bladder, but held aloft by constantly whirling, massive blades.

From across the square, coming from a much wider alley, she heard another roar. Reinforcements, she had to guess, though if they weren't the bears that had seen her, they wouldn't know what to look for.

Except I'm the only human here, she realized with a start. *That complicates matters.*

Her only chance was to disappear from the streets, to find a building to hide in. So she made a straight line for the nearest one, the glowing sign above the door unreadable to her, and she shoved through the hanging beads at the door and into...

A pub.

Coming up short, Sira gaped at what she had come into. An alien world, filled with countless non-humans, with customs and laws that she *clearly* didn't fully understand, and yet after having come all this way, she found herself in a pub not unlike a tavern in Daruun.

The ground was hardened sandstone, which she only just then realized was the same as what the ground outside was like, and the back wall looked like the start of a cave, but the rest of the pub was built of regular wood. A bar on the left side ran the entire length from door to cave-wall, a good fifty feet, and from the bar to the far wall was another eighty feet, filled with an assortment of round and square tables, chairs of every make imaginable, including a strange throne-like chair near what looked like an entertainer's stage.

Like the rest of the Bazaar, the pub was full of an assortment of creatures, though none of them towered like the bears or bull. The one who caught her eye the most, however, was the woman who at that moment trounced up to the throne-like chair and, in a fashion that boasted a cavalier attitude, sat down and crossed her legs, flourishing her arms to the cheers of those nearest her.

Sira thought she was human, or at least, she looked human enough. Long, dirty-blonde hair was let loose, spilling over her shoulders and down her back, and from where Sira stood, across a dimly-lit pub, her eyes looked dark. Her clothes also stood apart from what Sira was used to seeing – a pale-blue bodice with a v-neck cut that showed off more cleavage than Sira would have ever thought appropriate, along with olive-green trousers with leather trim, and leather boots that nearly reached the woman's knees.

One of the other women in the crowd, decidedly *not* human with yellow skin and orange and black eyes, threw a tripoint hat up to the woman, who deftly caught it and placed it neatly atop her head, before flourishing her hands to the applause of everyone present.

No one else in the pub was human. All were *humanoid,* but that woman, that one woman, was like a beacon in a haze of the unfamiliar.

"She's pretty, too," Raida chirped in her opinion.

Sira blinked, startled by Raida's reaction, but looked away and around at the pub. The urgency she'd felt from fleeing the guards had faltered, but rushed back into her chest when she realized she hadn't moved from the door. A simple glimpse through the bead curtain would reveal her presence, and the chase would be on again.

So she did the only thing she could think of – she moved deeper into the pub, wading into the overcrowded floor, past full tables, looking for anywhere she could to sit or hide or simply find an excuse to keep her back on the door.

"At least if anyone looks for a human in here, they can point to the throne lady," Raida volunteered helpfully.

Good point, Sira smiled nervously.

Her eyes darted back and forth at each table and chair she passed, desperate for an empty seat, but everything was full. And as she passed by each strange-looking person, she started to feel pinpricks on the back of her neck.

That was when she realized the noise had died down, and the eyes of all present had turned towards her.

"Well, now," a low, alto voice spoke into the silence that had fallen upon the pub. Sira looked up at the 'throne,' and saw that the human woman had uncrossed her legs and draped her right one over the arm rest, elbow resting on her knee. Now that Sira was closer, she could see that the woman had deep brown eyes, and they very slowly, very methodically looked Sira down and up. Something showed in her eyes that made Sira uncomfortable, but at some point, she had frozen in place, and now felt her cheeks flush. "Hello, there," the woman met Sira's eyes. "Pretty eyes."

Some of the crowd jeered and cheered, and Sira quickly realized what was happening. More than once, she'd seen it happen in taverns on Halarite, and for that matter, had been the *subject* of such attention.

Except, that had always been from unsavory men.

Usually when she was on the hunt for a bandit or other outlaw.

"Um, hi," she said, her right hand clasping her belt buckle, very close to the hilt of her sword.

"Out of the frying pan?" Raida asked, worry tinging her sarcasm.

"Alas," the woman let out an exaggerated, high-pitched sigh. "Not a poet to go with that lovely face. But no matter," she slapped her knee, and then bounced up onto her feet. "Perchance, you could tell me why you're here, young lass?"

Young?! Sira thought. *She's younger than me!*

"Or the same age," Raida suggested. *"But I like her. She thinks we're pretty!"*

"Um," Sira started again.

"Is that your name?" the woman asked. Sira's cheeks burned. "Madam Um? Or, wait," the woman stepped down from the throne and approached Sira carefully, her eyes darting to Sira's sword. "Shall it be Commander Um?"

Narrowing her eyes sourly at the woman and feeling the burn of indignation, Sira replied, "I'm Lieutenant Sira Reinar, if you must know."

"Oh, I *must*," the woman grinned. "And manners, manners, manners. I am-"

The woman was cut off by the sound of heavy footsteps and a sudden commotion at the entrance that Sira had just walked through. Sira froze, her heart thudding in her chest.

"Oye," the woman shouted over Sira's shoulder, her forehead scrunching into a cute little frown as she pushed past Sira. "This here's a private party, fellas."

Wait, Sira thought. *Did I just think of her frown as cute?*

"No," Raida corrected, *"I did."*

A gruff, deep, booming voice replied, "We're looking for a human woman."

A soft, velvety hand brushed against Sira's, and she looked down and right with a start. A grey-with-black-striped fur-covered woman, wearing a cotton white blouse and very worn trousers, both stained with black splotches, looked up at Sira with blazing yellow eyes, and then looked to a recently-vacated seat, the previous occupant having stood up and walked past Sira to follow the human woman.

"Sit," the furry woman hissed.

Sira didn't have to be told twice, and as she quickly occupied the seat, she heard the human woman reply, "Well, congrats, fellas, ya found one!"

"Not you," the booming voice sounded annoyed. "Witnesses on the street say she ran in here."

"Oh, you mean that platinum-haired lass?" the human woman replied. Sira felt her chest constrict.

I guess we're running again, Sira thought to Raida, her eyes darting around madly for another exit. There wasn't even a window on the front of the establishment, and with intense dismay, she realized she was trapped.

"Don't give up yet," Raida said. *"That pretty lady might help us."*

Why would she help us?

"Aye, she ducked in here," the woman told the guard. "And out the back. Isn't that right, everyone?"

The pub crowd all shouted out an affirmative at once, including the furry woman next to her, and Sira's eyes widened. Had they just covered for her?

"Only, uh," the woman paused, "ya know, someone of your…ahem, *stature,* might not be able to squeeze through here. Might wanna go get one of your foxy buddies to help out, eh? If she sticks to the back alleys, ya might not be able to catch up with her."

There was a very long pause, and Sira's hands clenched into fists. Maybe, with Raida's help, she could fend off the city guards long enough to escape, if they didn't buy the woman's story. But then she'd leave empty handed. No Kemila, no information on Nuuldan's location. She will have failed. All over a stupid misunderstanding.

"If I find out you're lying," the guard growled.

"Yeah, yeah," the woman replied flippantly. "You'll banish me from the bazaar, *again.* I've heard this one before, remember?"

"Maybe this time we'll impound your ship," the guard threatened.

Something shifted subtly amongst the gathered crowd, and Sira swore the temperature in the pub fell precipitously.

The woman's voice had changed to ice when she spoke her next words. "Over. My. Dead. Body."

"If necessary," the guard said smugly.

The sound of dozens of chairs scraping across the floor grated, as every single person seated in the pub, except for Sira, stood up. Sira's earlier suspicions were correct – the pub was full of a singular group, probably some sort of outlaws, and the woman was their leader.

Oh, gods, the last thing I want is to get involved in a tavern brawl, Sira thought.

"Oooh, I've never seen one before! Can we stay and watch?"

"Gents, ya might wanna go look for your platinum-haired lass," the woman spoke with only a slightly warmer tone of voice. "You know, unless you *want* her to get away."

The air was thick with tension, and Sira, despite having trained all her life for combat, suddenly felt more nervous. This wasn't a battlefield, this wasn't a sword fight. This was something worse.

She was being protected by the worst sort of persons, on the wrong side of the law.

This wasn't her.

And yet…

There was something…*fun* about it.

Raida…is that you influencing my thoughts again?

"Um, maybe?" Raida mentally shrugged. *"If so, I'm not meaning to!"*

"Fine," the guard finally relented. "But I'm warning you, Kemila." Sira's eyes shot wide open, and she couldn't help but gape at the woman. She instantly realized her mistake, but thankfully, the standing crowd hid Sira from view. "If you harbored a criminal…"

"Yeah, yeah," she could almost *hear* Kemila waving her hands flippantly. "Off with ya, now."

Another long, deafening pause, and the eyes of all of Kemila's crew glared at the guard, or guards, if more than one had stalked in after Sira. Finally, booming footsteps shook the ground, and the beads covering the door rattled once, twice, three times. Three guards.

The tension, and for that matter the cold in the room eased back. Sira shivered as goosebumps rose up on her arms, warmth caressing her face. It hadn't been her imagination. Someone in the room was magical, and had dropped the temperature considerably, intentionally or not.

The crew resumed their seats slowly, and more than a few eyes kept a wary gaze on the entrance.

The velvety, furry woman next to Sira remained standing, patting Sira's shoulder for a moment, before she walked away, leaving her seat empty. Until Kemila sat in it with a sigh.

Propping her elbow up on the table, Kemila rested her cheek in the palm of her hand, and stared at Sira. "Well, then, that was all manner of unpleasantness, wasn't it?"

Shock, fear, uncertainty, all of it bubbled inside of Sira. If she wasn't careful, if she said or did the wrong thing, the entire pub might turn on *her* next. But she forced those feelings down, swallowing her fears and shoving them to the bottom of her gut, not giving them the attention they cried out for. Now wasn't the time to let fear get the best of her. Not when her goal was literally sitting next to her.

"Yeah," Sira nodded. "Thank you so much for your help."

"My pleasure, darling," Kemila smiled. Sira wasn't sure why, but she felt her cheeks burn with a blush. "Spend enough time 'round here, you'll find out soon enough that some of the Bazaar guards are here to protect the peace, and others, well, they look for any excuse to exert their power over others."

Thinking back to the bull-like guard she'd met earlier, Sira was suddenly glad that he had been the one to welcome her, and not one of the bear-like guards.

"So," Sira narrowed her eyes. "Kemila...of Gevron?"

Cocking up an eyebrow, Kemila nodded. "Aye, that's me."

A smile blossomed on Sira's face. "Perfect! I actually came here to find you."

"Oh, my," Kemila touched her breastbone, a wry grin stretching up one corner of her mouth. "Looking for me, darling? Well, then, seems as though fate brought you to the right place."

"Oooh, she's good," Raida crooned. Something stirred inside, a strange burn that Sira *knew* wasn't her. *"I really like her, Sira!"*

Can we focus, please?

The warm burn turned to exasperation. *"Oh...fine..."*

"So what brings ya to me, lass?"

"Well," Sira glanced around warily, and leaned in closer to Kemila. The woman seemed to enjoy this idea and, removing her tripoint hat and holding it up to block others from seeing them, she leaned in closer to Sira, too. "I heard that..." Raida's thoughts strayed, and took Sira's with them. Her eyes dipped low, down Kemila's neck, down her v-cut neckline, down...

Stop that!

"What?!"

"Yes, darling?" Kemila leaned closer.

Sira blushed.

"I...heard...that you, um, know where to find a...um, dragon."

Kemila's advance stopped cold. She blinked, her expression sagging.

"A Dark Dragon," Sira clarified.

All flirtation melted away from Kemila's face, replaced by a cold terror. Her hat dipped low.

Revealing that the table next to them watched with quiet anticipation. Sira looked at them, felt her cheeks burn ever brighter, and pulled away from Kemila.

Before she knew what was happening, Kemila had pulled a small dagger from who-knew-where, and had its point pressed against Sira's neck. Panic and confusion rushed through her, dousing Raida's...*enthusiasm.*

The entire pub took notice, and all ambient noise ceased.

"Who sent ya?" Kemila asked, her voice turned to steel.

Resisting the urge to reach for her sword, and somehow not repeating the same mistake she'd made by the elven ship, Sira eased backwards, holding her hands up defensively. Kemila followed with the dagger, never letting the point leave Sira's neck.

"Wha...what do you...I mean," Sira stuttered.

"Who bloody sent you?!" Kemila bellowed.

"A Star Dragon!" Sira replied in a panic. "A Star Dragon sent me."

Kemila scrutinized Sira, scanning her with piercing eyes all over again. "A Star Dragon? Not the Darksteel Army?"

Blinking in surprise, Sira asked, "Darksteel Army? Wha...what do they have to do with Nuuldan?"

With a frown, Kemila eased back on the dagger. A trickle of warm blood ran down Sira's neck, and she realized that, once again, the temperature in the room had plummeted.

Drawing in a deep breath, Kemila let it out as a deep sigh. "I'm not getting involved," she said quietly. If the pub had been as lively as it had been moments ago, Sira wouldn't have heard anything she said. "Not again." The dagger disappeared from sight, and Kemila stood up. "Tell your friend I'm not helping. You'll have to find your Dark Dragons on your own."

Kemila's words registered as blows, one after another. Especially her last words.

"Wait, what?" she stood up and grasped at Kemila's arm. "Dark *Dragons*?"

"Aye," she nodded. "At least a couple of 'em. And I will *not* let them find me." Looking out into the pub, she shouted, "Pack it up, folks!" She looked again at Sira, and a little quieter said, "We're leaving."

Chapter 16

PROMOTION

When the meeting with Tana and General Arkad concluded, it was with a promise from Cardin that he would arrange a meeting with the Allied Council in haste. The next general meeting wasn't due until tomorrow, but Cardin knew he couldn't wait until then to talk to the Council.

As he, Dalin, Amaya, Nia, and the rest of Amaya's team gathered on the edge of the orc town, Cardin considered his next words and actions carefully. Time was short, and they would only have one chance to get everything right.

"Dalin," he looked to his friend. The former Wizard gave him his full attention. "I know that tensions are high between you and the Council of Masters, but if you're willing, I need you to go to the Wizards' Guild now and tell them we need to arrange an emergency Allied Council meeting this afternoon."

Dalin's mouth opened a little, a silent and almost imperceptible display of his surprise and protest. After a long pause, he sighed, resignation drawing down his face. "Very well," he nodded.

"Meet us back in Archanon," Cardin nodded, stifling his guilt, "and say nothing about why the meeting is being called except that it involves the impending invasion of the Darksteel Army."

As Dalin stepped away to create a portal, Cardin turned to Amaya. "I need you to come with me, but I'd like volunteers from your team to continue to stay here as liaison with the orcs."

"I can do that," Elic volunteered. "We've already been here a couple of weeks, so I'm welcome and used to being here."

Cardin nodded, but then glanced at Nia, before asking Amaya, "We'll also need a Wizard here in case the orcs need to communicate with us."

Amaya nodded, and asked, "Nia?"

Bowing, Nia said with a muted tone, "It will be my pleasure."

"Which leaves the rest of us to return to Archanon," Cardin turned and willed magic into his body. The power flowed easily, and in seconds, a glowing blue-white column of light opened before them. Amaya and the remainder of her team preceded Cardin through it.

Before he stepped through, Cardin turned and looked out upon the sprawling orc town one last time. A few of the children, their skin more uniform than their mottled-skinned parents, watched in awe. He smiled at that at first, but then something else worked its way into his chest.

Fear.

Fear of what was coming. Of what those children might have to face. Of what the children of Edilas, and all of Halarite for that matter, would have to endure.

Looking one last time upon Elic and Nia, Cardin marched through his portal, and was immediately graced by cooler weather and a vision of the western gate of Archanon. Amaya and her team waited patiently for him, and as soon as he stepped through, the portal closed.

Cardin took the lead, and cringed only a little bit as the guards watching from the wall above blew horns announcing Cardin's return. As he stepped through the gates purposefully, city guards from the guardhouse just inside and to his right streamed forth and formed up on either side of Cardin, while the busy main street of the Market District buzzed with activity and excitement.

"Make way for the Prince!" one of the guards shouted.

Marching straight ahead towards the Upper City, Cardin tried his best to ignore the looks the citizens of Archanon gave him. Some still looked at him in awe, but others were less pleasant. He had yet to prove himself as a leader, he knew, but worse still, some blamed him for all of the hardships that had fallen upon them. Or if not him outright, then the Sword of Dragons, still strapped to his back, an ever-present reminder that he had brought the attention of so many other worlds and evils down upon Tal.

Maybe they're not wrong, he thought, his mind wandering back to when he first encountered Kailar, when he failed to take the Sword from her. When he failed to stop Klaralin and his orcs.

When I failed the world.

He caught sight of a young child, no older than five, sitting upon his father's shoulders, watching as Cardin and his Guardians marched past, surrounded by soldiers intent on ensuring Cardin, above all others, remained safe. The child was completely oblivious to the politics and the failures and was just in awe to catch a glimpse of the new royalty of Tal.

A steely resolve set in, and Cardin shoved down those feelings of doubt and inadequacy that he had lived with for so long. He wouldn't fail that kid. He wouldn't fail his people.

Not again.

Thinking back to all that had already transpired today, Cardin asked Amaya, "How many other Guardians are you aware of?"

Seemingly surprised by his question, she replied, "Um, none, actually. Just those of my team."

That was unfortunate, and Cardin grimaced. Then he looked at her sheathed sword, lashed to the right side of her belt. "Do you have any contacts in the Archanon Guild?"

Her brow creased inwards at his question. "A few, yes. Though I'm unfamiliar with the new general."

They quickly came upon the gates to the Upper City, and Cardin stopped the entourage there. Looking Amaya dead in the eye, he said, "I need you to ask the General to assemble as many Warriors at their Guild complex as they can. Tell them it's about payment. If he refuses," Cardin nodded at her right bracer, "Don't be afraid to show that off and tell him it's a command from his Prince."

Nodding, Amaya replied, "As you command, Sire," and then motioned for the rest of her team to follow. Cardin was uncertain about the wisdom of taking her entire team, a show of force to the General who might view it as a threat.

But with only days left to organize defenses, Cardin knew there wouldn't be time to play politics with the Warriors or the other Guilds. The thought he had been mulling over in his head since his meeting with the farmers and merchants yesterday became the only clear path forward.

And it would shake the very foundations of their society.

First and foremost, he had to see to the defenses of the city now, as well as the rest of Tal.

With his entourage of guards, Cardin marched up into the Upper City, past the wealthy houses, and to the castle. As he stepped up onto the terrace before the main doors, Cardin was pleasantly surprised to see the house steward waiting for him.

"Kai," he smiled. "Exactly the person I hoped to see."

"Sire," she bowed, her grey and white dress prim and proper and not a hair out of place, as always. "A runner was sent from the front gate to inform me of your return."

That would save Cardin time. "Has Reis Kalind of Daruun arrived yet?"

"Just an hour ago, yes," she replied primly.

"Good." He looked over Kai's shoulder, past the doors and towards the throne room. Where he'd spent so very much of his time over the past few months.

Maybe a change of venue was in order. Looking right to a long row of windows facing west, he smiled. "Please have Reis brought to the library."

Bowing again, she replied, "At once, Sire," and with perfect grace, she spun on her heel, and retreated into the castle.

Nodding to the guards around him, Cardin said, "The rest of you are dismissed. Thank you for the escort."

"Yes, sire," one of the guards said.

Without waiting for them to disperse, Cardin walked ahead and into the castle, and immediately turned right. After turning down a few hallways, he found himself in the south wing, where the old Allied Council meeting chamber sat unused, but more importantly, where the castle's library was built.

There was no such thing as a more comprehensive library than the Grand Sanctuary, now half-destroyed, but the kings and queens of Tal had certainly curated an extensive collection all their own. Upon entering, Cardin was greeted with bright sunlight from the rows of windows to his right and straight ahead, and set into the wall on the left was an elaborate stone fireplace, disused now due to the warmth of summer, but he could imagine someday curling up in front of it with Sira and reading one of the library's many unique tomes.

Sira...

He wondered how she was faring on her adventure with Endri. As Cardin strode right and back into a little nook where couches and a low table waited him, he stared out into the courtyard in front of the castle and thought of her. Of the changes she had endured.

Of the fact that he may have somehow failed *her* in all of this.

She had done so much for him over the past year, sacrificed or risked her life and livelihood, and now that she needed him, where was he? Stuck in the role of ruler of Tal.

Cardin didn't want to be here. He didn't *belong* here.

Father...where are you?

"My Lord," Kai's stern voice startled him out of his reverie. Turning, the pang of loss and guilt was momentarily replaced when he saw his oldest friend for the first time in months.

"Reis!" Cardin crossed the distance to the entrance in a heartbeat, but when Reis didn't return Cardin's joviality at his arrival, and rather gave Cardin an arched eyebrow of curiosity, Cardin came up short. His friend wore his long, brown hair in a tight ponytail, and he wore his usual leather and chainmail duty armor, his bronze-dyed sword secure in a sheath on his left hip.

Kai stood patiently next to Reis, awaiting Cardin's next orders. He hesitated, and then addressed Kai. "Thank you, Steward. That will be all." She bowed, and began to leave, but then Cardin thought of something else. "Wait."

"Sire?" she turned back to him.

"The Council Chambers, they once served as a war room, yes?"

That question piqued both Reis's and Kai's curiosity, and the latter nodded. "Aye, Sire, it was."

Maybe it was because he had just visited the south wing for the first time in a month. Maybe it was because of the war looming ahead. Either way, he ordered, "Then it shall be again. See to it that it is returned to that state, with an updated map of Edilas."

Without questioning him, Kai bowed once more, and left the library.

Leaving Cardin and Reis face to face.

His friend's expression was curious, but that soon changed to a

143

blank slate. For a moment, Cardin wondered if their past spat had somehow come back to the forefront. Was Reis mad at him for keeping some other secret? Was it over the privilege of Mages? Something else entirely? Cardin inspected his friend's duty armor, but was unsurprised that Reis had yet to receive a promotion to Lieutenant. Reis could be feeling bitter about that, and his angst towards Mages in general might have returned.

Snapping to attention, Reis saluted, and said, "Reis Kalind of the Warriors' Guild, reporting as ordered, Sire."

That's when it dawned on Cardin what was going on. Raising his eyebrows, he replied, "Oh, really? Going all formal now, are you?"

Reis held his salute.

For about a second.

And then a great big grin cracked across his face. "Should I not, oh great Prince?"

"Come here, smart ass," Cardin reached out, and Reis clasped his offered hand, wrist-in-wrist, before Cardin drew him in and embraced his friend.

"Hey," Reis shrugged after stepping back and folding his arms, "I didn't know what to do, given that you're all Princely and such."

"I'm still your friend, Reis," Cardin replied sourly. "A crown on my head isn't going to change that."

Scrunching up the bridge of his nose, Reis said, "Yeah, about that." Looking rather intently upon Cardin's head, he remarked, "I don't see a crown…"

"I don't wear it unless I'm in court," Cardin turned back to where he had stood in the nook moments ago, and as he sat on a couch with its back to the window, he motioned to the one across from him, and Reis took the offered seat. "To be honest, I hate it. I hate…*all* of this," he scowled. "I'm not royalty. I never wanted to be."

Silence met him. Reis's characteristic grin faded ever-so-slightly, and Cardin looked down at his hands.

They were a Warrior's hands. A soldier's. A survivor's. Calloused, scarred, a sign of all the hard work he'd done, the battles he'd fought, the decade spent surviving on the fringe.

How had he come to this?

"Trade places?"

Cardin blinked, not quite sure he'd heard Reis correctly. When he looked at his friend, the grin had returned full force.

"What?"

Giving Cardin a casual shrug, he said, "Hey, you don't want to be a Prince, but I'd love it. Do you have any idea what I'd be able to do in your shoes?"

"Not much," Cardin remarked. "Believe me, you'd be kept so busy you'd barely have time to visit the washroom when you needed to."

Reis gaped at him wide-eyed. "Uh, that's a bit more than I needed to know..."

"Believe me, it's not a glamorous job," Cardin sighed and leaned back. He looked at the table and contemplated putting his feet up. And then he realized, *I'm the Prince, I can do what I want,* and proceeded to kick back and rest his feet, crossing his legs at the ankles. "But, it does have its perks, I suppose," he remarked upon Reis's aghast look.

"Yeah, I guess so," Reis eyed the mud coming off of Cardin's boots.

"Speaking of perks," Cardin started, "I called you here to make you an offer."

Once again, Reis's grin faltered. "O-oh?"

Realizing the seriousness of the offer, of the entire situation surrounding Cardin and Tal and all of Halarite, Cardin grudgingly set his feet back down on the ground and leaned closer to Reis. "Aye. You see, I need people I know and trust surrounding me, especially in the days to come. Political enemies are one thing, but even worse..." He drew in a deep breath, held it, and then shook his head before speaking with the most serious tone. "Reis, we're in trouble."

What was left of his friend's grin vanished completely. "You...you've never exactly been overly dramatic."

"I know," Cardin replied. "And I'm sorry to lay burdens upon you, but I trust you."

Quirking an eyebrow up, Reis asked, "Even after...you know, everything?"

"Even though," Cardin affirmed confidently. "You see, the Darksteel Army is coming. Not in a few years. Not even in a few months. We have days, I fear. Days before they're banging on our walls. Days before violence the likes of which we've yet to see on Halarite befalls us all. We have precious little time to organize our defenses, and to be frank...I've yet to select a Captain of the Guard."

Complete shock crossed Reis's face, and Cardin knew that his friend recognized the implication. "I…C-Captain? *Captain?!*"

"There's more," Cardin went on quickly. "As I've learned over the past three months, I need someone who is more than just the captain of the city guard."

"Oh, *just*, you say," Reis intoned smartly.

With a grin, Cardin pushed on. "It turns out that as captain of the guard, my father was also the man in charge of the Guardians."

If Reis had a drink, he would have sputtered it. As it was, he did a good job imitating it in his utter shock. "He *what?!*"

Suppressing a chuckle, Cardin nodded, and waited for Reis to absorb that bit of info. It was understandable that it was a lot to take in. The Guardians weren't a secret, but they weren't exactly publicly acknowledged, either. Any form of leadership in Tal knew who they were, but beyond that, there were rumors and speculation, and a few whispered encounters.

The elite.

The best.

And most importantly, they could speak with the same authority as the King. *The* most trusted servants of the kingdom.

"Reis," Cardin leaned closer. "I need you to take on this role. There's no one else I trust as much to speak with my authority, and right now, I need someone to act decisively. There's more for me to attend to than just defenses, and I just…" He sighed and shook his head. "I can't do this without you."

Reis fidgeted nervously, and then after a few more twitches, he stood up, and started pacing the length of the library. "This is crazy," he muttered. "I'm waiting for a promotion to Lieutenant. I…" His voice caught. "I'm supposed to…but I mean, the Daruun Commander needs me. But, then, why hasn't he…" Reeling on Cardin, he pointed a finger at his Prince. "Are you asking me to leave the Warriors?"

"Yes," Cardin replied simply. Reis's panicked reaction wasn't what he expected, but he wasn't about to turn back now on this offer.

"But…that's been my dream, *our* dream, all our lives." Reis paused, and corrected, "Well, I suppose you dropped that dream."

"Oh, it gets worse," Cardin spoke hesitantly. "Much worse. Reis, I told you, the Darksteel Army is coming, in *days*. Which means what

I must do next, what I must do today, and tomorrow, and the next, will reshape everything. But it's the only chance we have."

Standing, Cardin crossed the distance to Reis and planted hands on his shoulder, halting Reis's quick pace. "Reis, I need you. And Sira. And Dalin. I need all of you to be at your best, and to help me, help us, help *all* of Tal and Halarite survive the coming days. There's no time for politics, there's no time for catering to greedy whims. There's only survival."

Reis shook his head, and he folded his arms up again. Until Cardin's words truly registered.

Gaping wide-eyed at Cardin, he asked, "What...what are you planning on doing?"

Letting out a sigh, Cardin clasped Reis's shoulders tightly.

"What I must."

Chapter 17

THE RUINS OF CORIAS

By the time Kailar finished gathering all the lords of Devor, the sun had passed midday, and she felt an impatient urgency growing within her.

That or she was just plain hungry, since she had eaten neither breakfast nor lunch.

The lords were not pleased about being summoned back to Tieran again so soon, and it didn't help when Kailar urged them on by telling them a new government had subtly threatened them, but then would say no more.

Unfortunately, most lords insisted they could not be interrupted in their current tasks, and to an extent, Kailar could understand. It wasn't every day that an entire continent stood up a new government.

But they had less than a day before Xavien returned.

She had less than a day.

So after pestering and pushing and shoving, Kailar finally dropped the last lord off. Unlike the others, she didn't escort him into the council chamber, she merely left him outside, and asked the two guards bracketing the doors to escort him in.

That left her to what she knew she had to do.

Intent on summoning a portal in the center of town, Kailar turned away from the city hall, only to come face-to-face with Letan. Somehow, in her hustle to offload the last lord, she hadn't heard him approach.

Kailar's heart leapt into her throat, and she stared across the ten-foot gap between them. It might as well have been a ten-mile-wide valley. He stood stoically, folding his arms. She noted that he wore unusually warm clothes, even for winter in the port. Fur-lined gloves, a lined overcoat, and a heavy cloak.

And he said nothing.

Looking around uncomfortably, she finally asked, "What?"

Glancing behind her, Letan finally spoke, "By my estimate, that's the last lord you had to gather."

"Yeah, what of it?" she bit back harshly.

"Yet here you stand," he started to pace around her, keeping his arms folded. "Outside. Not in there, by the Empress's side, acting as adviser."

And if Kailar didn't move quickly, Reyla would send a guard out to collect her. She didn't have time for this.

"Well whatever you're thinking," she started saying, and stalked off away from Letan, "It's none of your business."

He hurried after her, the sound of rushed, booted footsteps crunching on gravel behind her. "The hells it isn't," he called after her. "You're thinking of defying orders."

She wanted to stop and reel around to shout at him, but instead she kept going, knowing that she had to get away from the area before she was forced to defy the Empress more openly. So she snapped over her shoulder, "Go away, Letan."

He caught up and planted a firm hand on her shoulder. Incensed, she rolled her shoulder out from under his grasp, and batted it away with her right hand, while she summoned dark magic into her left hand and formed a ball of purple-black energy in it. Letan came up short, shocked by her response.

Kailar found herself breathing hard, her heart thundering against her chest. Realizing she was making a scene in the middle of town, she clenched her jaw, and forced the magic away from her hand. Relaxing her stance out of combat readiness, she drew in a deep breath, and told him, "You're not my commanding officer anymore. I don't answer to you. So do us both a favor, and back off."

She turned to go. He interrupted, "Take me with you."

That stopped Kailar in her tracks, as absolute shock took hold. Turning wide-eyed to him, she asked, "W…what?"

He looked around briefly and stepped closer so that he could lower his voice. "Take me with you. We're the only ones on Devor who have spoken to the Navitas, so maybe…I don't know, but maybe we both need to be there."

Drawing her features down into a steep frown, Kailar replied, "But…the Empress ordered-"

"Ordered you to stay," he quickly said. "She gave me no such orders."

The guards that had escorted the last lord in emerged from behind Letan and started scanning the crowds of people going about their business. No doubt looking for Kailar to bring her in.

She looked at Letan. "You sure?" He nodded.

Turning on the spot, she summoned a portal, grabbed his arm, and shoved him through before she followed.

It was colder in the far west plains, and the wind howled behind her, pinning her cloak to her back and sheering right through to her skin, setting her shivering. Letan had taken just enough steps past the portal to let her through, and was busy gathering his cloak around him.

Or maybe it was the sight before her that sent a chill through her body.

The ruins of Corlas.

Unsure how far the glow from the Crystalline Peaks had receded, Kailar had decided that Corlas was a good place to start, but now that she stood upon the eastern edge of the town, she wasn't so sure. She stepped up next to Letan, and together, the two silently surveyed what was left of what had been his home for over a decade.

Fire had consumed it, and places where the sickly green lightning had lanced out from the Peaks were now barren craters fifty feet wide. The inch-thick covering of snow over everything only marginally hid the carnage, and did nothing to hide the smell.

Rotting corpses. *I thought we'd evacuated everyone,* she glumly thought, pressing her hand into her chest, willing the sick feeling back down into her stomach, where it belonged. Beside her, Letan's hands balled into tight fists, clenching hard enough that even through the roaring wind, she could hear the leather skin straining.

The walls were burned to the ground. The buildings. *Everything.*

All that remained were coals and charred stone foundations.

An entire city wiped from the map.

But that at least gave Kailar and Letan a clear line of sight to the Crystalline Peaks. The skies were overcast, but the clouds were high, and she could see miles to the northwest where cracked, giant crystals jutted up from the ground.

A green, stomach-turning glow illuminated the clouds nearest the crystals, but so far, no lightning-

And then one struck. It was far from Corlas, but it startled Kailar, both because of how blinding it was, and because an eerie silence followed. No clap of thunder, nothing else to indicate it had ever struck the ground.

Somehow that was more disturbing than the roar of thunder.

The wind blew harder, and Kailar fought to gather her cloak around her. She looked at Letan, as he surveyed the wreckage. He noticed her staring and looked back at her.

The urge to take his hand overcame her, to hold it, to hug him, to do something to help alleviate the ache she knew he felt in his heart. It struck her as odd that she should feel such an urge, but then, their relationship had only ended a few months ago.

Relationship? She thought. *Could it really be called that?* They had traveled together, fought together, and brought down vast swaths of the criminal underground together. They had flirted, kissed, had sex.

But an actual relationship?

No.

So she did the only other thing she could. Kailar moved forward, stepping into Corlas, closer to the peaks, watching intently for another energy discharge. Her feet crunched in the snow, and she heard Letan following closely behind, but that crunch was drowned out when another burst of wind blew through the ruins, and snow swirled all around, blocking her view of the peaks momentarily.

Still, she saw another bolt of energy lance out, burning its impression upon her eyes. She watched where it struck, and saw that it was far, far away from Corlas, very near the Peaks.

"It looks like the strikes are tightly confined to the peaks," she yelled over the wind.

"So far as we can tell," Letan agreed. "At first I..." He stopped himself, and when she looked back at him, into the howling wind and blowing snow, through squinted eyes she saw his face droop, and he turned his head away.

Shaking her head, she sighed and turned back towards the peaks. And then she looked right, towards the north, pondering if this was a wise course of action or not.

Never-the-less, she was committed, and wasn't about to back down now.

Pushing out the energy around her to create a void, Kailar's dark magic powered the creation of a portal, whose magical wind born of intermingling energy contested with the natural winds, setting the snow around them into a blurring wall.

Looking back to Letan, she nodded and hollered, "We should keep moving."

He met her gaze, eye to eye, for the briefest of moments. Warm butterflies stirred in her stomach, defiant of the cold wind. Then he nodded and preceded her through the portal. She followed a moment later, right into the heart of the Crystalline Forest.

Only to find herself in a bewilderingly empty plain. No Navitas. No crystalline trees. Not even the wind from the distant storm.

Just the Peaks to the west, which they were much closer to now, and craters in the ground where the peaks had discharged their built-up energy.

The Navitas were gone.

Panic gripped her heart. Had they perished in their attempt to calm the storm? Were the bolts of lightning lethal to them, and they'd all shattered?

No, she shook her head, examining the snow-covered ground. She bent down, wiped away snow, and found brown, frozen grass beneath. But no crystal fragments. Nothing to indicate the corpses of Navitas.

Standing back up, she surveyed the barren landscape as a light snow began to fall. Kailar exchanged worried looks with Letan, and then she shouted, "Hello? Is anyone here?" The blanket of snow absorbed her words, so she shouted louder, "We need to speak with you!"

Oppressive stillness answered back.

Letan added his own voice, his baritone resonating into the void, "We want to talk to the Navitas!"

Still nothing happened.

Until a faint rumbling contested with the howling wind. The

ground shook, her feet vibrating with it, until an explosion of dirt and snow bloomed before them. A blue, faceted crystalline being climbed out of the ground, its long, gangly, sharp arms pulling itself up. The entity had no neck, its head forming directly into its tree-like crystalline body, and where eye sockets were, two points of golden energy gazed down upon them. The Navitas had emerged by itself from the ground, and it stood up to its full towering height, at least five times as tall as Kailar. As it moved, she heard the sound of grinding and cracking crystal. A fresh line appeared beneath its eyes, and when it opened its newly-formed mouth to speak, it was human-like, deep, but for the strange tang of metallic sharpness to it.

"The Powerless One," it said, and then shifted its gaze to Letan. "Neither of you should be here." A sickly-green bolt of energy lanced out from the mountain, pounding into the ground less than a thousand feet away from them, as if to punctuate the crystalline being's words.

While the Navitas had emerged a good twenty feet away, she still had to crane her neck to stare up into its golden orbs.

The Navitas were alive.

There was hope.

When she didn't speak right away, the crystal entity stooped lower to examine her. The howling wind and cold seemed not to bother it in the least. "Why have you come?"

Hesitating, realizing she hadn't actually thought about what to ask the Navitas, she started, "I...I wanted to ask you. I mean." She drew in a shuddering breath and wrapped her cloak around her tighter. *This isn't me. I'm strong, I'm direct. Don't let fear control you, Kailar.*

Gathering her wits, she pressed on with faux-confidence. "A dark army stands ready to invade our world. One that has invaded many before ours. But for some reason, they offer this land, this continent, our new government, peace. I believe they fear something. I believe they fear you."

The hollows of its eyes widened, and it stood up straight. "Fear us? But if it is an army powered by darkness, as you say-"

"Not powered by darkness," Letan corrected. "Though they wear armor made of darkened steel, their powers are like yours and mine."

"Ah, yes," the Navitas's head curled back and forth, an imitation of a nod. "Then they have every reason to fear us. With the power of our Collectors," he waved a sweeping, six-fingered hand out towards the Peaks, "we cannot be defeated so easily by conventional magics."

So she was right! The Darksteel Empire must fear the Navitas.

"Would you help defend us?" she asked bluntly. "If they attack us, will you defend this land from them?"

Narrowing its eyes at them, the Navitas hesitated, and then folded its arms while considering her question. Its eyes looked up, towards the peaks, and then back down at Kailar. Her throat caught, and she waited with bated breath.

"You must understand," the creature spoke, his words slow, his voice low and barely audible above the howl of the wind. "It has taken all of our strength to repair the Collectors. We still have work to do. If we divert our attention from it, it will take longer. The repairs may even become undone. We must focus on our work."

"But if they invade," she started, shaking her head. "If we face them now, with our army barely formed, with our defenses almost non-existent...they'll overrun us in days. We won't survive. They'll take this land from us, and then turn their attention on you."

"Mhm," the Navitas grumbled. "Yes. The last we spoke, you convinced us to stand our ground and not flee this world. We stood against the Dark One, side by the side with the Keeper of the Sword. Many of us died. Too many."

"But you succeeded," Letan pitched in, stepping closer to the Navitas. "I've heard about the Battle of Maradin, you worked with the Keeper to successfully drive the Dark Dragon away."

"We drove the Dark One away, yes," it replied. "But we did not destroy it. It may yet find us and exact revenge upon us."

"I have no doubt he will," she agreed, "if you stand alone. I remember what I said to you back then, and I hold to that. If you stand alone, if *we* stand alone, we are vulnerable. The Dark Dragon, this army that now threatens us, either could destroy us all. And maybe more will come after them."

"All the more reason to finish our work," the Navitas swept his hand towards the Peaks again. "In our current state, we are vulnerable."

"But the Darksteel Empire would be just as vulnerable, if they marched upon you," she nodded, and again, a bolt of sickly green, disturbingly silent lightning lanced out, this time less than five hundred feet away, gouging a fresh crater into the ground. Though there was still no thunder, the thudding WHUMP from impact shook the ground, and rattled Kailar. "The Peaks would endanger them if they dared approach you."

The moment she finished speaking, she realized her mistake, and Letan turned his head sharply towards her. The Navitas capitalized upon that. "Exactly true, and that is why we must remain here. We must repair. Without the Collectors at full capacity, we cannot bring our full might against them, but here we are protected by the very damage we seek to repair."

Kailar's shoulders slouched. By her own words, she had proven the Navitas's plan correct. She had doomed her own people.

My own people, she grimaced. *I've finally found a place in life, and now I have to watch it be consumed by darkness.*

"I am sorry," the Navitas crouched lower to them, resting its arms on its faceted knees. "Truly. However, if they do not invade because of our presence on this land, perhaps that will be enough to safeguard your people."

She nodded, the well of emptiness and despair growing inside of her chest, forcing a lump into her throat. She wanted to speak, to thank the Navitas, to curse it, something, *anything*, but she simply couldn't speak.

The Navitas remained silent and still for a moment, but then it stood, and turned towards the Peaks. As it took one long, great step towards the Peaks, another energy bolt lanced out, this time striking within feet of the Navitas. Kailar jumped, the lump bursting out of her throat in an unintentional cry of fear.

The Navitas paused mid-stride, and though it could not turn its head, its eye sockets cracked and screeched around to face her. "You should leave."

Were the energy discharges attracted to her? Or to the Navitas? Or was it merely coincidence?

Either way, the crystalline being was right.

Except.

Except.

"Wait!"

The Navitas had begun to walk again, but once more halted, one leg hovering mid-stride above the ground.

"Wait," she insisted, and rushed towards it. "Maybe we don't need your entire army to stand with us."

The Navitas backed up, setting its foot down, and then slowly ground around to face her. "What do you propose?"

A grin spread across her face, excitement and anticipation growing as an idea formed in her head. It was perfect.

But would her Empress go for it? Would the lords of the land? She glanced at Letan, who looked at her quizzically.

"Technically speaking, the Navitas are the lords of this land," she told Letan with a grin.

His brow furrowed for a second, but then realization dawned, brightening his face as his eyes and mouth opened wide. "Tomorrow's meeting," he reasoned.

"Exactly," she grinned at him, and then turned to the Navitas. "You see, the Darksteel Empire has not brought its army to our city. They sent an emissary. A representative. If they fear you and your people," she grinned up at the crystalline entity. "Maybe all it takes to safeguard our sovereignty is just one of you."

The Navitas's eye sockets opened wide. "Interesting proposal." He hunched down again, looking at Kailar thoughtfully. "There may be merit to your idea." He nodded, or rather bobbed his head front to back in a 'nod.' "Yes. One Navitas leaving will not significantly hinder our repairs."

"Plus," Letan added quickly, "avoiding confrontation altogether is far better than fighting in a war once it has begun. Better than facing an army if they dominate us before your collectors finish. Sending one representative now could save both of our civilizations from an invasion."

The Navitas considered their proposal, and then she swore the crack that served as its mouth creased up just a hair in a grin. "You both speak wisdom. Yes," the Navitas bobbed its body in another nod. "I believe we can accede to this request."

A broad smile drew across Kailar's face, and without realizing what she was doing, she grasped Letan's hand in excitement.

Hope was rekindled.

Chapter 18

FAST EXIT

"Wait!" Sira pleaded, following Kemila as the airship captain headed for the exit, the other patrons of the pub rising from their seats in a cacophony of squeaking and rubbing and vibrating. "Wait, where did you see them?"

Ignoring Sira, Kemila headed for the bar next to the exit, hefting a bag of clinking metal off her belt. "I think this should cover us," Kemila called to the pub owner behind the bar, who seemed entirely unmoved by the sudden exodus from their establishment.

The pub owner, a large fellow who looked like he could take care of bouncer duties just as well as any others, deftly caught the clinking pouch and peered inside. He grunted once, stashed the pouch faster than Sira could watch, and disappeared into a back room.

Kemila hadn't even broken stride and was at the exit, with Sira following right behind her, wanting to tug on Kemila's sleeve to stop the woman, but unwilling to incidentally incur another person's ire.

Surprisingly, Kemila came to a sudden stop and whirled on Sira. "Woh, hold it there, Pretty Eyes," Kemila cautioned. The captain's crew piled up behind Sira, confusion and explicatives ringing out. "The local constabulary are still looking for you. If I was you, I'd stay put until morning. You can duck out into the crowd then."

"What?" Sira blinked, then shook her head, "I don't care about that."

"I would if I were you," Kemila thrust her arm into the beaded threshold of the door, parting it. "They don't take kindly to those who break the laws around here."

No longer caring, Sira grabbed a handful of the hem of Kemila's bodice.

Kemila whirled, her hands and arms a blur as she grasped Sira by the wrist and twisted.

Sira, having lived the life of a Warrior, reacted on instinct, breaking Kemila's wrist hold before the captain could solidify her grip, and then she deflected the captain's arms before shoving her against the door frame.

A dozen hands grabbed Sira, yanked her back, and panic fell upon her. Raida gathered in power, and-

"Wait!" Kemila shouted, pushing off against the door frame and holding out a halting hand to her crew. The power Raida had gathered remained poised and ready. Sira could direct it into another defensive pulse, just like at the elven airship dock.

"You'd best stow that power of yours, Pretty Eyes," Kemila cautioned, her hand lowering slowly. The grip upon Sira's *everything* disappeared, and she was allowed to stand on her own. "I've no interest in seeing you hurt, and someone will sense that power and coming running for ya. So just do yourself a favor, and ease off. You'll not learn a shred of info, not when it can come back to me and mine," she waved back at her crew. "We're done getting involved, ya hear?"

Sira stepped closer to Kemila, and was met with the point of a sword. Not from Kemila, but from the fur-covered woman that had sat next to Sira earlier. It was a curved sword, similar to the ones she'd seen marines use aboard ship when she and Cardin had set sail out of Maradin. A scimitar, if she remembered the term right.

"You'll not lay a hand on the Captain," the woman growled at Sira. Literally *growled* afterwards, a deep, throaty sound she would never have expected from such a lithe-looking creature.

"Easy, T'Zina," Kemila's hand rested on the cat-woman's hand, forcing her to lower her scimitar. "Young Sira here isn't gonna hurt me, is she?"

Narrowing her eyes, Sira replied, "No. But I'm not giving up, either."

Kemila pursed her lips at that. "Aye, you're a stubborn one, aren't ya? All the good ones are, aren't they?" Her crew all took up a rowdy grumble of agreement, and then fell silent, waiting patiently on their captain.

"You mean to tell me, if I leave, you'll follow, no matter what?" Kemila asked.

Sira tensed, ready to defend herself, anticipating Kemila to tell her crew to subdue Sira and shackle her to a table or something. Sira nodded. And waited.

Kemila grinned. "Then I guess we'll just have to bring you aboard our ship, eh?" Sira's eyes widened in surprise, and Kemila whirled her hand into the air. "Wrap her up, folks!"

A surge of movement, giant hands grasping her arms, and she was jostled forward. Kemila led the way out, and before Sira knew what was happening, she was hauled out after Kemila, with the crew crowding in, the tallest of whom surrounded her.

At first Sira struggled against the tug and pull of the two bronze-skinned, seven-foot-tall men on either side of her, but then she realized what was happening.

They were covering for Sira again. They were taking her to the docking spire and ensuring that no outside eyes would see her as they traversed the open area between the pub and the spire stairs.

"Wait, why are you taking me on the ship?" she called out.

Kemila didn't answer, but Sira thought she knew. She knew Kemila's type all too well, and had arrested more than a few. The airship captain was afraid Sira's insistence would mean getting caught in the lie she'd told the 'constabularies.' Which would mean she would, at the very least, get slapped with a fine. Maybe worse.

The best option to protect herself? Take Sira and make sure she never talked to another soul again.

That's alright, she thought. *As long as I'm with Kemila, I can keep pressing her. And as long as I have my...*

Sira patted her hip. Felt nothing there.

Sword.

Looking around in a panic, she couldn't see it anywhere, in anyone's hands, and the press of airship crewmembers was so dense and chaotic, she couldn't hope to find it now.

Looking at one of the bronze-skinned men next to her, his ears long, thin, tapered, and translucent, she growled at him, "I'd better get it back."

Whether or not he knew what she meant, she didn't care, but something in the gleam in his eye told her he knew.

When they reached the encircling stairs of the steel spire, Sira knew things were about to get complicated. She also knew she had a choice. This would be the best place to fight for her freedom, now, at the bottom of the stairs, when the throng of crew around her would have to thin out to only one in front and one behind.

The question was, did she want to fight? Or cooperate?

Kemila was the first up the stairs, allowing Sira to view the woman again for the first time since they'd left the pub. And something stirred inside of her. A kind of trust she couldn't explain. And a stirring that she thought *had* to be coming from Raida, as her eyes unwillingly watched Kemila's backside sway back and-

Blinking and forcing her eyes away, she thought, *Raida!*

"*Sorry!*"

Either way, if she wanted answers, she had to stick with the airship captain.

Craning her neck back just as she was shoved up the first few steps, Sira sighed at the magnificent sight above her. The whirling blades. The metallic skin of the ship.

There was something beautiful about it.

Something that captivated her imagination.

And she willingly walked up the stairs, with about five or six crew members between her and Kemila.

Of course, the problem was that she was now in the open, no longer concealed by the throng of the crew. They were only halfway up the stairs when a bull roar echoed off the square's walls. Sira searched the thinning crowd in the square, and saw at least one bull-like officer and two bear-like officers hustling towards them, weapons drawn.

"Double-time it!" Kemila shouted.

With her heart leaping in her throat, Sira kept pace with the bronze-skinned men, the steel staircase a caucus of clanging as fifty people ran up. The climb was exhausting, and if she hadn't done her best to keep fit during her months of leave from the Warriors, she was sure they would have had to carry her up.

By the time they reached the wide platform at the top of the spire,

she was heaving breaths, her heart hammering against her chest. But there was no time to take stock, no time to take in the view of the Deadlands stretching out around them. Or the massive engines above them, thrumming and humming, the whirling blades blasting air down upon the crew, scattering Sira's hair into her eyes.

The bottom of the ship was a sort of balcony, the hull made of steel, the deck of wood, but she grimaced as they walked over the small deck and into another door that revealed another set of stairs leading upwards.

But they only climbed a couple of stories worth in the enclosed stairwell, the huffing and breathing of the crew making it feel even more oppressive. Finally, they spilled out into a much more open area, even if it was still inside of the hull rather than in the open air.

Except for the grand vista she received from the front of the ship, where paneled glass covered a good one third of the wall. Wood deck jutted out into that observation area, but she quickly realized it *wasn't* just an observation area. A wheel like that of a sailing ship's was dead center on a platform raised a good three feet above the rest of the deck, and Kemila was already at that wheel. A circular iron or steel...*desk?* Something like a desk surrounded the front half of the wheel, and Kemila jammed her finger onto that desk and shouted at it, "Cast off all moorings! We're leaving, folks, and we're not coming back, so secure all cargo and man your stations."

Kemila's voice somehow echoed from all directions, and the crew busied themselves quick enough, spreading out, some climbing stairs or ladders to higher decks, some going to work on this deck.

A double-thud that Sira guessed were moorings being released reverberated against the hull, and the ship jerked beneath her feet, nearly throwing her off balance.

A low hum in the ship that she hadn't noticed before increased its cadence, and the ship shifted again beneath her feet. And they began to rise. Higher and higher. The force of false gravity pulled at Sira's belly button, and though it was difficult to tell from this high up, as Sira found herself walking past Kemila's helm and closer to the windows, she saw that they were moving forward.

They were clear. Faster than Sira would have thought possible, but they were clear.

And the way the crew had so rapidly prepared the ship for departure? Sira had the feeling this wasn't the first time they had done something like this.

The design of the ship's bridge was unlike anything Sira had ever seen before. Her time spent on the Sea Wisp had taught her that the crew of ships usually had to busy themselves with sails, ropes, lines, all manner of ship workings. As they soared over another airship, this one with a massive bladder suspended above it, she could see that the other ship's hull was made of wood, and looked very much like a traditional sailing boat, but with the bladder instead of sails jutting above the deck.

Kemila's ship was different. *Very* different. And the crew manned other desk-like stations lining the edge of the bridge, pressed up against the grand glass vista, and they threw levers and pushed disc-like things into the desks, which would light up or go dim when they depressed them.

How am I ever going to describe this to others back home?

Kemila's ship picked up speed rapidly, and in less than a minute, the bazaar was far behind them.

Except, the glow of the sun, having already set, was directly ahead of them.

Which meant Endri was behind them.

Whirling around, Sira looked up at Kemila and said, "Turn around."

Kemila's eyebrows rose up curiously. "Oh? That's funny, I thought *I* was the captain of this ship."

"My friend is back that way," Sira pointed. That's when she realized that there was a solid wall separating the bridge from the rest of the ship behind them. The hatch they had come out of wasn't the only hatch on the back, and she saw corridors stretching further back into the ship, with crew members bustling about back there.

"I told you, I'm not getting involved," Kemila gave her a sour look. "But you're welcome to get off at any point. Just brace yourself, it's a long ways down." The crew jeered and laughed at the captain's joke.

Sira stomped closer to the helm, "You can't just keep me on this ship!"

Bronze hands grasped her arms and yanked her back away from the helm.

This time she very intentionally pulsed out magic, shoving the twins away from her.

The ship shuddered and shook, and Kemila yelled in surprise, grasping the wheel hard and turning it against the shuddering and shaking.

"Stop!" the captain glared at Sira. "Don't use magic on the bridge, ya daft lass!" The shuddering of the ship eased off, but the tension in Kemila's shoulders didn't. "You'll disrupt the magic currents powering her, ya could bring the whole damn thing down!"

The bronze twins approached her again, so she did the only thing she could think of – she upturned her palm, and silently asked, *Raida, I could use a show of force here...*

The dragonspirit obliged. A purple sphere of energy appeared in Sira's hand, surprising even her. The ship didn't shudder this time, but her intent was clear to the others, and the twins backed off. A line of sweat appeared on Kemila's brow.

"You wouldn't," the captain whispered. "You'd kill us all."

Sira stared stubbornly back. "Take me back to my friend. Now. He's on the eastern edge of the Deadlands. Big green dragon, hard to miss."

Kemila remained silent. Other than the hiss of escaping gasses somewhere nearby, the entire bridge was deathly silent. All eyes were fixed upon Sira and the sphere of energy in her hands. The captain's eyes kept darting between it and Sira's violet eyes. Then they dipped to Sira's neckline.

"You're tattoo is glowing," Kemila murmured.

Of course Sira couldn't see it, but she could feel power pulsing into her hand. Power she hadn't called forth from the Universe around her.

It was Raida's power, fueling a magic that Sira knew no Mage could have ever hoped to cast.

"Are you really so intent on this, lass?" Kemila asked. "Would you really sacrifice yourself in your pursuit of it? You don't strike me as the type, and I pride myself on my judgment of character."

"Oh really?" Sira asked. "Then consider this. A Dark Dragon wiped out an entire city on my world. Killed the most powerful Wizard we know and dozens of other Wizards. And threatens the man I love." Kemila's eyebrows twitched. "Not to mention my entire world and the worlds of my friends. So yeah, I'm going to do whatever it takes to get the information I need to protect them."

With a thought directed more towards Raida than to control her powers, Sira doused the energy in her palm, and clenched her hand into a fist before she lowered it. "All I need to know is where. You can drop me off here, I'll walk around the Deadlands and meet my friend. You need not get involved again. I'll tell no one you helped."

The hardness in Sira diminished, her face softening, and she felt despair and desperation take hold of her gut, cinching it into a knot. "Please."

The hardness in Kemila's eyes likewise eased, almost imperceptibly, but still.

"I don't know..." the captain started.

And then a voice Sira never expected to hear called out, "Sira?!"

She blinked back at one of the aft hatches, and was greeted by reddish-orange hair, eyes the color of a sunset, skin well-tanned, and pointed ears a lot shorter than the elves she had encountered at the other docking spire.

Sira clenched her eyes shut, rubbed them, and opened them again. "Elaria?!"

The Dareann Elf didn't smile, but she burst forward, coming at Sira fast, and wrapped her arms around the Warrior in a surprisingly strong hug.

"Is it really you?" Elaria whispered. And a moment later, Sira felt wetness on her cheek.

Pulling away from the elf, she saw tears streaming down Elaria's face.

Then she noticed the woman's armor looked torn in sections, pieces of the leather scales missing. Her travelling cloak was noticeably absent, and there was a fading bruise on her left cheek.

"Elaria...what are you doing here?"

A hollow, distant look overcame her expression, and she glanced at Kemila. Sira immediately thought the worst – had the airship captain abducted Elaria and tortured her?

Except, Elaria wasn't bound. She looked free to move about the ship.

So what else could it be?

"The Darksteel Army," Elaria whispered.

A deep, dark well opened up in the pit of Sira's stomach, and her mouth suddenly felt dry. "Oh, gods..."

Elaria looked down, swallowed hard, and then looked into Sira's eyes. They were haunted eyes, sending chills all through Sira's body, raising goose bumps up along her arms.

She said to Sira, "Darea has fallen."

Chapter 19

WARRIORS AND SOLDIERS

There's never enough time, Cardin thought, glaring at his shadow upon the cobbled roads of Archanon. The shadow was growing longer, the sun stubbornly marching towards the horizon. It was well past noon, and all he and Reis had managed to do was grab a couple of apples from the kitchen before heading out towards the Warriors' Guild complex.

The march from the gates of the Upper City into the Red District wasn't overly long, but it took them past the half-destroyed Grand Sanctuary, leaving a sour pit in his stomach. Even despite all that had been revealed, the lies, the half-truths, and even despite the fall of the Covenant, the people of Halarite still looked to the Order of the Ages for answers. For calm. And so they worked to rebuild the once-greatest library on all of Halarite.

But money was tight for everyone, except for the wealthiest, and only some of them had funded the reconstruction efforts. Scaffolding had been constructed, but only a handful of workers were hard at it today. Both volunteers and supplies were running short.

A sign of the times, Cardin grimaced.

And now they had crossed from the Merchant District into the Red District. Red for war. Red for blood.

Warriors lived in the Red District. The Warriors' Guild Complex was built there, long ago, a mansion amongst a dense collection of homes, shops, and other crowded buildings. The training complex was nearby too, along with the city dungeon and guard barracks, but the Guild Complex overshadowed it all in size and grandeur, its watchtower reaching as high as the city's outer wall.

A waist-high stone wall surrounded the complex, with only a handful of arched entrances into the grounds. Cardin could feel the buzz of energy flowing through those walls, and knew that a permanent magic barrier had been enchanted into them, not unlike the larger barrier present in the city wall. Any would-be intruders into the Guild Complex would have to go through one of the highly-visible and guarded arched entrances, as a shield would flare up anywhere else the moment someone foolishly tried to hop the fence.

As Cardin, Reis, and Governor Maral, surrounded by a small entourage of city guards, marched down the cobblestone street, he could see into the grounds. Assembled on either side of the main path leading up to the front doors were hundreds of Warriors, almost all of them in casual clothes. No armor, no sign of being on duty.

Another sign of the times.

Cardin's greatest hurdle yet.

When they reached the arched entrance, General Vellar greeted them, along with his aide, a young man that Cardin had only met in passing and whose name he couldn't remember. Vellar, Cardin noted, was the only Warrior in armor, his ceremonial plate and chainmail dyed a burnt orange color, and Cardin guessed his sheathed, two-handed longsword was as well.

Next to the general stood Amaya and her team, minus Elic and Nia. The look on her face was apprehensive, but he knew that Reis's was probably much worse. At that moment, however, Cardin didn't dare give in to his curiosity and glance at Reis. They both needed to put on a brave face, and neither could afford to look uncertain.

As much as Cardin hated to agree to it, Reis had warned that this would become a game. A deadly game. And Cardin had to be sure not to show his hand. If anything, he might even need to bluff his way through it.

"Prince Kataar," General Vellar bowed, as did his aide. "Per your request, I have assembled all Warriors present in Archanon that were available on such short notice."

Which, despite the courtyard being overfilled with Warriors, wasn't as many as Cardin knew there should have been. There were still thousands, despite their recent casualties in battle, and that meant either the General hadn't seriously tried to gather more Warriors, or he only gathered the highest-ranking Warriors, intent on disseminating Cardin's message through the ranks.

In a way, it didn't really matter so much, as long as all of the Warriors heard sooner rather than later.

Nodding to the general, Cardin said, "Thank you. As you know, these are desperate times."

Walking past Vellar, Cardin used a trick he had only recently learned from Dalin, infusing magic to boost the volume of his voice without straining himself. "It has been desperate and difficult times for us all," he addressed the assembled Warriors. Though they still stood at attention, they followed Cardin with their eyes.

Their Prince.

Their country's leader.

Cardin felt sick to his stomach to have so much riding on his shoulders. He wanted to shake, shudder, turn away from the Warriors, turn away from it all. Instead, he pushed on, and hoped he was at least as persuasive to the Warriors of Tal as he was to the Allied Council in days past.

"No one could have anticipated the challenges we've faced over the past couple years," Cardin continued, slowly walking along the line, hands clasped behind his back, silver crown heavy upon his brow. He never wore it unless giving an audience. Or unless he needed every scrap of influence he had. "And the Warriors of Tal have braved it all. You defended Tal against Falind when Kailar set them upon us. Then you worked *with* the Falind Warriors to defend us against Klaralin. You fought bravely against the orcs for six months, against overwhelming odds. You watched the skies burn, and then turned around and invaded Maradin, in the face of the undead and a Dark Dragon."

Cardin reached halfway down the line and halted, Maral and Reis stopping beside him, while Vellar, having followed them, remained back a good fifty feet.

"Through all of that, you stood vigil and protected the people of Tal," Cardin looked to his left, looked into the eyes of one Warrior, then another, and still another, until he had met eyes with at least a dozen of them. He turned his head to his right and did the same on the other side.

He saw curiosity in their eyes. Pride. Worry.

Where was he going with this? What was coming next?

"Three months ago, our country endured its greatest blows ever," Cardin spoke a little softer, magic still conveying his voice across the breeze. "It has shaken our once-steadfast kingdom to its foundations, and perhaps irreparably changed our future. I wish I could tell you the hardest times were behind us, but they aren't." Turning, Cardin leveled his eyes upon Vellar. "I know morale is low. I know the throne cannot pay you actual gold and silver. And I wish I could tell you that it'll get better, but something far worse is coming. An army." He held his gaze with Vellar, trying to read the general's expression, but Vellar's face was maddeningly mute.

"They come not just for us, but for all of Halarite," Cardin continued. "*They* are responsible for many of the hardships we have endured. Starting with Klaralin and his orcs." Reaching back absently, he touched the Sword of Dragons, and added, "They engineered Kailar's discovery of the Sword. All in an attempt to weaken us. To set us against one another. To attract other life to our world and disrupt our beliefs, our values, to make us question everything we ever thought we understood. And now that we are at our weakest, they prepare to invade us."

A murmur of disquiet spread amongst the Warriors, but Cardin didn't look away from Vellar. There was something there. A spark of smug indignation, as if the general thought Cardin was making up this new threat.

Vellar was dangerous. Not in the way that Idann was dangerous, but in perhaps a far worse way. Though Cardin addressed Vellar now, his message was for the Warriors. All of them.

So he turned to the Warriors, looked back and forth across the gap, and said, "I know that you cannot fight on empty stomachs. I know that your families suffer. So I make you all this offer. Attend to your duties, and you will be fed and clothed. Protect the merchants and farmers, and they will provide for you, until such time that we can return to our normal economic situation. I have made this arrangement with them in the hopes of ensuring everyone's future, and I ask you all to consider it."

Silence followed. Whether stunned or considerate, Cardin didn't know. All he knew, all he *expected,* was greed to win out on the newly elected Tal General.

Vellar's face was scrunched up into a sneer. "With all due respect, Your Majesty…it sounds as if you wish us to work for free."

"Not free," Cardin shook his head. "Work for food. Work for clothes. Work for supplies to keep your homes in good condition."

Stepping closer, Vellar scoffed. "Oh, and they would be providing us these goods and services out of the kindness of their heart?"

"As I've explained, General," Cardin narrowed his eyes, keeping his voice magically enhanced so that everyone could hear his words. "They will provide it in exchange for protection. Creatures terrorize them. Criminal elements in these lands have run rampant. Some have even begun to migrate from the colonies. Do you think it coincidence that the largely lawless colonies suddenly aren't as lucrative to bandits and crime rings as Edilas? Everyone suffers without the protection of the Warriors."

"Then pay us," Vellar stubbornly stated.

Vellar knew as well as anyone that the kingdom didn't have the funds to pay them. Tax collection had broken down in the wake of the wraith. Coffers were already empty thanks to the King's son, Idrill Beredis.

That was never Vellar's goal. Cardin had known that, but until that very moment, he hadn't known what the general's goal was. Not until just now.

And it frightened Cardin.

"Let me be sure I understand you, General," Cardin narrowed his eyes, and chose his next words very, *very* carefully. "You are refusing to accept food and supplies for your people in exchange for doing your job? All because you'd rather have gold?"

Vellar's stout expression faltered just a little. He countered, "Gold buys that which you offer, and then some." Cardin watched the General's hands. Waited for them to turn aggressive, but so far, they hung unthreateningly at Vellar's sides.

"Yet you know we have none to offer, not yet," Cardin replied. "Not while we continue to recover and reorganize. This is the next best solution. The one that ensures your Warriors survive."

His stubborn look further faltering, Vellar shook his head. "Your Majesty, you make it sound as if…"

"As if you are more concerned with lining your pockets? Tell me, General, how much *does* a General normally retain as part of their commission?"

"When our income is zero, not enough," Vellar spat.

"Oh indeed," Cardin nodded. "And Commanders? Don't misunderstand, with rank comes increased responsibility, and that should ensure a commensurate pay. But what about duty? Honor? Integrity?" He paused for gravity, and asked, "What about the Warrior code?"

It was a risk, bringing the code up. And the general responded exactly as Cardin expected. "Do not *dare* speak to me about the code," Vellar said in a low, angry voice. "Not when you spat upon that code twelve years ago."

Cardin nodded, and looked around at the Warriors. "Aye. He's right. I trained as a Warrior, side by side with some of you." He exchanged a glance with Reis. His best friend. One who had trained with Cardin, day in and day out. "Then I rejected the Warriors. I thought the Guild broken." He sighed, pacing away from Vellar for a dozen feet before he stopped and looked down. "At the time, I didn't know who was to blame. I saw greed. I saw privilege unrestrained. I saw us fight other Warriors from other kingdoms."

He turned and leveled his gaze upon the general again, and finished, "All in the name of money. So long as our kingdom paid us, who cared who we fought?" He walked slowly towards the General, passing by Reis and Maral. "I cared. I still do. And now, from the throne of Tal, I finally see who is truly to blame." He stopped, leaving only five feet between him and the general.

"Me?" Vellar frowned.

"No," Cardin shook his head. Stunned surprise crossed Vellar's face. "You, your greed, it's just a symptom." He gulped, and again addressed the Warriors at large. "This is our fault. The throne's fault. Not just recent, but millennia of kings and queens. I was right, when I rejected the Guild, because there was no way I could ever make things better as a member of the Guild. Because I would always and forever be subject to the whims of whomever sat upon the throne. The Warriors need gold and silver to survive. To fight. To protect. So they go with whomever can pay them the most. And until recently, that was the throne. You fought other Warriors at the commands of your kings and queens."

He drew in a breath, and then said, "Unfortunately, our backs are against the wall. We cannot afford to restructure the Warriors' Guild to ensure this never happens again. But by the gods," and Cardin used that phrase intentionally, banking on the rumors flying around the kingdom that he had met one of the Six, "if you're going to fight on the orders of the throne, then we might as well make it official."

There was a deafening pause, and Cardin let the implication roll around the Warriors.

He waited. Time and lessons from Jeric had taught him that sometimes silence said more than words.

Finally, Vellar asked, "What are you saying?" No propriety. No title. A flat question.

Cardin turned to him, and then looked around at the Warriors.

"As of today," Cardin said, "I am disbanding the Tal Warriors, and absorbing all who volunteer to do so into the Tal military directly."

Silence.

Cardin waited for the inevitable roar of outrage. Waited for complaints, refusals, something, *anything*. Especially from Vellar.

But when he looked at the general, all he saw was eyes wide open in shock.

"I make you all this promise, right here, right now," Cardin said to them all. "Any here who volunteer to willingly become a soldier of Tal will retain their rank and privilege. Your families will be taken care of. Fed, clothed, everything that can be done. You will be allowed to retain your weapons and armor. You will also be fed and cared for. Likewise, as the order spreads," he looked at Maral, who though she looked stunned by his proclamation, did not look ready to object, "all will be given the same choice. Retain rank and privilege and join the army. Or leave and find your own way in the world."

Cardin hoped for volunteers, willing volunteers who would fight for their kingdom of their own volition. That was why he didn't dare say anything else. He didn't dare say that if there weren't enough people who made the jump, if the ranks of the Tal army weren't strong enough, they would be forced to conscript soldiers.

He desperately hoped it wouldn't come to that.

"Y…y-you can't," Vellar breathed, just loud enough for Cardin to hear. The Prince turned to him and leveled an even gaze upon the general. "You can't do this."

"I can," Cardin all but pointed to the crown upon his head. "I have. It is done."

Vellar's eyes fell upon Reis. "You...you went along with this?"

Not at first, Cardin thought, thinking back to his lengthy conversation with Reis.

"Aye, I did," Reis nodded, folding his arms in such a way that his right index finger pointed to the brooch on his chest. Rank insignia. Captain's rank. "I've already transitioned to the Prince's personal guard."

Something shifted in Vellar's eyes. Stunned shock transformed to anger. No, *rage.*

His hand was on the hilt of his sword, his voice contorted into a vengeful sound as he growled, "Traitor!"

But Amaya was behind him. Before either he or Reis could draw weapons, Amaya had drawn a dagger, jabbed her other fist into the man's side with a pulse of magic, enough to knock the wind out of him, and then kicked the back of his knees out, forcing him down so that she didn't have to reach up to point the dagger at his jugular.

"I wouldn't do that if I were you," she hissed.

It had happened in less than a second. The general of the Warriors had lashed out irrationally, threatened either Reis or Cardin, or both. And Amaya, without Cardin even having to talk to her ahead of time, had anticipated it and acted.

Cardin hadn't even seen her come up behind the general before she acted.

Gods, I'm glad she's on my side, he thought with a mental gulp.

The assembled Warriors hadn't had time to react at first, but now everyone tensed, and Cardin felt his heart leap into his throat. He knew this action could have led to civil war. It still could. Would it? Or had his words convinced them?

He heard the clink of swords being pulled out of their locks, but no one actually unsheathed their weapons. The Warriors at the front looked from Vellar to Cardin and back, uncertainty playing over their eyes.

Cardin didn't reach for the Sword. Didn't show his fear or anxiety. He remembered Reis's words. Remain calm. Confident. *Be the leader they need, the solid foundation they can look to for assurance, even if you don't feel it yourself.*

But which was the best course of action? Chastising Vellar? Or sympathizing with him? He hadn't been the general for long, but did he already hold their allegiance?

Having more friends is better than having more enemies, Cardin thought. *And even if he'll never be a friend, I can at least work to ensure he doesn't create more enemies.*

"I know how you feel," Cardin said. "Change is…frightening. And we have seen so much change since the Sword of Dragons was unearthed." Though he meant to address all of the assembled Warriors, Cardin kept his gaze upon the general. He didn't dare approach him, should he lash out despite the dagger pressed to his jugular. "But now is not the time for division. For civil war. Now is the time to stand together."

Now he turned his attention to the rest of the Warriors, and began pacing up the line again, towards the mansion. "Enemies stand at the gate, ready to break it down and ravage the land we have fought so long and hard to protect. We do not know their strength, we do not know their numbers. All we know is that they come for all of our cities, all of our land. Not one or two. Not this kingdom or that kingdom. Not the devout or the atheists."

He spun around on his heel and looked hard down the path, his eyes meeting Vellar's. "*All* of us. Everywhere. To what end, I do not know. Will they kill us? Enslave us?" He shook his head and walked back towards the general. "I'd rather not find out. I'd rather we stand firm against them, united as we did against Klaralin! United as we did against the orcs! United as we were against the necromancers! I'm asking you," he came within five feet again, and reached out a hand towards the general. "General Vellar. I'm offering you, and all of us, the only chance we have at surviving the coming invasion. Stand with me, not against me."

Vellar frowned at Cardin's hand. The general looked into his Prince's eyes, confused, uncertain. Unable to comprehend at first.

"I need a general to command my army," Cardin insisted. "I need a general to oversee the transition from Warriors to soldiers. I need a general to prepare our defenses."

"Y…you would trust me with that task," Vellar said carefully, the bump on his throat bouncing against the edge of the dagger. "After what I just did?"

Cardin stretched his hand out further, closer to the general. "I need more allies," Cardin said. "Not more enemies. Will you stand with me to defend our kingdom?"

Vellar pressed his lips into thin lines, regarding Cardin's hand. Cardin looked at Amaya, raised his eyebrows. She looked uncertainly at him, but nodded, and withdrew her dagger.

Cardin stepped closer, leaving bare inches between them.

The general stared at his hand. Cardin waited, tense, watching for some hint that the general might instead draw his sword and swipe at Cardin. Sure, Cardin was strong with magic, but he wasn't invincible. Worse still, a move like that would probably set off a civil war.

But the general didn't draw his weapon. He reached, hesitated, and then clasped Cardin's hand. Cardin hefted the man up onto his feet.

"I'm with you." And then he bowed deeply. "My Prince."

Chapter 20

DAREA'S FATE

A somber mood had fallen upon the bridge of Kemila's ship, and Sira took hold of Elaria's hands to squeeze them. "How?" she asked the elf. "I mean…"

Swallowing hard, Elaria shook her head, cleared her throat, and said, "It was the dwarves. They let them in through the shields."

"Th…the dwarves?!" Sira gaped, disbelief reeling through her heart. Memories of Gilrin, the dwarf that had travelled into the ruins beneath Archanon, passed before her mind's eye. He had a chip on his shoulder, sure, but…

'The elves stole our power!' The last conversation she remembered having with him, after the wraith had been defeated and the Cronal secured. Gilrin blamed the Dareann Elves for his people's loss of power and status in the Universe. Worse still, he wasn't wrong to blame them.

If that same sentiment had spread throughout all of the dwarves on Darea…

"There was an uprising," Elaria continued, barely above a whisper, her voice shaking . "Civil war between the dwarves and elves. It started less than a month after we learned the truth. Worse still was the chaos in our own ranks. Some, like me, felt sympathy for the dwarves, and didn't want bloodshed." A sour look drew down her face. "I was arrested for my beliefs." Elaria's head sank, her shoulders slouched. "The Darksteel Army came as I was being escorted to my cell. The city shields went up, the Darksteel Navy fired upon them ineffectively, but then...the shields fell. And they invaded."

Looking up at Kemila, Elaria sighed. "We were lucky. It was a low overcast that morning, the clouds concealed Kemila's ship at the docking spire. I knew it was there, and I knew the Darksteel Army couldn't get their hands on her ship, so I took advantage of the chaos and ran for it, hoping to help them escape. I made it to the ship just as they were casting off."

Hardness at the edge of Elaria's eyes, and the dark look she and Kemila exchanged, made Sira's stomach flop. "And...the Dark Dragons you saw?" Sira asked.

Elaria met Sira's gaze. "They helped the Darksteel Army."

Kemila sighed, and looked over at a tall, lithe man off to her right. She nodded at him, and he climbed up to the helm, taking over and allowing Kemila to step down to their level. "Again, the clouds saved us," the captain said. "I saw those beasts laying waste to nearby settlements, and I knew we had only one chance. We dropped back into the clouds and made for the nearest portal gateway. Two of my crew went down to activate the portal and bring us here, but the Darksteel Army was already closing in. We couldn't pick them up."

The captain's jaw was set hard, her fists clenched. "Including my first officer," she said quieter. "And my..." Her throat caught, and she cleared it and looked away.

Whomever the second person was that had done the job, they clearly meant a lot to her. Sira wanted to ask, but if the captain couldn't bring herself to talk about it, especially in front of her crew, Sira wouldn't press her.

"We got away," Elaria nodded. "Just last week. We've been..." She glanced sideways at Kemila. "Strategically waiting in hiding at the bazaar."

Raising an eyebrow, Sira glanced back and forth between Elaria and Kemila, the latter of whom was looking out the broad windows into the darkening sky.

"I wanted to come tell you," Elaria said, drawing Sira's gaze back to her. "I mean, Halarite, the four kingdoms. I was going to, but..."

"I asked her not to," Kemila finally met Sira's eyes. "Demanded it, really. My crew and I, we've lost enough already."

Sira's jaw tightened. "Maybe so," she said, her mind quickly running through the facts that she had just learned, and coming to only one conclusion. "But you've also given me more answers than I bargained for. We always wondered who might have allied with Nuuldan," she nodded at Elaria. "We just didn't know it was this mysterious Darksteel Army." Frowning, she folded her arms under her chest and added, "But we still don't know how the Darksteel Army knew about the Grand Wizard Hall, enough to tell Nuuldan exactly where to go."

Elaria huffed out a breath and shook her head. "I don't know. The Darksteel Army seems to be comprised of a great many species. Fighting my way past their advanced units, I saw orcs, dwarves, humans, elves, and half a dozen other species wearing their colors."

Catching on Elaria's list, Sira frowned. "Humans? From Halarite, or..."

"Not likely," Kemila grimaced. "As I understand it, the Darksteel Army has invaded at least three human-occupied worlds. Including-" Her voice caught again, and she had to clear it. "Including my own."

"That's why Kemila was on Darea," Elaria said quietly.

"I'm a refugee," she sighed, idly walking past them. Sira turned to watch Kemila as she stood in the center of the bridge and stared out. The glow of the setting sun was almost completely gone, and despite the glow of internal lights from the ship reflecting off of the windows, they could see stars in the sky. "So's everyone else on this ship," Kemila lightly touched one of the bronze twins' arms as she passed by him. "We came together on Darea, brought our knowledge together to create a weapon that could stand against the Darksteel Army."

The captain tilted her head, turned back to face Sira, and flourished her hands. "And this is the result," she said with a grin, which did a wonderful job hiding the turmoil no doubt still turning within Kemila. "As captain, I officially welcome you aboard the *Starfire*."

Sira took a moment to look around and admire the bridge again. She still couldn't tell what any of the desk-like constructs were for, just that the crew members manning them had slowed their pace of lever-flipping and such, and they all kept glancing back at the ongoing conversation with guarded expressions.

Leveling her gaze upon the captain, Sira nodded. "I'd never seen an airship before today, but already I know it's not like the others I saw at the bazaar."

Wagging an enthusiastic finger at her, Kemila brightly said, "Too right you are, Pretty Eyes. Come here," she waved Sira over as she hurried over to the left side of the ship, squeezing between two of the desk-like apparatuses to gaze back along the length of the *Starfire*. Sira walked over and leaned closer to the captain to see.

Raida grew excited, but Sira suppressed the emotion as best as she could.

"See those engines?" Kemila pointed to one of the horizontal whirling contraptions. "Those rotors run constantly to keep the ship aloft, and changing the propellers' speeds and angle allows us to rapidly change altitude."

"Uh," Sira frowned. "I understood about half of what you said."

Kemila turned her head to Sira, their noses only inches apart, and the captain winked at her. "Well, I'd be happy to give you a more...*intimate* lesson on mechanics, if you'd like."

Elaria cleared her throat.

Sira, finding herself drawn closer to the captain, blinked and backed away. "What about, um, those other types of ships?" Internally, she lectured, *Stop it, Raida!*

Grinning, Kemila walked past Sira, lightly drawing her fingers across Sira's stomach as she went. Goosebumps pressed up on Sira's arms and warmth rose within her.

"It's not just me!" Raida countered defensively.

"The bladders keep their ships aloft," Kemila explained. "Through various tricks, they can change altitude with them, but usually not as rapidly. They also can't travel as fast as this ship can, and they're limited to light wooden constructs that don't weigh the ship down, and so are easy to damage. And the bladders?" Kemila scoffed. "With simple ones, one puncture and the ship goes down. More advanced, often military-grade ships have compartments in their bladders that allow for single or double punctures, but even then, it hurts their ability to operate and stay aloft." Sira unconsciously rubbed her fingers over where Kemila had touched while she listened. "Worse still, depending on what they fill the bladders with, a single spark near a hole could blow the ships sky-high. Pun intended," Kemila winked.

"And the *Starfire*?" Sira asked. "You said it's a weapon to use against the Darksteel Army?"

"Our hull is steel," the captain beamed with pride. "Thin steel, granted, but tougher than wood, and enchantments on the hull help protect it from magic attacks. No bladder to puncture. And her engine…" Kemila hesitated and glanced at Elaria.

Elaria nodded. "If we can trust anyone, it's Sira."

Kemila looked back to Sira and studied her for a moment. She appeared to mull something over, and then nodded. "Right. Well, the engine is the key. You see, keeping propellers and rotors constantly turning takes energy. Energy usually takes fuel of some kind to move the mechanical components. But this ship, unlike any other airship we know of, is powered by a magic engine." Grinning proudly, she added, "Literally magic."

It all sounded so strange to Sira. Engines? Rotors? Half of the terms Kemila used were ones Sira had either never heard, or never heard applied in such ways. "I'm sorry, but what exactly does that mean?"

"It means," Elaria said, "that this ship can fly indefinitely, if the mechanical components are kept tuned and well-maintained."

"And my crew's the best," Kemila waved her hands around at the bridge. The members manning their stations all turned briefly and beamed at their captain. "We launched from the Darea dry dock three months ago and haven't had to shut down once. The *Starfire* is stronger, tougher, and can outlast and outrun any enemy airship. We can fly above them and reign fire down upon them, we can outmaneuver them, and we can take a hit."

"The plan," Elaria sighed, "was to build a fleet of them, once the prototype proved itself. And if we'd had the time to, the Darksteel Army wouldn't have stood a chance against us. But then…"

Sira nodded. "The dwarves."

Elaria plodded over to the three steps leading up to the helm and sat down on them with a huff. She planted her elbows on her knees and cradled her head in her hands. Looking off darkly to the side, she shook her head, and murmured, "The signs were there. I was…blind." She glanced sidelong at Kemila, and said, "You warned us. We didn't listen."

Kemila's jaw set tightly, and she nodded. "Aye, I warned you.

But you can't blame yourself for your entire race's actions. Your leaders failed you, love. They ignored the growing unrest from the dwarves. They ignored the growing disagreements between the College of Serelik and the government. They thought it was all just internal strife. But that's how the Darksteel Empire works. They start slow, influencing through insiders and traitors."

Sira's heart stilled out of terror.

Halarite.

She looked at Elaria, who looked up at her. The haunted expression upon Elaria's face told her that the elf had the same thought.

"Halarite is next," Sira breathed. "Klaralin, the Orc War, Nuuldan's attack on the Wizards…"

Lowering her hands and sitting up straight, Elaria nodded. "I think you're right. It's all coming to a head now, isn't it?"

"You have no idea," Sira shook her head. "Tal's Warriors are refusing to serve the throne. Farmers are refusing to sell crops without actual gold exchanging hands and without Warrior protection. The Allied Council is at each other's throats."

"That sounds about right," Kemila said with a grimace. She silently walked over to Sira and placed a hand on her shoulder, drawing Sira's eyes into hers. "I'm sorry, Pretty Eyes. I truly am."

The horror and sinking sensation in her gut wasn't assuaged by Kemila's words. If anything, they made her feel worse. Cardin was right. He'd been right all along. She'd never doubted him outwardly, but inside, she wondered if the threat he saw, the threat that orc shaman had warned them about, was real.

But now, she knew.

Soon, everyone would know.

"You have to take me back to Endri," she pleaded with Kemila. "They don't know. Cardin is powerful, one of the most powerful humans in the Universe now, but…they don't know. They don't know the Dark Dragons are helping. They don't know there's more than one!"

"It doesn't matter, Pretty Eyes," Kemila shook her head and reached a gentle hand out for Sira. "Your world is gone already, you just don't know it."

"No," Sira batted Kemila's hand away and backed up. "No, I won't accept that." Panic grew within. "I *can't!*"

"If you go back now, you'll just be killed or captured with the rest of your people," Kemila held her hands up defensively. "But if you stay here, you'll..."

"What," she scowled. "Be able to hide? Survive while everyone I love perishes? I'm not a coward!"

That soured Kemila's mood. Her face went from sympathetic and hopeful to a dour scowl. "Neither am I!"

"Yet here you are," Sira pointed ahead, and noticed several artificial light sources on the ground ahead. Possibly their destination.

"Yeah," Kemila growled. "Here I am. Alive!"

"And running," Sira shouted. "Hiding! You could help us..."

"No one can help!" Kemila yelled back. "Don't you see? The Darksteel Empire is unstoppable. We had a snowball's chance in hell, but now that they're allied with Dark Dragons? Come on, Sira, what can we possibly do against that?"

"We stand," she growled. "We stand with the only person in the Universe who can defeat the Dark Dragons. The Keeper of the Sword of Dragons." Kemila stopped, her mouth hanging open in an unsaid retort. "And," Sira continued, lowering her voice, "he just happens to be the Prince of my kingdom."

Silence fell upon the bridge. That is, until the helmsman cleared his throat. "Captain," he said. "We're approaching the gateway."

Kemila looked up at him and nodded. "Prepare for soft-dock," she ordered. The bridge crew immediately turned back to their stations and started working again.

Sira involuntarily stepped forward, an objection on the tip of her tongue.

"Don't," Kemila held up a hand. "I'm leaving. You're welcome to come with, but if not, you can leave the ship while I barter passage through their portal."

Letting her mouth hang open for a moment, Sira shook her head. But then she reminded herself who she was dealing with. Whomever or whatever Kemila was before, she wasn't a Warrior. She wasn't a soldier.

Clenching her jaw, Sira huffed out a breath. "Fine. I'll leave your precious ship and crew to run and hide." The atmosphere in the bridge felt decidedly cooler upon saying that, and the creaking of chairs and shuffling cloth clued her into the fact that all eyes fell upon her. Unkind eyes. "I'm going to fight. And don't worry. Outside of Endri and me, no one will know you're involved."

"That's all I ask," Kemila said, and turned back to face the front.

Elaria stood up then, and took two steps to come up alongside Sira. "I'm going with her," she declared. Sira's heart soared.

Kemila didn't turn around, barely even inclined her head. "Whatever, love. Maybe that's for the best."

Elaria reached out and grasped Sira's hand and held tight. "It's not too late," she reached out her other hand. "You can still-"

"Get off my ship," Kemila growled.

Snapping her jaw shut, Elaria nodded. "As you wish. Captain."

Turning to Sira, Elaria nodded, and together they headed back for the aft hatch, and the stairs down. Just before they passed through the hatch, one of the crewmen came forward and produced Sira's sword, which she gratefully snatched from his hands.

Sira had vital information, and it would take probably hours to hike back to Endri in the dark. But a part of her couldn't help but wonder how things might have turned out, if only...

If only...

Chapter 21

FRACTURED ALLIANCE

Emboldened by his victory at the Warriors' Guild, Cardin confidently marched into the Allied Council Chambers north of Archanon, with Dalin, Amaya, and Reis accompanying him. The escort that always came with had already sauntered off to their holding barracks in the Alliance structure, but Cardin could only imagine how they looked as they strode in, and he felt his confidence burgeoning.

Emergency sessions of the Council weren't unheard of, and this would be the fourth that Cardin had attended since being crowned Prince of Tal, but as he expected, no one looked happy. In fact, the decidedly grumpy look upon King Sal'fe's face effectively trounced Cardin's mood.

Still, the day had already gone better than expected. With General Vellar on Cardin's side, reorganizing the Warriors of Tal into the throne's army would be a much easier, and more importantly, a much *quicker* task than it otherwise would have been.

Now, if he could just keep the Allies on his side, maybe, just maybe, they had a chance at mounting a defense.

Sal'fe, as usual, was alone at his table. Master Syrn was already present as well, along with three other Master Wizards. In fact, the only standing member of the council not yet present was Queen Leian.

Cardin nodded to the black-granite Tal table, and said to the trio accompanying him, "I'd like you all to sit at the table with me."

Dalin was unsurprised, but Amaya and Reis looked shocked at first. He looked back and forth between the two of them, not allowing his faltering confidence to show through – they needed a leader to look up to. They needed to know that he knew what he was doing.

Even if he didn't.

Especially if he didn't.

The trio nodded back to him, and the troupe sat at the table, with Cardin taking up his customary far-left seat, unable to take any of the others due to the Sword of Dragons jutting out past his left thigh. Reis sat next to him, followed by Dalin, and finally Amaya.

Cardin exchanged a nod with Master Syrn, and then waited for Leian.

The wait wasn't long. Dalin had met Cardin shortly after returning from the Warriors' Guild to inform him that Master Syrn had scheduled the emergency meeting for mid-afternoon. That allowed Cardin and the others time to eat and bring Dalin up to speed on what Cardin had decreed.

When Leian arrived, she looked flustered and rushed in, her General in tow, along with a forest-green robed Wizard. She apologized for her lateness, and she and her party took their seats at their deep-blue lapis lazuli stone table.

With the surviving members of the Council assembled, Master Syrn rose and gathered her robes about her. There was little idle conversation as it was, due to the hasty assembly and therefore the lack of spectators in the guest seats, but she waited patiently until all eyes were set upon her.

"Thank you for coming," she spoke, the strength of her voice unwavering. "I realize how inconvenient these emergency sessions are, but as you all know, they are almost always justified. Today we've been summoned by young Prince Kataar," she regally motioned a hand towards Tal's table, "regarding the suspected impending invasion of the Darksteel Army. His...messenger," she eyed Dalin, "insisted the matter was quite urgent. As such, unless there are objections, I yield the floor to Prince Kataar."

When no one objected, Syrn carefully sat back down, and Cardin rose. The familiar rushing sensation he always felt before speaking in front of the Council tingled through his body, but by now, he knew how to suppress it, shove it back down to the depths of his stomach, and control his body and speech carefully.

Stepping around his table, he took up the more familiar position in the center of the room, where he had once addressed the Council before it was even officially a Council, in the old Archanon war room. A year ago. A lifetime ago.

"Thank you for coming," he echoed Syrn's opening. He'd thought all afternoon about how he would bring the news to the allies, but no matter how he thought about it, he knew that none of it would be taken well.

So he started there.

"By now," he looked around, meeting the eyes of the other three delegates, "this Council is no doubt accustomed to hearing strange, disturbing, even world-shattering news." His eyes met Syrn's, and her eyebrows arched up slightly in acknowledgement. "So I won't try to banter around it. I won't spend endless hours working up to it, like I normally would. Besides," he grinned, and looked specifically at Queen Leian, who still looked flustered and rushed, her face a tinge redder. "I doubt any of us wish to endure it when we've so much more to attend to." She nodded her appreciation.

"So I'll start with the bad news," he looked to Sal'fe. "We thought we had weeks, maybe months before the Darksteel Army would come to Halarite." He paused. Sal'fe steepled his fingers and rested his chin upon their tips. "Information has come my way that suggests this is not the case." He spun slowly, looking from table to table, as he continued, "We may only have days."

And he waited for the expected outcry, outrage, the disbelieving statements.

They never came. Syrn and Leian's faces scrunched down into looks of concerns and even fear. But not Sal'fe's. His expression remained steady, unchanging.

That caught Cardin's attention more than anything else so far.

Finally, Syrn asked the obvious question that would lead Cardin to the next topic, "How have you come by this information?"

"That," he started, and drew in a breath, "is going to be the more difficult part to accept for this Council. Please hear me out."

He allowed another pause, which Leian took advantage of. "You are not exactly inspiring us with confidence, Prince Kataar," she remarked.

Glancing at her sideways, Cardin nodded. His confidence had faltered, and he'd let it show at the wrong time.

There was nothing left to do but trudge on. "I learned about it from an orc shaman."

Dead silence rang through the echoing chamber. The assembly stared blankly at him, and he gave them a moment to process what he'd just said, before he continued on.

"In the past day and a half," he started, "I learned that the shaman I defeated at the end of the last war was not the only shaman on Halarite. In fact, much of her power base had been eroded by the presence of another shaman, whose name I have come to learn is Tana. In fact, our swift victory in the war may be largely due to her influence and interference. She ordered all those under her power to leave the orc army and flee deep into the Wastelands, to not fight us, and to hide from both sides."

Syrn's brow was furrowed ever-deeper in thought, while Leian's expression turned to one of shock and disbelief. Unexpectedly, Sal'fe remained expressionless. *What the hells is he thinking?*

Before anyone could interrupt, Cardin pressed on, "Tana is apparently gifted with foresight. She once lived upon the orc home world, and foresaw the Darksteel Army invasion there before it happened, though she was largely ignored before being exiled. Now, she foresees a similar invasion here, and her latest visions suggest the invasion is at hand. She has proposed an alliance with the fou-" Cardin paused, and glanced again at Sal'fe. "That is, the three kingdoms." That sounded so strange to him, but as he finished his statement, Sal'fe frowned and lowered his steepled fingers.

It was Leian who replied first. "With *orcs?!*" Disdain filled her voice.

"Yes," he nodded, bracing himself. "With orcs."

"You cannot be serious," Syrn spoke quietly. "Orcs are our enemies."

"All orcs?" he turned and asked her.

"Yes, all orcs," Leian spat. "Every last stinking, wretched one of them!"

He did his best to keep his calm, but somehow, after all that he had seen at the orc village, after the children he'd seen playing, the craftsmanship, it rankled him. "Because of the actions of those we've fought?"

"*Every* orc we've ever come up against," Leian growled. "They only ever had one goal in mind, one thought. Kill all humans."

"Because *we* treated them like animals!" he barely restrained himself from shouting back.

Leian leapt to her feet, "They attacked us first! Three thousand years ago *and* last year, they attacked *us!*"

"Under Klaralin's direction," he countered.

"Not the Relkin Mining Camp." Sal'fe's voice was calm, but for the hint of unreasonable anger giving his tone a sharp quality to it. "That was at the behest of-"

"Of a shaman still loyal to Klaralin, even after his death," Cardin glared. Something twitched in Sal'fe's eyes, whether being interrupted or something else. "I've seen their village, I've met their shaman, their general. They are not an evil people, they are just *people*."

Sal'fe frowned, and asked, "Their village? You, personally, met with them. Placed yourself at their mercy."

"Without informing the Council first," Master Syrn added, indignation in her voice. "You parlayed with an enemy of the Alliance without consulting us."

His stomach sank upon her words, and he felt the air close in around him. The Grand Master had just honed in on what Cardin knew would be the worst offense, in the eyes of the Allied Council.

"Yes," he nodded, and resisted the urge to fold his arms stubbornly. "I did. As a member of the Council, and as the Keeper of the Sword, it is my duty to investigate anything that might threaten Edilas as a whole."

"As a member of this council," Syrn corrected sternly, "It is your responsibility to keep us informed of any and all negotiations concerning the affairs of the entire continent. A lesson I thought we had all been reminded of recently," she looked at Sal'fe.

As did Cardin.

His eyebrows arched upwards. "Oh yes," he nodded. "I broke precedent. But what I did pales in comparison to your offense, Keeper. What was the central condition of your retaining the Sword of Dragons?"

Feeling drained from Cardin's extremities, and his stomach sank ever lower to the bottom depths of his being. His memory was quite clear regarding those conditions, but he hadn't thought of those words in recent times. Far too much had happened, and far too much was at stake.

"Let me remind you," Sal'fe volunteered when Cardin said nothing. "You would never act as Keeper of the Sword without the approval of the Allied Council by vote." Slowly, as if he were a predator confidently stalking his prey, Sal'fe stood up and leaned forward, pressing his palms down upon his table. "You have violated your oath, Keeper."

Deathly silence fell upon the Council chambers, and Cardin felt himself begin to shake. This wasn't where the conversation should have gone. This wasn't a contingency he had planned for in his head, even though he now recognized that he should have.

"Look," he started, shaking his head. "I'll concede that point as long as we table it for later. We have more pressing matters to concern ourselves with."

"Yes, pressing matters indeed," Sal'fe narrowed his eyes. "You claim an army is mere days from invading, at the same time you flaunt your oath and parlay with our enemy."

"The orcs are *not* our enemy!" he insisted.

"It's true," Amaya's voice spoke up, the scraping of her chair echoing when she bolted onto her feet. Cardin whipped his head around to glare at her, but she continued on regardless, "I've spent enough time with the orcs to know, these ones are peaceful."

He wanted to curse at her, scream at her. She had just said exactly the wrong thing at the wrong time. And the inevitable question came, of course, from Sal'fe. "Who are you, child, and why have you spent so much time with the orcs."

Could Cardin order her to be silent? Or would that only make matters worse? The secrets and lies of King Beredis would not be welcomed here, not now, not under these circumstances.

"I am Lieutenant Amaya Kenla," she spoke. "A Guardian of Tal. Upon King Beredis's orders, I sought out the orcs shortly after the skies burned over Halarite, to prepare for the coming darkness, so that we might forge an alliance." A rumble of dissent and outrage grew in the chambers from the relatively small crowd, and Amaya, no doubt thinking she was helping, bellowed out, "King Beredis knew we would need their help to defend the four kingdoms, even without the gift of foresight! We cannot throw this opportunity away!"

"Amaya!" Cardin finally stopped her, raising a halting hand. "Enough."

"But, Your Majesty…"

"How long?" Sal'fe growled above the murmur of conversation. Something in his voice, a note of burning rage, drew the attention of all present to him. His gaze, venomous, was locked upon Cardin. "How long did Tal know that orcs still roamed the Wastelands freely?"

Cardin met the other's gaze stoutly, trying not to show his desperation and fear in his eyes, but knowing that the Wizard King would be able to see right through him.

The secret was out. Delaying revealing the truth any longer would only make matters worse.

So he honestly said, "Since before the end of the war." It didn't matter how he knew that, explaining it to them would make little difference, so he said nothing more.

Sal'fe's enraged gaze didn't falter. His eyes…his *eyes*. Cardin squinted back at the man, and he saw something in them. Something powerful. Something magical.

Something that felt familiar and alien all at once.

It wasn't emotion. It was something…

The Wizard King noticed Cardin's sudden interest, and looked away, breaking Cardin's brief connection. He looked to Master Syrn, and said, "It seems this Alliance has been a failure from the start."

Syrn's eyes widened in surprise. "What…are you saying?"

"I am saying that if we wish to hold this Alliance, we must act accordingly," he settled his gaze upon Cardin again, but did not meet eye-for-eye. "Cardin Kataar has broken his oath. He is no longer worthy of the role of Keeper and must be relieved at once."

A possessiveness strangled Cardin, and he defensively took a step back, his arm automatically rising towards the hilt of the weapon upon his back. Light as a dagger, but heavy as the weight of the world, he had wielded it with purpose and protected it with all he had for over a year.

Now…

"You cannot be serious," Syrn scoffed breathlessly.

"I am deadly serious," Sal'fe stated.

"It's not your decision to make," Cardin retorted.

Somewhere, somehow, the Staff of Aliz had made its way into

Sal'fe's grip, a blur of motion Cardin hadn't even noticed. It was all Cardin could do to keep himself from drawing his own weapon, as his hand gripped the handle of the Sword tightly.

A surge of energy and deafening boom echoed from Syrn, who likewise held her staff in a firm grip, having planted it upon the marble floor. She said nothing at first, but she didn't have to.

The blood-red gem at the top of Sal'fe's staff glowed, power having gathered in it. It was dangerous, and Cardin drew magic in, letting it flow through him in a growing river of energy, just like Dalin and Endri had taught him. Sal'fe responded in kind, as did Syrn a moment later.

So much magic stirring in the chambers drew up a torrent of wind, blowing ever harder, whipping around the room noisily, blowing clothes, robes, and hair in wildly different directions.

There was no doubt that the entire Wizards' Guild was alerted, and any Mage in the honor guards attending Cardin and Queen Leian would sense it too.

This could very quickly turn into a blood bath.

So Cardin didn't draw the Sword. But he readied a shield to protect himself. One unshielded blast from Sal'fe's staff would be enough to end his life instantly. And somehow, he doubted that any amount of money could ever convince Sal'fe to bring him back.

"Stand down, Sal'fe," Syrn ordered. The other master Wizards had likewise taken up their staves and drawn in energy, forcing a whirlwind of energy to swirl around their table stronger than anywhere else. Magic powered Syrn's voice, allowing it to boom over the howling winds. "It is not your place to relieve the Keeper of the Sword."

Equally powerful, Sal'fe's voice resounded back, "If this body will not act…"

"You have given us no time to act!" Syrn lectured.

"There is no time to consider!" he roared. The blood red gem flared brighter. "He must not be allowed to bring greater harm to our world."

Without a word, the four Wizards spread out, with Syrn only stepping in front of their table, the others giving themselves a clearer line of sight to the Wizard King. Winds shifted as they moved, becoming gale-force and threatening to blow anyone not holding on away.

One flinch. One miscalculation. That's all it would take. Cardin remembered the gatehouse in Archanon when the Wizards fought Klaralin, the explosion that ripped apart the inner section of the wall and rained clusters of stone upon houses and Warriors. It felt as if the same thing could happen here at any moment.

"We will act as a unified body, Sal'fe," Syrn replied. "We will vote on the fate of the Keeper, as we will vote on what to do about the orcs."

"No!" Sal'fe snarled, surprising Cardin. "No more voting! No more dallying in politics! We act now or we are broken."

"Stand down!" Syrn insisted, her voice rock solid. "Or will you fight every Wizard in the Guild at once?"

Sal'fe blinked first.

He looked at Syrn, and the blinding glow atop the Staff of Aliz dwindled. Cardin felt power ease out of the Wizard King. Sal'fe relaxed his stance, brought the staff closer to his core, and leaned against it.

The other Wizards followed suit, backing off their powers. But Cardin wouldn't trust Sal'fe. He maintained his readiness to cast a shield before him.

The horrible rage within Sal'fe, the power that backed it – he had never seen the Wizard King act so brashly, so *emotionally*.

Something was wrong. And if Sal'fe wasn't in control of himself…

"Very well," Sal'fe finally said. He no longer had to amplify his voice, as the torrent of wind and power in the room had dwindled to a minor breeze. "This Alliance has grown cumbersome," he continued wearily. "It no longer serves its purpose." He looked up at Syrn, and stated, "Falind and its vassal state officially withdraw from the Alliance."

Cardin didn't dissipate his power, but he eased his hand off the Sword. It was a shock even to him. It was a move that made no sense. Unless…

Unless he only joined the Alliance until he no longer needed us.

Reports from Tal spies flashed through his memory. Stone structures being built along the border between Tal and Falind. Sal'fe's recent, mysterious absences from the Falind capitol city.

Except…

"Your defenses won't protect Saran," he blurted.

Sal'fe looked at him, briefly meeting his eyes until he looked down to Cardin's collarbone. "That is not your concern."

"What are you playing at?" Cardin narrowed his eyes. "This isn't just some spat that's got you leaving the Alliance to position yourself better."

Scowling, Sal'fe merely replied, "I do not answer to you, *traitor.*"

"But you will answer me," Syrn replied sternly.

Cocking an eyebrow up, Sal'fe regarded her cooly. "Oh really, dear Grand Master? You cast me out three thousand years ago, remember? I do not answer to you, either." His cool demeanor shifted into a sudden scowl. "Thoughtless, trite whelps. I no longer have the patience to dally with you. Any of you," he swept his arm out, encompassing all. He leveled a finger at Syrn then and said, "Your people are no longer welcome on sovereign Falind lands."

Syrn looked shocked. "But…the portals. We are prepared to lock the portals in this world down, Sal'fe, you know this. Without one of our gateways…"

"You are incapable of understanding what I am actually capable of," he snarled. "I do not need you, and your gateways in Falind and Saran will both be destroyed. And you," he shifted his finger to Cardin. "You are an enemy to us all."

He kept his gaze, and his finger, on Cardin a moment longer, and then, quite dramatically, turned on the spot and planted his staff on the marble floor. There was a loud, echoing bang and a gathering of energy, and a portal appeared before the Wizard King. Without another word, he stalked through the wall of light, and it winked out of existence moments later.

Cardin stared after him, his eyes growing ever narrower, his thoughts shifting rapidly.

Something was wrong.

Something was very, very wrong.

And somehow, he doubted the timing of Sal'fe's tantrum was a coincidence.

"Prince Kataar," Syrn's voice brought him out of his inner thoughts. He turned to look at her, and she looked hard at him. "It would seem this Council still has much to discuss, even absent another member."

Cardin nodded. "That we do," he spoke quietly.

"While I do believe that you have acted far beyond what is

appropriate, I am prepared to allow you to keep the Sword of Dragons." She looked around Cardin towards Queen Leian. "Do you agree?"

Turning, Cardin stared into her deep brown eyes, wondering if their earlier conversation would serve against him. The Alliance was crumbling, and he had refused her attempt to counter Sal'fe's growing power by formally allying themselves through marriage, unifying their kingdoms.

What would she do?

Leian remained standing. In fact, everyone in the room was on their feet. She looked back at Cardin, her eyes unwavering from him as she considered what had transpired. After a long moment, she huffed out a quick breath and shook her head. "I suppose we have no time to absorb and consider what all has transpired here, do we?"

Cardin shook his head.

"Very well," she nodded. "Given the circumstances, I agree. Now is not the time to argue over whom may hold the Sword of Dragons. We must, however, decide what to do about the orc problem."

Cardin's hands drew up into tight fists. Forcing his teeth to unclench, he said, "They aren't a problem. They are potential allies."

"Indeed," Leian said dubiously. "And tell me, have they asked for anything in return for their cooperation?"

Cardin's jaw tightened a moment, and he nodded. "Yes. The release of all orc prisoners of war into Tana's custody."

Leian scoffed and sat down, shaking her head. "Impossible."

"No, it isn't," Cardin looked back at the now-empty Falind table.

"How do you figure that?" the Queen asked.

He turned to look at Master Syrn, and then, deciding that he was tired of turning around in circles, he walked back to Tal's table, urging Dalin, Reis, and Amaya to sit down with a motion of his hand. They did as he bid, Amaya and Reis having to sheath their swords first, but Cardin stood beside his chair.

"The only orc prisoners currently reside in dungeons or camps in Falind and Tal," he pointed out. "Falind is no longer a member of this Council, and I cannot currently do anything about that." He set his jaw tightly and looked back and forth between the only two other surviving delegates. "I am inclined to allow Tal's prisoners go."

Stunned silence followed for a long moment. Syrn and Leian

exchanged shocked looks.

"After all that has transpired, you would defy the will of the Council further?" Syrn asked.

His hands were still balled into fists, and at Syrn's words, he slammed one down on the table, startling everyone, even himself. Drawing in a deep breath, trying to calm himself, he shook his head. "Don't you two get it? The time for talk is over. The time for debate is over. The Darksteel Army is coming, and we cannot hope to fight them alone. We need allies. *Starting* with the orcs. We should also send a delegate to the Dareann Elves. We should ask anyone and *everyone* we can for help, or *all* is lost."

Neither replied, and he held his fist on the table, impatiently shifting his weight from one foot to the other. Syrn and Leian remained silent for a long time. So he pushed on. "Stand with me," he pleaded. "Stand together. We need one another now more than ever."

Uncertain eyes met his.

"Please…"

Chapter 22

THE PRICE OF DISOBEDIENCE

When Kailar and Letan returned to Tieran, she motioned her head for him to follow and started for city hall. "Come on, I wanna tell them all."

Letan followed beside her. They had portaled into the edge of town, mostly to avoid accidentally opening a portal inside of a passing person – Kailar had no wish to see what would happen if that ever occurred. As such, it took them several minutes to get back to the city square.

But when they arrived at the double doors into city hall, the two guards standing on either side surprised Kailar by stepping directly into her path and holding out hands. She and Letan came up short, both too shocked to utter anything at first.

"I'm sorry, ma'am," the one guard told her. "The Empress has commanded you not be allowed in until the meeting is adjourned."

"You...what?!" She blinked in surprise and felt more than a little indignant embarrassment. "Out of my way," she started to push past the guards, but they seized her by the arms and pushed her back. Kailar clasped her hands on her daggers, started to draw them, but Letan's hand landed on her shoulder.

She'd almost forgotten what that felt like, and a combination of old habits and old memories stopped her cold. Looking into his blazing blue eyes, she gaped.

"Don't," he said. "They're just doing their jobs."

Color and heat rushed into her cheeks. "I don't care," she growled. "We've got to tell them what's happened, what we achieved. It's relevant to the conversation they're having in there."

"I know," he nodded, and glanced at the soldiers. "Did the Empress only command that Kailar could not enter?"

"Yes, sir," the guardswoman nodded curtly. Kailar noticed her sword was partially drawn from its sheath. "You may enter."

"Good," he nodded, and settled his eyes upon Kailar. "I'll go in."

"But-"

His hand squeezed her shoulder, and he insisted, "I'll tell them everything."

She rolled her shoulder out from under his grip and backed away, the burn of annoyance, embarrassment, shame, all of it turning her empty stomach. A part of Kailar wanted to tell him off for thinking they could ever go back to the way things were. That he shouldn't even *try* to restrain her.

Looking at the guards, Kailar's fury died a quick death.

Her temper had nearly made her attack the guards. Guards that were soldiers in the imperium she had helped build and was meant to protect.

They're just doing their jobs, and I…

Clenching her jaw, she let out a quick sigh and nodded without looking at Letan again. "Fine."

He stood next to her for a moment, and then, when she didn't look at him again, he turned and stalked past the guards, opening one of the double doors to step through.

After a moment of brooding in the street, she looked at the guards, both still holding their weapons partially drawn. *I should apologize*, she thought. But her stomach roiled at the idea.

Instead, she turned her back on them and stalked off to find something to ease her hunger pangs.

A few minutes later, she was in Alric's Inn at Water's Edge. She'd missed the lunch rush, the better to brood in silence, and stalked past the handful of lingering guests at the bar to her usual place in the far corner of the bar, up against windows that looked out upon the ships moored at the docks.

Alric appeared from the back room a second later, somehow always knowing when a new guest had arrived, even when they were silent. And Kailar was anything but silent.

Tall and broad enough to usually scare drunks right out of even thinking of starting a bar fight, Alric was even tougher than he looked. He'd been a vital informant in Kailar and Letan's fight against organized crime on Devor, and at least once during all of that, someone had made an attempt on his life.

Kailar had helped hide the would-be assassin's body.

Just as stunning, Alric's meals were incredible, and whomever provided him the ale and mead he sold was a damned genius.

Spotting Kailar in her corner, he smiled through his thick, bushy moustache and asked, "Want the usual, love?"

She wanted to feel cheerful, and his familiar words and voice did manage to nudge a smile onto her face, but she didn't answer verbally. A slight nod of her head was all she could give.

His brow furrowed darkly, but he didn't ask yet, and merely ducked back into the kitchen. A minute later, a steaming bowl of stew sat before Kailar with some dried bread, and a second later, a full pint of ale.

Kailar hovered over the bowl and drew in a deep breath, the stew's meaty and spicy scent filling every corner of her soul with a soothing balm. She'd closed her eyes mid-breath and let calm wash over her.

When she opened her eyes again, Alric stood leaning against the back counter directly across from Kailar, idly drying a mug with a cloth.

Her cheeks burned again. She knew what that meant.

As the proprietor of an inn and tavern, Alric always felt it his duty to act as a sounding board, and he had a knack for getting people to open up to him. It was part of why he'd made such a good ally in the fight against organized crime.

People told him things.

He was smarter than most gave him credit for, too, and he'd put together disparate pieces of information to figure out enemy movements.

This time, he didn't even speak. He just kept on leaning, kept on cleaning, and waited patiently for Kailar to inevitably talk.

She wanted to scowl. But somehow, the scowl turned into a

bemused grin, and she set to eating up her stew. It was delightfully meaty and flavorful, just the way she liked it.

Finally, when her bowl was half-empty, she sighed and sat up straighter, wishing the barstools had backs to them just so she could slouch back for a moment.

"Why is it," she started, "that so often, doing the right thing means doing the wrong thing?"

Arching a bushy eyebrow at her, Alric asked, "How do you mean, love?"

"I mean," she started, and stopped. Frowning, she took another sip of her stew, and then soaked a corner of the bread in it while she thought about her next words. "I knew we needed an ally. I was ordered not to pursue it out of fear for my life, but I did it anyway. Now I'm..." She stopped, thought about the situation, and somehow laughed about it. "Now I'm being blocked from reporting my success out of some strange punishment. I can't report because the Empress is annoyed that I disobeyed her orders?"

Alric took the words in stride, but the two lingerers further down the bar perked up and gave Kailar strange looks. She ignored them, took a bite of soaked bread, and said around chews, "It's petty and ridiculous!"

Furrowing his brow, Alric asked, "I thought you admired our new Empress?"

"Oh, aye, I do," Kailar nodded, and then took a swig of ale to help get the soaked bread down. "But I'm tired of being held back like a...well..."

Alric finished for her, "Like an adviser instead of a soldier or Warrior."

Pressing her lips into a thin line, she shook her head. "Like a tool. I'm tired of being a messenger, a transporter, a ferry for Lords. I'm *powerful*, Alric, damn powerful." Memories of nearly blasting the Pranid out of the water, of the damage she'd incurred on its stern, flashed through her mind's eye. "More so than even I realized. I should be taking action, not sitting on my hands. And when there's something useful for me to do, she tried to hold me back, fearful not even really for my life, but..." She grit her teeth. "Fearful of losing the only person on the continent who can make portals."

Quirking a curious eyebrow up, Alric asked, "Wait, it bothers you that she doesn't value your life as much as your skills?"

Kailar thought about a second, and then snorted out a chuckle. "No, you're right, that part doesn't surprise or bother me." Nodding, she said, "But I'm more than just a damn tool."

"So let me see if I've got this straight," Alric said, slapping the towel he'd been using onto his shoulder and setting the mug he'd been cleaning onto a shelf beneath the bar. "You were told not to do something dangerous. You did it anyway, and obtained new allies or info or some such. You want to tell the Empress, but she won't see you right now?" He paused, and added, "She's in a meeting with the Lords right now and won't let you present your new information to them."

Alric was *very* good at piecing together information. She nodded. "Yeah. Which is beyond stupid, even for her. Just to prove a point to me? I mean, come on. Sure, Letan got in and is telling them what we did, and I know I can expect a lecture later, but to do something so petty as to bar me from entry?"

Alric stood up straight, towering over Kailar. "Is it?"

Eyeing him carefully, she asked, "Excuse me?"

"She's a new leader, right? In a new empire. She has to establish her power base, ensure no one questions her. And what do you do? You question her. You disobey her. Love, of course she's going to make a show of punishing you over it. Even if what you've done is ultimately right for us all."

Kailar opened her mouth to retort, but then paused and considered Alric's words. Grumbling, she slouched forward, and then took another swig of her ale. "I hate politics," she growled.

"Aye, who doesn't?" Alric shrugged. "But you once told me you wouldn't let what happened on Edilas happen here. You wouldn't let this place become like the four kingdoms."

"I won't," she said quickly.

"Then ya gotta play the political game. It's as simple as that." He frowned, and amended, "Well, nothin' is simple when it comes to politics, but you get my meaning."

She softly laughed. "Yeah. I think I do."

"Good. Now finish up," Alric nodded just as one of the other guests tapped his empty mug on the bar. Alric acknowledged them with a nod, and said, "You've got an empire to save," before he moved down the bar.

Kailar sighed wearily. She supposed she did.

A few hours later, Kailar found herself being escorted into city hall by a random city guard, whose name she couldn't remember for the life of her.

The guardsman had found her out behind Alric's, where she'd been training with the daggers, trying to hone her skills. She'd spent a lifetime learning how to wield a sword – daggers were something entirely different, and she didn't quite feel comfortable with them yet.

She'd expected Letan, not someone else.

Either way, the results would be the same. A lecture, no doubt, and then, if she was lucky, congratulations on securing the help of the Navitas.

The sun was creeping towards the horizon now, evenings coming early in the deep of winter. Smells of cooking dinners over fires in all the homes of Tieran wafted past Kailar, but her late lunch had sated her for now.

The guard stopped inside of the antechamber and motioned Kailar towards the council chamber doors, closed at the moment.

She grit her teeth, working the emotions over in her stomach, shoving the uncertainty down and doing something she hadn't done in a long time – she encouraged the rage to build up inside of her.

Stepping forward resolutely, Kailar yanked the handles of the double-doors and opened them with a flourish, feeling her cloak billow out from the sudden gust of air. Inside, Reyla sat at the head of the table, exactly where she'd been when she'd signed the papers making the Imperium official.

Reyla hardly glanced up at her, her eyes focused on a piece of parchment.

Faltering at the lack of reaction, Kailar uneasily stepped in, and then, unsure what to do next, simply stopped and folded her arms.

"Close the doors," Reyla commanded mutely, still not looking up from the parchment.

Part of Kailar wanted to refuse. To disobey further. But she acknowledged the childishness in that and closed the doors behind her. When she turned back to Reyla, still the Empress didn't fully acknowledge her presence.

Unsure what else to do, Kailar silently walked over to the fireplace and tossed a log onto the gently-crackling fire. Pulling off her gloves, Kailar set to warming her hands.

Finally, she heard Reyla shuffle some parchment, and then the Empress let out a long sigh. Taking that as a cue, Kailar turned to face Reyla.

Fiery eyes met her gaze. Anger seethed in Reyla, but it wasn't the scorching, all-consuming anger that often burned through Kailar. It was slower. Deeper. Like coals burning, the outer glow only hinting at the fury within.

And then, as their eyes met and held with one another, Kailar unwilling to back down, something shifted in Reyla's eyes. The deep fury calmed, and was replaced by something worse. Something more damning.

Disappointment.

"I ordered you to stay away from the Crystalline Peaks," Reyla said, staring down at her clasped hands. "I told you it was too dangerous."

Kailar's mind raced, and her heart sped up. She didn't know what to say or do, she didn't know how to deal with this. She'd rather Reyla was angry with her.

Mouth dry, stomach twisting, Kailar felt her arms fall to her side limply. "It," she started and faltered. Clearing her throat, she said, "It was necessary. And fruitful."

Reyla blinked her eyes up, stared at Kailar again with cool, steel resolve. "Be that as it may, when your Empress gives you a command, you are to follow it, without exception. Is that understood?"

Frowning, Kailar began to protest, "But I succeeded-"

Slamming her palm onto the table, Reyla bolted up onto her feet, and icily reiterated, "Is that understood?"

The frown on Kailar's brow deepened. Conflicting emotions swirled within, twisting around one another and tugging her in two different directions. The sick feeling in her stomach wanted to appease the woman who had taken her into confidence, even after the atrocities Kailar had committed. The rush of energy and defiance wanted her to lift her chin up and argue that she was right.

Reyla's open palm on the table drew up into a clenched fist. "What am I going to do with you, Kailar?" she asked. "How am I to rule an empire when my own adviser disobeys me?"

Shaking her head, Kailar found herself asking, "What did you expect?" Color and heat rushed into her face at her outburst, but as she ever always did, she pushed on, heedless of Reyla's widening eyes. "You knew what I was like," Kailar waved her hands out in exasperation. "You knew I wasn't one to step into line like a good little girl and do as I was told! I don't do that, I *never* have, remember? And remember that you wanted that quality? Because it was that quality which freed Devor from the dirty, slimy thumb of the underworld. I think you used the phrase 'make waves' to describe what I did, and you spoke favorably about my actions."

Letting out a huff of breath, Reyla rubbed at the bridge of her nose and shook her head. "I know that, Kailar, but you very publicly disobeyed direct orders meant to ensure the future of the imperium."

"Publicly?" she shook her head. "How was what I did a public affront to you?"

Frustration rekindled the fire in Reyla. "When you sent Letan in to report on your activities to the Lords and I. That was *precisely* what I was hoping to avoid."

"But it was relevant to any decisions they would make," Kailar countered.

"Yes, it was!" Reyla sharply replied, cutting Kailar off. "Very much so. Not in so many words, but you've made them realize just how fragile our government is. In fact, the Lord of Corlas was *very* keen to point that out! Naturally he would grasp at any bit of attention, now that he knows exactly how badly Corlas was destroyed." Reyla walked away from Kailar and started pacing up and down the length of the table on the opposite side. "One of our best sources of income, of crystal and diamond, one we'd hoped to rebuild after the Crystalline Peaks stabilized, but with naught but the foundations left? That'll be difficult at best."

Halting her pacing, Reyla faced Kailar and planted her hands on her hips. "He pointed out that we need to secure our position on Halarite, especially knowing that we cannot actually count on the help of the Navitas in any military encounters at this time. So he proposed we actually take the Darksteel Empire's offer for membership."

Any retort or response Kailar had died on her lips. As if a great blow had smashed into her, she staggered back a step, the color draining from her face. "He...what?"

"And now the other Lords are considering it," Reyla continued without repeating herself. The Empress stepped closer to the table and rested against one of the chairs. She looked exhausted, more so than Kailar had ever seen her. "We've adjourned for now so that they may consider the proposal and refresh with dinner. We meet again in about an hour," Reyla shook her head and looked up, meeting Kailar's gaze, "and I imagine our meeting will go long into the night as we argue the matter."

"But...but they can't do that," Kailar shook her head. "You're the Empress, your will, your *command* is what..." She stopped herself, realization dawning upon her.

"My command seems worth very little," Reyla curtly reminded her. "As you have demonstrated. I rule at the behest of the people. If the Lords decide a course of action and I decide to ignore that decision, to act of my own will, they will turn against me." Reyla wasn't a martial person – she didn't train in physical combat, as far as Kailar knew, and didn't do anything to build up muscle. Yet her grip on the back of the wooden chair was so tight now that the wood groaned under the strain. "After all, if I cannot make my trusted adviser, who happens to be the *most powerful person on Devor,* obey me, I must be weaker than they originally thought."

Kailar was still so stunned that Reyla's words barely registered. When they did, it only deepened the feeling of shock she felt, and she slowly, carefully sat down. Even then, she almost fell off of the chair she had, at some point, pulled out, though she didn't remember ever actually pulling it out.

"But...we've only just started," Kailar shook her head and rubbed at her face, trying to massage life back into her senses. "We just established the Empire. To change direction so rapidly..."

"We are but a fledgling state, the first new government in millennia," Reyla shook her head. Her voice sounded weak. Defeated. "Nothing is solid. We have only our history of surviving neglect from Edilas and surviving abuse by the criminals of Devor to build our foundation upon. We needed more time. More stability. Anything and everything could change in an instant now."

Reyla walked over to the heavy curtains and peeked out the windows. An icy breeze blew in at that opportunity, and Reyla shivered and scowled before shoving he curtains back into place.

Looking to her Empress, Kailar suggested, "Let me help. Let me stay for the rest of the meeting. Maybe I can convince the Lords that-"

"I think you've helped enough," Reyla's glare fell upon Kailar.
"But..."

"Go," she commanded, turning away from Kailar again.

"Your Highness," Kailar tried again.

Reyla didn't reply. She simply stared at...at nothing in particular. At anything but Kailar.

The giant well of nothingness within Kailar's chest threatened to implode. She wanted to scream at Reyla. She wanted to beg. Neither appealed to her, and neither would solve anything.

She had failed. In doing what she thought was right, she had failed. Maybe so spectacularly that the Devor Imperium would surrender itself to the Darksteel Empire.

Carefully standing up, Kailar sighed, and instead of acting on emotion, she did the only thing she thought right. She bowed, even though Reyla didn't look at her, and said, "As you command, Empress."

With that, she turned, and left the Council Chambers, despondent of the future she had helped create.

Chapter 23

OVERPOWERING

After the *Starfire* had docked at a spire rising up from the jungle surrounding the Deadlands, Sira and Elaria had climbed down ahead of the crew, slowly and carefully descending a spiral staircase to a stone foundation. They were greeted by a dock worker, who bore four arms and six eyes, and thanks to the dim lighting, terrified Sira more than he should have.

It wasn't just that there were ample magically-powered glow lights on the dock, it was also the planetary rings – they shone bright and pale, casting diffuse light across everything. Raida wasn't able to translate the dock worker's language right away, a series of clicks and howl-like tones, but Elaria understood, and responded back, "We're not the captain. She'll be along presently."

At first Sira was confused by Elaria's use of Halarite's common tongue, but then remembered that the elf always wore a translation pendant that worked two ways – it allowed Elaria to understand any language spoken by another, and when she spoke, whomever was close enough would hear their own language.

The dock worker blinked its eyes in unison and looked up. Coming down the metal staircase, Kemila clanked down, and called out, "I need passage off-world."

Renewed anger flashed inside of Sira, and she turned and stormed off, only to have Elaria yank her back. She had almost walked off of the platform, which she only now noticed was raised up from the jungle floor. Far, *far* below was the distinct edge of jungle brush coming up against the barren Deadlands.

Following the gentle tug of Elaria's guiding hand, they walked over to their left, and found stairs that led down into the jungle. Before they descended them, Sira realized it would be wise to get her bearings now, and looked up ahead. The platform was at the edge of the Deadlands, only a good two or three hundred yards into the jungle from it, and not a single tree stood between them and the bazaar.

She glanced back and up, first at the *Starfire,* hovering high above them, and further into the jungle where...

She came to a sudden stop after only descending two steps, and gawked. Made of stone and rising high, a giant archway loomed a hundred yards further into the jungle.

It looked just like the one that the necromancer ships had passed through on Halarite, when she had been their prisoner. That archway, the city ruins on Trinil, they had been ancient, beyond the written history of Edilas, according to the elven archeologist that they had eventually rescued.

And this archway looked identical. The gleaming, flickering light at the base of it told her there was a river running through it, too, though she couldn't hear it above the whirring rotors of the *Starfire.* She looked right, then left, and then saw that the river passed the landing platform there, and then curved away, so that it didn't pass through the Deadlands.

"What's wrong?" Elaria asked, having descended several steps before tugging on Sira. "We should go."

Sira shook her head, and gaped at Elaria, whose face looked ghostly pale in the glow of the rings.

"That arch looks identical to the one on Trinil," she explained. "On Halarite. I mean," she looked back again, seeing several glow lights attached along the outside of the arch, lighting up details, runes, worn smooth by the passage of time, but still...

Elaria glanced back, and then tugged on Sira's handing, "Yes, it is. They're everywhere."

Blinking in surprise, Sira stumbled down the stairs before she caught her balance, with Elaria's help. "They are?"

After only a short descent, they came to a small landing, and then stepped out onto the uneven jungle floor. "Indeed," Elaria replied while looking down at her feet, treading carefully over roots and through ferns. "Civilizations have existed for tens of thousands, maybe hundreds of thousands of years, and empires have risen and fallen in that time." The elf motioned up at the rings, "In fact, the planetary rings were caused by-"

"A crazy ruler who used magic to draw down the moon and break it apart," Sira interrupted. Elaria looked back at her, stunned, and then tripped over a bulge in the ground. Her arms pinwheeled through the air, and Sira had to grab a fistful of Elaria's tunic to keep her from falling flat on her face. Wincing sympathetically, Sira hissed, "Sorry, sorry..."

"It's not your fault," Elaria shook her head. Then stumbled again. Cursing, she suddenly drew one of her mysterious hidden daggers. A pulse of magic echoed through the world, and the blade of the dagger suddenly illuminated bright white, casting better light around them.

Taking a moment to breathe deeply, Elaria nodded, and then they set out for the Deadlands again. After a moment of silent walking, Elaria asked, "Endri told you about that?"

Nodding once, Sira replied, "Yes. It's...a terrifying story." She almost glanced back at the portal again, but then remembered Elaria's almost-tumble, and kept her eyes focused on the task of navigating the flora-covered jungle floor. They had to push ferns and other plants out of the way, and weaved in and around larger bushes – it was excruciatingly slow.

Thinking further on it, Sira mused, "I guess it makes sense, though. The portal, I mean. I just didn't realize..." Frowning, she asked Elaria, "What do you think it means? Such a portal being on Halarite, and that ancient city?"

"I think Baenil would have wanted to spend more time there," Elaria replied. "I think that a past empire, once spread across the Universe, had a seat of power on Halarite long ago. And, knowing that, I think it's no coincidence that the Darksteel Army finds itself interested in Halarite."

Sira mulled that thought over for a moment. Then, inwardly asked, *Raida? Do you know anything about such ancient civilizations?*

"No," the dragonsoul replied. *"Nothing like that. No one in the village*

ever mentioned ancient civilizations, other than the Star Dragons."

Grimacing, Sira wondered what other secrets might lie in the jungle of Trinil. Or further inland. Explorers were still charting the Trinil shoreline, and it was proving to be a much larger landmass than any other known continent on Halarite. In fact, she recalled that when King Beredis and Draegus Kataar had been stranded in the Catacombs, before finding the dwarven city, they had found an ancient map set in stone that depicted the entire world. The king had described Trinil as being four great landmasses with channels of sea water separating them, and what looked like bridges connecting them at certain points.

It would take lifetimes to fully explore such a great land, even if it wasn't all covered in dense jungle.

Despite Sira and Elaria's languid pace, they quickly found themselves leaving the rich, lively jungle edge, and soon found themselves walking out onto barren, red soil.

The lack of life, of ambient magical energy, chilled her soul, but she was grateful for the easier terrain. It also meant that they had a clear view of the entire Deadlands, and the mountains to the east, where she knew Endri awaited.

"Alright," Elaria brought them to a halt. She lowered her dagger and let the bright white glow fade away. "Are you able to figure out where Endri is from here?"

"Um," Sira replied intelligently. She surveyed the eastern mountains again. At least, she was pretty sure that was east. Without moons or known stars or geological features, it was near impossible to tell. And without being fully familiar with the magic fields, she couldn't even really use magic to tell cardinal directions. It was frustratingly disorienting.

"I know we came to the world amidst mountains," Sira waved vaguely towards the ones on the opposite sides of the Deadlands. She thought further about it, remembering that the *Starfire* had been flying towards the glow of the setting sun, which meant they'd gone in the opposite direction of Endri. "I think almost directly on the other side of the Bazaar from here." And then she realized that while there was no moon, the remnants of the moon could point the way. She looked up at the rings, bright in the sky, and realized that they formed almost a straight line towards the bazaar, and the distant mountains. "In fact, yeah, if those rings go east to west, then that's exactly where to go."

"Good enough place to start," Elaria nodded, and stashed her dagger. The elf closed her eyes for a second, and Sira felt a sudden, intense stirring of magic. Thanks to Raida, Sira had a better sense of magic than she used to, and could feel it gather first within Elaria, and then felt it projected out ahead of them.

A flash of white light followed, as dead soil blew up into a whirlwind around them. A second later, a column of blue-white light stood before them, with tendrils of harmless lightning dancing around it.

"You first, my friend," Elaria opened her eyes and waved Sira on.

Sira walked forward and passed through the wall of light, and emerged miles away, facing the darkness of the jungle. After ensuring she left room for Elaria, she peered into the black beneath the jungle canopy, and shivered.

She felt more than heard Elaria emerge behind her, and the portal closed. The elf stepped up next to Sira and huffed out a breath. "I don't suppose we'll find him all that easily in the dark, will we?" she asked Sira.

Shaking her head remorsefully, Sira sighed. "No, not likely. I can't even feel his presence this far away. He wanted to stay out of sight of the Bazaar, fearful of drawing unwanted attention."

"That was probably smarter than even he realized," Elaria said with a grimace. When Sira looked at her questioningly, she explained, "The Dark Dragons are allied with the Darksteel Army. If they learned of a lone Star Dragon, one that could be corrupted or destroyed by Nuuldan, they would report it to their ally immediately, and he'd come looking."

A terrifying shiver ran down the length of Sira's back, raising goose bumps on her arms. She shivered, despite the relative warmth of the Deadlands, the memory of seeing that colossal Dark Dragon towering over them in Maradin flashing through her mind.

If it was up to her, she'd never see Nuuldan again.

"Well," she wrapped her arms around herself, "I'd rather we not delay."

"I agree," Elaria sighed. "How do we find him?"

Sira thought about it for a moment, and then remembered that Endri could hear Raida's words. *Raida, do you think you can project your voice out for Endri to hear? Let him know to connect with me and guide us to him?*

"I can try," the dragonsoul replied hesitantly. *"But I didn't even know I was doing that in the first place. So I don't really know what I'm doing. Yet."*

Smiling warmly, she thought, *I believe in you.* Raida sent soothing warmth through Sira's soul at that. Sira looked at Elaria, and spoke aloud, "Raida will see if she can find him."

Staring at her, Elaria frowned and asked, "What is it like having her with you?"

"It's…strange," Sira admitted. *No offense, Raida.* "There's a constant presence. A constant voice, like having a companion. Only…" Her thoughts drifted to Kemila. To how she had reacted to the woman's presence. To Raida's apparent attraction to Kemila, and how Sira was, too.

It wasn't unusual on Halarite. Not anymore. Same-sex relationships had been banned in the early days of history, but these days, it was only a small minority that was set against it.

But Sira had never felt attraction towards women. Not really.

So why now?

Raida was the only thing she could think of. Even if the dragonsoul wasn't doing it on purpose, the fact of the matter was, she was still trying to find her sense of self. Trying to define where she ended and Raida began.

Was that even possible anymore?

Who am I?

She felt a general sense of confusion from Raida. *"You are Sira Reinar."* A momentary pause. *"Aren't you?"*

Sira chuckled, despite feeling lost. Elaria raised a curious eyebrow at her. "Nothing," Sira shook her head, her cheeks burning in embarrassment.

"Okay, I think I know what to do," Raida said. *"I'm going to try now. You'll feel magic flow into you again."*

No sooner had Raida told her that, than did she feel magic drawing in from the Universe, gathering into Sira's shared body. Elaria must have sensed it too, her expression turning to one of confusion and even concern.

Power kept growing.

Gathering.

More and more.

And even more.

Something wasn't right about it.

Raida…

And then a white flash of searing pain, shifting into aching agony. The world simply blinked out for a second, and when Sira's senses returned to normal, she lay flat on her back, and every muscle and joint in her body ached.

"E-Elaria?" she looked over, and felt her heart drop out. The elf lay crumpled on the ground ten feet away. "Elaria!"

Sira tried to rise, but her head swam, threatening to pitch her backwards and empty her stomach at the same time. Groaning, she rolled over and pushed up onto her hands and knees, slowly, achingly crawling towards Elaria.

The elf's chest rose and fell, assuring Sira she still lived. When she reached Elaria's side, Sira placed her hand on the other's chest and felt for a heartbeat, only to realize she could barely feel anything of her own body.

Raida, what happened?

Her breath paused. Raida didn't answer at first.

And then, *"I'm so sorry! I…I didn't mean to."*

What happened? Why did I pass out? What happened to Elaria?

The elf groaned and pressed her hands to her temples. When she turned to look up, Sira gasped at the sight of blood trailing out of Elaria's nose. "Wh-what happened?" Elaria managed to ask.

Sira couldn't feel the stirring of magic, and so was startled by the sudden updraft of wind around them, and then she heard, over a ringing in her ears that she hadn't realized was there before now, the flapping of leathery wings.

From the shadows of night, Endri suddenly appeared overhead, landing practically on top of them. His starlit eyes gazed down upon them, and while Sira normally found herself lost in those eyes, now she could sense his fear. Sense his fear and concern over her own feelings and physical sensations.

"It was too much," Raida explained. *"I used too much magic, too much power."*

Folding his wings and lowering his massive head down to inches above them, Endri blew out a breath that billowed up red dust around them. *"Far more than you realize,"* Endri's soothing voice had an edge to it that pressed at Sira's nerves. *"It knocked these two senseless. Everyone with even a moderate connection to magic in the Bazaar likely felt it.*

Are you three okay?"

Sira blinked her eyes, tried to shake her head, and immediately regretted it when a sudden headache washed over her. She wavered on her knees, and it was all she could do to keep herself from falling over. "Oof. I...I don't know. I think so."

Elaria wiped blood from her face, stared at her now-bloodied hands, and blinked hard. "I'll be okay. I just need...a moment." Her head settled back down in the dirt.

Sira's senses began to return. Her touch. Her hearing, though there was nothing to hear outside of Endri's heavy breathing. And her sense of magic. Endri's presence grew stronger, a reassuring, familiar soul that practically enveloped them in a protective cocoon when he was so close.

"I'm so sorry," Raida intoned. *"I just...lost control of it. I wanted to make sure you heard me, Endri."*

The Star Dragon nodded and backed away from them. *"I heard you. I fear more than I did."*

The world felt steadier. Sira's legs felt stronger, recovering from the magic overload with every passing second. Forcing down the bile at the back of her throat, Sira pushed up onto her feet, and tried to dust herself off, only to feel dizzy again. She almost fell, but somehow managed to keep her feet under her. Elaria sat up and rubbed the bridge of her nose.

Another wave of dizziness overcame Sira, the world pitching to the side, and sending her down with it.

"Wha...I..." She muttered.

Her stomach emptied.

Darkness engulfed her.

Chapter 24

OF LIFE AND DEATH

The Allied Council was fractured.

There was hardly a shadow left of its former state, and Cardin knew that was by design. As he sat in the dining hall at Archanon Castle, shoving steak and potatoes around his plate without feeling the desire to actually eat it, he sulked.

He should have been starving. The Council session had lasted until sundown, and none of them ate dinner while they debated and discussed and planned. But in the end, he had only achieved marginal success. The Wizards and Erien would not side with the orcs. They were unsure if they could rely upon the Dareann Elves, knowing the political strife no doubt wreaking havoc across their world following the discovery of the Cronal's history.

Cardin didn't dare bring up his other ideas for alliances. If the remnants of the Council couldn't be convinced to work with the orcs, then he feared even the mention of another former enemy would only make matters worse.

"Hey, you awake over there, Princely?"

Cardin blinked when a hand waved in front of his face. Stirring out of his reverie, he looked to Reis, sat to Cardin's right, who frowned back at him. "Wha?" Cardin stirred.

"You haven't heard a thing we've talked about, have you?" he asked.

Cardin blinked again, looked around at the head table. Next to Reis sat Amaya, and to Cardin's left, scooted further away to stay out of poking range of the Sword's scabbard, sat Dalin. "I, uh…" Shaking his head, Cardin sighed. "No. I wasn't listening."

"Obviously," Dalin mused, and sipped at stew. "Perhaps you would care to share with us your musings?"

Half-laughing, Cardin simply shook his head, and shoved his plate away, knowing he'd never keep the food down. As much as he loved steak, he was too anxious, too nervous, too scared.

"What else is there to think about?" he asked despondently.

"Which is why we were talking about that very topic," Reis stated. His plate was long empty, and Cardin wondered if the full mug of ale that a servant set down before him, before taking his plate away, was his friend's third or fourth. Or more? How long had Cardin been lost in thought?

"Right, sorry," he shook his head and drew in a deep breath.

When he remained silent after that, staring at the grain of the wooden table, the others glanced at one another over his head, and then Reis nudged his arm. Or rather, shoved it, nearly toppling Cardin off of his chair. "Hey!"

"You heard the Wizard," Reis grated. "What were you thinking?"

Resisting the urge to shove Reis back, knowing it would do nothing to help the situation, Cardin grit his teeth, looked back and forth between his two friends, and then said, "I was thinking about the fractured Council. About how our current state is exactly what the Darksteel Army wanted. But then…" He trailed off and frowned. "It makes me wonder if we'd actually somewhat foiled their plans when we established the Council in the first place."

"I sincerely doubt it was a part of their plans," Dalin spoke thoughtfully. "Imagine what chaos would have been sown had we not allied ourselves? Or for that matter, if Klaralin was receiving support from the Darksteel Army, they probably hoped to seize control of Halarite without having to lift a finger of their own."

Nodding absently, Cardin planted his elbow on the table and rested his chin on his knuckle. "Hmm. I suppose you're right. It's a good bet they didn't want the Star Dragons involved, either."

"And I doubt they counted on Sal'fe and the Staff of Aliz," Reis added.

That triggered a whole slew of other thoughts, and without realizing he was doing it, Cardin mused out loud, "Right. Aliz... Sal'fe had me retrieve it from Kailar's cave before all of this started. Before I knew about the Sword." A deep frown furrowed his brow. "Sal'fe was a staunch supporter of the Alliance. He reveled in the role it gave him, as savior of Falind, though why he played that card specifically, I can't begin to fathom. But where did Kailar find the Staff?"

Silence followed. None of the others present could answer his question, and it suddenly nagged at Cardin. Looking at Dalin, he asked, "How was the staff lost in the first place?"

Raising his eyebrows, Dalin replied, "I am afraid I do not know. You would probably have to ask the Grand Master Wizard about that."

"Hmm," Cardin slouched and resumed staring ahead at nothing. "Something just doesn't feel right here. After almost a year of steadfast support, Sal'fe began to resist working together with the Council. He started even missing sessions now and again, or was late to some of them. I thought it was because he disagreed with my becoming Prince of Tal and a member of the Council, but..."

Reis quirked an eyebrow at him. "But what?"

He tried to think of something, *anything*, to give voice to what nagged at his subconscious. He tried to figure out how to describe the unsettling feeling he had that someone was pulling the strings on all of them, even now. In the end, all he could say was, "It just doesn't make sense. Sal'fe is intelligent. Strategic. Careful. He wouldn't throw away the Alliance when we need it the most like this, would he?"

Letting out a slow sigh, Dalin gently placed his spoon on the bowl of stew and pushed it forward, apparently finished. "I wondered about that too. I have a theory, although it certainly does not entirely fit all of the facts."

Raising a curious eyebrow, Cardin shifted his head on his fist to look at his friend. Dalin looked him in the eyes, and said, "Perhaps he played us from the start. All of us. With the Staff of Aliz, and the subsequent war against the orcs, he was in a position to extract considerable sums of gold from the other kingdoms. He trained Mages to become more than Mages. He commissioned and helped build new defenses along the border. By our own spies' accounts, the infrastructure in their capitol has been vastly improved. Perhaps he has sucked dry all that he needs from us, and now is content to remain lord of his own little corner of the world."

For several long moments, Cardin considered Dalin's theory. It had the ring of some truth to it, or at least of logical reasoning, but still, something in his soul told him that wasn't it. There was something else at play.

Then Cardin recalled Dalin's exact wording, and a broad smile drew across his face. Dalin frowned. "What is it?"

"Nothing, nothing," Cardin sat up straight and chuckled lightly. "It's just that...you said 'our spies,' not 'Tal's spies.'"

Dalin blinked once, twice, and then a sheepish grin pricked up the edge of his mouth. "Well, I am no longer a Wizard. Since I live in Tal, in the castle for that matter, then I am a citizen of Tal, am I not?"

Cardin laughed, and nodded. "Indeed you are, my friend," and he clasped Dalin heartily on the shoulder.

The levity was welcome, and Cardin felt his heart feel a little lighter, if only for the moment. He sat against the high back of the chair and looked over to Reis and Amaya. The Guardian had remained mostly silent throughout the evening, and he wondered about that. "Lieutenant."

She looked at him, and replied, "Sire?"

"Any thoughts?"

She furrowed her brow to ponder for a moment, and then nodded. "Yes. A question, really. When we die, if we don't ascend, where do we go?"

Cardin's eyebrows rose, and he glanced at his friends. Dalin asked, "Oh is that all? Well, if you are prepared for an hours-long discussion on the matter..."

Reis chuckled, and Cardin saw Amaya's cheeks redden. She turned to hide her reaction, and Cardin shot a heated look at Dalin. "Why do you ask that question?" Cardin asked, ensuring his tone was one of genuine interest.

"It's...well," she hesitated, "I was just wondering about what happens when Sal'fe uses the Staff of Aliz to take away one's life."

The thought caught Cardin off guard. It was a good question. He looked expectantly to Dalin, whose earlier humor instantly vanished.

He screwed up his face into one of thoughtfulness, and he shook his head a moment later. "I do not know. That is an excellent question."

"Aye," Reis said bashfully. "Sorry, I shouldn't have…"

When he didn't finish, Cardin backhanded his shoulder. "Shouldn't have what?"

"Sorry," Reis shook his head. "I mean I shouldn't have laughed."

"Nor should I have teased," Dalin bowed his head. "Perhaps I have spent too much time amongst lowly humans," he said with a mischievous wink.

Another light smile touched Cardin's face, but it vanished a second later. He was tired, and before he knew what was happening, a large yawn overcame him. It started a chain, with Reis taking up the call to yawn, followed by Dalin and Amaya at the same time.

It was summer and the sun had set, which meant the hour was late. He was used to it, but he also knew he had another long day ahead of him.

A day of forging a new alliance, whether the Allied Council wanted it or not.

"Well," he said, and clasped Reis on the back. "I think we should all get some rest. Reis, can you inspect our defense preparations in the morning? And make sure all the guards and soldiers know about our special guests arriving tomorrow?"

"Of course," Reis pushed his chair back and stood up. Cardin, Dalin, and Amaya followed suit. "Sire," he added with a smirk, and then sauntered off.

"Amaya, Dalin, I'd like you two to accompany me tomorrow morning. We're leaving at first light."

"I shall be ready," Dalin bowed, and left.

"As will I," Amaya mirrored Dalin's actions.

Cardin turned to look behind him, out of the broad windows into the castle courtyard. Everlasting torches and lanterns burned in the darkness, illuminating the bushes, trees, and pathways. He missed nature. He missed being out amongst the trees, the flora and fauna of Daruun Forest.

Things were hard back then, but they had also been so much simpler.

Sighing for possibly the hundredth time that day, he headed for the bedroom.

Except that night, he barely got a wink of sleep.

All he could think about was Amaya's question. It bothered him, and he didn't know why.

When he did finally sleep, it was a fitful rest at best, and full of dreams of invading armies, and of Sal'fe, laughing in a fashion he had never heard from the old Wizard before.

The laughter of insanity.

Chapter 25

RISING SHADOWS

When Steward Kai knocked on Cardin's door, he practically screamed himself awake. Darkness pressed in on him through the four-poster bed, and for a moment, he forgot where he was. This wasn't his home in Daruun...

And then he remembered. The weight of the Sword upon his back, the crown upon his head, even if neither were there now. He rolled over on the bed, infusing magic into his eyes and giving him the night vision he first unlocked in the jungles of Trinil, and grasped the Sword from its resting place beside the bed.

It was still there. He hadn't lost it.

He hadn't failed in his most important duty.

Another knock at the door, and Kai peeked her head in. "Sire?" her curt, business-like voice called into the gloom of his room.

"I'm okay." He heaved a sigh, tightening his grip upon the Sword's scabbard. "Just a...a dream." He looked at Kai, her sharp features easily visible with his night vision. Frowning, he asked, "Don't you ever sleep?"

"Only when my duties are completed," she replied. "You asked to be woken at the first pre-dawn glow, Sire."

"Yes, thanks." He swallowed down a lump in his throat, and

nodded, even though he doubted she could see him. "I'll be out shortly."

"I could send servants in to help you dress..."

He grinned. Kai asked almost every morning, and he usually acceded to her request. This time, however, he replied, "No thanks."

Taking that as dismissal, Kai closed the door, and left Cardin to the growing sick feeling in his stomach.

He pressed his hand to it and frowned as it audibly grumbled and growled. Not from hunger, but from the ill feeling he felt about today.

Shaking his head, he climbed off the bed, and without ever lighting a lantern or torch, he dressed in his traveling clothes for the day – thin dark-grey trousers, forest-green tunic, and after strapping the Sword's scabbard onto his back, he donned a tan travelling cloak.

Several minutes later, without really thinking about where his feet led him, Cardin found himself in the dining hall, where Dalin and Amaya groggily sat waiting. He greeted them without really thinking about it and sat down. But when servants brought out freshly-prepared porridge and thick sausages, Cardin's stomach did back flips, and he didn't touch it.

Dalin noticed. "Are you okay?"

Cardin gave his best placating smile and nodded. "I am. Just bad dreams kept me awake."

The former Wizard's eyebrows arched upward. "Dreams, or visions?"

Shuddering at the memories, Cardin shook his head. "I don't know." A pause. "I hope just dreams," he whispered.

After managing to force down a single sausage, Cardin, Dalin and Amaya headed out. A cold chill crept down Cardin's back before they even stepped foot outside, and somehow, when the castle doors were opened by two guards, he expected to find an army outside.

Nothing.

Predawn had shifted into diffuse morning, with the sun still hidden behind the Ilari Mountains, so it was a cool, humid morning as they walked out of the castle and onto the road bound for the western gate. Puddles in a gravel side path indicated that it had rained during the night, and the air smelled fresh, clean.

He breathed in that scent, letting it wash over him and sooth his frayed nerves. *Everything's going to be alright. Today is just another step towards gathering our allies. Just another…*

Stopping his thoughts, he shook his head. He was about to tell himself that it was just another day. When had society-altering moments in history become normal?

When you picked up the Sword.

Cardin waved off a retinue of guards that tried to accompany them from the Upper City gatehouse, telling them he would not need them today. They looked tired, and he figured they were the night crew, not yet relieved by their daytime counterparts.

The march across Main Street in the Market District was largely uneventful. Vendors with temporary carts were just setting up their stalls, and doors to stores were opening, but few patrons had ventured into the markets yet.

When the trio reached the massive, fifty-foot-tall outer wall, they were greeted by a pleasant face. Reis stepped out of the guardhouse at the base of the stairs climbing up to the wall, directly next to the massive ironwood gates, and smiled at them. "Well, then, looks like you managed to drag yourself out of bed before the crack of dawn," Reis said with a smirk.

Cardin returned the look, and tried to think of a snarky comeback, but the dark sense in his stomach made that impossible. His grin faltered, and when Reis noticed, his did too. "Cardin?"

Shaking his head, he drew in a deep breath, and looked out the gates as they clicked and groaned open, to the road stretching into the valley, towards the farms and the Daruun Forest beyond. Shadows of memory shaped into countless heads, countless weapons, marching on the gates.

Shivering, he replied, "I'll be okay. But…" He frowned, stopping in his tracks and staring down at his hands. Then he looked up at Reis. "Have the wall on high alert."

All remnants of humor left Reis, his characteristic grin fading completely. He swallowed hard, and nodded. "Will do. Good luck."

"We'll be back shortly," Cardin said.

"We'll watch for you," Reis said, before turning and heading back into the guardhouse.

Dalin and Amaya watched Cardin carefully, both of them with narrowed eyes and furrowed brows. His friend asked him, "Are you sure you are well?"

Giving Dalin another placating smile, Cardin started to nod, and then halfway changed it to a negative shake, the smile disappearing. "I don't know. No. Maybe." Looking again at Amaya, he said, "We're all coming back today, your entire crew that we left there. As soon as we arrive, get them."

Worry lines etched deeper into what should have been a young face, but Amaya nodded. "Of course, sire."

Drawing in a deep breath again, Cardin led the others out of the gates, crossing the threshold of the protective barrier surrounding Archanon, the one that prevented any and all star magic-based portals from forming, and then stopped them.

Without even reaching back to touch the Sword, Cardin drew in power, and almost effortlessly projected it before them, producing a shaft of blue-white light. Dalin passed through first, followed by Amaya, and then Cardin.

They appeared in the exact same place they had left, on the outskirts of the orc village. This far east, the sun was already several degrees above the horizon, and the village was alive with daily activity.

An outer patrol of orcs wearing darkened-steel armor spotted them, and broke into a run towards them. Cardin tensed, and started to reach back for the Sword, but then caught himself and forced himself to relax.

These weren't his enemies.

The orcs slowed to a trot, and then a walk as they approached.

With perfect diction, the largest of the orcs, who was still considerably shorter than General Arkad, looked down at Cardin and said, "Prince Kataar. Our Shaman told us to expect your arrival this morning. She awaits you in the longhouse," he motioned towards the same path they had taken during their previous visit. "Please allow me to escort your party."

"Of course," Cardin nodded.

Amaya added, "Kilack, may I go to my team?"

"In fact they await us in the longhouse with the Shaman," the orc identified as Kilack replied.

"Perfect," Amaya smiled.

Cardin didn't share her smile. The Shaman knew Cardin would return, but he had not told her when. And if she had ordered guards to watch for their return, and had already gathered the rest of Amaya's team, left behind to act as emissaries, then had she endured bad dreams last night as well? Prophetic dreams?

As Kilack and the other orcs escorted them through the village, Cardin felt a distinct difference. Children still played in the streets, but their voices were quiet, they weren't shouting playfully or chasing one another around. The adult orcs watched them go by, somber looks in their eyes. The ringing of hammers could be heard from every direction, and somehow, Cardin knew those were armor and weapon smiths, readying equipment for an inevitable battle.

The troupe reached the longhouse and ducked inside to find Tana, Nia, and Elic sitting around the same long, smooth wooden table they had sat around for hours talking during Cardin's previous visit. They immediately stood and greeted Cardin and the others, with Tana bowing respectfully to Cardin, and he to her in turn.

"Welcome back, Prince Kataar," Tana spoke with a strange gravely quality to her voice. She looked exhausted, with her mottled grey skin gathered up beneath her eyes and her mouth turned down in a grimace.

Kilack and the other orcs remained outside, surprisingly, but as Cardin, Dalin and Amaya walked further in, a hulking form followed. Arkad must have seen them passing through the town and quickly came to join them.

He was in full darkened-steel armor.

No, Cardin thought. *It isn't just darkened-steel. It is Darksteel. The same armor the enemy will wear.* Klaralin had gifted the orcs with Darksteel armor and weapons, and could have only done so with the help of the Darksteel Army.

It nagged at him again, like it did yesterday. Amaya's question nagged at him. Sal'fe's actions nagged at him.

But now wasn't the time.

"Shaman," he returned her greeting. Then he noticed that Elic was likewise wearing leather and chain armor, and two full traveling backpacks were set off to the side, against the wall of the longhouse.

"I believe you have important news to pass on?" Tana asked, while Arkad drew around to stand just beside and behind her.

"Um, yes, I do," he nodded. "Though not necessarily the best of news. The Allied Council has…well, political infighting over your existence and King Beredis's secrets surrounding you has fractured the Council. I've done all that I can to hold things together, but, well," he shook his head grimly. "I'm not really good at the whole politics thing." He debated mentioning his suspicions about Sal'fe to her, but decided that, for now, the details of the Allied Council's infighting was an internal matter.

There were more important things at stake.

"And the prisoners of war?" Arkad asked, his voice deep and rumbling.

Cardin glanced at him, but every time he did, he remembered the dead miners at the Relkin camp. The burned Warriors in the last battle he fought against Arkad. So he focused on Tana. "The Council does not agree to your terms," he said, "but I do."

Tana frowned. "I do not understand."

Thinking of his dream last night, Cardin swallowed hard. "I know we need all the help we can get against what's coming. I know that, especially as fractured as we are now, we don't stand a chance. I know we need your help, and you need ours. So, in the interest of cooperation, and to be frank, in the interest of giving you as many troops as we possibly can to help stand against the Darksteel Army, I'm going to release all Tal orc prisoners to you."

Tension in Tana's shoulders that he hadn't noticed melted away, and she huffed out a breath in relief. From a human's point of view, the smile that drew across her face was somewhat hideous, but Cardin tried not to think of her in that way. She looked up at Arkad and rested a hand on his log-wide forearm, before she focused again on Cardin. "I am gladdened to hear that, Prince Kataar. It is what I hoped *and* what my feelings told me would come to be."

So he was right. She had known, at least to some degree, what to expect from Cardin's visit today. "I feel I should provide full disclosure, several orcs were captured during the war behind Falind's border. Falind has officially broken off relations with the Alliance and closed their borders to us. I don't know that we'll be able to convince King Sal'fe to release his prisoners." Hot anger flashed in Arkad's eyes, but Cardin forged on, "However, I'd say the large majority of prisoners are in Tal's borders."

"Then we shall begin there," Tana nodded. "We are prepared to accompany you."

Cardin blinked. It was going to be his next suggestion, but it seemed as if Tana was already ahead of him in that regard. "You are?"

"Of course," Tana nodded. "I fear that if you try to escort any number of prisoners here yourself, they will fear execution or worse, and will resist. However, if I am there, they will be compelled to obey me."

Cardin felt his own tension ease up. "That's what I was hoping you would say. Well then," he clasped his hands together, and glanced at the travel packs again. "When would you be available to depart?"

"At this very moment," Tana replied.

It was better than Cardin could have hoped for.

He and the others parted, allowing Tana and Arkad to precede them out of the longhouse. Elic and Nia grabbed the backpacks, and then exchanged greetings with Amaya. Cardin noticed a brief hand touch between Nia and Amaya just as they ducked out of the longhouse. It was so brief that he thought he'd imagined it.

Once outside, Arkad spoke brief orders to Kilack, and then the orcs that had escorted them dispersed, leaving only Arkad and Tana to escort them back to the edge of the village. Once on the outskirts, Cardin drew in power, and projected another portal home. If his portal opened precisely where he intended it to, they would emerge only a hundred feet away from the outer gates.

He probably should have opened one further away, given the guests they were bringing, but he still felt nervous, with the dark shadow of fate pressing down upon him.

"I think it best if the rest of my people go first," Cardin stated, and nodded to Dalin. The Wizard preceded everyone else, and was soon followed by Elic, Nia, and Amaya, leaving Cardin alone with the orcs. Motioning to the portal, Cardin said to them, "After you."

Arkad grunted, and walked ahead of Tana protectively, and she followed behind. Cardin looked back at the village one last time, and then headed through the portal. The instant he touched it, he felt his shoulders tighten up anxiously, expecting the worst.

But again, upon emerging on the other side, there was nothing wrong. The portal closed, and he looked out into the valley again, expecting an army.

Nothing.

They were safe.

Heaving a sigh, he turned back to the gates. Several soldiers manned the wall, looking down upon them all cautiously from fifty feet up.

The new arrivals had spread out, not just further towards the gate, but to the sides, waiting for Cardin to lead them into the city. Drawing in a deep breath, he marched forward. Just inside of the gates, he saw Reis and General Vellar, the latter of whom wore his official, ceremonial plate armor, resplendent with a black and white tabard and black cape, waiting for them expectantly. Additional soldiers stood by them, ready to escort them through the Market District and into the Red District, where the city's dungeon, with two dozen orc prisoners, awaited.

Larger prison camps existed outside of other, southern cities, as well as near Valaras, but Cardin thought it appropriate to start with the few prisoners still left inside of the capitol.

Carding marched forward, passing through the gathered travelers and towards the gate. Looking at Vellar's ceremonial armor, it only just then occurred to Cardin that he should have worn something more official today. It was the first action of appeasement between Tal and the orcs, and he knew that the denizens of Archanon would not take well to seeing orcs walking freely amongst them. He would need all of the authority he could muster today.

But that was why he had arranged for an escort of soldiers. To surround them and protect Tana and Arkad from any attempted retaliation from the citizens of Tal.

Peace with the orcs was not going to be easy to endure for Archanon. Cardin intended to address the people as soon as possible, but there just wasn't time.

Never enough time.

The travelers followed, with Tana close behind and beside him, until they passed through the safety of the gates. Cardin stopped before Vellar, and nodded, "General."

"Prince Kataar," he bowed, before looking pointedly at Arkad, and then Tana. The hint of a sneer drew across his lips, but he quickly recovered and looked again at Cardin. "We stand ready to escort you to the dungeon, sire."

Cardin nodded, and looked back. All of the travelers had just entered the gate, and the tension he'd felt upon passing through the portal eased even further. They were safe inside of the walls.

"Let's go," Cardin ordered.

"Sire," Vellar nodded, and then looked to his troop. "Standard escort formation!" he barked.

The troops immediately complied, surrounding the travelers. Then, side-by-side with Vellar, Cardin lead the retinue past the guard shack and into the city.

But they only made it a hundred or so feet. Cardin brought the assembly to an abrupt halt when he felt an overwhelming surge of magic. It pressed against him like the tsunamis that had drenched the coasts when the skies burned.

Magic.

Magic everywhere, all around them. Such intense power that it momentarily overwhelmed his senses.

Tana cried out and grasped her head with one hand, her chest with another.

"My shaman?" Arkad asked in alarm.

The Mages in the area felt it, too. Something was wrong.

It felt like...

The first warning horn blared from above the main gate.

Another echoed from somewhere else along the wall. Then another. And another.

Cardin looked just as the gates began to close, and his heart nearly stopped. A wall of light shimmered in the valley, a thousand feet away. Not a small doorway like he was used to conjuring, but a wall as wide as the valley, and nearly as tall as the Archanon wall itself.

A portal.

Large enough for a dragon to pass through.

Or an army.

The first person to emerge through that portal was unexpectedly familiar. She was tall, and clad in Darksteel plate armor from head to toe, her head concealed in a helmet, her armor segmented, edges sharpened or pointed, and claws extended from every finger.

The same woman who had battled them in the village on Stella.

The same woman who had nearly killed Sira.

And she drew in magic even as she marched ahead of a line of eight or ten foot tall brutes in full plate armor behind her.

The gates hadn't closed yet, and the city shield couldn't be raised until they were.

The enemy knew that. That was why the clawed woman unleashed a blue-white ball of energy five feet in diameter by thrusting her clawed hands forward.

The Sword was in Cardin's hand even as he fueled his legs with magic and leapt into the air. He covered the distance back to the closing gates in one leap, and then he thrust his left hand, palm-first, out ahead of him, just in time to project a wide shield and intercept the energy ball before it slammed into the gate.

The sphere exploded against his shield with thunderous force, and actually *pushed* Cardin back two inches, nearly knocking him off balance. He imagined the woman snarled when her attack failed, and she charged up again. Cardin recovered his lost ground and prepared another shield. The gates were closing at a frustratingly slow pace, but he knew they were fully automated by magic, and it was no one's fault.

The woman unleashed another energy ball, and once again, it intersected Cardin's shield, only this one had more power behind it, and it actually knocked Cardin backwards and onto his butt.

The doors groaned and clicked close.

"Raise the shield!" a guard shouted.

A flux of energy, and the bricks of the great wall of Archanon shimmered, while a blue-white, almost-transparent wall of energy reached up into the sky.

Shaking his head, Cardin looked back at the city guards and the travelers. All were unharmed – if he hadn't been there, he had no doubt the doors would have been destroyed, and the guard house along with them.

That had been the Darksteel Army's plan. Destroy the gate before the city shield could be raised, allowing them to stream in through the gate.

What of the Southeast gate?!

He bounced up to his feet, and heard more warning horns wail all around the wall.

With his heart thundering in his chest, Cardin looked at the stairs leading up to the top of the wall, and then thought better of it, and surged magic into his legs and beneath him. He looked up, and leapt fifty feet into the air, to land with grace that surprised even himself atop the wall.

It was fifteen feet thick at the narrowest, with two turrets that reached out on either side of the gate. He bolted to one of the turrets, pressing in between the gathering soldiers preparing to defend the wall, should the shield fail for any reason.

And he saw row upon row of troops emerge. By now, the clawed woman walked ahead of a column a hundred across and ten deep, and more rows emerged from the wall of light. The woman charged up another ball and unleashed it with her full might against the gate. It thundered against the shield, causing it to flare brightly, but it held.

More thunderous explosions rocked the morning air from behind and all around Cardin, and he looked back. The city was several miles in diameter, and this segment of the wall was protected on either side by the natural cliffs, so he couldn't see what was going on elsewhere.

Looking south to the shorter tunnel carved into the mountain, Cardin raced off of the turret and into the tunnel, surging more magic into his legs to give him unnatural speed. He passed by rushing troops and a small barracks, and emerged on the other side of the mountain in seconds. From there, he got his first view of the true strength of the Darksteel Army.

More hundred-person-wide walls of light had appeared at the edge of the forest a thousand feet away, and from some of those portals, columns of soldiers, all clad in pitch-black armor, had already emerged, with more following. The mix of soldiers was dizzying – all shapes and sizes. Tall, small, wide, skinny, some with four arms rather than two, some with four legs rather than two.

And from still others, siege weapons were drawn forth, pulled along by creatures thirty feet tall and covered in foot-long, brown fur. The creatures let loose terrifying howls. They were larger and more terrifying than any qrishag the orcs had tamed, and the siege weapons, surging with enchanted magic, required four of the creatures each to pull through the portal into the field of battle.

Cardin kept running. The shield was up, so he hoped that meant the southeast gate had successfully closed, but he still had to check, still had to be sure.

As he raced along the length of the wall, covering miles in minutes, more enemy troops emerged, and the siege weapons reached their designated places and prepared to unleash their fury upon the oldest enchanted structure on Edilas.

When he came into view of the guard house at the southeast gate, he heaved a sigh of relief. The guardhouse was intact. When he was close enough, he leapt down and looked, just to reassure himself, and was pleased to see the gate intact.

But there was blood. And wounded. But to say wounded was an

understatement. Torsos without legs, blood and guts splattered on the road. Soldiers attended wounded, calling for help. He rushed up, wishing, hoping he could heal the soldiers, but even as he looked upon the wounded, faces smashed to unrecognizable pulp, he gaped in horror and knew that even his healing magic couldn't help.

"What...what happened?" he demanded of one soldier pulling half of a body away from the gate.

"Sire!" the soldier cried, and let go of the wounded man only to fall against Cardin, smearing blood and other, less savory material onto the Prince's tunic and cloak. "They came...without w-warning, sire. The enemy emerged, un...unleashed th-th-their power against the gate. They," he breathed out, and waved a hand towards the bodies, "they stepped in the way, cast Mage shields. Th-th-they stopped the enemy from d-d-destroying the gates, but...it was too much."

Cardin huffed out a breath, and gripped the soldier's shoulders tightly. But the man had already lost the will to stand. He slouched down to his knees, out of Cardin's grasp.

Men and women had given their lives to ensure the gate remained intact.

Had given their lives to ensure the shield could be raised, and the city protected.

Thunderous explosions and bright flashes, even in full daylight, caught his attention, as the enemy siege weapons unleashed their fury upon Archanon's wall.

He had seen how many had come. Tens of thousands. Hundreds of thousands. Dozens of behemoth-sized siege weapons.

And they surrounded Archanon.

The city was safe, for now. The shield was up.

But how long could it hold out against this?

Chapter 26

EMBASSY

A fresh blanket of snow had fallen upon Tieran Port in the night, and then, just as the sun rose over the horizon, the overcast clouds moved on. Orange rays of light reflected off of the powder, blinding Kailar whenever she looked east. The disc of the sun was still low enough to be a hazy orange, but she tried to soak in any warmth it could give her. She wore fur-lined clothes beneath her dark cloak, but it seemed to do little good.

Today was particularly frigid, and she thought with ire, *Of course, today of all days, the temperature plummets.* She, along with Empress Reyla, Letan, General Querlin, and the Lords of Devor, stood just outside the western border of the city. Throughout the night, soldiers and servants had brought the long table and multiple chairs from city hall out to a flat, snow-covered area just off of the main road out of town. Knowing how cold it was in the dead of winter, the servants had also built up four large stacks of wood, and only a handful of minutes ago, Kailar had used magic to ignite the logs and start the fires warming the area.

The snow in the area had also been cleared, but knowing that mud would be inevitable, several large rugs had been placed beneath and around the table and chairs. A sacrifice to the important meeting at hand, as the rugs would likely be unsalvageable afterwards.

The outside venue of the meeting had been a necessity – when the Navitas representative arrived, it would be impossible for them to fit inside of City Hall, given how high they towered over humans and human-like beings. Kailar also thought, with no small amount of amusement, that the residents of Devor were used to the chill winter, even if they didn't like it. The Darksteel ambassador, she hoped, would not likely be so accustomed to it.

Suddenly every magic-capable person in the gathering looked west at once, and the motion drew Kailar's attention that way. There must have been a stirring of star magic that she couldn't sense, as the powdery snow suddenly began to whirl into a small cyclone. Except, unlike the previous night when the Darksteel representatives had arrived, this was much further away from town, much further down the road – at least half a mile away.

And when the wall of blue-white light winked into existence, it wasn't a small shaft or a five-person-wide opening.

It was a *wall*. Twice as wide as the road, at least forty or fifty feet tall, it was one of the largest portals Kailar had seen, and she felt ice form in her veins, her stomach constricting.

Xavien and his honor guard couldn't possibly need a portal that large. *Something's wrong,* she thought.

Without thinking, she drew her darksteel daggers, and they set to humming immediately as she drew in dark magic. Following her lead, Letan and the General drew their swords. Closer to town, a retinue of soldiers had been ordered to stand by just in case, and Kailar heard the ring of swords being drawn.

"Hold!" the Empress commanded, slashing out her right arm, as if to hold the panicked soldiers back.

"Empress," General Querlin hissed, "I can't imagine they would make such a large portal unless-"

"Unless they intended to intimidate us," she interrupted. "That is precisely what this…"

She trailed off, as the first…*things* emerged from the portals. Not Xavien, not his honor guard, but something much, much larger. Giant, four-legged creatures, towering in height and covered in brown fur, lumbered through the wall of light, with harnesses attached, and chains, not rope but *chains* with links as big as Kailar's torso, trailing behind into the portal, taut with heavy tension.

"What the hells," Reyla breathed.

One of the creatures howled, a terrifying, resonating sound that vibrated Kailar's chest.

And then the structure they towed began to emerge. That was the most apt description. A structure on giant, metallic wheels almost as wide around as the creatures were tall. It was literally a building, made of grey stone bricks reinforced by Darksteel. Battlements were visible on top, and as the entire building emerged, towers with turrets that reached up to the full height of the portal appeared.

In Edilas, the structure wouldn't have been all that impressive, especially compared to Archanon's towering walls. But on Devor, next to Tieran, it was imposing.

The moment the structure's back wheels cleared the portal, one of the chains, which reached onto and over the structure's wall atop smooth arches, pulled in, and the creatures veered left. The heavy wheels dug into the road as it passed over, damaging the only well-traveled thoroughfare in and out of Tieran, which Kailar immediately identified as a threatening move.

When the structure cleared the portal, Kailar's heart rate doubled, as at least two dozen persons, all bearing dark colors, most wearing armor, followed. In the exact center, and the last to emerge from the portal, was Xavien. The wall of light collapsed into nothingness behind him.

The giant creatures pulling the mobile fortress drew closer, turning back to walk parallel to the road, and loomed over the assembly, their deep, dark, goat-like eyes stared down at Kailar and the gathered Devor representatives. Most present instinctively took steps back, once, twice, barely holding it together. Kailar could feel their panic in the air, and it took every measure of control she had not to follow suit. Finally, the monsters' chains clanked tighter, and the creatures brought the fortress to a lumbering halt.

Xavien and his much larger entourage paraded up the road, though their precision pace was interrupted when they had to step across the deep ruts carved into the road by the fortress. They resumed their march immediately after, and looked entirely unperturbed.

Reyla's earlier surprise was absent now, and she stepped ahead of Kailar and the rest with an air of confidence. And more, Kailar realized.

Reyla was angry.

As Xavien's entourage drew to a halt fifty feet away, Kailar took stock of his additional company, and was unsurprised that they all looked like battle-hardened veterans.

She recognized the four honor guards from before – the two lean, ghostly magic-users and the two eight-foot-tall brutish guardians with the T-shaped openings on their plate helmets.

The rest were more likely common foot soldiers, though they still represented threats. They wore less plate than the larger soldiers, more chain, all of it Darksteel, and bore weapons of varying design – swords, axes, maces, one soldier that looked possibly elven bore what looked like a half-staff, half-sword weapon.

But even with enchanted weapons and armor, which she knew they would all have, ten soldiers was not enough to invade even Tieran.

Kailar glanced at the structure. Were there more inside?

The Darksteel gates facing the road groaned outward, and several men and women hopped down to the ground and ran to the corners of the structure, to the wheels.

Reyla observed this, and then set furious eyes upon Xavien. "What is the meaning of this?" she demanded.

Raising his arms disarmingly, Xavien stepped ahead of his retinue, and replied, "Peace, Empress Aurin. We come in good faith for the meeting you requested, to negotiate a treaty between our people."

"Yet you come bearing a siege weapon and soldiers ready to fight?" Reyla asked.

Kailar noted that they, too, were ready for a fight. Kailar, Letan, none of the soldiers present had sheathed their weapons.

No doubt Xavien noticed this too.

"This structure is not a siege weapon," Xavien motioned towards the roving castle, just as the men and women that had run to the corners began to work mechanisms to lower the base of the structure down. "It is an embassy."

Kailar narrowed her eyes suspiciously and glanced up at the turrets. "A well-fortified embassy," she remarked.

Xavien glanced at her, glanced down at her Darksteel daggers, and then back up at her, the slightest hint of a frown on his face. "Yes, well, we aren't just in another foreign land, are we? Those of my people assigned to the embassy will be on a strange *world* with threats that could come from anywhere. We must be allowed to defend ourselves, should the need arise."

As if to punctuate his statement, the Darksteel Embassy settled with a whoosh of wind and a thump that startled one of the larger beasts, and it stamped its thick, circular, flat feet hard, shaking the ground.

But it was trained well enough to do nothing else, and it didn't strain against its chains.

"Ambassador," Reyla started, her voice curt and severe, "your embassy's arrival is premature. We have not concluded negotiations nor signed any treaties yet. Worse still, you have damaged one of our major roadways in doing so, which one could construe as an attempt to cripple our infrastructure, which I would interpret as an act of war."

Xavien gave her a placating smile and held his hands out disarmingly again. "I assure you, Empress, that is not our intention. We would be happy to assist you in repairing your roads, as we have incurred the damage. In fact," Xavien turned and looked at one of the lithe casters next to him, "Inform the commander to immediately begin roadway repairs."

Bowing slowly, the man said quietly, "At once," and turned and strode away, in no apparent hurry.

Turning again to Reyla, Xavien's smile never wavered as he said, "Of course, we could negotiate an agreement that would ensure you never have to rely upon roads again, Empress. We could construct static portals between every major city on your continent, perhaps even to every village as well, if you have something valuable to offer in return. Or," his eyes darted to the assembled Lords, looking each one in the eye before looking again upon Reyla, "if you were to become a member state of the Darksteel Empire, we would do so without requiring any recompense beyond the cost of membership."

A murmur broke out amongst the Lords as they looked to one another, excitement in some of their eyes, caution in others. There were only three Lords, after all, but Kailar was not happy when two of them, the Lord of Corlas and the Lord of Edingard, looked excited.

Even Kailar's head whirled with the possibilities of static portals. Trade and commerce could thrive under such circumstances. No more long wagon rides and hikes between Corlas and Tieran every few months, not when they could simply haul goods daily between one place and the next. And emergencies could be better tended to when reinforcements and supplies from a dozen settlements were only a step away.

Better still, the empire would no longer need to use Kailar as a tool.

It also highlighted the powerbase that the Darksteel Empire and its army likely enjoyed. If constructing such portals was a standard practice for them, they could have infrastructure setup like that across multiple *worlds.* Trade and commerce could thrive, and their armies could rapidly mobilize as needed to invade or crush any resistance.

Which made Kailar wonder just how powerful the Navitas were, if the Darksteel Army was, indeed, worried about them. She couldn't fathom any other reason for peace talks with Devor, but surely an empire as powerful as the Darksteel, they couldn't possibly be afraid of just one species.

Could they?

Only one way to find out, she thought, and she looked west. Hoping that the Navitas would show up soon.

Once the conversation amongst the Lords quieted, Reyla addressed Xavien again. "Thank you for that additional information, Ambassador. Now, shall we sit?" She motioned to the conference table, to which Xavien visibly frowned. "I am afraid that there are not enough seats for your entire retinue."

"That is no concern," Xavien replied, his face returning to a neutrally pleasant expression. Turning to the other lithe, elf-like attendant, he waved his hand dismissively. The attendant barked orders in a foreign language, and the bulk majority of the Ambassador's retinue snapped to attention, and then with military precision, turned and marched towards the embassy, where the other men and women had finished stabilizing the structure and had begun to unchain the giant beasts.

Only the two giant brutes and the lithe attendant remained, but as Xavien walked towards the table, they remained where they were, apparently uninvited to join them.

"I must admit," Xavien remarked, "I am surprised by the change in venue. Would it not be warmer and more pleasant indoors?"

Reyla didn't answer right away, and instead turned to her troupe and ordered, "General, Kailar, with us. Lieutenant Velethar, please hold the soldiers in reserve."

General Querlin and Letan both sheathed their swords at the same time, and Letan saluted, "Yes, Empress." He marched to the waiting soldiers, ordering them to sheath their weapons.

Kailar only reluctantly put away her daggers. She, Reyla, and the General turned and walked after Xavien, while the Lords followed behind. Once they reached the table, Reyla answered Xavien's question, "It would, indeed, especially on this particular morning. However, one of the Lords of Devor would be decidedly uncomfortable with the notion."

As he came to the end chair at the far side of the table, Xavien quirked a white eyebrow up and replied, "Oh?"

"Indeed," Reyla took up position at the other end of the table. Kailar stayed on Reyla's left, while Querlin stayed on the Empress's right. "They shall join us momentarily."

A flutter of surprise flashed across Xavien's face, almost imperceptible, but then he bowed his head, and then, with a flourish, sat in the wooden chair at his end. Reyla likewise sat, and everyone took that as a cue to assume their seats.

The original City Council had once numbered around a dozen, so even with Reyla, Kailar, Kent Querlin, and the three Lords, there were still plenty of empty seats, leaving Xavien strangely lonesome looking at his empty end of the table.

"Shall we wait for this additional party member, then?" Xavien asked, his voice calm and even, but for a hint of impatience.

Reyla nodded, "Indeed. They should be along any moment now." The Empress's eyes didn't dart towards Kailar, didn't give anything away, but she could see the tension in Reyla's crow's feet. She was worried the Navitas might not come.

Even Kailar was concerned. The Navitas wasn't necessarily late, but the presence of so many Darksteel troops, and the fortress, set her on edge.

That unease was probably exactly what Xavien wanted.

"I must commend you," Xavien addressed the General. "Your troops showed great restraint facing something wholly new and frightening."

Kailar narrowed her eyes. She'd been right – everything the Darksteel Empire had done today had been a calculated move to evoke a reaction, and now Xavien was pressing on that tension.

Kent let the barest sneer curl up one corner of his lip. "They're professionals, well trained," he replied.

Glancing behind them at Letan and the other soldiers, Xavien gave a plaintive smile. "Indeed."

His tone was unreadable, but Kailar could read the Ambassadors expression – he was unimpressed.

Kailar glanced towards town, hoping to catch Letan's eye for a second. She hoped she hadn't totally miscalculated. She hoped that hers and Letan's short venture in the Crystalline Forest had been worth it.

He saw her look, and nodded. She looked behind him, and was unsurprised to find that many townspeople had begun to gather behind the soldiers to gawk at the embassy, the creatures, and the new arrivals. That drew a grimace across Kailar's face – if the Darksteel Army decided to attack at any point with that gathered crowd, the number of innocents caught in the battle would be staggering, and would distract the Devor soldiers as they tried to protect the civilians.

Letan must have had the same thought, and he approached the civilians and ordered them to go back to their business and to stay away from the edge of town.

And then the ground began to rumble. The two lumbering beasts shifted uneasily and bleated nervously, and Kailar looked west, a grin pulling up one side of her lips.

Not much closer than Xavien's portal had appeared, on the opposite side of the road from the embassy, the ground suddenly opened up, and a blue-white, crystalline head appeared, followed by a torso, arms, and legs. The Navitas appeared to simply push up from the ground, rather than climb out, and towered above the Darksteel retinue, many of whom abandoned their positions in and around the embassy and drew weapons.

The Navitas did not react, it simply stared down at the Darksteel brutes, and then looked at the seated assembly. Xavien had stood up upon the emergence of the Navitas, and the first look of real surprise was planted on his face.

Kailar grinned triumphantly.

Speaking with that strange, almost-metallic-like voice, the Navitas said, "Empress Reyla Aurin." Its torso cracked and scraped as it bowed, pressing a spindly hand over its glowing core as it did so. "I hope I have not arrived too late."

Reyla's expression never cracked, never changed. She stood up and walked around the table to stand closer to Xavien. She replied, "Not at all. Your arrival is timely, Lord Navitas."

Xavien's shocked expression redoubled, and he gaped at Reyla.

Shock. Surprise. All those words. But the one thing Kailar didn't see was fear.

Not yet.

Reyla turned to Xavien and motioned a hand. "Ambassador Xavien, may I present to you the final Lord of Devor, the Navitas."

The surprise vanished, though Kailar swore it took several precious seconds. Xavien looked up at the Navitas, drew in a deep breath, and then nodded. "It is an honor to meet you," he called up.

And then he looked at Reyla with something else in his eyes. Displeasure, maybe. Not respect, not acquiescence to her move, just displeasure. And malice.

He didn't say it, but Kailar could see in his expression. 'Well played. But unwise.'

They hadn't won this battle of wills yet.

Not by a long shot.

Chapter 27

AIRBORNE SAVIOR

This is a dream, Sira thought. *It has to be.*

She could see herself, lying on red dust. The world around her was alight. Elaria lay next to her. The giant form of Endri stooped over her. And she looked down upon her body, as her eyes opened and flashed light into the world.

Her body stood up of its own accord, entirely outside of her control. She watched it happen, frowning curiously at the strangeness of it. She saw her mouth move, but could hear nothing.

The blink of an eye, and they had moved closer to the jungle, and lit a campfire. Sira's body sat cross-legged in front of it. Her eyes still glowed, but this time she could see color – deep, vibrant purple.

Something stirred the wind and Endri, hidden in the jungle, emerged and looked sky-ward, as did Elaria and Sira's body. Sira followed their gaze, to see a shade descending from the starry sky. No, not a shade.

An airship.

Held aloft by whirling blades.

The blink of an eye.

New figures had joined them around the fire. It looked like Kemila. She could hear murmurs of talking, but couldn't make out the words Kemila and Elaria said to one another.

Sira's eyes still glowed purple.

Another blink, and she felt fear. Terror.

Her body clambered up the ladder dangling from the *Starfire*. Something gleaned through the hazy morning predawn glow, bounced off of the hull of the ship with a noisy thud that left a scorch mark and a slight buckling of the metal.

The distant echo of a roar drew Sira's gaze, both her out-of-body eyes and her glowing eyes from the body that climbed up a rope ladder. Endri soared through the sky. He folded his wings, and dove upon an advancing column of siege-like weapons towed by giant, hairy monsters. He lay waste to them with ease.

And then a dark blight appeared in the sky, overshadowing all light, even the light of Sira's eyes. Overshadowing all hope.

And then Endri was gone.

An acrid, bitter smell was the first thing to greet Sira when she awoke. Her eyes flashed open, and for a brief moment, a violet haze appeared to cover everything.

When the haze dissipated and darkness engulfed the room, she realized it hadn't been a haze – it had been illumination.

From her eyes, her *body*.

But the room she lay in was not fully dark. A soft, luminescent glow panel cast a low light onto the bed she lay upon and the soft covers she was curled up beneath.

Then there was the sound that greeted her ears, coming to her as if clearing water from them finally – a soft, regular thumping sound. She recognized it, but could scarcely believe it.

Grumbling, she slowly sat up, allowing the covers to fall from her. She still wore her same tunic and trousers, though her cloak was not present, and her traveling pack was, she noted, leaning against the side of her bed. Her vision cleared further, and she saw in the low light that the room she was in was relatively small, smaller than her bedroom had been at her parents' house in Daruun.

And the walls were made of metal.

Groaning as a headache washed over her temples and forehead, she rubbed her face, and then reached inward. *Raida?*

"*...I am here, Sira.*"

Are...are we on the Starfire?

A pause, and a sense of discomfort came from the dragonsoul, accented when the bed, perhaps even the entire ship, rocked lightly. *"...Yes..."*

Sira thought of her dream and frowned. The *Starfire* had shown up in her dream, but hadn't Kemila left the planet behind? Why were they back?

A metallic *clang-clang* startled Sira, and she looked at what she assumed was a door. "Uh," was all she managed, before it clicked and swung inward, revealing a well-lit corridor that stung her eyes, and Elaria's worried face.

"Sira?"

"I'm awake," she nodded, but then hesitated, and amended, "I think."

"You are now, I promise."

What do you mean 'now'?

"You are," Elaria confirmed. "I see that your eyes are back to normal...ish." Which Sira took to meaning they were back to their new 'normal' violet-tinge. But if that was her new normal...what had they been before?

Wait...

"What happened?" she asked. "How'd we get on the *Starfire*?"

Elaria pressed her hand to a small crystal inset into the wall next to the door, and the glowing panel above Sira grew brighter. The ship rocked again, a little more violently than last time but still relatively light, and the glow panel flickered, but then stabilized. Sira's eyes had already begun to adjust to the light from the corridor, so it didn't hurt as much, but it didn't help her headache, either. Then the elf walked in and moved to sit on Sira's bed by her feet, still under the covers. She slid her feet over to give Elaria room, who sat down gently.

And then Kemila appeared in the door.

"I came back for you, Pretty Eyes," the Captain said, folding her arms and leaning casually against the door frame. "Turns out I couldn't say goodbye to that lovely face after all."

Sira felt herself blush, despite all her desires not to, and then felt annoyed at her reaction. Turning away from Kemila, she looked again at Elaria. "How? I mean...how...well...but...that means..." She tried to ask multiple questions at once, and found herself stumbling over her words.

Sighing in further frustration, she clenched her hands into fists, closed her eyes, and took in a deep breath.

"One thing at a time, lovely," Kemila said.

"Kemila felt bad for leaving us," Elaria grinned, glancing at the Captain. "Or maybe she was just lonely."

When Sira opened her eyes, the fire in Kemila's glare actually made Sira chuckle.

"Oye, stuff it," the Captain growled over another rocking of the ship. "Yes, yes," she waved her hands around, "I felt bad, okay? And I just couldn't leave you two to wander the Deadlands in the middle of the night." She folded her arms again, but then her posture slackened, and she pushed off of the wall to walk into the room, before she bent her knees and crouched low to look Sira in the eyes. The fire in her glare was gone, replaced by something more terrifying, something darker. "As I was climbing back up into the *Starfire,* a wave of energy surged through the Universe. A wave of energy from you," she pointed at Sira. "It damn near knocked me off of the docking spire."

Sira's eyes widened.

"Please tell her I'm sorry!" Raida suddenly said in a panic, sending Sira's stomach into a swirl of guilt and panic. *"I didn't meant to hurt her, or anyone else, I didn't mean to draw them here!"*

Draw them here? Draw who here? "Wait, wait," she shook her head. "So I wasn't dreaming?"

Elaria and Kemila exchanged glances. Elaria replied, "Dreaming about what?"

She shuddered. "The *Starfire's* return, someone attacking us, and Endri defending us."

Grimaces drew down their faces, and Sira felt herself mirroring their expressions, while her stomach dropped out to the bottom of her soul. Kemila replied, "No, lovely, you weren't dreaming. You...weren't exactly at the helm through it, but it all really happened."

Sira gaped at her. Elaria explained, "It was Raida. When you lost consciousness, you stopped breathing altogether. We thought you'd died. And then you woke up, your eyes glowing like a dragon's. And...you spoke. Well, I guess," she glanced again at Kemila, "not *you.*"

More guilt welled up inside of her, opening a maw of a pit in her stomach. But it wasn't her guilt. It was her companion's. *Raida, calm down. Tell me what happened, please.*

"I had to do something," she 'heard' her own voice in her head. The dragonsoul sounded dreadful, and Sira felt her heart ache for her companion. *"I'd shocked your soul so badly that it disconnected from your body, and your body couldn't survive in that state, so I asserted control until you could recover. It's...it's all my fault, Sira, I'm so sorry, I didn't mean to, it was too much, too much power, oh my stars but I almost killed you!"*

Woh, woh, calm down, Raida, it's okay! I'm alive, thanks to you!

Shaking her head, she tried to push both conversations forward, and said to Elaria, "So...I, or rather Raida, climbed up the ladder, and..." She squinted her eyes, recalling the dream. "Someone attacked us." She shook her head, and then immediately regretted it and clutched her temples as a fresh headache washed over her. "Oof. It's all so disconnected, there's gaps in my memory of events..."

With cold dread, Kemila answered her unasked question. "It was the Darksteel Army."

Sira opened her eyes, as horror sunk deep into her. The numbness she felt before returned, and suddenly the room felt far too small as the reality closed in around her.

"They found us?"

"Aye," Kemila whispered. "If I had to guess..."

The captain trailed off, leaving it to Elaria to finish, "They must have been drawn here by Raida's pulse of magic. Which means it went further than just the local area. It...must have been felt on nearby worlds."

Raida didn't speak again, didn't apologize. She didn't have to. The remorse swirling in Sira's gut was so strong now that it nearly made her sick. She held her stomach tightly as waves of nausea washed over her.

And then the ship lurched hard, the glow panel blinking off and on several times, and Sira couldn't hold it in. Kemila must have recognized the look on her face, and she grabbed a tin pale next to Sira's bed, allowing her to empty the contents of her stomach, which wasn't much, safely into it.

She gave the Captain and Elaria credit, they didn't back out of the room at the sight, sound, or stench of it. In fact, after handing her the bucket, Kemila helped keep Sira's blonde locks from getting in the way.

"Wuh…w-what's going on?" Sira managed to ask after a minute. "W-why's the ship keep d-doing that?"

Elaria grabbed a cloth from somewhere near the foot of the bed and handed it over to Sira, while Kemila took the bucket away and set it outside of the room before coming back in.

"The Darksteel Army sent forces into the Deadlands," Elaria explained. "They must not have known exactly where we were, just an inkling, and so invaded the bazaar, while searching the outlying areas. They found us before we could escape onto the *Starfire,* and then must have summoned the Dark Dragons the instant they saw Endri defend us."

"One appeared through a portal," Kemila continued, "before we could make good on our escape. Endri…he put himself between us and that Dark Dragon. Kept the Dark Dragon from attacking us. But now the Darksteel Army holds the bazaar and the portal. And they brought reinforcements. Including airships and more Dark Dragons. We ran as fast and as hard as we could, and got lucky. *Very* lucky."

The ship lurched again, but this time Sira managed to hold her stomach at ease.

Barely.

"We made it to the nearby ocean," Elaria explained. "And found a storm. We're riding in it to stay hidden. You're feeling updrafts and maybe even lightning strikes."

"And," Kemila beamed proudly, "the only reason you're not feeling worse is thanks to my ship's design. We can stay here for a while, though," she looked warningly at Elaria, "not forever. Meanwhile their airships are just standard run-of-the-mill bladder ships. They'd be tossed around like banners in this, and the first lightning strike would breach their bladders. Both the ship's and the crew members'," she added with a mischievous wink. When neither Elaria nor Sira laughed or smiled, her grin faltered, and she cleared her throat. "Anyway, the Dark Dragons would be the only possible threat, but as I understand it, they can't sense star magic, only other dark magic, right?"

Elaria shrugged. "So I've gathered, thanks to Cardin and Kailar."

Sira felt her insides twist. *Cardin.* She had to warn him about the Dark Dragons and the Darksteel Army. She had to warn the Star

Dragons. She had to warn everyone.

Endri... "What about..." She swallowed hard and looked up at Elaria and Kemila. "Endri? Do we know...?"

Elaria's eyes dropped down, and Kemila slowly shook her head. "No," Kemila replied, "we don't know what happened to him."

The waves of remorse coming from Raida redoubled, and Sira held her stomach tightly. She cinched her throat and shook her head. *This isn't your fault, Raida. And even if it is, you've got to stop letting the guilt overwhelm you.*

"How? How can I not feel this way? I let you down, I let everyone down by thinking I could do something I wasn't ready for. And now I'm responsible for the fall of a Star Dragon, Sira! Me, my fault! He's...he's gone because of..."

We don't know that! We don't know what's happened to him!

The moment she thought it, she realized that was somewhat untrue. They didn't know much about Dark Dragons, since they'd been absent from the Universe for over three thousand years, but they knew enough, thanks to Astaria, the oldest dragon and the mother of Raida.

"I think Endri is alive," she said aloud, and met the surprised looks from the others. She swallowed hard and drew in a deep breath. "Whatever Dark Dragons have arrived will try to turn him to dark magic. Which means we have to save him."

Kemila blinked once. Twice. Clenched her eyes, rubbed them, and then stuck her pinkies in her ears and rubbed them. "I'm sorry, lovely, I think I misheard you. You wanna rescue a Star Dragon...from a Dark Dragon?"

Sira stared evenly at her. "You heard me."

The guilt rolling around in Sira's stomach abated, even if only a little. Raida asked, *"Can...can we even do that?"*

"I don't know," Sira replied aloud, and then realized they hadn't heard Raida. "I don't know if we can do it. But we have to try. There may not be much time left."

"Well, no offense," Kemila replied, "but I don't think we've the talent for such an endeavor, lovely."

Sira began to give a hot retort, but Elaria interrupted, "She's right, Sira, and you know it. Even with the *Starfire,* we don't stand a chance."

"I know," she nodded. "Which is why we have to go get the Keeper of the Sword. We have to get to Halarite."

"Oh, is that all?" Kemila laughed in an exaggerated fashion. "Here I thought you wanted us to do the impossible thing. But no, not at all, you want to do the *other* impossible thing." She planted her hands on her hips and bent over to stare nose-to-nose at Sira. "Love, they have control of the closest portal that my ship can go through. And even if I knew where another one on this world was, the only thing keeping us from a fleet of airships is this storm."

"I thought you said this ship could fly faster and higher than theirs," Sira frowned. "Was that an exaggeration? Is this ship really not all that great after all?"

Kemila's eyes widened, and she stood back up and folded her arms. Then she narrowed her eyes and pursed her lips. "Aye, this ship can do better than they can."

"So we have a choice, then," she nodded. "We either stick with you and try to get the *Starfire* safely to Halarite. *Or* Elaria and I step through a smaller portal and then come back."

"But if we did that," Elaria replied, "we'd have no way of getting in touch with the *Starfire* again, since she'd constantly be on the move."

"So then here's the question," Sira stood up, and then almost lost her balance when the ship shifted beneath her feet. Elaria and Kemila caught her, and she felt her cheeks burn. She'd meant her standing up to be more moving, to push her point. Sighing in frustration, she worked to control her stomach, and then looked directly into Kemila's eyes, while keeping her own expression resolute and hard. "Do you want to say goodbye to us again? Or do you want to help?"

Kemila looked at Elaria, and then met Sira's gaze again. She chewed her lip, then realized what she was doing and clamped her mouth shut, only to start chewing on the inside of her cheek, her mouth moving up and down with the motion.

She sighed in frustration and planted her hands on her hips again.

Sira's eyebrows rose up. "Well?"

"Oye, I'm thinking about it, Pretty Eyes, give me a minute."

"Good," Elaria leaned away from Kemila and folded her arms, staring at the captain with intent eyes. "While you're thinking about it, consider this – you won't necessarily have to come back. We get you safely to Halarite, and you don't have to run anymore."

"Until they invade Halarite," Kemila pointed out.

"So you'll have time to plan out your next move, and decide if you're going to be part of this fight or not," Elaria clarified. "And then we can come back here with Cardin and rescue Endri."

"Mmm," Kemila nodded. "It's a good plan. And besides, I dunno just how much lightning this ship can absorb before it starts to degrade our systems." As if to prove her point, the ship lurched hard, throwing them all into the wall, while the glow panels, in the room and in the corridor, shut off for a second, before finally fading back on.

The clatter of a crashing and rolling bucket drew a grimace down everyone's face.

"Crap," Kemila sighed. "That smell will linger forever…"

"So how 'bout it?" Sira asked. "Are you in?"

Kemila arched an eyebrow. "Well that's a harsh question to ask."

Sira frowned. "What?"

Grinning mischievously, Kemila shook her head. "Nothing. Nothing. Alright, lovely, you've got me, for now. In exchange for safe harbor on Halarite, I'll find a way to get you there. I make no promises beyond that."

"Deal," Sira nodded, and held out her hand.

Kemila accepted it, gave it two good pumps, and then suddenly lifted Sira's hand up and gently kissed her knuckles.

Sira's cheeks turned scarlet. "Uhm…"

"Come on," Kemila grinned. "Let's get to the bridge and figure out how we're gonna get off this rock."

Chapter 28

THE WAR ROOM

The initial assault on Archanon's wall was furious, with the siege weapons being augmented by the tens of thousands of soldiers surrounding the city – all of them throwing magic of one kind or another against the wall. From atop the battlements, Cardin watched in sick horror as the enemy ranks, already formed when they came through, fell into order – those with short-range magic approached the wall, while the longer-range casters, or those with longer-range enchantments on their weapons, stayed back.

It was as if every hell in existence were released at once.

The draw of magic was overwhelming, and at one point, Cardin even swore he felt a sort of thirst, as if the magic he had continually drawn into himself and expelled was being tapped by the enemy. Elemental, arcane, all of it burst against the wall or the shield extending above the wall.

The sound was thunderous, deafening.

The light show it created was dazzling and petrifying.

But the wall held. The *shield* held.

After only an hour of furious magic, orders were shouted down the lines to hold back amongst the rank and file. The siege weapons continued their bombardment, and as Cardin, eventually joined by the General, Reis, and Amaya, toured the battlements, they soon counted ten siege weapons. It didn't sound like much, but their size, combined with the fact that they flung giant, enchanted boulders that exploded upon impact, more than made up for the relatively low numbers.

The troops dispersed, and dozens flooded into the foothills forest, cutting down trees, carving them up with rapid efficiency, and using branches to begin to erect shelter.

Cardin understood what that meant, as did they all.

The siege of Archanon was underway.

The few farms to the east had been overrun and demolished already, the fields trampled to make room for troop tents. They never knew what happened to the farmers living at or tending to the farms, but Cardin suspected, with a sickly twisting of his stomach, that they were already casualties of wars.

Innocent casualties.

The turning in his stomach soon shifted to fury.

Once again atop the western gate, Cardin stared down at the Darksteel Army. At least two hundred were still present, and though no siege weapon faced the gate, the gathered forces took turns pelting the wall, while camp was being set up. The rest of the forces that had followed the clawed woman had dispersed out of the valley, into the surrounding farmlands and towns. They couldn't see those farms from here, concealed by the towering mountains, but every now and then, Cardin saw wisps of smoke rising into the air from the distance.

Jaw clenched, teeth grinding against one another, fists tight, Cardin spun around to face his retinue and barked, "Bring Tana and Arkad to the war room." He didn't know where they had been taken after the initial attack, but now he needed them.

He needed everyone.

Cardin could have leapt down off of the wall, and was sorely tempted to, to get away from everyone for just a minute, to let his temper stew and let himself wander further into his thoughts without risking anyone else sensing his rage.

For now, he stayed with the group, and used one of the stone stairwells cut into the bracketing mountains to descend to the main road.

The market district was eerily empty. Outdoor shopkeepers had fled, and while troops marched up and down the road, scrambling to prepare in case of a shield failure, it was orderly, and completely unlike the bustling atmosphere he was accustomed to seeing in the market.

Marching ahead of everyone else, Cardin stayed off to the side, ensuring he didn't get in the way of the soldiers at work, and his mind wandered.

Everything had changed. *Again.* It kept happening, over and over. Edilas hadn't been given a chance to breathe in over a year, not since Klaralin's return, not since the Sword of Dragons.

He wanted to blame the Sword, but now, with Edilas caught unprepared, he felt like blaming others. Sal'fe for dividing the Council when it needed unity the most. Leian for springing a marriage proposal on him and distracting him. The former Prince, for allying with a wraith and destroying the people's faith in the throne. Former general Idann Kale for going along with it and always being a thorn in Cardin's side.

There were so many more he could blame.

So many more he *should* have blamed.

Maybe it wasn't right to, but he didn't care.

Because once again, he felt like one of the few who could see what was right, what was *needed*, and now it was up to him to clean it all up. Him, the Keeper of the Sword, potentially the most powerful human on Halarite, and Prince of Tal.

Cardin had given too much of himself to protecting Halarite to let it all fall apart now.

He clenched his fists again, and he felt magic flowing through him faster and faster. He used to only store magic he needed, and otherwise not let it flow through him regularly, but Dalin and Endri had taught him the value of always pulling in and expelling magic, like they always did. It ensured that if he ever cast magic, he wouldn't need to 'recharge the well,' as more magic would already be rushing in. It let him cast more magic faster, and more powerful spells were easier to prepare.

But the strange sensation of feeling how he altered magic as it passed through him gave him a moment's pause. It felt different all of a sudden.

Tainted by his anger.

He was letting his anger grow stronger, and the ill feeling this gave to the magic passing through him made him literally stumble in his steps.

"Your Majesty?" General Vellar asked, rushing up beside him.

Cursing softly, Cardin shook his head and trudged on. "I'm fine."

He was. He had to be. They needed him to be.

It didn't matter how he really felt.

The march through the Upper City was considerably shorter and somewhat strange, with servants still working the gardens and hedges of the rich houses like nothing was wrong. Except he could *feel* their nervousness.

The retinue quickly made its way to the war room, the former Allied Council chambers now returned to its former state. A large, wooden table had been setup in the middle, as he'd requested, with an updated map of Edilas set upon it.

Soldiers had already begun to place figures surrounding Archanon on the map, indicating the siege troops around them. Other figures were spread across Tal, indicating where known Tal soldiers were and what their strengths were, but beyond that, they had no knowledge of how widely spread the enemy invasion was.

Cardin stepped up to the table and leaned heavily against it, while the others joined him so that they could all see. An everlasting torch chandelier hung above the table, providing ample illumination.

That's when he noticed that Amaya hadn't joined them, but a few minutes later, she appeared at one of the entrances, escorting Tana and Arkad. The three of them joined Cardin and the others around the table, and stared at the map for a moment.

"This is all we know," Cardin grumbled, and looked at Arkad. "We have no way of knowing where else the enemy has invaded. But you said you were on your home world when it was invaded, General Arkad. What can we expect?"

Arkad grunted at him, and then looked back at the map for a moment before he replied, "They will have opened portals surrounding or even within every major city, every capitol city on this world, or at least on Edilas. For your kingdom, I can guarantee you that they have invaded Valaras, Freemount, and Daruun."

Cardin's fists clenched again, a surge of fear and anger passing through him. He looked at Reis, who looked back with a mortified expression.

Reis had just been there. If Cardin hadn't called him here, his best friend might have been killed…

"What will they do in those cities?" Cardin asked, turning back to Arkad.

"Anyone who fights, dies," Arkad replied gruffly. "They will announce this, suppress any resistance, and then declare martial law once all resistance is squashed. They accomplish this through sheer numbers, quickly and efficiently. Once they control the major cities, they will send forces to all outlying towns and villages to assert total dominance of the continent."

Cardin nodded. "What about cities with shields? With fields that block portals?"

"Archanon," Arkad grunted. "You already know. They will lay siege, and do all that they can to breach your shield. They will not stop until your shield falls, either by force or willingly."

Cardin nodded. "So, Archanon and the Wizards' Guild are safe for now, but also unable to send troops out and about. And based on recent info from spies, the Falind capitol likewise is protected. Three holdouts. That's all we have."

He looked up towards Lassil on the map, the new capitol of Erien. Queen Leian wouldn't be safe. "Erien will fall, possibly today, depending on how hard the remnants of her army fight," he spoke with a grimace. "And Saran had no defenses to speak of. Falind installed a border of shield emitters all along their territory, but if the Darksteel Army already penetrated that border, then it would only be the Falind capitol that would be spared, and I've no doubt that Sal'fe will do nothing to protect Salas, despite his claims to do otherwise in the Allied Council."

"Even if he wanted to," Dalin stated, gripping his staff tightly and leaning heavily on it, "I doubt he can. His city will be closed off like ours, and even he won't be able to portal in or out to command troops."

Cardin nodded. "Archanon's city shields has served us well, but now they are as much a hindrance as they are a help." But then, a sly grin drew up the corner of his lip. "But now we have an option none of them have."

Everyone looked at him, and he pointed to Archanon on the map. "Beneath us lies the ancient dwarven city. I've…" He glanced around, and then realized that the time for secrets amongst allies was long past. "I've had a special project going. The ancient underground road that was supposed to lead out of the dwarven city and to the surface, I've had teams excavating it since I assumed the throne. Largely in secret, to ensure *no* one outside of the trusted circle knew about it." That trusted circle being Dalin, Sira, Reis, and a handful of others, including those working the project.

But those who didn't know about it, including Vellar, Arkad, and Tana, all looked at Cardin with concern. Even before Arkad spoke, Cardin already knew what the orc was going to say. "If they breach the surface, it will provide an avenue for the Darksteel Army to invade," Arkad warned. "You should stop it at once."

"I intend to," Cardin nodded. "However, assuming the city shield doesn't extend that far underground, we already know that the magic field preventing portals doesn't extend beyond the dwarven city's border."

Dalin's eyes brightened. "We can use portals to begin to assess the situation outside of Archanon."

Cardin nodded. "And eventually organize a counter offensive."

"Hah!"

Arkad's laugh startled everyone. It was loud, short, and almost sounded like a vicious dog bark. Cardin looked at the General, and asked with a rather curt tone, "Do you have something to add, General?"

The orc folded his arms and stared at Cardin with his one good eye. "Counter offensive? I promise you, *human,* that will never happen."

"And just what is that supposed to mean?" Reis asked, mirroring Arkad's pose.

"It means that you're too late. We all are," the orc General flung his arms out in exasperation. "The Darksteel Army is here, they'll already have assumed control of most of your major cities, and you can't communicate with the few they haven't. What counter offensive do you truly hope to establish?"

Red crept its way into Cardin's peripheral, and he clenched the edge of the table hard enough to set the wood groaning. "And here I thought you orcs didn't give up without a fight," Cardin growled.

Arkad's fist pounded the table. "I've been here before, human! Remember?"

"General," Tana's gentle hand caressed Arkad's bicep.

"You've seen into my dreams, my memories," Arkad looked at

Tana. "You know what we face. Had the *humans* acted quicker," he set an accusing glare upon Cardin, "we might have stood a chance. But now? Now the Darksteel Army is here. Now we have no chance."

"We don't *know* that, you coward," Cardin retorted.

"Coward?!" Arkad stood up to his full height, and his hand reached for his axe.

"Yes, coward!" Cardin stood up too, though his five foot ten height paled in comparison to the general's nearly seven feet. "You want to run away again, hide and hope they never find you."

The moment Arkad's hand gripped his axe handle, Tana's hand flashed, and Arkad barreled onto his backside, smacking his head against the stone floor. The guards bracketing the entrances moved to draw their sword, but General Vellar yelled for them to hold their positions.

Then Tana spun on Cardin, and hissed, "That was hardly appropriate, Prince Kataar!"

"You said you wanted to be our allies," Cardin pointed a finger at her and spoke quickly. "You said we would stand side-by-side when the Darksteel Army came. Well they're here. So what's it going to be? Can we count on the orcs or not?"

The shaman narrowed her eyes at him, her jaw set tightly. Arkad rubbed the back of his head and sat up, which was still enough for him to see over the table top and glare at Cardin. Tana gave him a warning look, and then closed her eyes for a moment. Cardin felt the stirring of magic around and within her, and he wondered what she was doing, what magic she used to 'see.' It felt like star magic, but it felt...different. Sickly, almost, at least compared to what he was used to.

Then she opened her eyes and nodded. "We cannot run. We have nowhere to run to. So we must stand with you, if there is to be hope."

"My shaman," Arkad began to protest, but was silenced by another glare from Tana. His gaze dipped low, and he sighed with a grumble, before he pushed himself back onto his feet. It had been a calculated risk, calling Arkad a coward, and in hindsight, Cardin realized he'd acted upon anger. But impugning the General's honor had worked, even if it had been Tana who had finally forced the General over.

"We've faced terrible odds before," Cardin looked at everyone. "We've mostly come out on top."

"Yes, my Prince," Vellar said, hesitancy in his voice, "However in one matter, I...I must agree with the orc General." The tone of his voice when he agreed with Arkad was one of disgust. "This is different from anything we have faced in the past two years."

"I agree," Dalin said. "In the past, we managed to bring all of Edilas together, all our forces, to overwhelm our enemies. This time, our positions are reversed. Even if all standing armies left on Edilas were able to unite, including the orcs," he nodded respectfully to Tana, "we would still be outnumbered, if General Arkad's report from his home world is accurate."

"I assure you it is," Arkad rumbled.

"I'm sure it is," Cardin replied, holding up a hand. "However, there's one enemy right now that's greater than all, and is probably how the Darksteel Army manages to work so well."

"You mean other than ridiculously overwhelming numbers?" Reis asked.

"Yeah," Cardin replied. "Lack of information. General Arkad, I'm guessing part of what they do when they invade cities, then towns and villages, is keep all citizens within the boundaries of their cities and towns? Disrupt all trade?" The general grunted affirmatively. "They want to keep any information from flowing. They want to keep everyone from organizing. So we need to resist that as much as possible, and we need accurate information to plan our next move."

He paused, long enough to ensure everyone hung on his next words. "That is why I'll be using the tunnel to portal out and visit as many places as I can, gather as much information as I can."

"My Prince, you cannot!" General Vellar immediately replied.

"I agree, that is a bad idea," Dalin added.

"Your place," Vellar continued, "is here, Your Majesty! You must be here to lead!"

"You're here to lead," Cardin said. "Lead our troops. Lead our defenses, ensure the shield stays up and the enemy doesn't somehow slip in."

"But the *city*," Vellar started, "the citizens, they..."

"They have Governor Maral," he replied. "They have city shields to defend them, they have the bulk of the Tal army. The rest out there don't. They need to see that they aren't alone, that I'm here, that I'm alive. More than that, I'm the most powerful. I'm the only one who has a chance of fighting off Darksteel soldiers if I'm discovered, long enough to escape."

Dalin cleared his throat. "With all respect, my friend, you are not yet the most powerful person here."

"But I have combat experience," Cardin replied.

"As do I," Dalin countered.

"Alright," Cardin acceded, "but you've no *known* authority to command Tal troops, or to treaty with our allies."

"Indeed," Dalin nodded, "which is why I am going with you."

Cardin opened his mouth to protest, and then stopped.

"As am I, Your Majesty," Amaya replied. "As a Guardian, it is my duty."

"Yeah, what she said," Reis quickly added.

"No," Cardin countered, and then said more harshly, "No!" when Reis began to protest. "First, the more people with me, the harder it'll be to remain unnoticed. Second, I need you two here to try to identify as many other Guardians from the King's days as you can. We'll need all the Guardians we can get. And General Vellar, you need to stay to organize the troops."

Then he looked at Arkad and Tana, and considered his options for a second. "I think our first stop should be to the Wastelands, to see if the Darksteel Army found your village. At the same time, this will allow me to deliver on my promise, and let you go back with the few prisoners of war that we have here in Tal."

Arkad and Tana both visibly let out breaths and relaxed. "I intended to ask you for as much," Tana replied.

"Then I'll start in Tal, and work my way around, until I can then try to look in on the other kingdoms. I'll return before dark."

The room was silent after that, and Cardin took that as everyone agreeing to their assignments. It still felt strange to him, commanding others, but he was glad that they kept their objections to a minimum.

"Alright, then," he looked at Dalin. "We travel light. And…" He looked the Wizard up and down, taking in his robes. "I know you rely upon the embroidered runes, my friends, but I think we need to get you something a little less…obvious."

Dalin raised an eyebrow, and then nodded. "Perhaps something from your own wardrobe?"

Cardin grinned. "If it fits. General Vellar, Amaya, please escort Tana and General Arkad to the city dungeon to release the prisoners, then take them to the entrance of the Catacombs."

"At once, Sire," Vellar bowed, and then escorted the two orcs out.

"The rest of you know what to do," he said to the others. "We have a lot to do, and maybe not a lot of time to do it in. So be swift, be sure. This is the time to be at your best." Nodding, he finished, "Dismissed."

Chapter 29

NEGOTIATIONS

Xavien was a master manipulator.

Kailar hadn't quite appreciated just how talented he was before, but now, as she listened and watched him, she began to see the subtle signs more clearly, signs that Reyla had caught and pointed out to Kailar before.

It didn't help that from the get-go, the Lord of Corlas was enthusiastic about full membership in the Darksteel Empire, just as Reyla had warned her. It was fear that compelled the Lord, that much Kailar recognized, but even still, to give up the autonomy their fledgling imperium had just attained seemed foolish, even for a fearful Lord.

Xavien seized upon the Corlas position, promising help in rebuilding, pointing to the steadfast, mobile fortress that had preceded Xavien's arrival as evidence – that fortress supposedly had been constructed in less than two days, thanks to the near-endless supplies and labor that the Darksteel Empire enjoyed.

Kailar doubted the construction timeline very much. Just having to let the mortar between bricks cure would mean construction couldn't possibly have been accomplished that fast.

Unless…

Unless they used magic.

For the twentieth time that day, Kailar glanced at the fortress, feeling the rising burn of frustration in her gullet. If the fortress was enchanted, she had no way of sensing it. No way her dark magic could tell, except perhaps in close proximity. Maybe then, she could feel the push of magic against the emptiness she maintained inside.

Drawing herself back to the conversation at hand, she caught something she had missed before – a look between the Lord of Corlas and the Lord of Edingard.

A look as if asking, 'is this right?' Not as in morally, but as in…

No, she shook her head, and then caught herself. Kailar glanced at Xavien, but if he'd noticed her motion, he did not react. *Why would they collude over something like this?*

Especially when Edingard had been a stout critic of the promises of the Darksteel Empire all morning.

But Reyla was playing middle ground. Not committing to joining the Darksteel Empire, nor pushing for the treaty. Kailar watched her Empress, saw how Reyla observed with a keen eye, and challenged the Corlas Lord as frequently as she did the others.

And the Navitas? They stood like a sentinel over the proceedings, offering little in the way of conversation.

Until Xavien asked directly, "Tell me, Lord Navitas…" He hesitated, and Kailar knew that to be for show and nothing more. "Do you have a name to yourself, Lord?"

Cracking and screeching echoed from the Navitas as its body shifted and changed, its head arching down and its glowing eyes fixing upon Xavien. "Not in the manner which you would consider it. My identity, my moniker is pure energy, pure thought."

"I see," Xavien nodded thoughtfully. The Navitas gave nothing back, no segue for the Ambassador to continue, so he forged his own way, "May I simply address you as Lord Navitas?"

"That would be appropriate," the Navitas replied simply, "for I represent the interest of all Navitas in this matter, and my voice speaks for all."

"I see," Xavien again nodded thoughtfully. "Tell me, then, where do you stand on this matter? I confess, when I arrived this morning, I anticipated merely a treaty with Devor, but now the issue seems divided between a simple treaty and full membership in the Darksteel Empire."

"So it would seem," the Navitas replied. Kailar couldn't help but grin when it said no more. She knew just enough about them to recognize that the Navitas was intentionally giving Xavien little to work with, as a way of showing how little they thought about the Darksteel Empire. As if their Empire were beneath the Navitas.

"Yes, so my question," Xavien pressed. "Do the Navitas wish to join? If the other Lords join, would you go along with it?"

Golden eyes turned up to look at Reyla, then settled back upon Xavien. "Our understanding of humanoid customs and laws would indicate that it is not for the lords to decide. It is for the Empress."

Once again, the Navitas had avoided answering Xavien's question directly, and Kailar had to feign scratching her nose to hide the grin that drew up the corner of her mouth.

Xavien managed to remain patient, on the outside, and went along with the Navitas's answer. "Indeed, that is true. However, if I understand *human* precedents," he looked at Reyla, "you will listen to your people's thoughts and opinions and take them into consideration?"

"Of course," Reyla nodded. Which put her in a corner, Kailar suddenly realized. Reyla looked up into those glowing, golden eyes, and said, "Lord Navitas, your thoughts on this matter are important to me, and if you have any thoughts or opinions, I welcome them. As do we all," she motioned to the assembly.

The Navitas stared at her, and then at Xavien. Kailar saw a subtle shift in its eyes, a brief glance towards her, before they settled again upon Xavien. "We ask only to be left alone." Kailar tensed. Her bringing the Navitas in on the negotiations had been a move to curtail Xavien's influence, but now…now the Navitas were admitting the worst thing they could. "We ask for independence and autonomy." But then, the Navitas stooped low, as if to look Xavien in the eye. "If that requires us to defend the land, to defend our neighbors and uphold their wishes, then so be it."

Kailar's panic subsided, and again she had to hide a smile. *That* was more like it.

Xavien, however, took it in stride. "And if the rest of the Imperium should decide to join our Empire?"

Again, the Navitas's eyes darted at Kailar, and then at Reyla. "As long as we are left peacefully alone, we will abide by your wishes, Empress."

Part of Kailar cheered the Navitas on for addressing Reyla, not Xavien. Unfortunately, the rest of her felt despondent. Once again, by asking the right question, Xavien had steered the conversation into a victory.

If the Imperium sided with joining the Darksteel Empire, the Navitas would allow it. They wouldn't care. As long as they weren't bothered.

That left the ball entirely in Reyla's court, Kailar realized, and Xavien knew it too. The smug look of victory in his eyes was subtle, imperceptible, but the way he turned to look at the assembled Lords and leadership, his straight back, his jutting chin, his sharp eyes…oh he knew it. He knew he'd just obtained a vital victory.

And then his eyes settled upon the Lord of Corlas again.

A short time later, as stomachs began to growl, Reyla halted all discussions. "I think it would be best if we recessed for a short midday meal."

Kailar couldn't have agreed more – despite the growing unease she felt, her stomach rumbled hungrily.

"Yes, now is an appropriate time to break," Xavien nodded his assent and stood. "However, I would like to request the recess to last the remainder of the day." That shocked Kailar more than anything else that had been said so far. Xavien had seemed eager, even *hungry* for the meeting to continue, to spout all about the wonders and ease of life for the Darksteel Empire, and how Devor could share in these luxuries.

Reyla was likewise caught off guard, but she recovered quickly. "For what reason, Ambassador?" she asked evenly, only mild curiosity in her tone.

"I admit I did not expect today's meeting to last so long, or to take the turns that it has," Xavien replied. Kailar narrowed her eyes, suspicious doubt crawling its way through her chest. "I must report to my superiors. I promise to return in the morning."

Standing to meet Xavien's posture, Reyla said, "Very well. Unless anyone objects?" She surveyed the table, and then looked up at the Navitas.

"I may remain another day," the Navitas said. "Perhaps two at the most, and then I must return to the Collectors."

Kailar wondered about that. Did the Navitas need to recharge every so often, or was it simply eager to return and continue efforts to repair the Crystalline Peaks?

"I am certain we shall conclude our business by tomorrow," Xavien flashed a smile at the assembled.

Reyla narrowed her eyes. "That would be a surprise, to be honest, but we shall see how things proceed. In any case, shall we meet at the same approximate time tomorrow?"

"Yes, of course," Xavien nodded, impatience in his tone and gestures. "Now, if you will excuse me," and without waiting for an answer, he spun on the spot, and marched towards the mobile fortress. His retinue nearby snapped to attention, and then joined him, leaving the Lords of Devor with their Empress.

That act left Kailar stunned. All of his patience, all of his influencing, all of his subtleness suddenly gone. Had something changed?

It left most of the assembled Lords looking equally stunned. Except, strangely, for the Lord of Edingard. She looked entirely nonplussed about the Ambassador's change in behavior, and in fact stood up and said through a smile, "Well, then, where shall we eat and discuss this interesting meeting?"

Reyla and Kailar looked at her wearing equally steep frowns.

"He deceives," the Navitas spoke quietly. "He conceals."

Startled by his statement, Kailar, and everyone for that matter, gaped up at the Navitas. But it wasn't looking down at them. Instead, its eyes followed Xavien and his entourage.

When no one asked for clarification, and the Navitas didn't volunteer anything else, Kailar asked, "Who does? And what does 'he' conceal?"

Turning its multifaceted body back to Kailar, the Navitas stooped low, hovering over the table, and said quietly, "The Ambassador. He conceals communication through magic."

Kailar blinked in surprise. "He…what? What do you mean?"

"I felt someone connect to him moments before you suggested the recess," the Navitas said to Reyla. "Someone communicated with him through the currents of magic, and he in turn responded."

It was something Kailar didn't even know was possible, and as her eyes searched Reyla's, she saw that the Empress likewise did not know. If there had been a connection, there was no way for Kailar to have sensed it, not through dark magic. Had anyone else sensed it?

As she searched the eyes of the Lords or the General for any hint that they had likewise sensed it, she stopped upon the Lord of Edingard. Who looked up at the Navitas with venom in her eyes.

There was something strange going on. Something that centered not just around Xavien, but upon the Lords of Corlas and Edingard. She couldn't think of his name. She didn't know *any* of the Lords' names. She hadn't bothered to learn them.

But now, thinking about matters, remembering how the Lord of Corlas had looked to the Lord of Edingard as if seeking approval, Kailar decided she was long overdue in getting to know the Lords of Devor.

Chapter 30

FALLING STARFIRE

Yesterday, Sira had flown for the first time, astride Endri, and had seen what the world looked like hundreds of feet in the air. Today, she discovered a new perspective – seeing a storm from above.

She gazed out in wonder from the bridge of the *Starfire,* taking in the blanket of white spread out before her. It wasn't anything like she expected. Within the storm had been darkness, broken by the occasional flash of lightning, and turbulent winds, and rain. But up above?

Peaceful. Quiet. Pure, white fluff as far as the eye could see. Except to the ship's starboard side, where they could see a very defined, very peculiar hole in the clouds. Kemila had called it 'the eye.'

"This is incredible," Sira breathed.

"Aye, it is," Kemila said, her face lit up in a beautiful smile. "I'd forgotten how much I loved showing people views like this for the first time. To see your reaction, to see those pretty eyes light up with life…"

Sira looked up at the captain, and when their eyes met, Kemila sighed contentedly. "Aye, that's the look…"

Blushing, Sira turned away again, and stepped ahead of the helm to get a better view.

Instead of flying out of the storm, Kemila had chosen to bring the ship up above it to get their bearings.

Almost immediately, a crew member using a telescope spotted an enemy airship, its bladder painted pitch black, but they had stayed far away from the actual storm itself. If the enemy had noticed the *Starfire* popping up out of the clouds, it made no move to indicate as much, and Kemila took them higher.

"Reverify seals," Kemila ordered. It was the third time she'd called that order out, and Sira frowned.

"Seals check out okay," a crew member manning a station to port reported. "Pressure is steady."

"What seals are you talking about?" Sira asked.

"Pressure seals," Kemila replied, somewhat nervously. "See, the higher we go, the less air there is, less pressure. We're high enough now that we had to seal up the ship good and tight, to keep pressure and air in, otherwise we might start to slowly suffocate."

From beside Sira, Elaria added, "It's one of this ship's advantages. Being constructed the way it is, with metal and rotors, we can go higher than enemy airships and not suffer what's known as altitude sickness."

"Um," Sira blinked. *Raida...any chance you can translate for me?*

But the dragonsoul didn't reply. All she felt coming from Raida were waves of guilt, slow and steady, unyielding. Raida refused to forgive herself for her mistake.

Elaria narrowed her sunset orange eyes, and then said, "You've been hiking in the mountains, yes?" Sira nodded. "Ever climbed to a tall peak, and felt like you couldn't catch your breath, no matter what?"

Thinking back to some of her patrols in the Ilari Mountains, Sira replied, "I've not climbed to mountain peaks before, but our patrols across the Ilari Pass during the Orc War sometimes ended up with Warriors collapsing from exhaustion, even if they've trained just as hard as the others. I certainly had a hard time breathing on that pass."

"Same concept," Kemila nodded. "Only we're several times higher than those mountain passes. Alright," Kemila's voice changed, and Sira recognized it as a tone of command, loud and confident. "If they'd noticed us, we'd probably have a Dark Dragon on our collective cute asses, so we're going to move out. All hands maintain high-altitude conditions, but be prepared to man battle stations."

After a few acknowledgements from the crew, Kemila turned the wheel, and the *Starfire* rolled left, or rather to port, and turned. The carpet of fluffy-looking white beneath them shifted, and Sira watched in complete fascination. Kemila rolled them out of the turn shortly after, and far ahead, hazy on the horizon, she saw red and green mountains jutting up from the deep blue sea – land.

And then Sira couldn't help it anymore. She started asking questions.

For the next half hour, as the tips of land grew closer, Sira asked Kemila about the ship, about how things worked. Kemila was extremely patient and seemed to revel in explaining new terms and new technology to Sira, even when Sira had to ask her multiple times about the same thing.

She learned about the 'consoles,' and that the button-looking discs on them were actually called *buttons,* which she found more amusing than she perhaps should have, while half the bridge crew chuckled at her amusement. She learned that the buttons and levers controlled various parts of the ship through means that she didn't quite understand yet, but she realized was similar to how the gates of Archanon worked – magic signals sent through a series of pulleys, or other such systems. Literal magic, according to Kemila, as magic was the heart of the ship.

Surprisingly, a lot of the terms Sira learned were similar to what she had learned aboard the Sea Wisp on their voyage across the oceans of Halarite. Port, starboard, bow, aft, all of them familiar, but with some new ones, such as 'dorsal' meaning top of the ship, and 'ventral' meaning bottom.

When things grew more technical, when Kemila tried to explain how the *Starfire's* rotors worked, Sira had a very hard time keeping up, and at one point felt completely and utterly lost. But Kemila was patient, and did her best to familiarize Sira enough that she at least had an idea of what commands Kemila was giving, what they meant.

And even Raida finally started emerging from her shell. She suggested a few questions to ask Kemila, and even helped explain how wings worked, and that the rotors were basically fast-moving wings to keep the ship aloft.

Sira only understood about half of it, but that was more than she had known before today.

And then the lessons came to an end, when it was time for Kemila to perform some 'daring maneuvers.'

Land wasn't far now, crystal clear rather than hazy, red mountains jutting up, covered in green jungle growth. Beneath them was pristine, blue water, and a handful of puffy, low clouds.

"Alright, here's the plan, just so no one freaks out too much," Kemila said. "We need to dive fast, so that no one spots us. To help conceal our dive, I'm going straight for that bit of cloud beneath us."

Sira walked forward to get a better view, and looked down...*way* down at a long, stretched out tuft of cloud, whose shadow was easily visible below, and made it look like the cloud was close to sea level. *Uncomfortably* close.

Glancing back at Kemila, Sira swallowed back a growing sense of unease. "Sounds like you've done this before," she said, hopeful.

"Heh," Kemila grinned, "Nope." Sira's stomach sank. "But the *Starfire* should be able to handle it no problem."

She said 'should,' Sira thought, her innards fluxing enough to make her regret having eaten a snack earlier. Hopefully she wouldn't need another bucket...

"Once we come out beneath the cloud," Kemila continued, "we're gonna fly as fast as we can into the nearest valley, and then we can finally slow down."

Gaping at the captain wide-eyed, Sira tried to keep her fear from her voice when she asked, "Slow down? What...if we can't turn fast enough into the valley?" She'd failed utterly, her voice almost sounding like a squeak.

Kemila shrugged. "If that becomes a problem...well, then our problems are over." She flashed Sira a charming smile, and then pointed a finger over to the port side of the bridge. "You and Elaria better grab on to something."

Sira saw a metal pipe attached to the only bare spot of wall on the bridge, just behind the windows. She glanced at Elaria, and without a word, both of them rushed over.

Kemila touched something on the small console to her right, cleared her throat, and then her voice echoed throughout the ship. "Attention all hands. Brace for extreme maneuvers. Monitor all seals. We're about to put the *Starfire* through her paces, but I'm confident. I'm confident in her, and I'm confident in all of you. So let's stick it to those Darksteel bastards one more time, eh?"

A couple of cheers erupted on the bridge, but they quickly controlled themselves, and set to work.

Kemila gave her full attention to the helm again, and then she pushed the wheel forward. The *Starfire* nosed down, and Sira had to hold on as all of a sudden, the deep blue sea filled their entire forward view, and that strip of cloud beneath them. Her stomach didn't want to stay with them, and she felt it rise up, and threatened to empty out. She cinched her throat tight and held on for dear life.

The engine pitch dropped a little, but mostly Kemila kept the propellers going enough to give them a speed boost, and the wind started whistling louder and louder, even through the *Starfire's* hull. They picked up more and more speed, and it was the strangest sensation, to have her feet wanting to fall *forward,* but her stomach struggled to catch up.

The cloud started to grow noticeably larger, *closer,* faster and faster, until it filled their entire view. The wind was howling now, and the metal structure of the ship groaned and creaked. And then they dove, nose-first at gods knew how fast, into the cloud.

"This is amazing!" Raida shouted in her head, elation mixing with Sira's terror to create the most exciting feeling she had ever felt.

"Hold on!" Kemila shouted, pulling back on the wheel.

Suddenly gravity returned to normal...and then became stronger. And *stronger,* weighing Sira down onto the deck of the ship, almost forcing her knees to buckle. She clutched tighter onto the bar, and she swore not even a few seconds passed before they zoomed out beneath the cloud, the water rushing up towards them at alarming speed!

The ship's nose tilted up. The engines grew louder as Kemila put as much power into the rotors as she could. The ship's hull creaked and groaned some more, and Sira feared the whole thing would come apart even before they hit the water.

Finally, with only feet to spare, their dive stopped, and Kemila leveled the ship out. Gravity returned to normal, but the wind still howled as the ship sped out from beneath the cloud, towards the rocky shores and mountainous peaks ahead.

Sira's heart thundered in her ears, and her ears *hurt.* "Pressure breach somewhere on deck two!" a crew member called out.

"Happened at about a thousand feet."

"We'll fix it later," Kemila growled out, her hands clutching the wheel tight, her teeth clenched.

Suddenly something popped in Sira's ears, and the pain she felt vanished. She sighed in relief, and looked back at Elaria behind her, whose grip on the bar was even tighter than Sira's. Elaria's jaw was taut, and her eyes intense as she stared ahead.

Sira looked ahead again, the mountains startlingly closer. The *Starfire* was moving fast, faster than Endri had taken them, faster than Sira had ever gone before in her life.

But the valley wasn't a straight shot. It dug into the mountains to the left, and they were coming at it at a sharp angle.

So Kemila rolled the ship to port, and pulled hard. Gravity played tricks on Sira again, and she gripped the bar with increasingly sweaty fingers. The ship didn't seem to want to turn, as they raced across the rocky shore and over the jungle canopy of the valley. Her nose pointed to port, true enough, but the ship kept heading towards the cliff face.

Seconds spanned eternity, and Sira's eyes grew wider and wider, terror and excitement mixing.

Something scraped the ship's hull, the top of a particularly large tree, startling her. But finally, with aching slowness amongst such incredible speed, the ship started moving to port, and while they might have grazed a couple more treetops, they made the turn, and started slowing down, fast enough that gravity seemed to pull Sira forward again.

The crew visibly relaxed then, with more than a few sighs of relief.

"YEAH!" Sira shouted, her excitement and glee bubbling up over now-vanished fear. "My gods, that was incredible!"

Her enthusiasm was contagious, and it spread to the rest of the bridge, as crew members cheered and patted one another on their backs. But most of all, everyone looked back at the helm, at their captain, with newfound appreciation.

The tall, lithe man, who was always near Kemila on the bridge, stepped up next to her and patted her on the shoulder. "Outstanding piloting, my captain," he grinned.

She grinned back at him, and her shoulders, bunched up with incredible tension, visibly slackened. "Alright, everyone, settle down," she called out soothingly. "We've passed one hurdle. Now we just need to-"

The ship lurched, hard, slamming Sira's torso into the pipe she was holding onto.

"Dammit!" Kemila shouted, struggling to keep the *Starfire* on course. "Where'd that fire come from?"

The ship lurched again, and Kemila turned them hard to port. The valley wall suddenly filled their view, but then she pulled it back around to starboard, enough that the other valley wall became visible. "There!" one of the bronze twins called out, pointing to an airship cresting over the valley wall to starboard. A blast of blue-white magic lanced out from the ship, and splashed against the windows, creating a tiny crack, but otherwise failing to breach the hull.

"All hands to battle stations," Kemila shouted, while leveling them out and pulling up. "Take them down before they can alert anyone else!"

Several more blasts of magic lanced out from the enemy ship, and Kemila turned the ship to port, and then starboard again, trying her best to avoid enemy fire, but mostly failing. Then Sira realized she wasn't trying to avoid enemy attacks, just trying to ensure they couldn't attack specific parts of the ship.

Oh gods, she thought with a start. *What happens if they hit those rotor engine things?*

"We fall from the sky," Raida replied with a mental gulp.

Sira started to let go of the bar to approach the helm, but when the ship lurched and she nearly lost her footing, she grasped at it again. "Captain, what can I do to help?"

"Nothing, pretty eyes," Kemila replied. "Trust me, we've got this!" Then, though she didn't say it loud enough, Sira swore she saw Kemila mouth, "I hope…"

Sira cursed, but the curse was lost in the panging of multiple strikes on the ship's hull. The enemy ship flashed before the forward view briefly as Kemila turned again, only they were almost on top of the ship!

And then it flashed by on their port side, with enemy magic attacks slamming into the glass and hull, creating new cracks in the glass.

"Damn, their casters are strong," Kemila cursed. "Did anyone get a hit in?"

"Two strikes on their hull, one on their bladder as we swept by," a voice

called over the air. Sira blinked, and then remembered Kemila talking to the whole crew from her console. Someone somewhere else must have had access to the same thing. *"But they aren't out of the fight yet."*

"Alright," Kemila called into her console. "We're gonna hit them from above this time, so I won't have to maneuver so much. But I'm not slowing down, either, just in case they brought friends. Get ready!"

"We're ready!" the crewmember replied.

That's when Sira realized that the jostling of the ship has ceased. And she knew then what had happened. When they had buzzed by the enemy ship, they weren't just moving fast, they were moving *up,* and the enemy ship's lighter-than-air bladder prevented their Mages, or whatever their equivalents were called, from shooting up at the *Starfire.* All Kemila had to do was stay above, which considering how fast and maneuverable the *Starfire* was, probably wouldn't be difficult.

Sira watched in awe as the captain turned the wheel and manipulated the throttle rapidly and efficiently. Crew members at consoles stood up and peeked over to look down, and shouted the enemy ship's position.

"Port side, slow," someone called.

"About to overshoot!" another called.

"That's it, Captain, we've got 'em!"

"Alright," Kemila spoke into her console. "Get ready, I'm gonna juke it over to starboard."

"Ready, Captain!"

After only a breath, Kemila yanked the wheel over, and the ship lurched underfoot, throwing Sira into the bar she was holding so dearly onto.

And then Kemila jerked the wheel back in the other direction, leveling them out quickly. "Fire!"

Sira never heard anything, not through the hull of the ship, but she felt the waves of magic unleashed from below. Crew members must have gone onto the open deck below, and were probably leaning over the railing to unleash hell on their enemy below.

And then the torrent of magic ceased.

"All hits confirmed, their bladder is deflating rapidly!" the voice cheered. *"We've got 'em, Captain!"*

"Alright, hold on, we're going back down!" she said, and turned the *Starfire* back into a nosedive.

"Hey, what gives?" Sira asked while holding on for dear life.

"Need to get below the mountain peaks again," Elaria explained. "Before another ship sees us, or worse, a Dark Dragon."

Sira's eyes bulged. In all the crazy action, she had forgotten about the Dark Dragons. The *Starfire's* enchanted hull could withstand some hits, obviously, but certainly not an assault from a Dark Dragon. Kemila had gambled when she brought them up above the mountain peaks for a quick kill.

The ship leveled out, again playing tricks with gravity, and Kemila eased back on the throttle. The pitch of the engines eased off and drew down low, settling into the more familiar cruising tone. Sira held her breath, waiting to hear a report of a dark blot in the sky.

Seconds ticked by. The bridge crew was silent. Kemila kept a firm grip on the wheel, and slowly scanned back and forth ahead of the ship for any hint of another enemy ship.

A minute passed. Two. The tension eased out of Sira's shoulders. No more attacks. No more jostling of the ship.

They were safe. For now.

"Alright," Kemila sighed. "Time for phase two." She slouched just a little at the helm, but then stood up tall and looked over at Sira and Elaria. "You two ready to do your part?"

The duo exchanged looks, and then nodded together at the captain. "We're ready," Sira affirmed. "Let's go home."

Chapter 31

GLIMMER OF HOPE

Cardin and Dalin waited by the entrance to the catacombs. It had been mostly repaired after a meteorite had collapsed it, but there was still evidence of the strike. Still a crater in the ground. New grass had grown in, softening the blow, and Cardin marveled at that.

Marveled at how nature continued on, renewed life from death.

The magic of nature.

Then he looked up at Dalin, and grinned as the former Wizard shifted uncomfortably. Dalin donned a pair of black trousers, a little too short in the legs for him, and the strapped-on leather shoes he wore did little to cover his rather bony ankles. A gray tunic topped with a dark blue (of course) vest completed the Wizard's outfit, and it looked strange on him. Comical, even.

The first time ever that Cardin had seen Dalin outside of Wizard's robes.

Dalin tugged at the vest, adjusted the black leather belt over it for the hundredth time, and then hefted the weight of his leather backpack, before gripping his staff tighter.

Looking at Cardin, the former Wizard narrowed his eyes. "Amused, sir Prince?"

"Mildly," Cardin grinned. "You look fine, Dalin. Stop fussing."

"A Wizard does not fuss," he replied, jutting his chin out. Faltering a moment later, he amended, "Even former Wizards."

"Indeed," Cardin arched an eyebrow. Then he looked at Reis, who was meant to see them off. And Cardin knew why. His friend normally was of greater cheer, and would have joined in the teasing banter. But now, Reis just stared at the entrance to the catacombs longingly. With his heart heaving with regret, Cardin said, "I'm sorry, my friend."

Reis blinked, looked at Cardin. "Hm?"

"I know you wanted to see her," Cardin continued, clasping a firm hand on Reis's shoulder. "But I need you up here."

The 'her' he referred to was Anila Kovin, former guardian of the secrets of the Covenant, and now steward and leader of the expedition in the dwarven city. She was also somewhat of a love interest for Reis.

At least, I think she is.

Frowning, Cardin realized Reis and Anila had never officially declared their relationship, and he wondered if their past conflict meant that they wouldn't.

Shrugging one shoulder uneasily, Reis replied, "I know. You're...not going to take her with you, are you?"

"No," Cardin shook his head. "As valuable as her skills and powers would be, I need to keep the scouting party small."

Visibly relaxing, Reis sighed and nodded. "Then at least she's safe. I'll see her again."

Squeezing Reis's shoulder, Cardin caught his friend's eye and said, "Yes, you will. So stay alive while I'm gone, okay? No heroics. The General will keep the shield up. You keep your wits about you. Don't let the Darksteel Army get an upper hand."

"I won't," he nodded stoutly. "I'm too stubborn for that."

Letting out a short breath of a laugh, Cardin replied, "Damn right, you are."

Only a few moments passed before he saw General Vellar and about a dozen and a half soldiers escorting a large group into the open field. The ruins of the Grand Sanctuary towered behind them, and Cardin watched with no small amount of intrigue. A view he never thought he'd see.

Over thirty orcs, walking as free men in the streets of Archanon. The escort was largely for their protection against the citizenry of

Archanon, who still feared orcs and would look for any outlet for their fear and anger amidst the siege of Archanon, and as if to punctuate his thoughts, the violent 'BOOM' of another siege burst against the shield forced Cardin to clench his jaw. But the former prisoners themselves were under control, thanks to the tiny, powerful woman leading them.

Tana was a force of nature, and Cardin was glad to have her as an ally, even if he didn't fully trust the orcs.

Not yet.

Reis and Dalin turned to watch the approaching group together, until Vellar led them across the broad, mostly flat grassy area, and came to a stop before Cardin. Tana, Vellar, and Arkad stood at the front, and Vellar bowed. "Prince Kataar. The orc prisoners as ordered, shackle-free."

Cardin nodded. "Thank you, General. You and the other soldiers are dismissed."

Vellar glanced at Tana, at Arkad, obviously uneasy about following Cardin's command. But he did so anyway and shouted orders for the troops to follow him.

Once they marched away, Cardin turned to Tana and Arkad again, and forced a friendly smile onto his face. "Shaman. General. The journey to the bottom will take some time. It is important that no one wanders from the group, as branch tunnels twist and turn below, and it is easy to get lost in."

"I understand," Tana spoke in her raspy voice. "I swear that my orcs will follow our lead."

"Good," Cardin looked behind her at the group of orcs. They were the more typical types he was used to, long-armed, long-legged, muscular, hairless, mottled, and they wore only basic leather thongs and chest pieces. In short, seemingly uncivilized.

Virtually none of the more intelligent orcs, donning Darksteel armor and weapons, had allowed themselves to be captured during the war. Only the 'rabble,' as he once called them, were ever captured. *I shouldn't think of them that way anymore,* he thought. *Now, they're allies.* He looked at Arkad, and barely contained a shudder. *All of them.*

"Well, then, if you'll follow me," Cardin motioned to the Catacomb entrance, and then led them down into the darkness.

The journey through the Catacombs was uneventful, but Cardin was grateful for that, and it made the natural stench of the orcs almost bearable. The constant thumping of the siege weapons attacking the shield faded, until they were so deep that they could no longer hear it. That was long after they passed through the Tomb of the Ascended.

Everlasting torches were setup along the entire route, guiding them, until they came to the once-hidden narrow entrance into the dwarven city. The traces of the enchanted door could still be felt all around them, but it had been dispelled over six months ago, and nothing prevented them from walking through the tunnel, and into the wide-open, ancient, abandoned city of the dwarves.

Cardin led Tana and Arkad out onto the platform overlooking the city, and watched as the two orcs gaped in awe. A line of floor-to-ceiling stone columns were illuminated leading all the way to the capitol building at city center, and then from there to the tunnel being cleared on the opposite side. Cardin knew that the pillars were being regularly powered by Anila's magic, as was an enchanted device atop the dwarven capitol that kept the giant arachnid-like kiklar away.

The dwarves had carved every building out of stone, and as far as Cardin could tell, they had done so from the existing stone in the cavern. None of the buildings looked like they had been assembled from materials brought in from the outside world. The outer edges of the city were comprised of smaller buildings packed in tightly, while further in, the buildings grew taller, higher, more elaborate, indicating a clear hierarchy in their ancient society. An inner wall separated the richest from the rest, similar to Archanon's Upper City wall.

"Welcome," Cardin said, sweeping his arms out, "to the ancient city of the Dwarven Empire."

"Incredible," Tana mouthed. "This looks as grand as our once greatest city, Akaida."

Cardin keyed in on that name, never having heard them mention it before.

While Cardin led them down the curved stairs carved into the outer wall, Tana and Arkad gaped up at the ceiling. Arkad, he noted, eyed the thick webbing, once pristine and white, now covered in dirt and dust.

"Something other than dwarves lived here," the General

remarked.

"Aye," Cardin nodded. "They were known as kiklar."

Arkad and Tana's heads whipped around, looking at the webs, looking all around, before focusing on Cardin. "The kiklar? And they let you and your people move freely in the city?"

They had reached the bottom step, and Cardin paused to regard them. He scratched the back of his neck and winced. "Not exactly. The dwarves once built an enchantment that drove the kiklar away. All we had to do was give it some energy to work with, and it cleared them all out."

"Ah," Tana visibly relaxed. "So *that* is the regular pulse of magic that I feel." And then the orc shaman stepped off of the last step, touching the ground of the dwarven city. And instantly collapsed to her knees.

Something else, not the enchanted anti-kiklar device but another source altogether, pulsed. Cardin felt magic thrum in the ground, rumbling like a sword charged with magic would vibrate. Without even trying, he could *see* magic suddenly swirl and gather all around Tana, seeping up into her body, into every nook and crevice of her soul.

"Tana!" Arkad bellowed, falling to his knees beside her and holding her. "What is it? My shaman?" His yellow-red eyes looked sharply at Cardin, hate and rage seething from him. "What have you done?!"

The other thirty orcs growled along with their general, and Cardin realized that Tana's hold over them had faltered. He stepped away from Arkad, and the thirty who could pounce on him from the stairs. Behind the thirty, Dalin, still atop the platform at the entrance, readied his staff.

"No!" Tana breathed, holding up one hand. "It is alright. I'm fine…" She swayed, even on her knees, but the gathering magic ebbed in its torrential flow. And much of the gathered magic within Tana began to seep back out into the world, carefully controlled by the shaman.

She was overloaded, Cardin realized. "Too much magic," he said aloud. "Too much rushed into her…"

Looking up at Cardin with strained eyes, Tana's eyes glowed bright red, almost completely occluding her irises. "What…what lies beneath? What great power thrums below the deep earth of

Halarite?"

Cardin's jaw tightened. He'd been reaching for the Sword, he realized, so he consciously lowered his hand. The thirty orcs settled, but he could see tension in their muscles. They were ready to defend Tana at a moment's notice.

But Tana's words. The sensation of magic, welling up from a powerful concentration. It could have been only one thing.

Should he tell her? Tell *them*? The orcs, once enemies, now uneasy allies...could he trust them with perhaps the greatest secret beneath Archanon?

The truth about the Order of the Ages.

The truth about the Cronal.

That which had nearly destroyed everyone and everything.

And had left his father an empty shell.

The glow within Tana's eyes receded, and after a prolonged gaze, they finally returned to normal. Cardin held his eyes steady upon her, debating, deciding. Was it his place to tell her?

Who else's would it be? You're the Prince of Tal, and the Keeper of the Sword.

Sighing, he held a hand down towards Tana. Arkad looked ready to rip it off, a deep, rumbling growl escaping his throat. Tana gave the general a sour look, and then accepted Cardin's proffered hand. She was as light as a feather, and hefting her onto her feet took as much effort as lifting a down pillow.

Less, even.

Drawing in a deep breath, Cardin looked up at Dalin, who no doubt hadn't heard Tana's question, but could have guessed. The former Wizard stood ready to defend against the thirty orcs, but they paid him little attention. Their eyes were focused upon their shaman.

Looking towards the capitol, which was barely visible over the smaller dwarven structures, Cardin sighed. "Walk with me to the capitol, and I'll tell you," he beckoned.

And that was how Tana, last Shaman of the Orcs, learned about the Cronal, and the access it provided to the Great Library. All knowledge. All *power*.

It was also why Cardin barely sensed a presence in time to stop another catastrophe.

Head whipping around, Cardin shouted, "Anila, no!"

A shadow wavered on the edge of the light. The procession came to a halt, and Tana and Arkad followed Cardin's eyes. From the shadows emerged a figure, clad in a dark cloak and holding a long, thin, curved sword, which Cardin had finally learned recently was called a katana.

Anila Kovin lowered her weapon, and then pulled her hood back to reveal jet-black hair that only helped hide her in the darkness, and blazing blue eyes. She stood half of a head shorter than Cardin, but she was pure muscle, pure power.

She was also more than she seemed. A half-human, half-Wizard hybrid whose powers exceeded a Mage's, but fell far short of a Wizard's.

And somehow, despite lies and mistrust, she had become a trusted adviser to Cardin, and the only person he knew he could leave to a project as vital as protecting the secrets of the Cronal.

"Prince Kataar," she bowed before him, before slipping the curved weapon into its matching scabbard. "I...wasn't sure what was going on. Orcs?"

"Our allies," he nodded. "Anila Kovin, this is the shaman Tana, and General Arkad."

She regarded the orcs coolly before she gave them the same respectful bow that she had just given Cardin. "My apologies for nearly attacking."

"Apology accepted," Tana returned the bow.

"Status of the dig?" Cardin asked.

Stepping further into the light of the nearest pillars, Anila replied, "Tunnel clearing is on-going. If I had to guess, we are halfway through to the surface."

Nodding, Cardin set his jaw for a moment, and then said, "I need you to halt all efforts immediately."

Raising an eyebrow, Anila asked, "May I ask why?"

Exchanging a quick glance with Tana and Arkad, Cardin drew in a deep breath, and told Anila about the Siege of Archanon.

Anila took the news quite well. While Cardin filled her in on all that had happened, they closed the distance to the dwarven capitol, passing through one of the arched entrances into the 'upper city,' and up the steps to the capitol. A few of the workers under Anila's leadership were present, and were startled by so many orcs suddenly streaming into the capitol square, but Anila calmed them down, and then ordered them to get back to the work site and order the men and women to cease work.

As they ascended the stairs, Tana's brow scrunched further and further down.

Until they walked into capitol building's main hall, where the workers had setup camp. The glow panels in the hexagonal room were lit up, though a few were 'burned out' from damage when Reis and his party had fought the guardian statue.

The same statue that had somehow been moved away from the central platform and the stairs leading down into the Cronal chamber below. It, or rather pieces of it, were pushed up against the wall opposite of the room's front entrance, leaving the stairwell clear for access. Two soldiers guarded the stairs and were startled upon seeing first their Prince, and then Tana and Arkad enter. The thirty orcs were left outside, under Dalin's watchful eye.

And like a moth drawn to a flame, Tana walked, slow step by slow step, towards the stairs, as if drawn.

"Tana," Cardin rushed towards her while the Warriors drew their swords. "Stand down!" he barked at them. "These are our allies, now. Tana," he stepped in front of her and hunched down to look her in the eyes. "What is it?"

"This...Cronal," she tried looking over his shoulders. "Its power. Its knowledge. Its connection to everything, everywhere. It draws me in..."

Cardin looked back towards the stairs. He knew the danger, and a creepy feeling crawled up the back of his spine. Regardless of whether or not he could trust Tana, he knew it was dangerous allowing *anyone* access to the Cronal. A literal spiritual library of everything that was, is, and could be. Infinite knowledge. And wraiths anxious for a ride into the real world.

A lithe hand touched his shoulder, and then squeezed with surprising strength. He looked back at Tana, and she looked into his soul. Not just his eyes, but he *felt* her penetrate his soul, for a brief moment. His mental and magical defenses reacted instantly and shoved her out.

But whatever she had been looking for, she found it.

"My dear Prince Cardin," she smiled lightly. "The answers you seek so desperately are already before you. Or rather, *beneath* you."

Tilting his head to one side, Cardin asked, "What do you mean?"

Raising her eyebrows, or rather the skin where eyebrows would have been on a human, Tana released his shoulder. "Your father."

He faltered, and stood up straight, towering over the tiny orc. "What about him?" he asked, his voice tight, his words crisp and warning.

"Whatever his current predicament is," she said. "Does it involve the Cronal?" Cardin's stomach roiled uncomfortably, but at the same time, something inside of him clicked. He nodded in answer. "The Cronal, as you have described it to me, temporarily separates a soul from its body. His soul is *here*, Cardin Kataar. I feel it, as strongly as I feel your own." He blinked in shock, and looked up at Anila, who stood beside the towering orc General. "I know it must be his because of how similar your souls are to one another, and I know this – if you wish to revive your father, you *must* bring him here again. You must create a bridge between where your father's soul is, and your father's body."

Hope kindled. A rushing sensation bubbled up inside of Cardin, and he turned towards the stairs, gaping down at them.

His father. Still alive. All he had to do was...

Breach the shield on the Wizards' Guild and bring him here.

Cardin's fists tightened, hard enough that even through leather gloves, he could feel the pain of his fingertips digging in.

Finally, after so long trying to find answers, trying to find a way to bring Draegus Kataar back, he had a solution. But he had no way of carrying it out.

Gods dammit, he thought, and ground his teeth together.

Maybe, just maybe, Cardin could have found a way through the Wizards' shield. If he'd learned how to open portals using dark magic. He didn't know that for sure, but if it let Kailar open a portal within Archanon, it stood to reason that one could pass through a shield, too.

But Cardin was Prince of the damned kingdom of Tal. Too busy to practice magic, to learn how to use dark magic. Too busy to save his father. Too busy to save anyone, when it was his responsibility to save *everyone*.

Keeper of the Sword.

Prince of Tal.

He wanted none of it.

He just wanted his father back. And then, he would no longer have to rule over the kingdom. Draegus knew politics better, had served side-by-side with King Beredis for years.

They all needed Draegus Kataar to return.

But how?

He hung his head. For all he knew, the Wizards' Guild had already fallen.

Which brought him back to his mission. He had to return the orcs to their village, and then he had to scout. Daruun, Valaras, Falind, Erien's cities. But most importantly, he had to check on the Wizards' Guild.

He had to be sure his father's body was still safe.

I'm coming, Father, he vowed. *Just hold on…*

Chapter 32

ESCAPE

The rest of the voyage aboard the *Starfire* went without incident, and Sira's stomach was ever so thankful. The ship flew through the jungle valleys with a slow, deliberate pace, and it took them over an hour to finally reach their destination.

Which was to say, the ship came to a 'hover,' as Kemila called it, one valley over from the portal apparatus. From there, they lowered a rope ladder, and Sira and Elaria descended into the jungle below.

The sun was already marching towards the horizon, and it was swelteringly hot beneath the jungle canopy. Creatures cawed or howled into the thick, moist atmosphere, and the smell of flowers mixed with decay and soil stung at Sira's nose, threatening a resurgence of nausea.

From there, they trudged. That was the most appropriate word Sira could think of. In the undergrowth, wary of both flora and fauna, they *trudged* through the valley, heading for the ridge that would lead them over to the next valley.

Much like the jungle on Halarite, this one's floor was a mixture of tiny, six-inch-tall ferns and six-foot-tall ferns that they had to navigate around or under or through. Blurs of creatures swung across vines or branches above, but Sira only ever caught glimpses of them, brown shapes zooming for just a moment, but hidden the moment Sira tried to look directly at them.

"Uh, do we need to worry about some animal attacking us?" she asked Elaria.

The Dareann Elf shrugged. "Not that I know of." Sira relaxed, tension easing from her shoulders. "But if all of my time exploring other worlds has taught me anything, it's to expect the unexpected." Tension returned instantly.

"She sure knows how to make us feel better," Raida remarked.

Oh good, your sense of humor is back.

The dragonsoul let out a wave of renewed guilt at Sira's remark. *"I'm sorry..."*

Stop that, Sira lectured, furrowing her brow, and then looking self-consciously at Elaria. Her hiking companion didn't seem to notice Sira's sudden change in expression. *Stop feeling guilty. You made a mistake, it happens. The best thing we can do now is face the consequences of that mistake together.*

"But how am I to learn from my mistake if I don't think about how it was made?"

Thinking and learning about a mistake is one thing. Dwelling on the guilt you feel is another. Sira thought of Cardin, of the crippling guilt he had felt after refusing to join the Warriors' Guild. Sira had dwelt on her anger, he on his guilt, and their relationship, and any chance at a friendship for nearly ten years, had suffered.

Now, did he feel a similar guilt? She needed him, now more than ever, didn't she? As she struggled to regain her sense of self over Raida's presence, as she continued her leave from the Warriors, feeling more and more worthless and useless and...

Hmm. Which of us is truly feeling guilty?

The question had been meant to compare herself to Cardin, but the surge of emotions from Raida made her realize she'd thought that 'aloud.' And then giggled at that turn of phrase, eliciting a strange look from Elaria. Sira shook her head. "I'm sorry. It's just...a strange thing, having another voice in your head all the time."

Elaria's scrutiny softened. "I have no doubt of that."

The duo, or perhaps it was more accurate to consider it the *trio*, continued on through the jungle. Sira peered at her physical traveling companion, and wondered before finally asking aloud, "In all of your travels, have you ever encountered anything like Raida?"

Considering her question for a moment, scrunching her nose up thoughtfully, Elaria shook her head. "Not *exactly* like your situation, no. The closest I came was to meeting a species on another world who shared their body with another, physical creature, in a sort of symbiotic relationship."

Sira arched an eyebrow. "Symbiotic? I know that word, but it's been used to describe certain animals helping one another survive, or providing for one another without intending to."

"Same thing," Elaria nodded. "You see, the larger species, the...I suppose you would call it *humanoid* species, named the Kesla, were born without a companion. It was only once they came of age that they were given a Primsa."

Sira frowned. "Primsa...the name of the other species?"

"Indeed," Elaria nodded. "Though I never got to see one, they are tiny, but intelligent, and usually live for generations, hopping from one host to the next as one host died and another came of age. When they do, their personalities...I guess you could say they merge, from what I was told. Experiences of the younger Kesla blend with the Primsa, and according to what I was told, neither personality remains solely the same, they blend to become someone new, a culmination of the Kesla and Primsa."

Sira shuddered. "They...they do this voluntarily?"

"Yeah," Elaria paused in her stride, her head jerking to one side. Sira halted, her stomach jerking along with her, and together, she and Elaria scanned the jungle. The elf must have heard something that Sira had missed.

Moments passed. Then minutes. But nothing else happened.

After she was satisfied that they were alone, Elaria waved Sira on, and they set out again.

Lowering her voice, Elaria continued, "They looked forward to it. This one young little girl was only a year away from receiving her Primsa, and she was giddy over the idea of finally gaining that experience. Hated how awkward she was in her youth. She told me she would benefit greatly from the wisdom and experience of the Primsa that her great grandmother would give her."

Sira frowned. At first, when Elaria had begun to describe the Kesla and Primsa, a sense of unease began to worm its way into her stomach. Was that sort of 'blending' happening to her and Raida? Was she losing who she was, and Raida was losing *her*self, to become a one, whole, new personality?

But what of the advantages? The experience and wisdom that Sira brought, coupled with the soul of a dragon, whose insight didn't just include an entire village of far-ranging species, but the sage wisdom from the essence of the Universe itself. Wouldn't that be worth the price to pay?

Is it worth losing who I am to become something more?

"*I don't know,*" Raida replied, even though it hadn't been a question meant for the dragonsoul to answer. "*I…I'm still a child, as far as dragons go. I'm not sure I'm able to truly contribute much to this…relationship of ours.*"

Sira frowned. "Elaria…what about when a Kesla blended with a newly-born Primsa?"

Elaria smiled. "They would become something new *together*. Gain wisdom together. Become *more,* together. Instead of blending an old personality with a new, they were able to make wholly new discoveries about themselves *together*. It was at least as revered as the blending of an old Primsa was."

Then, Elaria's smile hardened, and she stopped again, before suddenly ducking. Sira followed suit an instant later, soundless.

After several more moments passed by, she finally heard what had set off Elaria's senses. Boots trudging through the jungle.

A lot of them.

Waving for Sira to follow, Elaria kept herself bent low and quickly traversed over to a dense growth of ferns. Sira followed, eyes searching, ears alert, magic senses augmented by Raida. She sensed points of magic not far ahead, and when she stopped next to Elaria, she tapped the elf's shoulder, pointed in the direction she sensed the surge of magic from, and held up five fingers to indicate that she sensed the presence of five magic-wielding persons.

Elaria nodded, and then they waited. Sira closed her eyes a moment, and asked Raida, *Can you mask our presence in magic?*

"*I think so, but you won't be able to sense them anymore, either.*"

Better than them honing in on our stronger-than-usual presence.

"*Right. Okay…*"

And then the world felt dark. Empty. As if Sira's connection to magic had been severed.

Moments later, the approaching footsteps halted. Now they would have to rely upon Elaria's superior physical senses to know if they were in danger. But at least the approaching group, whom Sira assumed were Darksteel soldiers, couldn't sense her or Raida anymore.

Distant murmurs of voices reached Sira's ears, and she strained to listen, but couldn't make out the words. Elaria screwed up her forehead in concentration and listened, while Sira waited impatiently. Were they in danger?

But Elaria's hands never disappeared into her cloak, never emerged with her curved, exotic daggers. And after a minute, the voices stopped, and the footsteps continued.

Except that the footsteps started moving *away* from them.

Elaria's shoulders visibly slackened, and she slowly let out her breath. Sira relaxed, and sighed.

Looking at Sira, Elaria whispered, "Maybe we should keep conversation to a minimum."

"Yeah, I got that impression too," Sira replied.

Elaria tilted her head and listened for a minute or two, and then nodded before standing up. Sira followed, and the trio continued into the jungle, slowly following the patrol that had come so close to finding them.

The rest of the hike was spent in relative silence, with only Raida to keep Sira company. Even then, they hardly spoke to one another, fearful of diverting attention. As time went on, and Sira tried to grow accustomed to the lack of magic senses, she started to suspect that it was an even bigger strain on the dragonsoul.

Dodging patrols was relatively easy for them, especially with Elaria's superior hearing and vision, and only once did a patrol get too close for comfort. That was also the only time Sira was able to see their adversaries, and she noted that while four of the patrol members were large and fully armored, the fifth, the leader, wore more cloth than metal, and lacked a helmet. That man was an elf, though far paler than Elaria, almost frost-white-skin and blue-white eyes.

Raida, is it a universal truth that all elf variants have superior hearing and sight?

The dragonsoul never replied, and she wondered how long her companion could keep up the veil.

But thankfully, the elf marched on with his retinue, and Sira and

Elaria remained undiscovered.

They finally made it to the jungle's edge. The sun was getting low, the days and nights shorter on this world, and soon she and Elaria would be cast in the shadows of the mountains. Which meant their timing was almost perfect, but they didn't have time to thoroughly scout and plan.

Coming out of the valley, they had climbed up a little to one side to get an elevated view of the portal platform and the docking spire. There was a single airship docked at the spire, a large, bulbous, black-skinned bladder with a black-painted, wooden ship beneath that looked like a repurposed sailing ship.

Looking down at the platform around the giant portal apparatus, Sira counted at least six men and women wearing Darksteel armor, and another cloth-bearing person, but not elven. It was a species she didn't recognize. Taller, eyes glowing bright orange, visible even in broad daylight from a couple thousand feet away.

Elaria said, "That tall guy is going to be the real threat." Then she jutted her chin up towards the airship. "Same with whatever reinforcements they might have on the ship. We'll need to take them both down at the same time."

Recalling the battle on Stella against the invading Darksteel Army, Sira concurred. "Agreed. I don't see any of their heavy hitters, so we're lucky in that regard, but I'll bet there's some on the ship. Plus we saw at least two in the patrols. So we need to hit fast and hard, and get the *Starfire* through."

For a moment, Elaria was silent. She looked at Sira, and smiled. "I don't know how, but until just now, I'd somehow forgotten you were an experienced military commander."

A small smile edged Sira's mouth, a mixture of pride and embarrassment swirling through her stomach. She wasn't an active Warrior now, and her future as one was still questionable.

But the mentality, the training, that was all still there. While most of her experience was in overt actions, such as patrols meant to be seen and frontline battles against orcs, she had training appropriate to their current situation, and she knew enough to extrapolate.

Clasping her hand over her white-dyed longsword strapped to her left hip, Sira said, "I'm better able to hit distant targets with more power. Your daggers make you more of a threat in close range. So we sneak over to the platform. You get up and take out the caster, and the moment you do, I hit the airship's bladder. I rush in, help you finish off the other guards. Then, while you open the portal, I signal the *Starfire*."

Elaria nodded. "Sounds good. What could go wrong?"

Sira grimaced and felt a distinct sinking sensation in her stomach. Groaning, she said, "Gods, don't say that…" Elaria grinned mischievously. Sira paused, and then looked Elaria up and down before she asked, "I haven't asked, but your armor…it looks worn and torn. Will it still work?"

The elf's grin shifted down into a grimace. "Not as effectively."

Nodding, Sira asked, "Can you still make yourself nearly invisible?"

Considering Sira's question for a moment, Elaria scratched at her cheek, and huffed out a breath. "Yes, but not as effectively. The armor channels that ability, helps me refine and maintain it, and with the damage," she glanced with a grimace at a tear on her left arm, "it'll make it ten times harder to maintain. I'll only have a few seconds of near-invisibility, and from there it'll degrade fast."

"Still, that'll let you get in close."

"Aye, it will," Elaria nodded, and then closed her eyes. "Sorry. Been spending too much time with Kemila." She stooped low, and passed in front of Sira, saying, "Come on, the nearest patrol is still moving away. We need to hit them now."

They maneuvered through the jungle quickly and silently, Elaria somehow knowing exactly where to step to minimize their visibility from the platform and keep the noise they made to a minimum. Sira was in awe of the other's ability, but she knew from watching Cardin that experience went a long ways, and Elaria had spent a lot of time exploring other worlds, no doubt sometimes having to avoid being seen.

In fact, Sira wasn't even sure how old Elaria was. She looked no older than Sira, but it was a well-known fact that the more powerful a person was with magic, the slower they aged. Plus she swore she remembered Elaria mentioning that elves lived for millennia.

They reached a spot of brush and trees closest to the platform and peeked around one of the tree trunks. One of the guards stood at the edge, surveying the jungle to their right. Elaria held her hand up to hold Sira back, though Sira didn't need that, and they waited, patiently, cautiously.

Sira had participated in guard duty all of her life. She knew how boring it was. Knew how easily distracted guards could become. So she knew to expect…

Sure enough, the guard yawned, and turned away from the jungle, walking away at a leisurely pace, until he was no longer visible.

Waving her hand to follow, Elaria darted out from cover, and Sira followed, doing her best to precisely follow the elf's tracks. They reached the stone platform and pressed against it. Sira's heart thundered in her ears, adrenaline surging and helping her stay alert.

But she needed magic. Soon.

Raida, get ready to drop the veil. I'm going to need all the magic I can get in a minute.

The dragonsoul didn't reply, but Sira trusted her companion.

Once they were sure the nearest guard hadn't heard their approach, Elaria led them along the wall to the left, heading closer to the control mechanism and the spire, where they'd last seen the lead guard standing.

They circumnavigated the platform, and when they turned the corner and started towards the Deadlands, the ground pitched down, the better to conceal them from those upon the platform. The airship loomed overhead now, the bladder filling much of the sky, but it was eerily silent. Sira had grown accustomed to the constant whirling of the *Starfire's* rotors and the sound of her engine running. The Darksteel airship was deathly silent.

Finally, they made it to the next corner, and the stairs that they had taken down from the platform only a day ago came into view.

As one might have expected, two more guards that they hadn't seen before stood ready at the bottom of the steps, facing out towards the Deadlands and the Bazaar.

And from their vantage, Sira got her first really good look at the Deadlands since the Darksteel Army had arrived.

Six Darksteel airships hovered over the bazaar, and black smoke billowed up into the air. The giant creatures she vaguely remembered seeing while under Raida's control were far in the distance, now disconnected from the siege machines they had been towing. The air was hazy with red dust, but she imagined an army of soldiers were also present.

The Darksteel Army had seized control.

She squinted into the distance, trying to catch a glimpse of a Dark

Dragon, or of Endri, but neither were visible from her vantage. It was possible, even probable that if Endri was still there, he'd be secured either on the far end of the Deadlands, where he had first brought Sira in, or he would be secured down in the bazaar.

A sick feeling twisted in her gut, and she looked at the black smoke. That couldn't be from a burning corpse, could it? Bodies didn't usually burn pitch black, not even orc bodies. But what about a Star Dragon's?

No, she thought furiously. *Endri is alive. He has to be...*

Turning her attention back to the guards, she looked at Elaria, and motioned towards them, then pointed a finger at Elaria, and motioned her hand up and over.

The elf seemed to understand and nodded. The base of the platform was not a perfectly flat wall, but had an angle to it, albeit a steep one. But for someone like Elaria, it proved no challenge. She stepped back, produced her two signature daggers from somewhere under her cloak, and then half-ran, half-scrambled up the side of the wall, incredibly silent. As soon as she reached the peak, Elaria vanished from sight.

Sira silently drew her sword and started to edge along towards the stairs, getting closer to the guards. She looked up at the airship and nodded.

Alright, Raida, get ready!

Again, no word, and she felt her stomach lurch. If this went wrong...

The sound of ringing steel. A cry of surprise, a gurgle, and a thump.

NOW, RAIDA!

The world flourished back into her senses, life suddenly pressing in, along with magic, *power.* Sira drew it in as rapidly as she could, surged it into her sword, and just as the two guards turned towards the sounds from above, Sira thrust her sword straight up, and unleashed a purple-hued arcane attack. It pierced the airbladder, bottom and top, sizzling through the material with little resistance.

And then it exploded, with a loud *THUMP,* sending a shockwave and instantly followed by a deafening roar. The gas in the airship had been flammable, and her attack had ignited it, she realized. As the ship heavily listed away from her, she heard the groan of bending metal, the docking spire resisting the ship's sudden movement, and then the *SNAP* of mooring lines breaking.

There wasn't time to see what happened to the airship next, the guards had drawn their swords, saw Sira, and came at her.

"I've got you!" Raida said, and Sira felt the rush of magic into her arms.

The first enemy reached her, and she held up her hand, channeling the energy into a shield. The Darksteel soldier's blow glanced off of the sword, barely registering as an impact on Sira, and then she pirouetted around and used her magically-charged sword to try to slice into his chainmailed torso.

Experience with Darksteel-armored orcs allowed her to expect the sword to not cut, but the discharge of magic made her opponent stumble, and she pressed the advantage, thrusting her sword tip into his exposed armpit, and out through his shoulder, back into his neck. Grey blood spurted. *That's new.*

She'd managed to position her first opponent between herself and the second guard, so when she withdrew her sword, she gave the man a kick, and sent him stumbling into his partner. Then she rushed in, pressed her advantage, and while he tried to throw his partner off, she thrust into his torso with all her strength and power.

Only the barest tip of the sword penetrated his armor, but it was enough. She unleashed more pent-up magic, and without any armor between it and her opponent, it blasted his chest to a crumpled mass, and he blew backwards, arched over the steps, and landed on the other side.

It should have shocked her. Even for a Mage, she'd just used more power in three seconds than most Mages could cast in a minute. Not number of attacks, but sheer *power,* enhancing her sword, her strength, her shield.

She knew she had Raida to thank for it.

And then the airship crashed, a good quarter of its fiery remains smashing onto the corner opposite of Sira, and the rest collapsed into the jungle. The repurposed wooden ship that had hung beneath it never stood a chance, and neither did the crew.

Ringing steel on steel drew her attention, and she hopped over the edge onto the stairs and ran up. Taking stock in an instant, she saw the lead guard by the apparatus that controlled the portal had his throat sliced open, and another guard was already dead beside him.

And Elaria was twisting and turning and ducking amongst five other guards.

Sira rushed in, and though one of his companions tried to warn him, Sira took the guard with his back to her by complete surprise. She sliced another weak point of his armor, behind the knees, which drove him down to her height, and allowed her to swing hard at his neck. It wasn't an easy task, beheading a person, but with magic enhancing her sword's edge and her muscle strength, she easily accomplished the task, and moved on to the next opponent.

There was a lull in their movements, surprise at her attack, and Elaria took advantage of that, leaping up at another guard and sinking her daggers into the base of his neck.

Sira ducked under the swing of a wicked-looking mace, past another man's battle axe, and then she unleashed a pinpoint blast upon the axe-wielder, sending him sprawling away. Then she faced the mace-man, and disarmed him a moment later, literally, before finishing him.

Elaria and Sira faced the remaining standing guard and closed together. To his credit, he tried to use a shield to block both of them at the same time, but they worked past it and ended him.

A surge of magic was all the warning Sira got, and she grabbed Elaria and spun her around to put Sira between the elf and the axe-wielding opponent, just as a blast of fire engulfed her shield. Heat seared all around them, scorched the platform, but didn't harm a hair on Sira's or Elaria's heads.

The instant the flow of fire ceased, Elaria darted to the side, and threw her dagger. It twirled through the air and bounced harmlessly off of their opponent's hastily-erected magic shield.

Sira turned, rushed, with Elaria beside her, and unleashed a blast. His shield absorbed it, but the attack was strong enough to physically push him back. Elaria unleashed her own magic attack, and it again shoved the man back. Sira did again, and then finally they closed the gap, and the duo descended upon him mercilessly. He survived for maybe two seconds longer after that.

They stood over his dying form, breathing heavily. Fatigue began to edge at Sira, the amount of magic she'd been throwing finally getting to her and Raida, but they had succeeded.

Now they had only moments. "Go!" Sira shouted, and looked around, spotting Elaria's deflected dagger. "I've got your weapon, get that portal open!"

Horns sounded from the jungle, and from the bazaar. The rest of the enemy knew they were under attack. It was no surprise. They'd have an infinitesimally small window to get the *Starfire* to safety before a Dark Dragon made its way over.

There just wasn't time.

Except, as Sira picked up Elaria's dagger, she frowned and looked towards the Deadlands.

She felt…something strong. Powerful.

Warm.

Endri.

She hadn't felt his presence before, but she felt it now. He was alive. And still a Star Dragon.

There was still hope.

Twisting around, she charged up her sword, and unleashed the brightest flare of magic she could towards the setting sun. The signal for the *Starfire* to get moving.

Not waiting to see when they popped up over the ridge, Sira ran to Elaria's side, and observed as the elf planted her hands on the apparatus. It was a simple stone desk-looking thing, a *console* if she used the same terms that Kemila had taught her, except there were no buttons, no dials, no levers.

Just a flat surface, and two quarter-sphere impressions, which Elaria's hands were pushed into. They glowed, and Sira felt the surge of magic from her friend. Her brow furrowed in concentration.

Then, her eyes darted open. "Dammit," Elaria muttered, and looked at Sira. "Did the meteorites take out the portal structure near the necromancer city?"

Sira blinked. "Uh, I don't know? We haven't sent an expedition back to the city yet. Been a bit busy."

"I can't make a connection to it," Elaria grit her teeth. "Which means I'm going to have to do this the hard way."

Elaria closed her eyes and looked like she had to focus harder, so instead of bothering the elf, Sira asked Raida, *What's she talking about?*

"As I understand it," Raida replied, *"A Great Portal like this can open a large portal anywhere, but unless you connect to another Great Portal, it takes more will, more effort to do so. And precious seconds that we might not have…"*

Sira glanced back towards the Deadlands and noticed that all five of the other airships were turning towards them. She searched the horizon for a dark form, but still no sign of a Dark Dragon…

Whirling blades and the sound of engines turning drew her attention in the opposite direction, and she felt a thrill of elation as the *Starfire* descended rapidly from the mountainous jungle off to her left. The ship would circle around and, if Elaria could get the portal open in time, would pass through without slowing down.

They were only moments away from their first pass.

"Elaria..." Sira warned.

"I know, I know," Elaria grumbled. "I'm trying. It's not as easy..." She trailed off.

The *Starfire* passed the portal, rushing out towards the oncoming airships. Those gas-filled behemoths were slower, sure, but after experiencing an attack from one, Sira was sure there was only so much damage the *Starfire* could take, and they couldn't just pop up above the ships to handle them, not with Dark Dragons lurking about.

Where are they? While glad for the slow response from Dark Dragons, she still worried...

Something in her stomach turned sour. Something in her *soul* turned sour. It hit her like a hammer, and she staggered, then collapsed to one knee.

It wasn't her that felt it.

It was Raida.

"Oh no," Raida murmured in her head.

An explosion of emptiness. Words that should never have been used together, but that was the only way Sira could think to describe it. Then it crawled, slunk, stole up into her gut.

Something was very wrong.

Darkness.

Emptiness.

For a brief second, a flicker of energy combated it. The portal opened. The hum of engines filled the air, and with a whoosh of wind, the *Starfire* plowed through the open portal at full speed.

Sira looked up just as Elaria pulled her hands away from the apparatus, and the portal closed. When the elf looked down at Sira, horror crossed her face. Sira thought, *Why is Elaria's face turning violet?*

Then she knew. Her eyes must have glowed again.

And Raida spoke through her voice. *"Darkness. Darkness has infected Endri."*

That was why no Dark Dragons had risen to attack the *Starfire*.

They had been focused on corrupting Endri.

And now Endri was fighting the darkness.

"We have little time left. The Keeper must help!"

Sira swallowed the overwhelming sickening sensation back down into her stomach. "Alright," she spoke with her own voice. "Alright. Elaria, get us back to Halarite." She looked into her friend's eyes with an intensity she had never felt before. "Now!"

Elaria grabbed the other dagger from Sira's hand, stowed her weapons, and then turned on the spot to face towards the ruined docking spire. Magic rushed through her being, and Sira felt it, more clearly than ever before, a distinct rush of light in a burgeoning darkness.

The shaft of light appeared, and then Elaria's hands pulled Sira up. She supported Sira and walked her over to the portal, and together, they passed through.

The temperature change was subtle, but the sudden lack of humidity was a shock, and Sira felt instantly cool.

She blinked, getting her bearings.

They'd come somewhere familiar. Two-story walls surrounded them, made of stone and brick. A courtyard of trampled grass, wooden training dummies on one side, some with arrows sticking out of them.

And shouts. Shouts of combat. Ringing of steel. Pulses of magic.

Battle.

They were in the Daruun Warriors' Guild complex, the designated arrival location for portals in Daruun, after the assault against Elaria and Gilrin a few months ago. Protected. Safe from angry citizens.

Now under siege. A portion of the wall exploded from the inner city, and Sira instinctively put up a shield, allowing the pellets of stone to bounce harmlessly off them.

Looking up on the walls, she started.

There wasn't a single Warrior manning the defenses.

Just Darksteel soldiers.

The Darksteel Army was defending the Daruun complex.

But from what? From whom?

The freshly-blasted hole on the wall had left a cloud of dust and dirt in the air, but it rapidly cleared. And an instant later, a familiar, blood-red flash drew her eyes.

Cardin Kataar, Prince of Tal and Keeper of the Sword of Dragons, rushed into the complex, and blasted a section of wall where the Darksteel soldiers had retreated to.

Then he looked at Sira and Elaria, before doing a double-take.

"S...Sira?!"

Chapter 33

DEVASTATION OF DARUUN

Cardin's head continued to swirl, his stomach turned, even when he, Dalin, and the orcs reached the tunnel. Anila rushed ahead, further into the tunnel. It gradually curved upward, towards the surface, towards the light. The 'road' was made of cobblestone, ancient and enduring in the shadows of darkness.

Reports from the dig over the past few months had revealed that not *all* of the tunnel upward had collapsed, but much of it had, and it had taken considerable time and effort to break the collapsed rock up and move it into the city.

Even though he was tempted to simply send the orcs on their way and not follow, an urgent desire to move on pressing him, Cardin knew he had to make sure the orc settlement was still safe. And of all those present, he was the most likely to hold out against overwhelming enemies until he could escape.

"Dalin," he turned to his friend. "I'll go first, if you'll open the portal."

The former Wizard arched an eyebrow at Cardin and looked ready to protest. But then he hissed out a patient breath and nodded. "Very well."

"If you don't see another portal immediately come back, you'll be safe to come through," Cardin said to Tana and Arkad.

Dalin stepped further into the tunnel, further away from the incredibly deep shield that prevented portals. Cardin wondered about how that field dug so deep into the Earth, and yet the magical physical shield didn't.

While Cardin's friend summoned a portal by planting his otherworldly staff into the ground and projecting his power outward through it, Cardin narrowed his eyes.

The wall itself had been enchanted thousands of years ago, meant to ensure the wall survived any bombardment. But the shield that extended above the wall? That was a later addition. In fact, it had been added three thousand years ago, by Klaralin during his occupation.

Same with the field that blocked portals, he had thought. Was it even older? Was it a result of the Cronal instead?

Power coalesced before them, and a blue-white shaft of light appeared. Dalin nodded in satisfaction, and turned to await Cardin.

The Keeper of the Sword pushed his thoughts about the wall away for now. Klaralin was dead, and whatever his motivations had been, whether or not he had known about the dwarven city below and the dangerous secret, his machinations had long-ago failed to come to fruition.

Cardin reached back with his right hand and grasped the hilt of the Sword of Dragons, and then he marched forward into the portal.

The transition was staggering, from damp coolness to sweltering heat, from dim torchlight to full morning sunlight.

And the orc village was before him. Peaceful. Safe. Not a single Darksteel soldier in sight. Smoke rose from countless campfires and kilns and forges, but nothing that shouldn't have been burning was alight.

The enemy hadn't found the orcs yet.

Sentries noticed the portal and Cardin emerging alone, and they marched towards Cardin. He stepped aside and waited. By the time the sentries were within spitting distance, they had their hands on their weapons, ready to demand what Cardin was doing there alone. Seconds later, Tana, followed by Arkad, emerged. The sentries drew up short, fury on their faces turning to surprise, then relief.

Tana and Arkad stepped aside, and soon after, more orcs followed. Arkad barked orders at the sentries to find food and shelter for the new arrivals, but no sooner had he done so, than did multiple other orcs in the village notice what was going on, and they rushed over to help.

It was a stark contrast, seeing the villagers next to the prisoners. The prisoners in their simple leather thongs, the villagers in their refined, well-tailored clothes.

It drove home the realization that the humans had grossly mistreated the orcs.

And yet, Tana was willing to stand with humans. Maybe that fact, and that the orcs followed her despite the bad blood between orcs and humans, was a testament to the power she exerted over her people.

The question was, could Cardin do the same? Not just over the people of Tal, but all of Edilas? All of Halarite?

Not likely.

But Tana's reasoning was valid, even brilliant. There was no way the orcs could stand alone against the Darksteel Army, they'd already failed once. And there was no way the humans could, either.

He narrowed his eyes, an idea sparking in his mind. Realization. Memories spilling into the forefront of thought.

Memories of a ship adrift at sea, and a lone scout in her hold. Memories of an ancient, advanced city, and the undead filling it.

Halarite was home to more than just humans. More than just orcs.

Focus, he reminded himself. *One mission at a time.*

Once the last orc was through, Dalin followed, and the portal closed.

The two pairs faced one another, and Cardin nodded. "I will begin my scouting mission at once, and either myself or someone I know and trust will return to your village soon, once we know more about what's going on. We'll begin to more closely coordinate after that, and maybe, if we're lucky, figure out a plan."

"Until then," Tana nodded. She and Arkad turned as one and followed their rescued companions into the village.

Cardin then turned to Dalin and clenched his fists. Dalin once again arched an eyebrow. "The Wizards' Guild?" he asked Cardin.

"Yeah," Cardin replied, and turned on the spot to summon the power necessary for a portal.

"I recommend we approach from the forest," Dalin said, his voice cautioning.

"I know," Cardin replied. "Can't very well show up in the middle of the enemy army, can we?"

Even though a part of him, the part growing with anger and rage at those who trampled all over their world, wanted to attack full-on. Destroy as many of the enemy as they could. Make them pay for what they'd done.

But not now. Not yet.

The portal winked into existence effortlessly, Cardin's anger fueling his magic. And then he followed Dalin into it, traveling from the Wastelands all the way to the north, and the towering, swaying trees of the northern Daruun Forest.

Though the Darksteel Army had scouts patrolling the forest west of the rebuilt Wizards' Guild complex, they were easy enough for Cardin and Dalin to evade. This section of the forest, thankfully untouched by the meteorites half a year ago, was too far north for Cardin to be completely familiar with them, but he'd spent enough time in the wilderness that navigating it and using it for cover wasn't too difficult.

This far north, the trees were taller and broader, and shaded more of the floor from sunlight. There wasn't nearly as much undergrowth here, but that didn't matter so much. There was plenty for their needs, and the terrain was hilly enough that they had enough time to hide the moment they sensed anyone or anything approaching.

Within half an hour, they made their way to the edge of the forest, and they snuck to that edge for a closer look. As expected, a massive army, not quite rivaling the one surrounding Archanon, was arrayed around the domed magic shield of the Wizards' Guild.

That many troops here, more around Archanon, and who knew how many more elsewhere, but Cardin reasoned that similar units were deployed all around Edilas. The size of the Darksteel Army was staggering, and he couldn't begin to comprehend how they kept such an army fed and watered, or armed and in good repair.

It was a juggernaut. Unstoppable.

Eight siege weapons were arrayed against the shield, and each one took a turn at unleashing enchanted boulders against the shield. One launched every minute without fail. The boom was deafening, but somehow being on the other side of such an assault diminished the sound and the jarring effect it had.

But the Wizards were safe.

Cardin's father was safe.

For now.

Cardin motioned for Dalin to turn around, and then he dug around in his friend's pack, in search of the proper pre-set parchment. He found one that had a hastily made overhead drawing of the Wizards' Guild and its surroundings, and then he pulled out two small charcoal pencils. Spreading it out on the ground, he and Dalin began the laborious task of drawing estimated enemy positions and strengths.

This process was slow for the most part, since they had to remain as hidden as possible, and they had to relocate once to hide from another patrol.

But finally, as the sun marched further along its path, they finished, gathered up the parchment and stuffed it in Dalin's pack, and then silently moved back into the forest.

"It is as bad as we feared," Dalin whispered.

"Yeah," Cardin agreed. "I mean, we knew their numbers would be vast, but this…" He shook his head. "I don't know how we can possibly expect to repel such an enemy invasion."

Dalin eyed him curiously. "You do realize, do you not? This is not an invasion."

Cardin frowned at him. "What do you mean?"

"This is an occupation," Dalin said. "The invasion was swift and is already over."

His furrowed brow deepened, and Cardin glanced back at the Wizards' Guild. "Not yet," he corrected. "Not so long as Archanon and the Wizards' Guild stands against them."

"Cardin, those are but two holdouts," Dalin waved backwards. "And they cannot expect to hold forever. Anywhere else that does *not* have a shield? The fighting is already over."

"Stop!" Cardin held up a cautioning finger, halting in his tracks. "Don't. Don't even go there, we're *not* giving up!"

Dalin walked past him, and then turned around to face him, planting fists on his hips. "I did not say we should give up, Cardin. I am merely pointing out that we cannot approach this as we have fights in the past."

That killed Cardin's next words before they left his mouth.

"You...what?"

"You see the forces arrayed against us," Dalin said, again motioning to the besieged Wizards' Guild. "And while I know we still have much more scouting to do, I fear that everywhere else we go, the fighting will be finished, the cities and towns and villages occupied, with maybe the exception of the Falind capitol. They occupy the majority of Edilas, my friend. We cannot simply gather an army and march against them as we have our enemies in the past."

Cardin drew in a deep breath, thinking about how he could refute his friend and adviser's point.

But he couldn't. Dalin was right.

When Kailar had taken control of Falind, it had been traditional warfare at first, augmented by Wizards and summoned drakes. When Klaralin had marched orcs upon Archanon, it was one army against another on a single field of battle. Same with the necromancers — they occupied a single city on Edilas, and Cardin was able to inspire the Allies to quickly mobilize on a united front. The war against the necromancers had ended in a day.

This? This was something else entirely. The humans of Halarite were outnumbered, by a ratio that Cardin couldn't begin to calculate yet. Worse, the Allies were divided, isolated, and right at the key moment, just before the enemy invasion, they had turned on one another.

"Alright," he nodded. "What do you suggest we do?"

"I do not know just yet," Dalin shook his head. "But I do know that we must not face this threat in the same way we have faced others, or we will be doomed to fail. Furthermore, we need more information to even begin to form a plan."

Cardin nodded. "You're right. So let's stick with our current course, and scout out the next location." He paused, and his eyes flicked up at his friend's. "Daruun?"

"Indeed," Dalin grimaced. Neither wanted to see it, but at the same time, they had to. Cardin's home. The place where he and Dalin had first met, over a year ago.

And besides, there was an advantage in Daruun. Cardin knew of at least one house that was unoccupied at the moment. They could see what an occupied town looked like from within, and hopefully not bring an army crashing down upon them.

It felt strange, but Cardin took the lead, and summoned a portal to his house as easily as opening a door. If his portal was precisely on target, they would enter into the open space between the kitchen table and the weapons and armor racks.

It was a risk, he realized, as the house could have been destroyed in the invasion. But somehow, he doubted that an empty house would have been targeted. Nevertheless, as Dalin stepped up to Cardin's portal, he likewise stepped up close behind his friend. If there was a war on the other side, he needed to protect his companion.

Glancing back at Cardin, Dalin nodded, said, "Here we go," and one after another, they stepped through.

It was thankfully empty. The fireplace was clean, the candles unlit, and dust and cobwebs indicated that no one had been around to clean it in a while.

He glanced at his bedroom door, open and unoccupied, and then looked out the window when he heard shouting outside. As his portal closed, he and Dalin rushed to either side of the window, counting on the shadows and reflective glass to keep them hidden, and glanced outside.

As feared, Daruun was occupied. Troops of varying species, all bearing Darksteel armor, marched outside, and not a single citizen was in sight. Not near his house, anyway.

Dalin's eyes opened wide, his gaze over Cardin's shoulder, but Cardin couldn't see around the corner without risking exposing himself. Frowning, Cardin whispered, "What is it?"

Loud bangs shook the front door in its frame. A gruff, deep voice outside ordered, "Come out at once!"

"I think they must have detected our portal," Dalin murmured.

Of course.

He should have known that would happen, and in that instant, he realized his stupid mistake. Desire to see home, to see something familiar had blinded him from the obvious.

The door shook hard in its frame again, and he was thankful he had paid a local group to repair his home in recent times. "I think we should leave," he pushed off of the wall and prepared to summon a portal.

"Agreed," Dalin rushed past him and stood before the door, magic gathering into his staff, ready to defend.

Before he could cast his spell, however, a sudden rush of energy directly *above* them startled him. It felt immense, and he immediately recognized the feeling as that of a portal, but the amount of energy pouring forth from it was much more than a single personal portal.

It had to be at least as large as the portals that had brought the Darksteel Army upon Edilas.

But it was from *above!*

"Look!" someone outside shouted. The banging on the door ceased. He heard the sound of armored boots stomping away.

And then a gust of wind blasted down on the house, rattling the shingles and the entire house in its frame, as an incredible *noise* suddenly was simply there. And windows rattled and shook, until the one front window actually shattered.

"Airship!" someone outside shouted.

The portal closed.

And without the glass between Cardin, Dalin, and the outside, they were easily visible to the troops, though for the moment, their gazes were all fixed upon something moving above.

"Airship?" Cardin asked his friend.

Dalin gave him a blank stare and shrugged.

And then the Darksteel troops raised their weapons, or rather those who could cast long-range magic from them, and they unleashed a torrent of power into the air.

"Well whatever it is, they don't like it!" Cardin declared, and rushed to the front door to open it. "This I've gotta see!"

"Cardin, wait!" Dalin planted a halting hand on his shoulder. "We'll expose ourselves!"

He wheeled on his friend, rolling his shoulder to break the former Wizard's grasp upon him. A fury inside, boiling since the invasion had begun, spilled over, and he declared, "Someone they don't like just came through a massive portal, they might need our help!"

"We don't know that," Dalin cautioned. "They could be..."

But their argument had drawn the attention of their enemies, and Dalin thrust his staff past Cardin, erecting a shield just in time to deflect a blast of powerful magic. A blast that bounced into the house and exploded against the frame, blowing out the door and a large chunk of wall with it.

Too late.

Cardin's hand automatically went to the Sword, and with barely a thought, he freed it from its scabbard, charged magic into it, and pointed the tip outside.

At what looked like a full company of troops.

Dalin's shield dissipated. Cardin unleashed his blast. And then he rushed out of the way, grabbing Dalin around the waist as he did so and yanking him down, while his blast exploded on the ground in the midst of the enemy soldiers, sending chunks of earth and *soldiers* flying through the air.

And they returned in kind, unleashing arcane and elemental attacks upon Cardin's house.

Upon his *home*. Chunks blasted off. Ice pelted holes through it. Fire ignited anything flamable. His table. His walls. His weapons and armor, disused and left behind. His bed.

His father's bed.

His family's home.

And Cardin's restraint broke.

Fury infused his magic and he unleashed wave after wave of arcane power, while Dalin shielded them from the falling roof.

The enemy soldiers took the blows surprisingly well, at first, but never before had Cardin felt such unbridled rage. He stepped over the remnants of his home's wall and unleashed another blast into the enemy shields. They stopped attacking Cardin.

He remembered the siege weapons pelting Archanon, and the remains of the troops he'd found at the Southeast Gate, and Cardin let loose another blast. The enemy soldiers shielded themselves, unable to retaliate now, their entire focus upon Cardin's attacks.

He saw his father, lying pale and unconscious in the Recovery Ward. A way to save him now known, but he was cut off. A stronger blastwave from the Sword tore up the ground, deflected off of the enemy shields and into neighboring houses.

He saw orcs bearing Darksteel armor and weapons tearing through the Blue District of Archanon. Another blast, and this time the enemy shields all failed at once.

And he saw Sira, her back tore up from the claws of an enemy commander, near-death, but for the soul of a Star Dragon.

Another wave tore *through* the enemy soldiers. Through and past them, into the homes of innocents behind them.

Almost two hundred enemy soldiers fell to his rage-fueled assault.

He was shocked by his own power, but then he noticed, with some relief cooling his rage, that the homes he'd just half-destroyed were empty.

He looked around at his hometown and saw columns of smoke billowing up into the air. The buildings he'd accidentally destroyed weren't the first to have fallen. The Darksteel Army hadn't been kind to his city.

Maybe because Daruun never gave in easily to assailants. Millennia of enduring Lesser Wars as a front-line city had induced a stubborn resistance to would-be invaders, but as Arkad had pointed out, the Darksteel Army didn't treat resistance kindly.

Dead Warriors and soldiers lay upon the ground, bloodied, battered, broken.

If reason hadn't already left him, it did now. All he could think of was finding and rescuing any survivors. And if there were any holdouts, they'd be holed up at the Warrior's Guild.

So Cardin, Sword held menacingly at his side, stalked forth. To Dalin's credit, he didn't try to stop Cardin, didn't try to invoke reason. Maybe he was just as furious over the sight. Maybe he just knew better than to try to stop Cardin. And just maybe, the magic rolling out of Cardin let his friend know just how much fury he felt.

Only a dozen steps later did Cardin look up to see the strange craft, which the Darksteel soldiers had called 'airship,' flying away. It looked metallic, and it weathered countless arcane assaults against its skin, but it flew hard and fast. Then it banked left, and started coming around, and unleashed arcane assaults upon the Darksteel army.

The questions that should have burned in Cardin barely registered – who or what was it? Why was it here? And seeing the Darksteel army occupying the city, why wasn't it fleeing?

It didn't matter, but knowing that it had come through a portal gave Cardin an idea, and he stopped. In the blink of an eye, he opened a portal from his home street to the western edge of town, where the fortified Guild hall resided.

He didn't wait for Dalin, so as he stalked forward, his friend rushed with him, and together they passed through.

Cardin's rage didn't abate. On the contrary, when he came through and saw the ironwood doors sealed and Darksteel soldiers upon the Guild's battlements, he roared in rage, and unleashed another blast from the tip of the Sword, blasting a section of the wall to rubble.

Magic from a portal inside of the Guild complex barely registered in his rage-fueled mind. The soldiers atop were mostly focused on blasting the airship circling the city, but Cardin's assault on the wall got more than a few to pay attention to him.

He saw too much red to consider a shield, but Dalin's mind must have been clearer, and he erected a shield ahead of them. Together, they stalked forward. And Cardin's stalking turned into a jog, and then a run. He ran past Dalin's shield, and with a roar, he leapt into the air and unleashed pinpoint precision attacks upon those who attacked him.

Pinpoint except his powers were stronger in his rage-fueled mindset, and chunks of the wall were blasted away as Darksteel armor crumpled and bodies were crushed. Cardin landed next to the hole he had blasted in the wall, and he climbed up it, anticipating reinforcements through a portal to be on the other side.

Except it wasn't.

Platinum blonde hair. Sunset orange hair.

Two people he would never have expected to see here, now.

Cardin gaped, and said, "S…Sira?"

She stared back at him.

"Cardin!"

Sira and Elaria had just come through a portal, and looked completely unprepared for the battle around them.

Blasts of magic rained down upon the battlements, the attack from the airship suddenly focusing on their location, and the ship swooped down, turning sharply and coming right towards the Guild complex.

"It's the *Starfire*," Elaria declared. Cardin quirked his head to one side when he heard the name and watched as people on the bottom platform of the strange-looking craft unleashed furious attacks upon the Darksteel troops. Hitting targets with incredible accuracy, he noted.

And then two rope ladders unfurled as the thing's whirling blades blew up dust and debris around the guild, the airship coming to a surprisingly rapid stop directly overhead. People above waved their hands, and he heard a woman's voice, no doubt enhanced by magic, call down, "Come on, Pretty Eyes, we gotta go!"

Arcane blasts panged against the metallic skin of the ship, but he knew the contraption wouldn't last long enough for anyone to climb up it. Sira waved at Cardin, "Come on, we need to get aboard that ship!"

Cardin blinked in surprise, looked up, and then at Sira.

"Wait," he called to her. "I've a better idea." He and Dalin rushed to their sides, and he barely resisted the urge to embrace her. And then, calling upon magic reserves that were fast dwindling, he summoned another portal, this one onto the bottom platform of that ship.

"Go!" he shouted, and turned when he felt a surge of magic. While maintaining a portal to the strange ship above, he raised a shield wide enough to cover all of his friends just as half a dozen enemy soldiers poured out from within the fortress's dungeon area and let loose a torrent of magic.

Fatigue hit him. Darkness threatened him – not unconsciousness, but dark magic. It wanted to assert itself, but he knew that now was not the time, not yet. He held on to the light.

Elaria rushed through the portal, followed by Dalin. Sira hesitated only a second, the purple of her eyes flashing for a moment.

She was through, and he felt his focus waver. He couldn't maintain the portal and the shield at the same time.

The crew of the ship came to his rescue, as a deluge of magic rained down upon the enemy troops.

Cardin puffed out a breath he hadn't realized he'd been holding, looked up at the ship, and then rushed through his portal.

The lower deck of the ship was crowded, between Cardin and his friends and the six crew members manning it. None of the crew were human, he realized, and a cat-like, fur-covered humanoid slapped her palm on something next to a ladder leading up *into* the ship and yelled, "We're all here, Captain, go!"

The ship surged forward, and Cardin grasped the metal railing surrounding the deck. The hum of its whirling blades grew in pitch.

But they weren't out of it yet. Blasts of magic lanced upward at them, slamming into the ship's hull with distinct 'pangs!' and jarring the ship, leaving dents and scorch marks upon her hull. One blast almost hit Cardin, and he unconsciously raised a shield big enough to cover the entire deck and all aboard it.

The ship rose up, creating false gravity that weighed upon Cardin, while it surged forward and rolled right.

Giving Cardin and his friends an unfettered view of Daruun from above.

For all of his rage-induced damage, Cardin had barely contributed to the ruin of his home city. While sections that had been leveled by meteorites over six months ago were being rebuilt, other sections lay demolished or burned.

Sira came up next to him and wrapped her arms around his, clinging tightly as she gaped down upon what was left of their home city. She shuddered. "My gods, Cardin…" Their eyes met, and despite the strange violet color of her irises, her gaze momentarily penetrated the cloud of his rage. "That's…our home."

He forced down a lump that had rolled up into his throat and nodded. "I know…" And he wrapped his arms around her, and they watched as the ship rose higher to the safety of the sky.

Daruun disappeared in a wisp of clouds.

Chapter 34

THE LORDS OF DEVOR

When the assembled Lords of Devor broke for lunch, Kailar walked to where Letan watched over the guards and stepped up next to him. He eyed her curiously, but she waited, patience winning out. For now.

Kent came by shortly after and ordered the troops dismissed and to attend to their normal duties for the remainder of the day. Which freed Letan.

"Say," she looked at him, injecting as much intensity into her eyes as she could, "How about lunch at the Water's Edge?"

Purpose and reasoning gave her voice an edge, and Letan cued in on that. "Uh," he glanced at Kent, who frowned at both of them. With his pale cheeks turning rosy, Letan nodded. "Sure?"

Unfortunately, Reyla had other thoughts. "Kailar," she called.

Gritting her teeth, Kailar turned and saw Reyla, along with the Lords, sauntering back into town, the shadow of the Darksteel 'embassy' a disturbing backdrop. The creatures that had towed it into place snuffed and stamped their feet impatiently.

Looking back at Letan, she held up a finger, "One moment," and then she rushed over to Reyla.

The Empress didn't stop walking, with the lords conversing

behind her, mostly complaining about the cold and musing over what they would eat for lunch.

"Yes, Empress?" Kailar fell into step next to Reyla.

"We will be having lunch in the former city hall building," she stated simply.

Kailar waited for her to say more, but when she said nothing else, she realized Reyla meant for Kailar to attend, no doubt to discuss the turn of events and the meeting. She glanced back at the meeting table as the Navitas watched them leave. Would he stay in the area?

After glancing at the lords, especially the Lord of Corlas, she turned back to Reyla. "With respect, Empress," Kailar started hesitantly, "I have other things I must attend to that will be vital for tomorrow's resumption of negotiations."

Reyla didn't look at her at first, and simply walked along, forcing Kailar's stomach to turn. After their discussion yesterday about Kailar's disobedience, she half-expected Reyla to deny her. But then she turned her head towards Kailar, and ever-so-slightly glanced back at the Lords.

Kailar nodded.

"Very well," Reyla nodded. "I expect a full report by dinner tonight."

Stopping and bowing as the Empress walked along, Kailar replied, "Yes, Your Highness."

The look that the Corlas Lord gave her as he walked by incensed her, and her blood boiled.

But she held back. She had to.

This was too important.

General Querlin and the troops fell into formation, flowing around Kailar to surround the Lords and their Empress protectively, leaving Kailar alone with Letan, who stepped up next to her.

"So," he sighed and folded his arms. "What trouble do you have planned for us now?"

With a wry grin stretching across her face, she winked at him. She didn't actually have anything dangerous planned just yet, but she didn't let him know that. "Come on," she walked ahead of him, headed for the Navitas.

Letan rushed to catch up to her, and a moment later, they stood before the Navitas, who looked down upon them, the crystalline structure around his faux-neck cracking and scraping. "Powerless

One," he acknowledged her.

She stopped at that, remembering burning skies and Dark Dragons. Recovering quickly, she asked, "Can you tell us anything about whom the Darksteel ambassador was communicating with?"

Slowly, deliberately the Navitas turned to look upon the embassy, and its eye sockets narrowed in an approximation of a frown. "It was someone on this world."

Kailar waited patiently for the Navitas to continue, but when it turned back to face her and said nothing more, she huffed out a breath impatiently. "Okay. Someone nearby?"

For a moment, it simply stared back at them. Then, "Please define 'nearby.'"

Her hands clenched into fists and she exchanged an exasperated glance with Letan. He took up the challenge, "Someone in this city? In the meeting?"

"No," the Navitas replied. "Much further. I cannot discern exactly how far, but this other exists somewhere upon this landmass."

Thinking about its words, she interpreted, "Somewhere on Devor? But not in proximity to Tieran." She looked at Letan. "That makes me think there's someone else working for the Darksteel Empire on Devor."

Letan nodded, his ginger eyebrows scrunched up while he idly stroked his goatee. "Agreed. And that's more than a little disturbing. Do you...do you think they're occupying us here with negotiations while they invade the rest of Devor?"

She hadn't considered that possibility, but as inky and deceptive as Xavien *felt*, she wouldn't put him past it. On the other hand, the actions of the Lords of Corlas and Edingard had her wondering something else. "Maybe, or maybe they've had an insider here all along."

Letan cocked his head to one side. "Come again?"

She gave him an icy look as pieces connected in her head. "What do you know about the Lord of Corlas?"

"Lord Tass Beckitt," Letan replied. "Well, he was born on a ship bound for Devor over thirty years ago. His family was sent by Falind to help administer Corlas specifically."

"Falind?" she asked. "No wonder I don't like him."

Letan gave her an exasperated look. She smiled innocently.

"Anyway," he continued, "he grew up knowing he would be Mayor of Corlas, and let me tell you, he wasn't afraid to flaunt that fact. But other than an arrogant demeanor, there's not much else remarkable about him. Not anything that would paint him as suspicious, anyway, if that's what you're asking."

Kailar frowned at that. She wasn't sure what she had expected to learn, but the picture was incomplete. She glanced up at the Navitas, but it patiently, stoically watched and listened. "Okay, does he know the Lord of Edingard?"

Letan gave her another exasperated look. "What?" she asked.

"You know they all have names."

"So does everyone else in town," she shrugged, "but you can't expect me to remember everyone's names, now, can you?"

Sighing, he replied, "Kailar, they're the most influential people on Devor, aside from the Empress."

"And?"

Planting his hands on his hips, he grumbled, "Kind of worth knowing their names." Thinking about it a moment longer, he nodded. "Yes, Lord Beckitt does indeed know Lord Vara Penn. As I recall, they take turns visiting one another's cities every three months. They would request only a minimal Warrior escort when they did."

"Interesting," she mumbled.

He heard. "What's interesting?"

"Uh, that they knew each other. What do you know about Lord, um. Pin?"

"Penn," Letan corrected. "Not much. I never actually met her myself until you and I started fighting the criminal underground, and even then, it was just to keep her informed of our activities. She seemed amenable to our actions, especially given how rampant violent crime, especially murder, was in Edingard."

Kailar felt her innards twist with guilt, and she quickly looked away from Letan. She didn't want him to see the shame in her eyes. Didn't want him to ever know about what she'd done in Edingard.

Sighing, she looked up at the Navitas, but had no more questions for it. She would have preferred it to support Devor's independence from the Darksteel Empire, but she understood its position. It wanted to protect its people, and as long as they were left alone...

Left alone.

The Darksteel Empire was afraid of the Navitas. Their power was greater than she knew, though if they ever found out about just how vulnerable the Navitas were, they might launch a pre-emptive attack. What if they destroyed the Crystalline Peaks? Would the Navitas survive without their 'collectors?'

And why, if they were so afraid of the Navitas, would they risk coming to Devor in the first place? Was Edilas, Asirin, and Trinil not enough?

"Gods dammit," she hissed out, folding her arms.

"What?" Letan asked, surprised by her outburst.

"I'm missing something, some key piece of information." Looking up at the Navitas again, she asked, "And you're sure there's no way you can pinpoint who the Ambassador communicated with?"

"That is beyond my ability," the Navitas patiently replied.

She nodded, resisting the urge to curse about it. She didn't know if the Navitas felt emotions the same way humans did, but it wasn't its fault, and it had already given them more information than they otherwise would have had.

When she looked again at Letan, his nose was scrunched up in thought. "What is it?" she asked.

"Well," he hesitated. "It's just that...he was so damned impatient yesterday and this morning to get us to sign a treaty, right?"

"Yeah, I thought he'd have forced us to conclude negotiations today," she replied.

"So why the change?" he looked at the embassy. "Why the delay? What piece of information did he receive, and more importantly, what's he waiting for next?"

Kailar followed his gaze to the embassy. Four guards stood outside of its draw bridge, and half a dozen more attended to the giant beasts.

"Maybe we watch them and find out," Kailar suggested.

Letan grimaced. "Let me guess, then."

She huffed out a sigh. "Yeah. Long night ahead of us."

Letan visibly shivered against a frigid breeze.

Chapter 35

THE FLIRTY CAPTAIN

Daruun lay in ruins.

Sira's heart ached, and the swirls of her despair and Raida's lingering guilt twisted her stomach. The *Starfire* leveled out her turn, but kept rising higher and higher, and Sira knew they'd soon go too high for them to breathe.

So did the *Starfire's* officers. The cat-like person, T'Zina, laid a velvety paw upon Sira's shoulder. "We need to get to the bridge," she rasped.

Sira nodded, "Right." Still in Cardin's arms, she looked at him, and he at her. She felt him drop the shield protecting the ship from counter strikes below, and then she squeezed him harder, nuzzling into the nook of his neck.

She'd missed this. Sira hadn't realized until that very moment just how much she missed him. Their home, and if she had to guess, their *world* burned beneath them. Everything was falling apart, and she felt more lost than ever.

"Come on," she pulled out of Cardin's arms and tugged his hand to follow her.

She came up short when she realized the other person with Cardin was Dalin.

But he wasn't wearing Wizard robes.

Commentary would have to wait until later, she realized, as the *Starfire* picked up speed and the blasting wind made it impossible to hold a conversation.

Preceding Cardin and the others up, she ascended to the bridge deck and led her companions into what had become a familiar surrounding for her. Kemila was at the helm, and her crew worked diligently at their consoles.

From everywhere and nowhere, she heard T'Zina's raspy voice call up to the bridge, *"Captain, we're all sealed up down here, but we never identified the breach on deck 2."*

"Right," Kemila replied. "We'll have to level out now, then. Get on it, T'Zina, we need our altitude advantage back."

As Sira led Cardin, Dalin, and Elaria further forward, Kemila heard them coming and turned. Arching her eyebrows up, she nodded to one of the other crewmen, who took the helm from her so that she could step down to their level.

"Right good job, Pretty Eyes," Kemila smiled at Sira, and a mixture of flirty embarrassment and guilt swirled inside of Sira's stomach. "You too, gorgeous," she added to Elaria. "And who might these two strapping lads be?"

Sira cleared her throat. "Captain Kemila of Gevron, may I introduce Prince Cardin Kataar-"

"Oh my, a prince!" Kemila's hand touched the bare skin of her collarbone, drawing everyone's gaze in that direction. "As far as stowaways go, that's a new one."

Sira coughed. "Yes, well, he's...um, also," she flustered, now feeling unsure about Kemila's attentions towards Cardin. Did she even have a right to feel jealous?

And who was she truly jealous over? Cardin, or Kemila?

Cardin took it in stride and bowed.

Dalin cleared his throat.

"And, um, this is Dalin, former Wizard, and adviser to Cardin," Sira finished.

"So you're all from Halarite as well?" Kemila inquired.

"Yes," Cardin replied.

"My my," Kemila smiled at Elaria. "If you had told me so many good looking people were here, I'd have come sooner!"

Now it was Elaria's turn to cough.

Cardin looked around, and said, "This is a...uh, fine ship you have. I've never seen the like."

"And you probably never will again," Kemila winked. "She's one of a kind. Now, I did my part, lovelies," Kemila glanced between Sira and Elaria. "Does having a prince onboard mean we can make it official?"

Cardin frowned. "Make what official?"

Sira felt flustered, and realized that in all of the craziness, she hadn't had a chance to fill Cardin in on any of it. Before she could begin, Kemila said, "My crew and I seek asylum. Although..." Kemila glanced behind her, out into the blue skies and at Edilas at large. "It looks like it may be too late for that."

"Cardin," Sira started, and then her voice caught. "I...uh. Darea. Darea has fallen."

She saw his face blanche, as did Dalin's. They both looked at Elaria, and it was as if Cardin truly saw her for the first time. Saw her disheveled look.

But then his jaw tightened. "The Darksteel Army?"

Elaria's eyes downturned for a moment, but then flashed up to him. "Yes," she whispered. Wetness accumulated around her eyes, but no tears streaked down. Not yet.

"It gets worse," Sira added, and the whole reason they risked everything came back to her at once. "Cardin, the world we just came from, Endri..."

Turning back to her, Cardin looked mortified. "Oh no...what happened?"

"Endri," she shook her head. "He...it's the Dark Dragons. They're....I mean." She sighed in frustration.

"Calm down," Raida admonished. *"Breathe! Just breathe, Sira."*

She sucked in a breath, then let it out slowly, and repeated that exercise over and over.

"It's okay," Cardin soothed and took her hand. "Just tell me what..."

"The Dark Dragons are allied with the Darksteel Army," she finally spat it out. "And they have Endri. And just before we left, before we escaped, we felt...Raida and I, we felt it. Cardin." She squeezed his hand. "The darkness has already infected him." Cardin's eyes widened. "Raida felt it. He's fighting it, but you know what'll happen if we don't rescue him! It'll consume Endri, and the dragon we know and love will…"

She didn't finish. It wouldn't kill him, they knew that, but death would almost be preferable. Star Dragons were not meant to interact with the darkness, the void between stars.

It would corrupt Endri. Drive him insane.

Endri would cease to exist.

But then Sira's heart weighed down to the bottom of her chest when she realized what was happening. The Darksteel Army was here too. Halarite was under siege.

Before Cardin started talking, she already knew what he might say, knew the war that raged within him even now. "I…" He started, stopped, and walked past Kemila, staring out at Halarite below. "Hellfire. It's all happening at once. Too much. Too much at once."

She walked after him, tried to take his hand, but it was cold and lifeless. As if all life had drained from him. Glancing back at Dalin, she asked, "What's happened here?"

"They attacked this morning," Dalin explained. "We've only scouted two other locations, the Wizard complex and the orc town."

In all that had happened, Sira had forgotten about the orcs. "Attacked this morning," she whispered. "Archanon?"

"Is safe," Cardin replied absently. "For now. So is the Wizards' Guild, both locations got their shields up in time. They were luckier than-" His voice caught, and his hands furled into fists, crushing Sira's hand. She held tight, ignoring the pain of his strength.

"We don't know yet about other locations," Dalin shook his head. "Not yet."

"Scouting will have to wait," Cardin stated, determination hardening his voice. "We need to act. And we need more information." His head popped up. "Darksteel Army, and the Dark Dragons. You said dragons. Plural."

"There's more than one now," she said. He looked at her, stunned.

"Sira…I could barely hold my own against Nuuldan," he shook his head. "And that was with help."

"But that was before you mastered dark magic," she insisted, stepping closer to him.

"Dark magic?" Kemila gaped at them. "You can use dark magic?"

"I wouldn't say I've mastered it," Cardin shook his head. "But yes, I'm able to use it."

"You're his only chance!" she insisted. "We'll lose Endri if we don't do something *now!*"

"Even if I can summon my avatar," he shook his head, dread and regret filling his voice. "I can't take them on alone."

"Then we get help," Dalin said.

"From who, the Navitas again?" Cardin asked. "That'd take time we don't have, just to convince them to help, let alone-"

"The Star Dragons," Raida said.

"The Star Dragons!" Sira echoed excitedly. "It's perfect! They can help us, on all fronts," she swept out her free hand, encompassing Halarite. "If the Dark Dragons are allied with the Darksteel Army, then this invasion affects them too, *and* they can help you rescue Endri!"

Cardin stared at her, and the hint of a smile creased his lips. "Yeah. You're right!" Looking excitedly between Sira, Kemila, Elaria and Dalin, he said, "We need to get to the Celestial Spires."

Kemila's hands shot up. "Don't look at me, Princely. We'd have to find another Ancient Gateway to get this ship there, unless you can open a big enough portal. Besides which, I've already done more than I bargained for."

A scowl drew down Sira's face, and she looked at Kemila with more than a little disappointment. But she knew that the *Starfire's* captain was right. Maybe Cardin could create a portal that big, but he didn't need to.

"It's okay," he shook his head. "You brought Sira back. You saved Elaria. Thank you. I would say on behalf of all of Halarite, but really from me, thank you *so much.*"

Kemila faltered in replying. "I…well, you're welcome, handsome."

Sira felt her cheeks burn, but she shoved her jealousy down deep for now.

"We promised her asylum if she brought us here," Sira stated. "But with the world in flames now…"

"The orc town is safe," Cardin suggested. "For now. If the Darksteel Army knew where it was, they would have invaded it right away."

Dalin nodded. "Agreed. But we also do not know precisely where it is, just generally."

"Generally is better than they have," Cardin replied. "You've been there twice now, do you think you could lead the Captain there?"

Eyes widening, Dalin objected, "I will not leave your side-"

"There's no time to argue," Cardin cut him off sharply. "We have to go. Now. You and I are the only ones here who know where it is, you're the only one who can guide them."

Closing the distance to Cardin and Sira, Dalin whispered, "I promised Master Valkere I would not leave your side."

"I know," Cardin reassured, pressing a hand on their friend's shoulder. "I know. But these are desperate times, my friend, and I need your help." He nodded at Kemila. "They need your help."

Dalin grumbled and clenched his jaw, working it back and forth. "Very well," he nodded. "I will see you at the orc town, then."

"Sounds good." Cardin then turned to Sira. "Are you staying with them, or-"

"I'm going with you," she clenched his hand in hers. "We're going to rescue Endri *together*. Besides, I know the lay of the land. Uh," she glanced at Elaria. "Sort of."

Elaria smiled and nodded. "I'll go with, if you'd like."

"Alright," Cardin nodded. "The three of us." He turned to Kemila and said, "Please...please take care of my friend."

Kemila sidled up next to Dalin and took his arm in hers, gently patting his hand. "Oh don't worry, silver-hair and I will watch out for one another, handsome."

Cardin nodded and turned, but the moment Sira felt him gather power, she said, "Wait!" The power gathered in Cardin faltered for a moment. "It's not safe to cast magic on the bridge."

Kemila beamed a smile at her. "You learn fast, Pretty Eyes."

Cardin's eyes widened. "Wait, she's been calling *you* 'Pretty Eyes?'"

"Am I wrong to?" Kemila asked. "I mean, just look at those gorgeous colors and that smile and that...oooh," she squirmed a little next to Dalin, and the Wizard shifted uncomfortably away from her.

Sira blushed.

Raida grew excited.

Not now!

"Then when?"

"Um," was all Cardin could manage.

"Helm, drop to twenty-four pressures," Kemila ordered.

"Aye, Captain," the person at the wheel stated, and gently tilted the wheel forward. The ship angled beneath them, and the view of the ground filled their view. Pressure built in Sira's ears, and then popped a moment later.

Abandoning Dalin, Kemila sauntered over to Cardin and Sira and smiled. "I figure you don't want to be gasping for air down on the open deck when you go summon your portal." She reached up and gently caressed Cardin's cheek. "I don't think blue would do your lips justice, Handsome."

"Uh," Cardin sputtered.

"Hey," Sira growled.

Kemila winked at Sira. "Easy there, Pretty Eyes, just making friends with your...lover? Boyfriend?"

Sira didn't reply. She didn't know how to, and that fact startled her. They were *together* now...weren't they?

Looking at him, hoping he would answer, she felt her heart seize when he stumbled over words, but never actually managed to say anything.

"Exterior pressure steady at twenty-four, Captain," the helmsman declared, and the *Starfire* leveled out.

Kemila quirked an eyebrow up. "Well, then. Saved by the helm. Go on, you two," she smiled. "Go have fun together."

Turning on her heel, Kemila headed back for the helm, but then paused as she passed by Elaria. She looked at the elf, and then leaned forward and kissed her cheek before rushing past and up to the wheel. The helmsman yielded to her, and Kemila took over, keeping her eyes forward.

Refusing to look at either Sira or Elaria.

I am never going to understand that woman, Sira thought.

"Indeed," Raida agreed. *"I like her!"*

Sira shook her head, and then looked at Cardin, who stared blankly at the captain. She snapped her fingers in front of his eyes. "Hey, wake up, Keeper, you've got a dragon to save."

"Right," he shook his head. Glancing one last time at Kemila, who refused to look at any of them, they headed aft.

Dalin walked with them to the hatch that led to the lower decks, and said to them all, "Be safe, my friends."

Elaria passed him and started her descent, and Cardin stopped long enough to clasp Dalin's shoulder. "You too."

Sira smiled at Dalin as she passed, and then they descended.

She really hoped this wouldn't be the last time she saw Dalin.

And a strong part of her really hoped to see Kemila again. The guilt within her was only overcome by the fear she felt for her friends.

Not to mention for herself.

Gods, are we really going to take on Dark Dragons?

"At least our lives are never boring."

Chapter 36

WHEN DRAGONS GO TO WAR

There was a part of Cardin that wanted to go numb. To stop feeling, to stop seeing, to stop noticing. How else do you cope with your world falling apart around you, your friends falling one by one?

Instead, a steely resolve settled over him. It smoldered his rage, set it to a blazing-hot pile of coals, ready to ignite again, but tamed for now.

Halarite was in trouble, but there wasn't much he could do for that just now.

Elaria's world was in trouble. While he didn't know the details, he reasoned that meant that Baenil, Ventelis, and Gilrin were, too. And he could do nothing for them.

Endri was in trouble. But maybe, just maybe, he could do something about that.

Pick the battles you can win, and maybe you can rack up enough victories to make a difference.

Elaria led the way down the enclosed stairs, doubling back on themselves every half a flight, until they reached the bottom and she opened the steel door. Wind assaulted them, relatively warm but still jarring, and Cardin's cloak billowed out.

The three of them filed out onto the strange balcony-type deck, and after Elaria secured the door, the two ladies gathered around Cardin. He looked down at the world around them, but all he could tell was that they were somewhere over the Daruun Forest, maybe further south toward Ironwood.

No sooner had he thought that, however, than did the *Starfire* roll into a bank. The three of them had to grab the hand railing on the ship's right, or starboard side if he remembered his naval parlance, but they leveled out again a few seconds later.

His magic senses told him the ship was now headed southeast.

Towards the Wastelands, and the orcs.

Dalin must have given them directions.

"Come on," Elaria insisted. "Kemila will want to get the ship back up to altitude in case the Darksteel Army brought their own airships."

Cardin felt color drain from his face, and he stared at his oldest elven friend. "They have ships like this, too?"

"Not like this," Sira replied, surprising Cardin even further. "But yes, they have airships."

"Fleets of airships," Elaria added.

Before today, Cardin never knew there was such a thing as airships. His mind reeled. Their enemy was more advanced, more dangerous than he could have ever realized.

Focus, Kataar! Concentrate on the battles you can win.

"Alright, let's get out of here, then," he turned towards the stern, and on the precious little space available on the lowest deck, he summoned a portal.

The exercise was unique – he had never opened a portal on a fast-moving platform before, but either his intuition or the Sword of Dragons immediately made him realize that the platform was stationary, relative to himself. After realizing that, it was easy.

Only a second later did he realize what he'd just done. His first portal to an off-world location. To a place he had only been once.

Gods I hope I did this right...

Terrifying images of Sira and Elaria plummeting to their deaths into steep, far-down, misty canyons terrified him, and he almost told them to stay aboard the *Starfire*. However, when he looked into Sira's otherworldly, violet eyes, he knew he couldn't.

She would never let him.

Sira smiled at Cardin, absolutely trusting in his power and his control, and she walked forward and was the first to pass through. Elaria followed a second later.

Cardin drew in a deep breath and stepped through. Just like he remembered when he passed through Endri's off-world portals, the feeling of electricity passed through his skin, and he swore there was a momentary pause between one side and the other, though he couldn't quite account for it.

His portal deposited them safely on the other side, and for the second time in his life, Cardin beheld the Celestial Spires, the meeting place of the Star Dragons.

They stood atop a great pillar amidst many, towering hundreds of feet above the landscape below and surrounded by six circles of expanding spires. They were made of multi-layered stone of reds, tans, and browns, and though no flora grew atop any of the flattened spires, he imagined dry, desert-like plants would.

If the dragons ever let anything grow upon their meeting stones.

Except, there were no dragons. Just like last time, it was where the Star Dragons met, not where they lived. He would have to find a way to bring them forth. Without the benefit of a dragon to roar out to the others.

He looked right, saw Sira smiling as she took in the vista, and then left, and saw Elaria's jaw hanging open, her gaze upwards. Cardin followed her line of sight, and saw above them a sky of pinks, purples, and blues, distant clouds amongst the stars that shone brightly. The ringed world they had seen last time they were at the Spires was gone, no doubt having set, and who knew how long before it would rise again.

But Elaria's gaze was none-the-less one of awe. When she noticed Cardin staring, she blushed and asked, "What?"

"Nothing," he shook his head with a grin. "I just…expected you to be used to seeing things like this, is all. How many worlds have you explored?"

Her blush turned into a smile, and she drew in a deep breath, taking in the smell of sage and the nearby saltwater ocean. "That's just it, Cardin. Every world I travel to, every new place, it's a new experience every time. Nothing is ever quite the same. This, *this* is why I do what I do," she held her arms out, encompassing the celestial vista. "This is why I explore."

Having only traveled to two other worlds, Cardin could

understand. Those two were so very different from one another, he felt like he'd barely scratched the surface of what the Universe had to offer. Soon, he would see another world.

He turned to Sira, saw the wondrous smile that lit up her face, and he took her hand in his, squeezing it, thankful to finally have another adventure with her.

Even if more rode on their next actions than ever before.

Even if their world was ending.

Her smile faltered. Had she read his mind? Or merely had the same thought?

"So," she looked around at the empty pillars. "How do we summon the dragons?"

That was a good question. Cardin thought back to when Endri had brought them here, only a few months ago. The dragon had roared out to call forth the Star Dragons, but even then, Cardin had felt that there was more to the roar.

It was magic. A call that Cardin couldn't hope to recreate...could he?

It was a Star Dragon's call.

The Sword of Dragons was crafted by the Star Dragons, infused with all of their knowledge, all of their magic. Betting on the fact that the Sword had just taught him how to create an off-world portal on a moving craft, and so the Sword had entered another active teaching phase, he closed his eyes and infused his memory of Endri's call into his heart, his soul.

Dalin always said that to cast magic, you didn't just have to know the magic, you had to *own* it. Make it a part of you.

Magic flowed through Cardin, and the moment they had stepped through the portal, the sense of that magic had changed. The source had changed. The star this world orbited was different than Halarite's, and thus the source of his magic was different.

But it was still star magic.

He knew what to do.

Releasing Sira's hand, Cardin clutched the Sword and drew it forth, and after channeling a significant portion of magic into it, he thrust it skyward and unleashed the call in the form of a golden beam of energy lancing into the heavens, deafening them with a clap of thunder.

The call rang out.

Come forth.

They waited. Moments passed. Cardin's confidence faltered. Had he cast it wrong?

Or was it something worse? Were the dragons already gone from this world? Or even more terrifying...had they already been defeated?

A breath of a sigh escaped his mouth the moment he felt the first portal open. A great, red dragon soared through. Another portal allowed a blue. Another, and another, one by one, as if the Star Dragons had choreographed their entrance, they all arrived in a circular pattern above them, slowly descending, until one-by-one, they landed upon the pillars, filling the inner circle, then the middle...

There were fewer dragons. Last time he'd been here, there had been twenty-six dragons, including Endri. Seven inner pillars, twelve outer, and seven more dragons only partly filling the third track. This time, none filled the third track.

Nineteen Star Dragons.

What had happened to the rest of them?

Cardin and the others turned to the largest red dragon on the closest inner pillar, and Cardin bowed low.

A voice in his thoughts spoke, calm and wisely, *"Greetings, Keeper of the Sword."*

"Firdal," Cardin replied, the dragon's name forever burned in his memory. How could he ever forget such a wondrous creature's name? Standing up straight, Cardin introduced, "You know Sira Reinar." She smiled to the red dragon. "And this is Elaria of the Dareann Elves."

"Ah yes, the one Endri told us about," the dragon's red-star eyes turned to Elaria. *"It is an honor to meet you, young one."*

Elaria blushed and bowed, "The honor is mine, revered dragon."

The mention of Endri's name drew Cardin's jaw tight, and he sucked in a deep breath. That was when Firdal looked to the skies, and then looked to the other Star Dragons, before he focused again on Cardin and asked, *"Where is Endri?"*

Cardin began to answer, but Sira interrupted, "He has been taken by Dark Dragons."

The sudden surprised shift that came from every single Star Dragon present was mesmerizing. The dragons looked to one another, and though Cardin couldn't hear their words, he sensed a wave of magic conversation amongst them.

"You are sure of this?" Firdal asked.

"We are," Elaria replied. "We were at the Teledin Bazaar when the Darksteel Army came, augmented by multiple Dark Dragons."

The red dragon's lips grew into a thin, grimacing line. Cardin had spent enough time with Endri to know that look, to know how Star Dragons imitated humanoid expressions as best as their reptilian builds would allow.

He was shocked, but not surprised.

What was he not surprised about? Any of it? Or just a specific part?

Before he could stop himself from asking, Cardin challenged, "Did you know about the Darksteel Army alliance with the Dark Dragons?"

Firdal quirked his head to one side. *"No, we did not. However, we knew that more of our kind had fallen to darkness, far faster than we could have anticipated. Including…"* He looked around the Spires, looked at how many empty ones there were. *"Including some we had gathered here, and were later lured away. We did not know they had left, until it was too late to save them."*

Lured away? How did a Dark Dragon lure a Star Dragon away? Unless…

"If a third party, the Darksteel Army as you call it, has helped Nuuldan," Firdal mentally sighed, *"Then that explains a great deal about how it happened."*

Dread filled Cardin.

"Oh gods," Sira echoed his thoughts. "Oh gods, is…was this intentional?" She gripped Cardin's hand tightly, and they looked to one another, both feeling fear. "Was this a trap for Endri all along?"

They looked to Elaria, but she only looked confused. "I don't understand. What's wrong?"

"They're using the Darksteel Army to lure Star Dragons out and trap them," Sira stated. "And Endri had said he heard rumor that someone who had seen a Dark Dragon was at the Bazaar."

Looking to Firdal, Cardin asked, "Did Endri tell you how he heard that rumor?"

"He did not," Firdal replied. *"However, it would stand to reason that he fell for the trap, the same as others have."*

Surging forward, Cardin declared, "We have to save him!"

The red dragon's head hung low. "It is too late."

"No it isn't," Sira shook her head furiously. "Elaria and I felt it, the darkness has tainted him, but he's still fighting it. He's still saveable!"

"I wish that were so," Firdal's eyes dimmed just a shade. *"Once the darkness touches a Star Dragon, there is no coming back. They can fight it, they can stave it off for a short time, but there is no coming back from it. Endri...is lost."*

Cardin gripped the Sword of Dragons tightly. He felt the darkness within, swirling around, ready to be allowed to come forth.

Balanced with the light.

A lesson he had learned from another red dragon, on Stella.

"No," he shook his head, and lifted the Sword up to show Firdal. The red dragon's head slowly rose, and the pinpoint lights of his eyes looked to the weapon in Cardin's hand. "It isn't too late. *I* can save him. I can bring the light back, banish the darkness within him."

Firdal blinked at him. *"You can?"*

Sira echoed, "You can?!"

Magic thrummed through the Sword, through his arm, through his *soul*. He didn't know if he could or not, truth be told. But he had to try.

So he projected confidence. "Yes I can. But..." He hesitated, looked around at the other dragons present, all of whom focused on him. Starry eyes ranging in color from blues to reds to oranges to greens and more all gazed into him, penetrated his soul, saw him for who and what he was. "But I cannot do it alone," he said to them. "I cannot fend off Dark Dragons and the Darksteel Army while also saving Endri. I need help." He looked at Sira, and then Elaria, and added, *"We* need your help. All of us."

Firdal looked hesitant, and he arched his neck forward, as if to look closer at Cardin. To look deeper within him. Could he see Cardin's lie? The half-truth?

True, he had no way of knowing if what he wanted to do with the Sword was possible, but he had to try.

He *would* try. With or without the Star Dragons.

Cardin wouldn't let the Dark Dragons or the Darksteel Army take one more thing from him, one more friend.

No more.

Something of his courage and determination must have shown

through. Firdal eased back on his perch, and blew out a puff of noisy breath. *"I believe you can,"* he spoke quietly, a strange effect considering he spoke through magic. He looked around at the other Star Dragons, and they looked to him. Cardin felt them converse amongst themselves.

Until they finished, and Firdal looked to Cardin. *"We will help."* His spirits soared, elation filling every fiber of his being. *"After all, what is the point of gathering so many dragons if we do not fight when we are needed most?"*

He almost remarked something snarky, but he held his tongue.

Looking to Sira, Firdal asked, *"The Teledin Bazaar, yes?"* Sira nodded. *"Then that is where we shall go. Come, my friends!"* And with a roar, all nineteen dragons took to the skies at once, flying in dangerously close formation as they ascended on natural updrafts. *"It is time for the Star Dragons to go to war!"*

Chapter 37

BATTLE OF THE DEADLANDS

Energy surged through Cardin. Confidence, boldness, courage, call it whatever you want, it resonated from the Star Dragons alighting upon the winds, swirling around the Celestial Spires hypnotically.

Cardin saw that same feeling in his companions, *felt* it echoing off of their souls. Sira's violet eyes lit up, and for the first time, he truly *felt* the entity within her, flexing its powers, vying to be with those dragons, lifting into the air, ready to give their all to rescue one of their own.

One of their own…Endri was one of them. Not the Star Dragons, but one of Cardin's people. One of Cardin's friends.

His family.

A single, great portal opened above them, and the Star Dragons streamed through, one after another after another, led by Firdal himself.

"Let's go, before we're too late to join the fun," Elaria remarked, and she opened a portal large enough for the three of them to pass through together.

Cardin brandished the Sword of Dragons, while Sira drew her white-dyed claymore, and Elaria drew her enchanted daggers.

As one, they rushed through.

And came out atop a stone platform in the middle of a jungle.

Cardin had no time to take in his surroundings, a giant of a brute sporting Darksteel armor and a great axe greeted him. He caught and blocked the brute's strike upon him, pushed away, and wielding the great Sword as easily as he would a shortsword, Cardin pirouetted and cut right through the enchantments on the brute's armor, slicing into his torso and startling his opponent.

He was out of the fight. The other ten weren't.

But while Cardin cut down the one, Elaria and Sira wasted no time charging at the others, and Cardin felt a surge of magic lance out of Sira's blade, blasting through a lithe, pale-faced caster's shield before she was upon him. He used his pauldrons to block her sword attacks, and then tried to blast her with magic, but Raida, it seemed, was powerful enough to defend her, for now.

Cardin tore his attention from her and went after the next eight-foot-tall brute, this one wielding a heavy mace, it's spikes big enough to rend Cardin's body in half.

He cast a shield, and though the brute's weapon was infused with ice-cold magic, it bounced off of his defenses. He felt the drain, felt the strength behind his opponents attack, and knew that he would be much better off dodging such attacks in the future than absorbing them.

But now he was inside of the brute's defenses, and he thrust the Sword up, into his enemy's chest, the tip coming out through his spine.

Blue blood appeared in stark contrasts to the red of the Sword.

As the brute fell, Cardin withdrew his weapon, and turned to the next enemy, another ghost-looking magic-wielder who was focused on Elaria. Counting on his enhanced control, Cardin pointed the tip of the Sword at the ghost, who felt Cardin's power and tried to shield himself.

But Cardin switched from star magic to dark magic. It took precious seconds, and the ghost tried to attack Cardin, but his newly-erected dark shield absorbed the attack easily, and then he blasted the ghost. His dark magic didn't deflect off of his opponent's shield, but rather sank into it, canceling it out, until there was nothing left.

With the enemy's shield down, Elaria was free to come up behind him and cut his throat.

And that was it for the battle on the platform. Allowing Cardin to figure out where they were and what they were doing.

The edge of a jungle, and as he turned towards where he felt incredible power flowing from a dozen and a half Star Dragons, he saw a land of death. A land where no life grew.

And a battle the likes of which he had never seen before.

Star Dragons and Dark Dragons, flying above steel spires and columns of smoke, circling one another, trying to overpower one another. He had seen a similar battle between his avatar and Nuuldan.

Nuuldan…he was here. Cardin felt the Dark Dragon's presence, same as he had in Maradin.

But he didn't see the form flying amongst the others. The four Dark Dragons he could see spiraling up, combatting the other Star Dragons, were much too small to be Nuuldan, whose size was only challenged by Astaria's on Stella. Even Firdal would have been dwarfed by the First Dark Dragon.

Cardin searched the horizon then, but it was dusty, hazy, impossible to see through.

But not to feel through. The metal spires in the distance, that's where he felt the dark presence.

No…not the spires.

Just past them.

He looked at Elaria, and then Sira. He wanted to tell them to stay here, to guard whatever this platform was. But then he realized that if there were Darksteel soldiers on the other side…

Which there was. He glanced back at the battling dragons and suddenly saw countless blasts of magic lancing up from the ground, helping the Dark Dragons hold off the Star Dragons.

He couldn't do this alone.

"Come with me," he ordered, barely remembering that not so long ago, Sira was the one giving *him* orders.

Without another thought, he opened a portal. It barely registered on him that he was still using dark magic, and that it was his first dark portal.

Sira and Elaria exchanged surprised looks, but they otherwise didn't hesitate, and with Cardin only a half-step behind them, they passed through…

Into chaos.

They were right in the middle of a battalion of Darksteel troops, including siege weapons like the ones pelting Archanon's wall and their accompanying furry monsters.

Their attention was skyward, and Cardin bringing them in with Dark Magic meant they hadn't sensed their arrival, not right away. Those of the enemy who were capable used enchanted weapons or gauntlets to assault the Star Dragons, to help give the Dark Dragons a chance at defending against the overwhelming odds.

The enemy hadn't counted on ground support.

Without pausing or taking stock of where they were at first, Cardin launched at the closest magic-casting ghost-like enemy, and cut her down.

Sira and Elaria likewise attacked, taking the enemy by surprise. But their enemy was well trained, and while Cardin, Sira, and Elaria managed to cut down over a dozen in seconds, the enemy forces noticed something was amiss quickly, and turned their attention to the ground.

Gone was the element of surprise, and Cardin had to keep his shield up constantly while fighting, as blasts of magic and swiping weapons came from every direction.

This wasn't what he wanted, and he realized too late that he had committed a serious tactical error. They should have come in further away, to assess the enemy strength and even assault them from the distance.

Cardin couldn't unleash his full powers, not without risking Sira and Elaria, and the battle wore on him quickly, even infusing magic into his limbs to revitalize himself. They would lose by sheer numbers if something didn't change. So he did the only thing he could think of.

He called to the Star Dragons, using the 'come forth' spell.

"I am coming," Firdal's voice echoed in his thoughts.

Above them, the red dragon broke off from the battle, and folded its wings to dive back towards the barren, red dirt at breakneck speed.

Firdal unleashed an incredibly powerful blast of white magic from his mouth and carved and rended into the ground around them, destroying any Darksteel soldiers unfortunate enough to get caught in the blast, and otherwise separating them from the rest of the warriors.

And then the great dragon landed with a thunderous, ground-shattering boom that sent waves of dust into the air.

While Firdal swiped and blasted at troops, Cardin and the others were able to focus on those left in the artificial island Firdal had made for them.

He killed a brute, a ghost, another, smaller, more powerful attacker, and then another brute, and then a half dozen foot soldier type enemies, until finally, they were clear.

Firdal wasn't so lucky. Two of the giant beasts, untethered from their siege weapons, charged at the red dragon. He swiped at one, easily batting it aside, its momentum carrying it into dozens of Darksteel troops and kicking up even more red dirt. The second beast plowed into Firdal, piercing his scaly hide with horns, and the dragon roared out in shock and pain.

Cardin charged his weapon with dark magic and unleashed a pinpoint powerful attack. It pierced the creature's thick hide right where he hoped its heart would be, and it stopped cold. Firdal disconnected and rolled once, twice, crushing more enemies.

A soft, green light covered the Star Dragon's side, and in only moments, its physical wound was healed. *Damn, they're fast at that,* he thought, and wondered if a Star Dragon could actually ever be killed in battle.

A flash of red, an impossible screech, and a blast of dark magic lanced out of the dust and struck Firdal right where he'd been trying to heal himself. The scream Firdal let forth was not just physical, but magical. Dark and light colliding, and without a shield to protect him, the darkness had directly assaulted Firdal's light.

It hurt to hear. It hurt to *feel* Firdal's pain. Cardin grasped his chest, feeling his heart seize in it for a moment.

Another red blast lanced out of the dust and slammed into Firdal, but this time the Star Dragon managed to get a shield up, absorbing the impact. But the blast did not abate, and just like Cardin's first battle with Nuuldan, it eroded the star-made shield, wore it down, drained it of power, until the blast pierced it and drove into Firdal, eliciting another magic-rending scream.

Cardin couldn't see where Nuuldan was in the dusty haze, and he had to cover his mouth to keep from coughing uncontrollably against the red sand, but the two blasts let him hone in on the Dark Dragon. Charging the Sword with more dark magic, he pointed the tip in that general direction, elevating it since he knew just how large the First

Dark Dragon was, and he unleashed the most powerful blast of dark magic he could.

A roar of surprise and pain. Nuuldan hadn't expected it! And he couldn't see Cardin anymore than Cardin could see him. He must have wounded the Dark Dragon!

But Cardin was just as vulnerable, his friends more-so. If Nuuldan could hone in on him as he had on the Dark Dragon…

With moments to spare, Cardin erected a dark shield big enough to encompass the entire 'island' that Firdal had carved for them, just as a wave of red-colored magic slammed into it. Nuuldan hadn't been exactly on target, and Cardin was grateful for that, as the glancing blow wore him down immensely. The blast ricocheted off of his shield and slammed into more Darksteel soldiers in the distance, and gouged into the ground, throwing up even *more* red dirt into the air.

Firdal's roar of pain had caught the attention of others, and before Nuuldan could unleash more attacks, Cardin saw blasts of multicolored light rain down from the sky towards the direction he'd felt Nuuldan. An impatient roar followed, and then the giant, eclipsing form of Nuuldan leapt into the sky, dark wings unfurling and blowing the cloud of dirt away as he rose to meet his challengers head-on.

Which gave Cardin the chance he needed.

Closing his eyes, he turned his attention away from dark magic and allowed the light of the stars to fill him again. The cold darkness gave way to the warmth of *being,* and he reached out his senses, allowing the light of magic to fill his vision even through closed eyes. He *Saw.* Saw Sira, Saw Elaria, and even Saw every single Darksteel troop and their giant, powerful creatures.

Most importantly, he saw the dimming light of a Star Dragon.
Endri.

"I have to get to him," Cardin told the others, and without waiting to explain further, he ran towards the dimming light, using his powers to leap over the wide gap and onto the rest of the Deadlands.

Breathing was becoming challenging, coughing became a norm, which made running harder. Dirt stung at his eyes, so he closed them and allowed the light of magic to guide him.

It was…eerie, strange even. He could see the light of the living, but he was used to seeing life everywhere on Halarite. The grasses, the trees, the animals. Here, the ground was void of life. Only the Darksteel army and Endri lit up. It was a stark contrast, but it made avoiding enemy soldiers easier.

Until, finally, the dimming light of Endri filled his entire being, and he risked opening his eyes.

The formerly green dragon was tethered to the Deadlands, great big, Darksteel chains were cast over him, the links larger than Cardin's entire body, with pikes dug into the barren dirt to hold his friend in place, including across his snout.

He was wounded. Great big rends in his scales, patterned in a way that Cardin knew that Nuuldan had done it with his claws. Dark, dried blood intermixed with fresh, and Cardin knew Endri hadn't been able to heal himself, either through Nuuldan's interference or dark magic interfering with Endri's powers.

Either way, his friend was hurt. Badly.

And when Endri opened his eyes, the light within was dim, so much so that even though there was little dirt in the air between them, Cardin could barely see them.

A rumbling groan escaped his friend's throat, and he tried to shift his head to see Cardin better, but the chains gave him very little play.

His voice was weak. *"Cardin..."*

"My gods," Cardin shook his head, and ran, faster than he'd ever run before, to his friend's side. He tried desperately to keep the images of Avall, the purple dragon he'd met beneath the Ilari Mountains, from coming forward, but the similarities were jarring and terrifying.

She had died then.

Endri looked worse.

He was larger than Avall had been, and standing beside the green dragon's head, he still had to look up to see Endri's eye.

That was when he noticed the darkness in his scales. Streaks, really. But he could feel the darkness within, creeping into the Star Dragon's soul, expanding.

"You are not real," Endri said. *"Another...illusion."*

"I'm real," he said, and touched his friend's scales. They were cold, far colder than they should have been. "I'm here. I'm going to save you."

"There is no safe," the dragon muttered. His voice sounded strange, echoing in Cardin's thoughts, as if he spoke twice at once. Then

Cardin realized why – Endri was speaking to him through both star magic and dark magic. *"There is no save. Save is illusion."*

He wasn't himself, Cardin realized.

An explosion caught his attention, and he looked left. What looked like a floating ship with a giant, bulbous bladder above it caught fire and was consumed by flame, but ten more floated near it, approaching the battle and unleashing magical strikes from their decks upon the Star Dragons.

He looked up, and through the haze of dirt, saw a Star Dragon take three blasts of dark magic simultaneously, and it fell from the sky.

They were running out of time.

This place wasn't safe to try to save Endri. He had to get him somewhere else.

Stepping away, Cardin looked at the chains and wondered what enchantments they might have. Could he safely destroy a link without hurting Endri further?

"The answers, Keeper," Endri muttered. *"Are in the questions. The darkness. The light."*

"Just hold on, Endri," he shuddered. "Hold on..."

If they were enchanted, then dark magic could easily break the chains. But that could further infect Endri. Was it worth the risk?

I have to save him.

So he pushed star magic out of him, pushed out all power, creating a void that filled with dark energy.

And he unleashed it with perfect accuracy, snapping the chain around Endri's head. Cardin repeated the exercise, snapped the next chain, and the next, until all chains released.

Endri stretched and lifted his head, and turned to Cardin. *"The question burns within you. A question of life. Of intelligence. Can darkness be life? Can stars survive the dark? Will they become living darkness?"*

The words, the questions, they caught Cardin off guard. "Wh...what? Living darkness?"

"Or will it end us all? The source of all life as we know it." Endri's gaze turned towards this world's sun. *"If they fall to darkness...do we all perish?"*

"I...I don't know," Cardin shook his head. "It doesn't matter now, we need to get you to safety. Can you stand?"

Endri looked at him, and then laid his head down and closed his eyes.

"Endri?" Nothing. "Endri!"

The dragon lived. He still had magic. But the darkness spread rapidly. It was as if Endri had given up the fight.

"No, no, no, not now! Not yet!"

"Then when?"

Cardin rushed to the dragon's side, saw that more darkness had spread across his scales. "No," he shook his head. "No, I won't lose you too, dammit!"

He planted his hand on the dragon's scaly cheek, and closed his eyes. Battle be damned, he had to save Endri.

So he looked within. Within himself. Within the Sword.

"The Shadow Quartz," Endri reminded him. *"That gives the Sword its dark power."*

Cardin blinked, looked up at Endri's eye, open again, but dimmer than ever. Red crept in on the edges. Just like Nuuldan's eyes.

Endri shuddered, and he closed his eyes. *"I told him that."*

Cardin felt dread wash over him. He looked up. Two more Star Dragons fell from the sky, and the hulking form of Nuuldan swept towards another.

He knew.

Nuuldan knew that the Sword of Dragons was partly made of the Shadow Quartz he sought.

"I had no choice, Keeper. He...infected my mind. He knows." Endri huffed out, blowing new dust into the air. *"He knows. About everything I know. Everything."*

The Shadow Quartz. A dark artifact that Nuuldan destroyed the Wizards' Guild over, something that was meant to darken the skies of every world, darken every star, and snuff out all star magic everywhere.

It had destroyed the Vestuul sun, driving the necromancers to Halarite.

It was what linked the Sword to the Dark Dragons.

It was what allowed the first Vrol to take up the Sword and wipe every conscious Dark Dragon from existence in one fell swoop.

That was the tale he had been told, the story Astaria had admitted to him.

What if that was the answer? Cardin hefted the Sword up, light as ever, but a heavy burden to bear, and he looked at the intricate runes carved into it, the beautiful ley lines inlaid. Somehow able to help both star and dark magic flow in and out of it.

The Sword of Dragons was balance. The bridge between light and dark. If the Shadow Quartz gave it its dark power, then what gave it its star power?

He didn't know the answer to that, but there had to be something imbued within it. Something of the Star Dragons, or something of the stars themselves.

Both contained within a single blade.

Coexisting, just like the disparate powers coexisted within himself.

The Sword was knowledge. And it gave that knowledge to those who wielded it.

So he did the only thing he could think to save his friend. He pressed the Sword of Dragons against Endri's skin. The first time in three thousand years that the Sword of Dragons ever touched an actual Star Dragon.

Endri reared up, tearing the Sword from his grip. The blade glowed brightly, searing itself against Endri's scales, and the dragon roared, roared through the physical realm, through star magic, through dark magic.

The blade flashed bright, and burst away from Endri as suddenly as it had fused with him, and summersaulted through the air to embed itself blade-first in the red earth a hundred yards from Cardin.

Every dragon, Star and Dark alike, felt Endri's roar, and light and dark eyes fell upon Endri. Upon Cardin.

Suddenly the Sword felt like it was a mile away. And while Endri writhed and contended with the new knowledge infused within him, Cardin raced across the dusty landscape towards the Sword, using magic to imbue his legs with greater strength and speed.

He heard and *felt* Nuuldan roar, and the Dark Dragon dove for him.

Cardin ran faster.

His heart raced, his vision blurred. No, he couldn't fail. Not in this.

Time slowed, the distance between him and the Sword stretched out endlessly.

Nuuldan pulsed magic into his body, Cardin felt the darkness swell, and he came faster.

Cardin would reach it first, he *had* to.

Until a dark portal opened just above the Sword.

Nuuldan slammed through at breakneck speed, shook the ground, sent up a plume of renewed dust, and Cardin lost his balance, tumbling along the Deadlands at speeds faster than any human was ever meant to endure. Something broke on his right arm, his shoulder.

Finally, he tumbled to a stop, with still a dozen yards between him and the Sword.

And Nuuldan inches above it.

He gaped, and feared. Nuuldan had wanted the Sword before...but to what end? He had hoped the Sword would have saved Endri, but Nuuldan was already entirely dark. What effect would it have on him?

Nuuldan snuffed at Cardin, and then lifted his paw, preparing to bring it down upon the Sword and do who knew what to it.

Endri slammed into him, barreling over the Dark Dragon despite the difference in their size and weight, and then he unleashed a blast of magic upon Nuuldan.

Magic that Cardin swore felt like a combination of both star and dark magic. Nuuldan howled in pain as they tumbled away from the Sword.

Cardin wasn't sure what to make of it, but it didn't matter. The Sword was still twenty yards away, so against the pain wracking his body, he crawled forward. His right arm hung loosely, pain surging throughout his body, so he infused magic into himself, and brought forth streams of healing power. A green glow covered half of his body, healing not just his arm, but wounds he hadn't even realized he'd endured.

More blasts of magic from Endri and Nuuldan vied for his attention, but he had to focus on the Sword.

Ten yards.

"It's mine!" he heard Nuuldan's terrifying voice in his mind.

A blast of red magic lanced out at him. He raised a shield, barely in time to intercept, but the blast was larger, encompassing, and anywhere not protected by his shield was blasted. Including the Sword. Another cloud of red dust exploded into the air.

He tried to find the Sword, but it had been blasted from its spot and wound up tumbling across the barren landscape.

Endri got in the way of the next blast, taking the full brunt of it and roaring in pain and shock.

Cardin ran after the Sword, his healing magic restoring more and more of his body and his muscles.

Darksteel troops were emerging from the dust, right near the Sword.

He ran faster, and unleashed a torrent of magic from his hands, blasting the enemy. They returned his attack, and his shield, weakened by the fact that he tried to heal himself, failed. A blast hit him full-force in the chest, stopping him cold and planting him square on his back, the wind knocked out of him.

His chest hurt.

Ribs. His ribs were broken.

Magic. He coursed magic into his body. Healed the ribs. They snapped painfully back into place. Darkness edged his vision – he was going to pass out.

But the Sword, he had to get the Sword.

So as much as he wanted to lie down and fall asleep, he instead pushed himself up, his body complaining every inch of the way.

The enemy prepared to attack him again. If he gave up on his healing magic to defend himself, then his body would shut down, and he'd pass out. He was dead either way.

Until a white longsword cut one down, and a pair of daggers pierced another, and then magic lashed out at the enemy troops.

Sira and Elaria had emerged from the dust, and they got the enemy's attention.

Endri kept Nuuldan busy.

His love and his friend kept the Darksteel Army busy.

This was his only chance.

It hurt, but he stood up.

He was tired, but he marched forward, step after exhausting step.

Until, finally, just as Sira cut down the last Darksteel soldier, he collapsed to his knees next to the Sword, and he picked it up.

The burden was his again.

He fell over, but Elaria caught him, and Sira helped them a second later.

Roars, furious magic, and shaking ground drew their attention, and Sira and Elaria helped Cardin turn to see the battle unfolding between the First Dark Dragon and Endri, whose form changed before their eyes.

Light and darkness together, not unlike Cardin's avatar.

Except, something was different. It wasn't stable. Darkness crept over parts of Endri, while green faded to white.

White glowed.

Dark absorbed all light, becoming darker than the darkest night.

Nuuldan unleashed a blast of dark magic upon Endri, but the blast passed into a void of nothingness. A moment later, a pulse of *being,* of *everything* lanced out, slamming into Nuuldan and sending him sprawling thousands of feet through the air, but that blast also tore up the ground, sending massive boulders sailing into the sky, and they rained down violently, one nearly crushing Cardin and the others, landing only a few feet away.

Endri roared. But it wasn't a challenge or a triumphant roar.

It was surprise, he thought.

But not terror.

Endri clenched at his stomach. The light became brighter, the dark became darker.

White noise rumbled through the air, through magic, light and dark magic alike. It grew louder, deafening, painful against their souls.

Cresting at a crescendo that eclipsed their vision, their hearing, all of their senses, Endri roared out one last time.

But his voice. His voice came to Cardin. *"My friend. Thank you."*

Barely able to think above the pressing *everything* against him, Cardin thought, *Endri?*

"Thank you for not giving up on me. Now let me protect you."

The dragon paused, and though Cardin couldn't see his friend, he could feel his presence, his power, his grace.

"Let me send you home. All of you."

A moment later, the deafening noise ended.

The light faded. The pressure released.

Cardin had closed his eyes, but as he felt the last of his healing magic fading, its job completed, he felt…

Stone.

He opened his eyes, and found himself lying on his back, staring up at a clear blue sky.

Broken a moment later by a curious-looking Reis, who hovered over him, frowning. "Uh, hello there," Reis quipped.

Cardin blinked. "R-Reis?"

Grinning, Reis nodded. "Yeah, that's me. You look like every hell rolled into one."

The healing magic was done, but Cardin still felt fatigue in every bone in his body. So when he tried and failed to stand up, Reis clasped his hand and pulled him up.

They were next to Main Street in Archanon, not far from the Western Gate.

They. Cardin, Sira, and Elaria, the others who were likewise being helped up by Archanon soldiers.

"What...happened?" he asked.

"Uh," Reis exchanged glances with the others present. "Yeah, I was hoping you could tell us. All of a sudden, there was a loud bang. I was up on the wall assessing enemy movements, and then I look back down here and the three of you were just...*here*."

Cardin shook his head, and then looked at Sira and Elaria. "It was Endri," he said.

"I know," Sira nodded solemnly. "I heard him, too."

"Yeah," Elaria agreed. "He...he sent us back here before..."

Cardin felt his heart cinch.

The green dragon was gone. He didn't know how, or to where or why, but Endri was gone.

But now...now they were home.

What was left of it, anyway.

No Endri.

No Star Dragons.

No hope.

Had it all been for nothing?

Chapter 38

SHATTERED

Kailar hated waiting.

Especially in the freezing cold of night. They had watched the Darksteel embassy all day, initially from the council meeting table, but after the fires died, they retreated into town to watch from a distance. The Navitas just…stood there. Staring at the mobile embassy, never moving, never blinking, just waiting for the next day's meeting with frustrating patience.

But Kailar didn't have that kind of tolerance. At one point, she left Letan to watch while she traveled to the other cities on Devor, just to make sure the Darksteel Empire hadn't invaded them.

All was peaceful. Eerily so.

After more waiting and watching with Letan, she then went to have dinner with Reyla at Reyla's house, as she had promised, even though there were no new insights to report.

The Empress, on the other hand, had plenty to discuss. Kailar learned that things were more or less deadlocked. The Lords of Corlas and Edingard were in favor of joining the Darksteel Empire, but the Lord of Neolas was not. Combined with Reyla's reticence to give up their sovereignty, and the Navitas being unwilling to choose a side, it left them in a difficult spot.

Over a savory meal of hot stew filled with meat and potatoes, they sat in Reyla's dining room, as big as she'd expect for one of the wealthiest persons on Devor. The Empress had always been a conundrum to Kailar, her wealth obvious in her mansion-like home, but her preference in clothes rather simple and unassuming.

Kailar and Reyla sat quietly for a moment, enjoying their meal and the warmth of a fire in the dining room's hearth.

Mulling it over in her head, Kailar couldn't figure it out. "Why?" she asked.

Reyla stared at her for a moment, and then asked, "Why what?"

Kailar blinked in surprise. "Uh, did I say that out loud?"

After another sip of hot stew, Reyla nodded. "You did. Speak your mind, Kailar."

She considered her question carefully before asking it. "Why are the Lords of Corlas and Edingard so willing to give up on our new empire?"

Reyla appeared to consider her question for a moment, and then shook her head. "They are not."

Kailar's brow creased down into a deep frown. "Then what are they doing?"

"Surviving," Reyla replied simply. "In a way, that is all any of us on Devor know how to do. You included."

Kailar's cheeks warmed against that statement, but she couldn't dismiss Reyla's observation.

Devor had survived *in spite* of a lack of support from Edilas. Had survived against rampant criminals.

And Kailar? She had survived more.

"That still doesn't make sense, though," Kailar shook her head, stirring her stew aimlessly. "This is the first time anyone on Devor has had something *more,* or at least a chance for more. Why give it away at the first sign of trouble?"

"Well," Reyla shook her head. "It's more than just a *little* trouble, to be sure. The threats of the Darksteel ambassador are veiled, but still obvious. The description of the breadth of their power is beyond anything we have ever known. We are a...well, a rather quaint society compared to their empire."

Kailar scowled. It was a distasteful description, insulting and demeaning.

Then again, she conceded that it was an apt depiction.

The Darksteel Empire boasted a vast interplanetary trade and commerce, and a military capable of occupying entire worlds, all supplemented by an ability to move goods and resources in the blink of an eye. Soldiers in the field could be fed without having to rely on local farms. Reinforcements could be summoned in minutes. Intelligence could be passed along just as quickly.

Worse still, she had the distinct feeling that right now, at that very moment, an invasion with those resources was playing out on Edilas. Maybe Asirin, too.

"We don't stand a chance," she murmured.

"No?" Reyla asked. "Not even with you?"

Kailar smiled lightly. "I'm not all-powerful."

"Indeed you are not."

The Empress's face drew down then, and she settled the spoon carefully in the bowl, her stew barely touched. "I fear, Kailar." Her voice tremored, and Kailar's eyes widened. Reyla had not admitted such fear before, and her steadfast demeanor, her stoicism, her confidence as a leader would have had Kailar believing she knew exactly how to get them out of this situation.

Turns out the Empress was as human as Kailar was, and despite everything, that surprised Kailar.

The Empress looked into Kailar's eyes, the fear stirring within her, passing between them both. "And so do the Lords," Reyla continued. "They fear the Darksteel Army. Rightly so. And while the Navitas may help one day, as you have learned, they cannot help now. They have their own matters to attend to. And it won't be long before the Darksteel ambassador figures this out, he is so clever."

Kailar conceded that as well.

And then stopped cold in her thoughts, and looked up at Reyla. Her stomach felt like it was dropping out as a sudden realization coursed through Kailar.

The Empress frowned at Kailar's sudden change. "What is it?"

"Did...did you tell the Lords that?"

Reyla's frown deepened. "Yes, of course."

The Lord of Edingard. If she knew...

"I have to get back to Letan," she threw her utensil down and bolted out of the dining room and out of the house, surprising servants and guards alike. Kailar paid them little heed as she ran, ran as fast as she could, as fast as her magic-enhanced legs would take her.

Snow crunched, her breath ran ragged, puffing into the freezing air. Without the moons to light her way, she was dependent upon the city's torches. So few compared to Archanon.

Racing down the main street, seeing the glow of the Navitas's eyes in the distance, she at least took comfort in the fact that it was still undisturbed. Maybe there was still time.

"Kailar!"

Letan's call startled her, but she held her balance as she slid across the well-packed snowy road. She saw him emerge into the light of a shop's windows, not where she had left him. "Letan?"

"I was coming to find you," he hurried over to her as she finally slid to a stop. "You won't believe who I just saw going into the embassy-"

"Lord Penn?"

He came up short, bewildered. "Uh, yeah!"

It still didn't explain what magic communication the Navitas had felt, but it fit her suspicions. "I think she's been in their pocket all this time, and she just found out-"

A flash of light from the embassy.

An explosion of crystal and energy unleashed in a shattering wave, demolishing the meeting table, scattering the embers of the fires, and rattling the nearest buildings.

The Navitas was gone, and in its place lingered a pulsing golden energy, rending out bolts of lightning, striking the ground in thunderous claps, and striking buildings, setting them blazing.

Kailar projected a dark shield just in time, as a bolt of golden energy lanced out at them, only to be lost in the void of her magic.

The bolts gradually tapered off to nothing, but the golden light lingered where the Navitas had stood.

"By the gods," Letan whispered, staring at the wound in the world, in magic.

The Navitas was gone. Slain.

"They know," Kailar whispered. "They know that the Navitas pose no threat."

Letan's face looked mortified as he gaped at her, but then his head snapped back towards the embassy, which she knew meant he sensed more magic that she could not.

And in the blink of an eye, a blue-white portal as wide as the embassy opened before it. And the first invaders of Devor marched forth in columns of ten. Giant brutes. Ghosts. And more. So many more different invaders.

One row. Two rows. They marched with military precision through fresh snow, giving the wound of the Navitas's death a wide berth, and coming straight for the city. For Kailar and Letan.

Reyla and General Querlin had not left the embassy unguarded, however, and the soldiers of the Devor Imperium, few as they were on night guard, streamed out of the shadows around Kailar and Letan and lined up beside and behind them in their own column.

A column of thirty against seventy. Eighty. Ninety. The enemy's numbers swelled, streaming through the gate unopposed.

War had not been fought on Devor. There were no siege weapons, and the walls were a joke, incomplete and inconsequential against such a force.

Kailar's daggers were in-hand, Letan's sword in his. Her blades hummed with dark energy, his with light. And all around, the soldiers of Devor drew swords, and what few Mages they had pulsed energy into their swords.

One hundred fifty Darksteel soldiers. One hundred sixty. They just kept coming.

Kailar couldn't comprehend it. Couldn't believe it.

Belatedly, a horn called out, one of the city watch's horns, alerting the rest of the soldiers, the rest of the city, many of whom stood at their doorsteps now, having been startled from their homes by the destruction of a crystalline entity. They watched in stunned horror, much as Kailar did.

She knew the city's strength, and it wasn't much. Less than five hundred soldiers, only about one hundred of them Mages. The largest city on Devor. The largest army in the Imperium.

More Darksteel streamed forth. Would it ever end?

"Hold," Letan shouted. She wanted to believe it was a challenge to the Darksteel Army, but Kailar knew better. They couldn't win this. The odds were impossible. Even if they somehow managed to defeat every single Darksteel soldier present, more would come. And more after that. Streaming forth from a dozen worlds or more, ready to fight, ready to burn the city to the ground, if necessary.

She looked right. Looked left. Down the line, past the soldiers, to the townspeople staring from doors and windows, unable to comprehend the fact that they should go back inside, that their lives as they knew it were over.

Kailar looked at them. Innocents, every one of them.

They would all die if the imperial soldiers resisted. Letan knew that. He had lived on Devor all of his life, he knew the odds, and he knew the people.

So he ordered the imperial soldiers, "Hold! Do not attack!"

The sound of the marching Darksteel was overwhelming, even in snowpack. Thunder held no sway over the rumbling of precision marching. How could they do that in powder or on ice? It was beyond impressive. It was beyond terrifying. And they drew ever closer. A hundred yards, and they came on like a juggernaut.

She wanted to attack. Wanted to unleash her most powerful blast upon the enemy. She could lay waste to them like she had the citizens of Archanon at the Wizards' Guild. Row after row would fall to her dark magic.

But they weren't enthralled peasants, and the portal was still open. More soldiers marched in, bearing enchanted armor and enchanted weapons.

"Letan!" someone shouted from behind. They turned, saw another soldier scrambling towards them, fully geared and no doubt part of the night watch. "There's another portal! Another army marches upon us from the northwest!"

So that was it. Even if Kailar wanted to. Even if she could stand up against the now-thousand-strong troops marching towards them, only fifty yards away, it wouldn't matter.

Following along behind that soldier was a harried-looking General Querlin, and behind him was Empress Reyla.

Kailar turned to the army. Twenty yards away.

She looked at Letan, and he at her. There was no fear in his eyes, and that shocked her. All she saw was determination. The look of a man who had spent his entire life protecting others, now willing to make the hardest call ever.

Ten yards, booming marching. The portal had closed at some point, but they were so close now, and so numerous and so many of them taller than humans that she couldn't even see the embassy now. Shadows against the snow, demons with no remorse, no regret, just the certainty that they had already won.

Five yards, and they stopped. No verbal command was ever given, they just stopped. Over one thousand troops, in unison.

More Devor soldiers had formed up. She could hear them shaking in their armor. Could feel their nervousness, even without star magic.

It should have pervaded her emotions too, but it didn't. No terror, not anymore. Just a steadfast resolve.

Kent and Reyla edged their way to the front of the imperial formation, Kailar and Letan pressing aside to allow them in.

And from the Darksteel army came a familiar face. Xavien strode between his troops, entirely nonplussed and exuding an air of absolute confidence. He stepped in front of this troops directly before Reyla and stopped, showing them his profile, as if they were beneath him.

Reyla looked to Kailar. To Kent. To Letan. Kailar couldn't read her expression. Or maybe she didn't want to. After so long working towards this, after so many years, so many miles, she couldn't accept the look within her empress's face.

But Kailar knew what would come next, and knew that she had no choice but to follow Reyla.

Kent's sword was drawn, and he looked at it with the kind of regret one showed when giving up their most prized possession. He and Reyla took a single step forward.

And then Kent planted his sword into the icy road. As one, he and Empress Reyla of the Devor Imperium knelt.

They never had to say anything. The act was enough.

A long, eerie grin stretched across Xavien's face, and he looked side-long at them. "Now, then," he said. "Let us discuss your future."

Chapter 39

DISQUIET NIGHT

Night had fallen upon Archanon, and Sira wondered if it would be their last night. Never could she have believed such a thought would ever cross her mind, but here, now, she thought it. She *felt* it.

BOOM!

The Darksteel Army continued their assault upon the shield. Even in the castle, the booms resonated and echoed. Only the dead could sleep.

And Cardin Kataar. He had passed out the moment his head hit the pillow in their room.

Watching from her favorite seat near the window, a single chamberstick illuminating the room, she thought *I don't blame him.* It had been a long day for everyone, but none among them had fought as hard as Cardin had.

They had spent the afternoon catching up with each other. She told him about the Teledin Bazaar, running from the guards, meeting Kemila and Elaria.

Elaria told him of the fate of Darea.

He told them of the meeting with the orcs, the initial invasion, and his scouting. He also told them about the chance his father had now, slim as it may be. But it was hope, nonetheless. Hope in a time when there was little to be had.

BOOM!

Another round from the siege weapons.

Sira shuddered and resigned herself to the waking world. For all she had endured, the fact was that she had slept for several hours before being rescued by the *Starfire,* and now was as wide awake as one could be.

So, leaving Cardin to slumber, she grabbed the chamberstick and slunk from their room to wander the castle corridors, her thoughts turning inward.

To Raida.

I still love him, you know.

"He's a loveable guy, most times."

No one's loveable all the time, are they?

"Well, no one except me, maybe."

Sira laughed aloud, and then caught herself as she passed a sleepy-looking castle servant. He gave her a wide berth in the hallway after that.

Shaking her head and trying to suppress her laugh, Sira wandered out into the gardens. It was a warm, late summer night, and she breathed in the fresh air. Fall would come soon, she realized, and it seemed like fall came faster in Archanon than in Daruun, no doubt thanks to being nestled up in the foothills of the Ilari Mountains.

BOOM!

Wandering the gardens in back, she swept past flowerbeds and trees, and thought, *This time last year, I was fighting in the Orc War. Now...now the orcs are our allies.*

She felt Raida stir with curiosity. *"You find this turn of events difficult?"*

Sira considered the dragonsoul's question for a moment, and wandered over to one of the fountains, its water bubbling and gurgling out upon a column and down into a stark, white basin. *Yes,* she admitted. *I grew up thinking of them as the enemy. I saw them commit atrocities during the war. It is difficult to think of them as anything other than monsters.*

"And what of the Darksteel Army? Are they monsters, too?"

Sira shuddered. Shortly after Endri sent them home, she had climbed up onto the city wall. Saw them in the setting sun, their new enemy, their greatest foe, moving about like shadows, setting siege weapons, making camp.

What had become of the outlying farms? What had become of the citizens of Daruun?

BOOM!

Yes, she thought. *They are.*

"*Regardless of what species they are?*"

Furrowing her brow, Sira sat upon a bench, the gentle glow of a lantern nearby and her chamber stick keeping her from total shadows. *What does it matter their species?*

"*What of the dwarves of Darea?*"

She started at that, and immediately thought of Gilrin. She hadn't spent much time with the dwarf, but he was a decent person. A little brash for a man who served an honored institute, but nevertheless, a noble man as far as she could tell.

Would he be absorbed into the Darksteel Army? Were all of his people monsters for turning against the elves, who had once already betrayed the dwarves in a heinous fashion far beyond anything she could truly understand?

Fair point, she conceded.

BOOM!

Fidgeting and restless, she stood up and started walking again. There were enough lanterns and everlasting torches throughout the garden that she could have left the chamberstick behind. Either way, somehow she knew that Raida wouldn't let her stumble around in the dark.

Eventually she found herself wandering to the wide terrace that ran much of the length of the front of the castle, and stared out west towards the gates, the twin peaks shadowed in the dark of night.

Except when another siege weapon lit up the shield.

BOOM!

A cascading wave spread across a quarter of the shield, and even from this distance, she *felt* the magic enchantments of the siege round.

Further along the terrace, she saw two figures stooped over the waist-high stone fence, looking over the Upper City pensively, the man's face gloomy in the shadows of the nearby everlasting torches, the woman's passive, thoughtful. Reis and Elaria were alone, and as Reis looked towards the western peaks, towards the entrance to the catacombs, Sira suspected Reis missed Anila.

After debating a moment, she walked over to them. The flickering candlelight drew their attention, and when they saw her coming, Reis stood up straight and drew in a breath of surprise while Elaria smiled. Reis started to speak, stopped, and then laughed. "I guess I shouldn't be surprised you're up, too."

Sidling up next to them and resting her bottom against the fence, she shrugged. "Only the dead can sleep in this."

"And Cardin," Reis agreed, eliciting a chuckle from Elaria.

Pressing an elbow into his side, Sira asked, "How are you holding up?"

"Um," he sighed and copied her posture, "I'm not? I mean, I get promoted to captain of the guard right when the Warriors are disbanded, and-"

"Wait, they *what?!*" Sira gaped at him, wide-eyed. Her stomach sank and she felt a void open up in its place. "Disbanded?" Elaria looked just as surprised, but stared out and let the two Warriors...*former* Warriors talk.

"Oh," he stopped, wide-eyed. "Right. I guess we forgot to tell you about that. Um. Well, a lot happened while you were gone. The Warriors continued to refuse to fight for Cardin without pay. Cardin made a deal with the farmers and merchants guild, but it depended upon the Warriors fighting for food and supplies rather than gold. And when the orc shaman told him about her visions of an impending invasion, Cardin knew he had to act quickly. So he disbanded the Guild, made an offer for everyone to convert to the army, and that everyone would be taken care of if they did. Sooooooo, yeah. I'm not a Warrior anymore, and, um, neither are you."

She took the new information in, tried to make sense of it, but it was difficult to comprehend. The Warriors, one of the longest-running institutions in all of Halarite, had been disbanded?

"Only in Tal, I believe," Raida pointed out.

Even still, Sira shook her head. "I can't believe it..."

"Hey, don't sweat it," he shook his head. "I've no doubt you'll be welcomed into the ranks again. In fact," he narrowed his eyes at her. "How do you feel about the Guardians?"

She stared blankly at him, her mind still reeling. Still unable to wrap her mind around it. And here Reis was half-jokingly offering her a job.

A job where she would answer to him.

She once commanded him. Once commanded Cardin. Now she would answer to both of them?

"No, thanks," she shook her head. "I'll...I'll find a way...my way."

He nodded. "I understand. Hell, if you and Cardin ever get married, you'll be Princess of Tal and still outrank me anyway." Elaria glanced at Sira. Reis shuddered, and looked into the city just as...

BOOM!

And Sira's last dream flashed into memory. Cardin marrying Queen Leian. Suddenly the dream didn't bother her so much, and that startled her.

Oblivious to Sira's musings, Reis added, "Assuming we survive as a kingdom."

She barely heard him, her thoughts seizing upon the dream. The dream that had woken her in a cold sweat, made her feel disconnected, disoriented, even a little jealous.

Now it didn't bother her one bit.

The idea of marrying Cardin, on the other hand, suddenly seemed foreign. Strange.

Princess Sira Reinar. Or as politics would no doubt demand, Princess Sira Kataar.

Why did that bother her so much?

Was it because of her experiences over the last few days? Or was it more? Was the line between her and Raida blurring further?

Gods, who am I becoming? What *am I becoming?*

Then, a reassuring echo from only hours ago and a lifetime ago, Raida said, *"You are Sira Reinar."* Simple, to the point, and reassuring. *"No matter what happens, you are still you. And I am still me."*

But...we're influencing each other, aren't we? Sira thought of the symbiotic species that Elaria had mentioned. *Becoming something different?*

"Is that so bad? I feel like I am becoming a more complete being, thanks to your guidance. Have I not had a positive impact upon your life?"

Sira considered that question, and hesitated maybe a bit too long, the swirls of guilt welling up within her stomach. Raida's guilt.

The truth of it was, however, that she couldn't deny it. She was a stronger Mage thanks to Raida, she was more open-minded. She saw the world through new eyes, thanks to Raida's wonder. Through all of her years as a Warrior, Sira had been so focused on rank and command, on tactics and skills.

A year with the Keeper of the Sword had started to change that, but she truly hadn't started to appreciate the simple things in life until Raida reminded her about them. So many things she had taken for granted, things a Star Dragon might never have experienced but now was able to experience through her.

Simple things like bacon.

Smiling inwardly, she nodded her head. *Yes. You truly have, my dearest.* Warmth blossomed through her soul, the first time she had felt Raida smile so fully since the incident in the Deadlands.

Turning to Reis and Elaria, her face warming with happiness, she saw them staring at her awkwardly. That warmth turned to a blush of embarrassment. "Y-yes?"

Reis grinned at her. "It's kinda funny watching your face when you're talking with Raida."

Narrowing her eyes at him, she elbowed him a little harder. "Don't make fun of me."

A chuckle escaped him, and he backed away when she moved to smack him. Waving his hands up innocently, "Hey, easy there! I'm sorry!"

"Yeah, I'll make you sorry," she playfully started towards him.

BOOM!

Brought back to reality, she started and turned east, catching the last light of the shield flare from another round just barely visible above the castle from her vantage.

Running bootsteps caught their attention, and the trio turned back west, towards the Upper City gates. Barreling down the main avenue up towards the castle was a Warrior...no, not Warrior, a *soldier*. Full armor, sword and shield secured, he came at full speed past the front fountain and bounded up the terrace stairs three at a time.

"Soldier!" Reis yelled.

The soldier blurted out unintelligibly in surprise and stumbled, nearly tumbling forward. He must not have seen them. They hurried over to him while he caught his balance and his breath.

"What's going on?" Reis demanded.

"Uh," the soldier started and stopped, his eyes darting amongst them, lingering on Elaria. "Well, s-sir, I, um, have orders to bring the

Prince t-to the front immediately. The Western Gate."

"Oh?" Reis asked and exchanged a curious glance with the others. "What for?"

"I'm s-sorry sir, I was explicitly told to tell n-no one else why."

He looked terrified that Reis, the new Captain of the guard and Guardians, would reprimand him. Sira wondered herself how the usual prankster would handle command.

"By whose orders?" Reis asked.

"General Vellar's," the soldier instantly replied.

The only man whose rank might be equal to Reis's, though they commanded separate divisions.

Reis frowned, but the soldier anxiously shifted and said, "Please, s-sir, it's urgent."

"We could go with him," Sira suggested. "Cardin can decide if we can be present or not when he delivers the summons."

Reis nodded. "Good idea. Come on, soldier."

The four of them rushed through the main castle doors and turned left towards the north wing, and quickly came to Sira and Cardin's room. The soldier was about to bang on the doors, but Sira stopped him and simply walked in, the others following.

Chamberstick still in hand, Sira walked over to the bed, and as she pulled the four-poster curtains apart, she loudly said, "Cardin! Wake up, Cardin."

"Bwah, huh?" Cardin stirred blearily, reaching for the Sword leaning against the post by his head. He saw Sira's face and relaxed, rubbing his face. "Whasgoinon?"

Arching an eyebrow, and feeling only a little bad for waking him, she asked, "Come again?"

Cardin cleared his throat and shook his head. She felt the stir of magic around him, and thanks to Raida, she knew he coursed power into his body to help him wake up. "Sorry. What's going on?"

BOOM!

They all started at that, but then Cardin noticed Reis, Elaria, and the soldier. "What'd I miss?"

"Sir," the soldier hesitantly stepped next to the bed and took a knee, bowing his head low. "With your p-permission, I, uh. Have…"

"General Vellar wants to see you immediately by the west gate," Reis filled in for the flustered soldier. "Though apparently the reason why is super extra secret."

"Yes," the soldier nodded sheepishly. "S-sorry. I can tell you in front of them only with your permission."

Cardin frowned at them and rubbed more sleep from his eyes. "Well, go on. You can consider them my most trusted advisers, they know what I know."

Except about the Warriors being disbanded, Sira grumbled inwardly.

"Let's give him hellfire about that later," Raida suggested.

Absolutely.

"One of the tower tunnels," the soldier stated. "In the northwest mountain. We, that is I, um, was on patrol in the tunnels when I heard something, and I went down tower tunnel two to investigate, and when I got to where the shield cuts off the tunnel, I saw…that is, I came across…"

Cardin, more awake now, crawled out of bed and stood beside the soldier, who was beside himself and just couldn't come up with a coherent sentence. Sighing impatiently, Cardin touched the soldier's shoulder and said, "Come on, up. Stand up, and breathe."

The soldier looked even more nervous, but he managed to get to his feet and nod. "T-thank you, sir. Sire. I mean, Your Majesty."

"Stop," Cardin shook his head. "And just tell me what you saw."

"The Darksteel Army," he stated bluntly. "I mean, their leader or general or whatever she is. The one with claws on her gauntlets."

BOOM!

Sira's neck twitched, and her jaw tightened. "Her…" Memories of blazing pain upon her back intermixed with the terror Raida had felt when her chrysalis was damaged echoed through Sira's soul.

"Y-yeah," the soldier nodded. "She was there. And so was…" He hesitated and looked at Cardin wide-eyed. "So was General Artula."

The shock that passed amongst Cardin, Sira and Reis was beyond obvious, and Sira felt Cardin's soul stir upon hearing that name. "Wait, the former general of the Tal Warriors?" Sira asked.

"Yeah," he shook his head. "B-but he was *with* the Darksteel General. Wearing Darksteel armor."

Sira blinked in even more surprise. And realized just how tired she was of being surprised tonight.

"That's why he went missing," Elaria muttered, realization and distress on her face. When the others looked at her, she explained,

"One of our own military commanders apparently went missing five years ago, missing without a trace. And then one of Kemila's crew told me that he spotted our general leading the Darksteel invasion of Darea."

"The Darksteel General demanded I get someone in power to speak with her," the soldier continued. "I found General Vellar and brought him, and then the Darksteel general demanded of our General to get you because she has something of vital importance to tell you."

Cardin looked to the others again, concern and curiosity edging his features, and Sira tried to figure out exactly what was going on. "Wait, wait," Reis shook his head, rubbing his temples. "The Darksteel General and General Artula asked you to get General Vellar just to ask him to get Prince Kataar so that he could come speak with the three Generals, and the Darksteel Army General could tell him something important?"

Sira's head hurt, and from the looks on the soldiers face, his did too. "Um. Yes. I think."

There was a joke in all this, and she could tell that Reis wanted to say it, but he held his tongue.

Cardin, on the other hand, was all business. "Then I suppose it's past time to treat with our enemy," he sighed. "I don't suppose there's time to get properly dressed..."

BOOM!

Chapter 40

UNVEILED

Cardin and his entourage hurried through the city towards the Western Gate, but they didn't run. He refused to show such hurry for an enemy, memories of diplomacy and negotiations barely-remembered passing through his head.

His entourage…gods, he still wasn't used to words like that. He still wasn't used to his life as Prince of Tal. Maybe he never would be.

This was war, however, and *that* he understood.

The streets of Archanon were quiet, except for the regular *BOOM!* that echoed incessantly, like a steady, terrifying heartbeat reminding them all that their enemy lived, and bore down on them with steadfast certainty. Golden-hued everlasting torches cast the Market District in a warm glow, and belied the terror only a few feet on the other side of the fifty foot wall. He could sense that dawn was nearing, and soon, the citizens of Tal would stir from restless sleep, and try to live their lives amidst an overwhelming siege.

Turning right, Cardin led Sira, Elaria, Reis, and the soldier up the stairs carved into the stone of the mountain, until they came out atop the Western Wall. Cardin glanced down upon the assembled enemy troops in the valley, illuminated by countless light sources. No torches, he realized, just camp fires and handheld implements that looked like miniaturized versions of the glowlights from the dwarven city.

Then they turned right into the larger of the two mountains bracketing the Western Gate, and walked down a deep, long tunnel, illuminated by smokeless everlasting torches. The tunnel followed the curve of the wall, and would eventually come across another barracks, but their journey would not take them so far.

They walked up to the second, small cross-tunnel they came across, wide enough for two people to walk side-by-side, and found General Vellar waiting, barring any curious soldiers who might wander by from walking down.

"Prince Kataar," he nodded solemnly.

"General," Cardin replied.

"You're dismissed, soldier," the General said to the summoning soldier. "But remember, keep your mouth shut about what you learned tonight, understood?"

Clacking his armored boots together and saluting, the soldier replied, "Absolutely, s-sir. T-thank you." Without waiting for further orders, the nervous soldier headed off towards the barracks at a brisk, anxious pace.

Watching the soldier go, Cardin lifted an eyebrow and wondered if he had been that nervous in his youth. Then he looked again to Vellar and asked, "So. Is it true?"

Vellar's head canted back and he considered Cardin's question, before he turned and headed down the tunnel, waving for them to follow. "See for yourself, Sire."

Cardin looked to the others, and then followed along, Sira beside him and Reis and Elaria behind them.

"Did you talk more with the enemy general?" Reis asked.

Glancing over his shoulder scornfully, Vellar nodded. "I did. And General Artula. It is…not what I expected."

"How so?" Cardin asked as they came around a slight bend, and he saw them ahead. The Darksteel general was stooped low, too tall to comfortably fit in the tunnel, and that helped diminish her imposing stature. Cardin tried really hard not to tense up upon seeing her, but it didn't help when he felt Sira's anger pulse into the magic around them.

"Well," Vellar shook his head. "It'll be best if she speaks for herself, I think."

And there beside the enemy stood the legendary General Geildein Artula, once Tal's greatest Warrior leader, and lost since the meteorites fell upon Halarite and the necromancer invasion.

As Vellar brought their troupe to a halt only a few feet from the visitors, Cardin felt the city's shield, passing through rock unhindered, but still strong enough to separate them from the visitors.

Just like when they first met her, the Darksteel general's entire body was covered from head to toe in Darksteel plate armor, segmented frequently to give her freedom of movement. Even her head, except for eye slits, was completely covered, and through those slits, Cardin could more easily see an orange glow in the gloom of the tunnel.

Now, up close, as she stooped to keep her helmet from scraping on the ceiling, she looked more imposing. She *felt* more imposing. Her magic was strong, Cardin realized. He hadn't taken the time to really measure her up on Stella, but now he could sense it. She was more powerful than a Wizard, even Grand Master Syrn. No Star Dragon, to be sure, but still a considerable threat.

The Darksteel general's fingers flexed, but her claws remained retracted, for the moment.

"Keeper of the Sword," she spoke, her voice raspy in the helmet. "At last."

Cardin drew up next to General Vellar and stood at his full height. "I am Prince Cardin Kataar of Tal."

Geildein Artula, whose helmet was held between his right arm and torso, shifted anxiously. "Prince Kataar," a voice Cardin hadn't heard in months intoned, but it was not a question. "I had heard as much, but it still surprises me." He looked upon Cardin's clothes, a simple blue tunic and black trousers.

Cardin regarded the General's Darksteel armor. Armor that Cardin had become all too familiar with over the past year and a half.

"General Artula," Cardin nodded. "I am beyond surprised to see you standing next to...*her*." His eyes flashed towards the enemy General, and he felt the rage from earlier in the day scourge the magic flowing through him. The Darksteel general flinched, and that confirmed his suspicions about how powerful and attuned to magic she was. Looking back to Artula, Cardin folded his arms and said,

"Last we heard, you were lost in the Wastelands after the meteorite shower."

Artula seemed unperturbed by Cardin's venom and distrust. "Indeed," he replied with resolute stoicism. "It would seem that the Darksteel Empire had spies within our ranks already, and when the skies burned, they took the opportunity to abduct me and take me to another world."

Cardin tensed upon hearing that. "To what end?" He again looked the General up and down. "To turn you against us?"

Artula's jaw tensed, but he nodded. "Precisely that, yes."

Cardin's veins turned to ice. Geildein Artula knew their strengths and weaknesses. He knew how the Warriors fought, and even though they were disbanded in name, the Warriors still operated in much the way they had.

Maybe that was why Daruun had fallen so easily.

"Well if you both expected me to surrender tonight," Cardin looked to the Darksteel general, "I intend to disappoint you."

"On the contrary," she replied, her fingers flexing again. "I had hoped you would be unwilling to surrender."

Cardin quirked an eyebrow up. "Oh? Anxious for another fight with me? I assure you, it won't go any better than last time."

"And I've gained a lot more power since then," Sira growled, stepping closer. Cardin felt her powers flex, and when he glanced back, her violet eyes glowed menacingly.

He wanted to tell her to back down, but he understood her anger, and shared it.

"I came to warn you."

Cardin felt his heart skip a beat. He looked across the shield, but the general's posture hadn't changed. Her voice had sounded completely serious. "Warn us of what?" he asked.

"Word has already spread of your victory over our ally, the Dark Dragon Nuuldan," she said. "And while he yet lives, he is wounded and will be nursing his wounds for some time, as will the other Dark Dragons, or rather, the ones that survived."

Cardin's mind reeled. He was keenly interested in learning about what had happened after Endri had sent them away, but he didn't expect to learn anything anytime soon. This was news, and he wanted to hear more. What happened to Endri? What happened to the other Star Dragons? Unfortunately, he didn't expect to learn more. Not yet.

Her explanation wasn't an explanation, however, and he pointed out as much, "Is there a point to you telling me that?"

"You are powerful, Keeper," she stated. "More powerful than we anticipated. After all, the Sword of Dragons was not built for your kind. Your ability to wield it effectively, to have saved the Star Dragon from turning to darkness gave him incredible power over both for the moments he lived afterwards." Cardin started upon those words, but aside from clenching his jaw, he kept his face as even and passive as he could. *Don't give them an advantage. Don't give them the satisfaction.* But he couldn't help it. His heart ached to hear the final fate of Endri. *For the moments he lived afterwards...*

"As such," the Darksteel general continued, "I have been given orders to accelerate our assault. You know what airships are?"

Frowning, Cardin nodded. "As of yesterday, yes."

"I was told to bring them to bear upon your world, but I held them back in reserve. Now, however," she shook her head, an awkward gesture in the relatively cramped quarters. "Now I have no choice. I have already given the order, and come morning, a fleet of airships will arrive."

Cardin frowned, and glanced at the others in his party, but they looked just as perplexed. "And what exactly will that do for your people?"

It was General Artula who answered, first by looking up. Cardin followed his gaze to the rocky ceiling.

Then he understood.

"Oh." He felt his face grow pale. "The shield."

"It extends only so high," Artula nodded to him. "The airships will be able to fly over the shield and invade the city from above."

Cardin narrowed his eyes. "You realize we can just...blast them out of the sky with magic, yes?"

"It will not matter," the Darksteel general shook her head. "My troops will descend with or without intact airships. They will destroy your shield mechanism from the inside, much as the Wizard Klaralin did. The shield will fall this morning. Archanon will fall. I can no longer delay it."

A mixture of surprise, fear, and determination coursed through him, and his arms fell limply to his sides. "I see..."

"Why warn us?" Sira asked. "Why would you help us? Why delay your invasion in the first place?"

"Because of why we have come to Halarite," she replied. "Because I do not wish to see what has happened to my world happen to Halarite, or any other world. There is little time, because I know there will be much for you to see to," she looked upon Cardin. "So I cannot explain it all right here, right now."

Cardin tilted his head to one side and considered her words briefly. "I see. So are you telling me that your world fell victim to the Darksteel Army, and you want to help us protect Halarite to keep us from the same fate?"

She did not answer at first, and her hesitancy worried Cardin.

"No," she finally replied. "My world did not fall victim to the Darksteel Army. My world *leads* the Darksteel Army. My world is the seat of power for our entire empire."

Startled, Cardin looked to his companions again, and then asked, "Then who are you? *What* are you?" Even though he didn't expect to recognize whatever species name she gave him, he wanted to know. He wanted a name behind the nemesis that had plagued Halarite, and so many other worlds, for so long. "Show yourself," he demanded. "Take that helmet off."

"I cannot," she replied cautiously. "I am trapped, you see. As much a prisoner within this armor as I am within the ranks of the Darksteel Army."

Cardin frowned. "I don't understand."

She sighed then and glanced at Artula. Finally, she said, "My name is Aezara Tanlen."

The weight she gave her words sounded as if she were telling them an important and terrible secret, but Cardin shook his head. "I'm sorry, should that name mean something to me?"

Now Aezara shifted as if surprised. "I would expect so," she replied. "The House of Tanlen is a name you should be very familiar with." Again Cardin shook his head. "Considering my grandfather once wielded the same weapon you now wield."

Her words took a moment to register, but again, it did little to clarify matters. "I don't understand. Before I wielded it, Kailar did, and before her, it was guarded by a Star Dragon. And before that…" He stopped cold, the realization of what she meant finally dawning upon him. "The only other person to have ever wielded the Sword of Dragons," he uneasily touched the hilt of the Sword over his shoulder, "was the person who first took up the blade from the forge, and used it to wipe the Dark Dragons from existence."

She did not confirm his line of thought, she merely stared at him, her glowing orange eyes steady and unwavering.

"You…you're a vrol."

Aezara nodded. "Yes."

"The…the vrol command the Darksteel Army?" Cardin shook his head, bewildered. "But…I don't understand."

"I know, Keeper," Aezara sighed. "I wish there was time to explain further, but know that the man who now resides over the vrol home world is not a kind or caring man. He is ruthless, and beyond cruel. As it is, this armor that serves as my prison has already induced considerable pain in my body as it detects I am betraying my oath to serve my emperor." Cardin blinked in surprise. He never would have guessed from her posture. But then, maybe that's why she barely moved. "I can only speak of a little more. We came here in search of something, I cannot say what and I beg you not to ask me." A new earnestness had entered her voice, and Cardin found himself stepping closer to the shield, intent on hearing her next words clearly. "But we do not know where on Halarite it is. What we do know is that there is a device in your possession that would lead us directly to it."

Cardin felt his breath leave him, his mind finally working clearly enough that he intuitively knew exactly what she was talking about. "The Cronal."

"You must disable or destroy it," she implored. "Perhaps it will only delay us, but we must do *something*. *You* must do something."

"But…" He shook his head, and suddenly felt very alone. He looked back at Sira, and reached for her hand. She took his and squeezed reassuringly. "What of Archanon?" he asked Aezara. "How can we save it?"

"You can't," Artula stated.

"Says you," Reis remarked.

Sparing a moment to give Reis a furious glare, Artula said, "Cardin, I am free of mind and body only because of Aezara's intervention. I am here to assure you that if we could stop the invasion of Archanon, we would. But it *will* happen this morning. And if not today, then as soon as Nuuldan recovers, *he* will come and bring down the city's shields. I doubt he'll leave much else standing after that, not if there's a chance he can get to you."

"So, what?" Cardin shook his head. "You want me to *let* you invade? Are you crazy?"

"No," Aezara shook her head. "I expect your soldiers to fight back, and many will die. I would never expect your people to allow us to invade without a fight. However, *you* must not be here."

"Excuse me, *what?!*" He shook his head furiously. "Why the hellfire would I abandon my city, my *kingdom*?"

Sira squeezed his hand. "Cardin..."

He looked at her, and she gazed back at him, the glow in her eyes gone, but the strangely beautiful purple still ever-present. And then he knew why he would leave.

A beach along a jungle in an abandoned village. Undead closing in all around them. Sira had given Cardin an order back then. An order to keep a dangerous enemy from obtaining the most powerful weapon in the known Universe.

"Keeper, we are vrol," Aezara explained. "The Darksteel Emperor is vrol. The Sword was designed specifically for us. The moment any of us take up the Sword, all of its knowledge and power will be bestowed upon us instantly. We can *not* allow the Emperor to have it."

Quirking an eyebrow up, Cardin asked, "And what of you? If you are trapped, as you say, couldn't you take it up and use it to stop all of this?" He wouldn't give it to her, of course, but he was curious...

"Oh I desire such power more than you could possibly know," she spoke quietly, her eyes fixed upon the black handle of the Sword. "I would rend the Emperor from this Universe and the next, tear him apart until only dust remained, and then reassemble him again just to do it all over. I dream of it every...single...day." The shuddering rage in her voice was tempered by pain, and Cardin realized that the armor must still be hurting her. "But I cannot. The armor would never allow me to connect with the Sword. Only once I am free could I hope to do so, but that is not likely to ever happen."

Cardin tilted his chin up. "Alright. Let's say I believe you. What do I do after I disable the Cronal? Where do I go?"

"It is better that you do not tell me," she replied simply. "As for what to do once you flee, I cannot say. Just know that I will hunt you."

Cardin's throat tightened. That actually frightened him.

"You must go," Aezara insisted. She looked up and around, and asked, "Surely you have noticed that our bombardment has ceased?"

Blinking in surprise, Cardin realized she was right. "Yeah…"

"Morning approaches. You have hours at best, minutes at worst. Go," she pointed behind Cardin, her claws coming within inches of the shield, which flared against her power. "Go now." She breathed heavily, and he realized this must have caused her immense pain. "GO!"

And then, turning around, Aezara stalked away.

Artula remained only a moment longer, and said, "I am so sorry. I will do everything I can from within, but they still do not trust me." Then he, too, turned and walked away from Archanon.

So that was it. Archanon would fall today.

Tal would fall.

Their world really was ending.

He turned to his friends. His companions. His love.

No, he shook his head. *Even if Archanon falls today, this is not the end.* His hands balled up into tight fists.

Sira looked at him uncertainly.

"Cardin?"

"We need to move if there's to be any hope," he said, but then stopped before he even started, and then he looked upon his friends once more, and felt horrible even before he asked it. "Before we go, however, there's one last thing I need to ask…"

Sira and Reis exchanged glances, and Cardin imagined that General Vellar felt entirely excluded, but for now that didn't matter so much.

"It's my father," Cardin said. "If…if we're going to dismantle or destroy the Cronal, then we only have this one chance to save him. No one has to help me, not with the fate of the city and the *world* in the balance, but…I can't just leave him like he is, forever disconnected." He reached out and clasped both Reis and Sira on their shoulders, and he looked from one to the other and then to Elaria. "Will you help me?"

Elaria did not blink or waver, her sunset eyes staring into his. "I will never abandon you," she firmly stated.

Sira smiled warmly, and gently touched his hand. "Of course."

Reis's usual sardonic grin was gone, replaced with an absolute look for determination. "Save the king before saving the world?

Hellfire, Cardin, you don't ask for much, do you? But I'm in."

Cardin nodded his appreciation, squeezing their shoulders before letting go.

Then there was the General. "Vellar," he nodded.

The General was pale, his face vacant, but he came to attention. "S-sire?"

Drawing in a deep breath, Cardin commanded, "Prepare the city for an invasion from above. Delay them as long as you can. Give me every moment you can."

Clamping his mouth shut, the General stood at attention, and nodded.

"It will be done, Sire."

Chapter 41

PRIDE AND POWER

Surrender.

The most dreadful term that Kailar could think of. A term she swore over a decade ago that she would never use, never say it, not unless she was demanding it of an enemy.

Today was a day of firsts. Letan had likewise planted his Warrior's sword into the ground next to Kent's, and as Xavien watched, and the Darksteel Army stood poised, the rest of the Devor imperial soldiers laid their weapons down.

Kailar looked at her Darksteel daggers, and knelt to set them down, but Xavien shook his head, "Hold, dark one." Pausing, Kailar hovered, holding the daggers only inches from the ground. "How have you come by those weapons? They do not belong to you."

"On the contrary," she intoned icily. "I earned them by taking the life of one who wielded them."

"Interesting," Xavien quirked an eyebrow. "It seems our ally was not fully forthcoming with us after all."

Our ally? But that would mean…

"Sal'fe."

Xavien merely smiled, and then waved to the Darksteel soldier immediately behind him. "Please relieve her of those weapons, they do not belong in the mud."

There was no mud to be had, only icy snowpack. But then Kailar realized what he meant – *she* was the mud.

Grinding her teeth, Kailar slowly stood up, and tensed as the soldier approached. It would be easy enough to rend him in half with a little extra dark magic, but...

"Consider your actions carefully, dark one," Xavien cautioned. "I would not want you to nullify your compatriots' surrender with a brash act."

The Darksteel soldier, one of the tall brutes, placed his double-headed axe on his back with little effort – a magnet, she guessed, or some magical means of securing it with ease. And then, stepping past Reyla and Kent, he stood before her, hands outstretched.

It was her moment of truth. What would she do? What *could* she do?

Could she really surrender? Or would she fight, knowing what it would cost the others? Cost Tieran Port? What would happen to all of Devor if she fought now?

There was wisdom in biding her time, in waiting. She wielded dark magic, whereas these so-called Darksteel soldiers did not. They could not sense her, and their ability to counter her surely would be limited.

Surrender. Could Kailar do it?

An impatient sigh escaped Xavien, and he waved to another soldier. It came forth, brandishing its axe. "If the dark one does not hand over her blades, kill the Empress."

Kailar tensed, and the second brute hefted the axe up.

"I give you moments, dark one, no more," Xavien cautioned, raising a finger and wagging it back and forth. "Give. Us. Those. Daggers."

Reyla. Not a friend, but someone more. Perhaps the first leader that Kailar had ever respected. The Empress had given Kailar the chance she had dreamed of, to make a difference, to change the world for the better. To form a new country, a *better* country.

And now this skinny, scrawny little filament threatened to take it all away?

A cold, life-sucking rage grew within Kailar. She had spent her life bowing to no one, *no* one!

So Kailar turned to her dark magic, powers bestowed by the

Sword of Dragon, powers no Star Dragon or other being of light could ever hope to counter or take away. She had learned to heal with it, just like she had with star magic, just as Kailar had relearned to make portals with it. New powers she had never possessed had even come to her, elemental powers.

So surely, she could rekindle another power she once possessed.

Her grip on the daggers tightened. She coursed dark magic through them, and reached out. Out into the ether, the void between magic. The void between her and the brute brandishing his axe. Her rage fueled her, gave her the focus she needed to push past, the barrier between *being* and *nothing*.

Like her, these were beings of light. However like Kailar, they could also be touched by the darkness.

So she penetrated deep into the pulse of magic in the soldier, and instinctively pushed right to where his thoughts were. Alien to some extent, and yet he was not so different from her or anyone else. He followed orders.

Kailar gave him *new* orders. When she had done so before the Star Dragons took her magic, she had not used any implements, but this time, she enhanced her powers with the daggers, giving her even sharper focus. And as the axe came down, she *made* him divert.

The axe planted into the icy snow with a *chunk*, and the brute blinked, shaking his head. There was a push against Kailar's will, but it was weak. Xavien frowned, but she knew that he could not sense her powers exerting her will over the brute.

Turning to Xavien, Kailar focused on him, penetrated his shields, ripping them down layer by layer. He was stronger, star magic encapsulated him. Growing fatigued, she immediately knew she could not control him, could not ever hope to reach his mind.

"What...are you doing?" he asked, staggering backwards.

Moments stood between her and an early death, as Xavien's confusion registered on the brute in front of her. He didn't even reach back for his axe, he lunged forward and wrapped his fingers around her throat.

Kailar gurgled, and then her airway was cinched off, and she lost her hold upon the axe-wielding brute.

"Kailar, stop!" Reyla pleaded.

She wouldn't. She *couldn't*. It was already too late, and if she didn't fight now, she would die.

With a pulse of will, a violet beam of concentrated energy lanced out of her daggers and easily penetrated the enchantments on the Darksteel brute's armor, hollowing out two holes in his chest. His grip immediately vanished, and she turned back to the other brute, who was shaking his head to clear her control.

The Darksteel army surged, all one thousand of them.

Kailar reasserted her control. The brute turned as the sound of a thousand footsteps boomed.

He turned to Xavien. The ambassador's eyes widened.

She didn't hesitate. The brute wrapped his hands around Xavien's throat, and didn't stop at choking.

He crushed Xavien's throat.

And just like she had done with mind control, she called forth another power she had not used since she had opened up to darkness.

Black drakes dove from the sky, miniature dragons, eyes glowing red, scales as black as the night, falling upon the Darksteel's front lines before they could take a second step, and rending through their armor with claws imbued with dark magic.

The presence of so many minds in hers felt familiar and alien all at once, but she could control the dark drakes as easily as she had controlled the ones summoned through star magic.

As long as she kept her focus, and remembered that dark magic worked the *opposite* way that star magic did.

The dark drakes lunged onto the next line of Darksteel soldiers. Darksteel ghosts attacked the drakes with magic, and they were powerful enough to hurt and even kill her drakes, but just like she had done over a year ago, she simply called forth more. And *more*.

The tide changed quickly. The perfect ranks of the Darksteel Army dissolved into chaos, and Kailar bid the dark drakes to start with the ghosts, those capable of casting the most powerful magics against them, and they obeyed perfectly. Dozens of dark drakes were killed violently, their dark magic unable to contend with the overwhelming power of the ghosts, but Kailar summoned more in their places.

Unfortunately this was only the first wave of Darksteel soldiers, and the second wave from the northwest approached, the steady clanking of their march echoing through the streets.

Kailar couldn't divide her attention, she was already straining to summon enough drakes to contend with the thousand-strong first wave. Thankfully, Kent recognized that, and drew his sword from the icy street and lifted it into the air. Amidst the flickering city torches and the bright flashes of magic from the first wave, Letan ordered, "Soldiers of Devor, to arms! About face!"

Behind her, Kailar heard the thump of a well-trained army turn.

"Letan," Kent said, just as the redheaded man pulled his weapon from the ice. "Get the Empress out of here!"

While Kent marched forward, past Kailar without sparing her a glance, Letan beckoned Reyla to go with him. She looked at Kailar, and Kailar spared her a quick glance, trying to discern if her Empress was pleased or enraged. Or worse, disappointed. However, if she felt anything, Kailar couldn't read her expression and Letan pulled her away.

Turning her full attention back to the battle, Kailar cursed as nine Darksteel troops broke away from the battle and went after Reyla and Letan, led by one of the ghosts.

"Get back here!" she screamed, and summoned two drakes in their path. They easily overcame the drakes, but Kailar had used it as a distraction only, giving her time to push as much dark magic into her blades as she could.

Unleashing the full fury of her powers upon them, two of the nine fell instantly. The others redirected their attention to her, just like she wanted. Trying to reserve as much of her concentration as she could for the drakes, she spun her blades around to face down, and prepared to battle the incoming seven soldiers.

Daggers weren't her strength. Neither were they her weakness.

The ghost leading the pack unleashed an arcane attack upon her, but instead of shielding herself, Kailar reserved her strength for the drakes and rolled across the snowpack, coming up in front of a brute and thrusting her dagger into his stomach before he could stop her, and then she unleashed a weak blast of magic. Weak, but from within the brute's body, it destroyed his innards and ended his life.

A soldier more her size and sporting long, elven ears swung a longsword at her, humming with magic. Kailar ducked, and the weapon reverberated off of the dead brute's plate armor. Kailar swept the man's legs out from beneath him, and then plunged another dagger straight into his throat.

This time when the ghost sent a bolt of lightning at her, she raised a shield and let the elemental energy vanish into the ether of darkness. And then she shoved forward with her shield, slamming it into the ghost and sending him sprawling.

Another brute and two soldiers were upon her, and she rolled out of the way, but as she came up out of her roll, the icy streets got the best of her, and her footing slipped. She fell to her knees and felt them pop and surge in pain.

A sword came at her, and she blocked with both daggers, but then an axe joined it. She deflected it with dark magic, feeling a drain from the star magic enchantments on her shield, but she held it a moment longer.

Struggling to get to her feet, she realized she had to get off of the snow packed street and into fresh powder. It wasn't ideal, but the ice was treacherous.

Backpedaling, her shield absorbed a blast from the ghost, and that was when her focus wavered, and the shield fell. It was too much. The drakes, the soldiers, it was too much. She was alone, and she was vulnerable.

Summoning new drakes was becoming too exhausting, so as she backed up and tried desperately not to slip, the remaining five Darksteel soldiers closing in on her, she called several out of the battle to fall upon them. The dark drakes were quick and agile, their claws digging into ice and allowing them to barrel into the enemy soldiers like battering rams. The ghost turned his attention on them, and Kailar used that opportunity to unleash a weak but effective attack upon the ghost.

This time, *he* slipped on the ice, and a drake fell upon him, rending his flesh apart and eventually separating his head from his body.

The other four didn't stand a chance against her drakes, and as she fell back into the easement between buildings, she leaned heavily against one of the structures and shook her head.

It was too much. She had been a fool. And now, her pride was going to get everyone killed.

Although Kailar sent her rescuers back into the fray, she couldn't keep up summoning more. No matter how angry or frustrated, no matter how much her blades let her focus her powers, she couldn't keep up. Searching through the eyes of her followers, she knew that over half of the first wave of Darksteel had fallen, but the number of drakes on the field at any time was dwindling.

Kailar was alone, and she couldn't hope to outmatch the Darksteel Army.

Nor could she summon a portal just now, she realized. She was too fatigued, too weak. Kailar needed time to recover, and then maybe she could regroup and come up with a plan.

Or worse, do the one thing she hated most – ask for help.

Distasteful as that thought was, she justified it with one additional realization – Sal'fe was allied with the Darksteel Empire. Did Cardin Kataar and the Allies know that?

They had to be warned.

So she turned away from the battle and ran to the next street. The battle against the second unit had spilled over to there, and she knew she didn't have the energy to face off against them.

Hiding in the shadows, she watched, and wondered how long she could stay hidden. If a ghost found her, she was dead.

"Kailar!"

A familiar, deep voice called to her, but it was the last one she expected. Looking over, she saw a man she'd not spoken to in months – Dillarn, the map maker. He stood at the back of what she realized was his shop, and motioned her over.

Glancing at the battle, she hurried to him, hoping no one else noticed. He rushed her inside the back door and closed it, dousing them in darkness.

Heavy breathing all around made her realize that there were more people inside, but she couldn't see nor sense them. Had Dillarn offered sanctuary to more people?

Striking a light, Dillarn, an older, skinny, balding man, asked, "Are ya alright?"

She wanted to say yes, but knew it would be a lie. Instead, she looked around and saw that there was indeed a group of people in the shop with Dillarn, at least six others, all huddled down low, all breathing quietly and shaking in terror.

"What's going on?" she asked. "Who are these people?"

"Explorers," he said. "Escapees."

"Escapees?" she frowned at him. "Escapees from what?"

"The Darksteel Army," one of them replied, a man around her age, his face weathered like a man who spent more time in the wild than inside comfort. "They captured us, and corralled us in here in secret."

Bewildered, Kailar looked at Dillarn. "In here? Why here? And how did…?"

"When you fought back just now, the ones guarding us left to join in," Dillarn stated. "Kailar, I don't know what, but they're looking for something. Just look what they did to my shop!"

It was difficult to see from only one candle, but Kailar took in her surroundings. While Dillarn's maps were legendary for their accuracy, he was also known as a collector and purveyor of strange artifacts found throughout all of Devor. Explorers brought them to Dillarn to appraise and determine if they were an authentic 'oddity' or just another explorer's lost relics.

His shelves were empty, many of the displays broken. Not a single relic was left.

Behind his counter, where he stored rolled up maps, were more empty shelves, and the counter itself was smashed and splintered.

"I don't understand," she frowned. "What could they possibly be looking for? And how the hellfire did they gather you all here without alerting the city guard?"

"Portals," the other man spoke up. "We were all brought here through portals. Dekker there was brought not an hour ago from Edingard."

A sheepish, young man waved his hand. "I'd just gotten back from an expedition, freezing my nuts off, I was. And that tosser Brask put me in shackles and held me until *they* came for me. Those ghostly-white fellows."

Kailar tensed. Was that the communication the Navitas had sensed, Brask calling them to come get another explorer?

"Brask," Kailar frowned. "Why's that name familiar?"

"I dunno," the young man replied. "He used to run a slave trade across the mountain passes, but when Kailar started going after the criminal types, he closed up shop and pretended to go legit."

"This *is* Kailar, dumbass," the other explorer that had spoken smacked the young man's head.

"Oh. *Oh!*"

Kailar rolled her eyes, but then felt her face pale. Brask. She hadn't found out about it until later, but Brask had been the man who ran the whole slave trade and mining operations out of Edingard. The young man she had murdered…

Shaking her head and pushing the guilt away, she focused on the tasks at hand. "Alright, so there are people here who were already working for the Darksteel Empire. Which means they've had people here a long time. But why are they gathering you all now? What could they possibly be looking for?"

"I dunno," Dillarn shook his head. "But they asked me over and over again if my maps were really as accurate as claimed. Asked where most of the artifacts I had came from."

"And you told them?"

"Well, yeah," he shrugged. "I figured there was no harm, they were just relics. If they had any enchantments, they're so old that they lost their charge."

Kailar scowled. "And where was that, Dillarn? Where do most of the artifacts come from?"

"The deep south, of course. Especially the Frozen Peaks in the Southwest."

Kailar's eyes widened. "How long have you been under their thumb?"

"Since before they even showed up to negotiate," he replied sullenly. "I've been a prisoner in my own shop for four days."

That explained a few things, such as why his shop had been closed, though she'd barely noticed.

It also explained how the Darksteel Empire knew to fear the Navitas. But Dillarn hadn't known how bad the Crystalline Peaks had been damaged. For that matter, no one had known that the Navitas had to focus all of their efforts on repairing them until Kailar and Letan had defied orders and went to find out.

Sinking to her knees, Kailar shook her head. This was her fault. All of this. Maybe they could have negotiated a peace if she hadn't let the Navitas' secret out. Maybe all of those soldiers outside, fighting for their lives right now, would have had a chance had she not let her pride get the better of her.

"Gods dammit all," she spat. "I've got to do something."

"Like what?" Dillarn asked. "I watched you and your dragon things fight out there, the Darksteel are too much."

"Yeah," she grimaced, just as she felt a release in her soul. "And the last drake just fell. I don't think I could summon more." Which meant the survivors of the first unit would be charging in to aid their second unit fight off the imperial soldiers. Maybe she could summon more drakes in a minute or two, but it wouldn't be enough. It would never be enough.

"What about their building?" Dillarn asked.

Kailar frowned at him. "What?"

"Their building they brought with them," he motioned to the west. "If I was a betting man, they've probably gathered all of the relics and maps there. Maybe we can find a clue as to what they're looking for in there? I'll bet they didn't leave any guards in there, or not many."

"What good would that do?" the young man asked. "They gonna kill us all even if we figure out what they're up to."

"Unless we can hold it, whatever it is, for ransom," Kailar stood up, feeling the slimmest hope rekindling in her. It wasn't much, but as the sounds of battle grew louder outside, she knew she had to do something. If she wouldn't take surrender before, she certainly wouldn't now.

"Well, then, let's go," Dillarn cracked his knuckles.

Kailar frowned and shook her head. "Oh no. I'm not gonna let you risk your life, this is my job."

"Oh, Aye," he looked at her curiously, "and just how familiar are you with all those relics, eh?"

She started to refute his question, but then stopped and sighed. "Fine. But the rest of you stay here. It's too dangerous out there."

"No arguments from us," the young man said.

Chapter 42

THE ENEMY'S FORTRESS

For the tenth time in as many minutes, Kailar thought, *What the hellfire am I doing?!*

Her new home city was under assault, her new *empire* was being brought to her knees, and she was sneaking around, heading away from the battle in some vain effort to hold information ransom?

It was foolish, it was *stupid*.

On the other hand, her only other options were to surrender or run. That wasn't happening.

So, as she and Dillarn snuck across less-traveled, and therefore annoyingly crunchier snow well away from the main road, she focused on the embassy looming ahead. It was sparsely illuminated, slivers of both moons having just risen ahead of the sunrise doing little to show off the dark grey bricks or the darksteel reinforcements.

The sound of battle behind them had almost completely died off, and Kailar tried not to think about what that meant. She was fatigued from summoning drakes and controlling just one Darksteel soldier, but she would finish her task. She would find *something*.

She had to.

Coming at it from this angle, they couldn't see the portcullis that had been so obvious before, and in the dark of night, the

384

watchtowers would not see them coming. Then again, looking up to those battlements, she saw no sign of a watch. Had they all foolishly left their post to fight the imperial soldiers?

It was hard to imagine such a well-trained, experienced military making that kind of mistake, but she had seen examples of worse offenses on Edilas. The Tal army had more or less won the last Lesser War, which should have meant the Tal Warriors were the best of the best. Yet this was the kind of mistake she had seen them make more than once, maybe even *because* of the arrogance and complacency of a post-war victor.

Steady, pale light peered through the slits of windows in the fortress, a sign that they used more of those glowing panels or glowing lights rather than torches, just like she had seen in the dwarven city. It would make moving around inside more hazardous – soldiers would be less likely to think errant shadows were simply from flickering firelight.

Worried that their luck would run out, Kailar rushed across the barren outskirts of town and pressed up against the freezing-cold stone brick…only to hear Dillarn huffing while still trying to cover the distance. She grimaced and looked up, but couldn't see the battlements – if they heard him or saw him, all this might be for nothing.

Finally, he made it to the wall and slapped up against it heavily, his heaving chest visible despite the half-dozen layers she swore he had put on before coming out.

Pausing and trying to hear over him, she worried his impact with the wall might have alerted someone.

Kailar also noted that all sounds of battle had completely stopped. If they were going to do this, it would have to be now.

"Come on," she whispered, glancing only a moment at the rising moons before crunching along towards the damaged main road.

They came to the back corner of the castle where one of the metallic, giant wheels still sat, and she peeked around the corner, but saw no sign of enemies. What she did see drew a grimace down her face – the magical wound of the Navitas, still pulsing with light where it had fallen across the street and closer to town. It flashed and blinked hypnotically with a golden-white energy, and she wondered just how long that wound would last. If rumors from Maradin were true, it might not fade for a long time, if ever.

More disconcerting for her, however, were the beasts that had brought the embassy through the portal. They lay motionless only a hundred yards ahead of the fortress, their massive chests rising peacefully as they slumbered. Apparently they cared little for the life and death struggle playing itself out on the streets of Tieran, maybe because the beasts were as much war veterans as the rest of the Darksteel troops. Still, from sheer size and proximity, she felt fear trying to claw its way up into her chest, and she did all that she could to shove it back down into the depths of nothingness where it belonged.

There was no time for fear.

On the bright side, the bulk of the creatures hid Kailar and Dillarn from town.

Waving Dillarn on, she bolted across crunching snow and came to the other forward wheel. She peered between it and the wall along the front of the rectangular fortress, and grimaced when she saw two brutes guarding the gate. *So they aren't complete idiots after all,* she thought.

If there were enemies within, all it would take was one to sound the alarm.

Then another thought occurred to her. The fortress was maybe forty feet tall. She craned her head up, and remembered leaping great heights and distances while fighting Cardin in Archanon. Just how high had she jumped?

It was difficult to remember – much of that battle was lost in the haze of adrenaline and the staggering aftermath. Maybe she could have leapt that high before, but could she use dark magic to do the same thing? She knew she'd already leapt further than she should have otherwise been able to.

Risky, she thought. *But maybe worth it, if I'm lucky.*

"Stay here until I clear the guards up front," she commanded Dillarn while stowing her daggers in their sheaths. Kailar then drew dark magic in, letting it power her legs, her awareness. Fatigue was still clouding her mind, but this was relatively easy.

Lowering down slowly, she tried to judge how much magic to use to infuse her legs with strength, and then hoping she got it right, she *pushed* with all of her might, and sailed high, high up into the night.

She barely made it, and slapped her palms onto the crest of the battlements. Then promptly slipped and nearly fell down, her heart leaping into her throat as she scrambled to grab a hold of *anything*, and barely managing to snag her arm in between the battlements.

It hurt, and she bit down on her lip to keep from screaming, managing to reduce it to a grunt. Something strained in her arm, but thankfully didn't break.

Pausing a moment, Kailar listened, hoping she hadn't just alerted any guards. When no alarming voices met her, she sighed, and then worked to free her arm and climb up over the wall. Peering around, she saw that the embassy was much as she had expected, a literal fortress. The top of the wall was a walkway a good three feet lower than the edge, with the slits in between meant to allow casters and archers a place to shoot down upon their enemies. As she had suspected and was relieved to find out she was right, no guards patrolled the top of the wall.

Hefting herself onto the walkway, she crept inward, and looked down into a courtyard, except that the courtyard was too close, too high up. She realized that the entrance gate below led *inside,* and the courtyard was built on the top level. If she judged correctly, especially accounting for how tall the brutes were, there were only two more stories beneath the courtyard, at most. Or a single really tall interior.

Like the battlements, the courtyard was unguarded. *Thank goodness for small mercies.*

Staying low, Kailar crept along the outer edge towards the gate side of the mobile fortress, and then when she was about midway, she hefted up onto the battlement's edge and looked over. Forty feet below stood the two guards on either side of the ramp. A ramp that was at least ten feet wide. No way she could take them both out. Not unless...

Could she summon just one more drake?

Worth a shot.

Closing her eyes, Kailar drew in a deep, frigid breath, and directed dark energy through her, into her daggers, and out into the world, picturing a drake as she had before. It had been *so easy* to summon them with the Sword, but now?

The world spun and Kailar lost her balance, falling back and bruising her backside. A great fog overtook her thoughts, and for a moment, she wondered if she could lose her *self* if she pushed her magic too far.

But it had worked. She found out when hot, stinky breath washed over her face, and a warm, slobbery tongue licked her cheek.

"What-? Gross!" Shoving the snout of the dark drake away, she scowled at it, but it merely looked at her curiously, tilting its head to one side and blinking in confusion, the reds of its eyes winking in and out as it did so.

With the drake summoned, it would take considerably less effort to keep it in the Universe. Still, she knew she couldn't keep it up forever, and she'd have to dispel it if she needed to open a portal. Assuming she even could open a portal yet. *Gods, I'm so tired...*

Sleep threatened to overtake her, but Kailar wouldn't let it. Groaning with the effort, she stood up and pressed up against the battlements again, willing the drake to follow her lead. It effortlessly jumped its front legs up onto the battlement and peaked down, identifying the two targets.

Timing would be everything. As would her landing – if she didn't maintain her focus, she might break her legs, or worse.

Get ready, she told her companion. It rumbled softly, sounding more like a purr than an actual growl, acknowledging her silent command. Kailar coursed magic into her muscles again, trying to push away the fatigue and give her the strength she'd need to safely make a forty foot drop.

Once atop the battlements, she paused, held her breath...and then fell.

The drake beside her followed, keeping its wings folded and allowing gravity to do all of the work.

Except as Kailar drew more dark magic in and tried to focus it on her muscles, she grew even more fatigued. She lost her connection to the dark drake.

Forty feet sounded far, but not when you're in free-fall – Kailar slammed into her chosen target, daggers sinking up to their hilts in the weak parts of the brute's armor.

The drake fell like a ton of bricks on the other brute, smashing him into the ground in a great clatter. It should have sunk claws and teeth into its opponent, but it was heavy enough that it ended up not mattering – the brute did not stir or rise again.

The dark drake, on the other hand, vanished.

Gods dammit, she sighed, and tried to stand up from her dead target. Except she'd twisted her ankle, and it gave out on her, sending her back down into the trampled snow, the barest hint of a scream issuing forth.

Waves of pain flowed up from her right foot, and she held on just above her ankle, her daggers discarded. "Oh, god's," she hissed between her teeth. Without magic to dull the pain, she was feeling the full force of the injury. Kailar tried to pulse magic down into it to heal it or at least deaden the pain, but it was getting so hard to control her powers.

Crunching bootsteps startled her, and she reached for one of the daggers, only to find Dillarn hovering over her. "By the gods, girly, you're crazy!"

Chuckling through the pain, Kailar remarked, "You clearly haven't spent enough time with me."

"Maybe," he sighed. "But then crazy might just be what we need right now. Come on, get up!" He clasped her hands and yanked her up, and it was all she could do not to scream when she put weight on her right foot.

"We need to get inside," she breathed through the pain. "Help me get my daggers."

Leaving her to hobble on one foot, Dillarn collected both daggers, then handed them to Kailar to stow.

With the map-maker's help, she hobbled up the ramp, cursing whomever built the thing every step of the way.

Inside, they found an elaborate antechamber, walls painted a deep, navy blue with black trim, and a gold and red rug half the size of the room set down in the center. Wooden chairs of the finest craftsmanship that took up twice the amount of space a chair should were situated around the corners, which was to say, the room was not made of four walls, but six, with diagonal walls ahead to the right and left, and each with a door inset into them.

If this was an embassy, she couldn't imagine what their palaces or castles on their home world looked like.

The paintings were of interest, too – each door was bracketed by paintings, and Kailar reasoned they were meant to impress visitors with the scope of the Darksteel Empire's forces. Paintings of armies, of vast trade markets, caravans, storefronts full of spices and fineries the likes of which she had never seen outside of Archanon, and even then a rarity.

The only open door was the one straight ahead, which led directly to a flight of stairs that ascended halfway, then split up to ascend along the back wall.

"So, where do we start?" she asked.

"Um, pick a room at random?" Dillarn suggested.

"And risk bumbling into the barracks, if it isn't on the levels above?" She huffed impatiently. "Come on, Dillarn, if this was your embassy, where would you stuff your most valuable trinkets?"

"Well, not on the ground floor," he replied casually. "I'd put it in the heart of the structure, make it harder for anyone to get to it, and harder still to leave with anything."

Kailar grimaced and glared at the stairs. "Hellfire."

With Dillarn's help, she ascended the first half of the stairs, wincing and cursing the entire way. When they reached the landing, they found that taking the stairs to the right would take them all the way up to the courtyard, but to the left would take them to the second level.

Nothing she saw in the courtyard looked like a safe or storage container, so Kailar directed Dillarn to take them left, and they ascended the rest of the way.

Rather than being sectioned off into rooms, the second floor was wide-open, with support pillars placed in an array matching the corners of the hexagonal antechamber below. Tables and desks were setup throughout the large room, each seeming to serve a different purpose – the first one they came across appeared to be a desk meant for writing upon, with blank parchment and inkwells. Further along was what looked to be a tailor's station, with threads and fabrics.

And in the center of the room were artifacts stored in or on displays.

Guarded, naturally.

Quiet as Kailar would have liked to be, she was in too much pain and too hobbled, so the single guard and his ward both turned towards Kailar and Dillarn.

Cursing the gods and wraiths in one breath, Kailar leaned heavily on Dillarn and drew a dagger, and channeled as much magic as she could spare into it. The Darksteel guard, a ghost, threw up his gauntlets in a cross and erected a shield just as Kailar unleashed a broad attack, the dark magic equivalent of an arcane blast.

It didn't penetrate the ghost's shield. He looked over his crossed arms at her and smirked.

And then surged on his feet as the sound of something sharp shinked into his back. He fell to his knees as blue blood trickled from his mouth, and then he fell over with an exotic dagger sticking out of his back.

Behind him stood the most unexpected familiar face – the same elf that had accompanied Elaria during the battle against Degrin at the Wizards' Guild.

"You!" she breathed.

Blinking rapidly, the elf replied, "Me? I mean, yes. But, um, y-you I didn't expect to s-see here."

She kept her dagger leveled at him, and with Dillarn's help, she passed around various workstations to close the distance. "What are you doing here?"

Eyebrows raising up, he motioned all around him, at several curiosities and artifacts that looked completely out of place among the Darksteel weapons and armors she had seen.

Confirming what she already suspected, Dillarn said, "These are from my shop."

Frowning, the elf remarked, "Are they? I was told they were collected from all around this land."

"They were," Dillarn nodded. "Brought to me by explorers."

"Ah," the elf plaintively replied. "That explains how they were so cleaned up. You do an excellent job in caring for ancient relics, sir."

She swore the old codger blushed. "Well thank you, sir. Um. If you are indeed a sir."

"I am," he nodded. "My name is Baenil of the Darean College of Serelik." That was the name – Kailar had completely forgotten. If she had ever bothered to learn it in the first place. "And to answer your q-question," his stutter resumed the moment he laid eyes on Kailar again. "I...that is, I am the foremost expert on h-human relics. W-well, I am now. My mentor was killed only two weeks ago..."

The half-crazy elf's face slouched, and he found a chair to sit on. That was the first time Kailar noticed the chains bounding his wrists to the central desk, clinking as he moved. Rubbing his unshaven face, the elf shook his head. "Ventelis would have sorted these artifacts in a fraction of the time it has taken me."

Kailar and Dillarn stopped at the edge of the elf's workspace, and she sighed. "You're a prisoner. They're forcing you to analyze the relics."

"Indeed," he mournfully replied. "The guard was meant to keep me working through the battle. He should have kept a closer eye on me." Fire ignited behind the elf's eyes, and he looked around the room in disgust. "I am a scholar, but I learned the hard way to defend myself when needed."

Kailar arched an eyebrow, and then shook her head. "So, you've had time with these relics – any idea what they're looking for?"

"That much they told me the moment they brought me here," Baenil shrugged. *Interesting that his stutter comes and goes,* she thought curiously. "They call it the Conduit. A pyramid-like structure left behind by an ancient civilization."

Kailar frowned and glanced at Dillarn, but he looked as perplexed as she was. "Pyramid?"

"Yes, triangular-type structure," Baenil explained, his tone that of an adult speaking plainly to a child. "Four-sided."

"I know what a pyramid is," she scowled.

"Oh, good, then," Baenil shrugged. *"They,"* he pointed to the dead Darksteel guard, "thought I could discern where it was from these trinkets. They thought because I had spent ten years on Halarite studying ancient ruins, I would know how to identify its location."

Kailar shook her head. "I thought the last pyramid was lost in one of those great storms. By that volcano in the southwest of Edilas. No other known pyramids exist on Halarite."

"On Edilas," Baenil corrected, lifting a halting finger. "Edilas, however, is *not* where most ancient civilizations lived on Halarite. I am rather surprised there is evidence suggesting ancient civilizations were on this continent. You have never found structures suggesting as much?"

Kailar hadn't a clue, but Dillarn did. "Not a one," he replied. "Just weapons, armor, cooking implements. Signs of advanced civilizations, but not a single ruin. Though explorers started pushing more heavily into the frozen south – if anything survived, I'd wager it would have been buried in snow and ice."

"A likely probability," Baenil said with a smile. "You and I will get along quite well, sir."

Kailar rolled her eyes. "So what is this pyramid exactly, and why are the Darksteel so keen to find it?"

"W-well, um, isn't t-that obvious?" Kailar impatiently shook her head. "W-what, um, do people, like you I might add, with power, I mean, want?"

Kailar sighed. "How would I know?"

"Power," Baenil simply said. "Historically, t-that is from what my research shows, um…those who get a taste for power inevitably want more, and to ensure they never lose the power that they have."

Thinking on it for a moment, she nodded. "I suppose that makes sense. So this pyramid thing…?"

"They tell me it is old." Baenil's voice had taken on a reverential tone. "Older than their civilization. Older than ours. Maybe older than the Star Dragons themselves, and its power siphons from the stars themselves."

"And you're just too happy to find it for them?" she asked, scowling.

Taken aback, he shook his head. "After they invaded my world?" Kailar's scowl faded instantly. "I held back. I didn't dare tell them what I already knew about it, even before they had me analyze these fragments."

Kailar barely registered his last words, focusing more on the fact that his world had been invaded. Dillarn, however, asked, "Where is it, then?"

Eyebrows rising up, Baenil shook his head. "To be frank, I would sooner tell the Keeper of the Sword than I would *her*," he narrowed his eyes at Kailar. She wanted to be insulted by his tone, but she also knew he had good reason to be suspicious of her. "You may not be allied with the Darksteel Empire, but Elaria has told me all about what you did, or what you tried to do."

Kailar didn't know how to reply. All she knew for sure was that they were at an impasse. If Baenil wouldn't tell her, then the secret was stuck with him. On the other hand, she had hoped to have something to hold ransom against the Darksteel Empire. And now she had just that.

"Come on," she motioned towards the elf. "Let's free him and get out of-"

Shouting from the stairwell drew their attention, and shadows from the glowlamps preceded enemy forces rushing up the stairs.

They were out of time.

"Dammit," she growled and pushed Dillarn out of the way,

wincing and practically screaming as she put her full weight on her wounded ankle.

Charging her dagger and setting it humming, she lashed at the chains binding Baenil to the desk. Dark magic canceled out whatever star magic enchantment bound it, and the links broke easily, freeing the elf.

The elf started, "Thank you, I-"

But as enemy troops flowed up and started to surround them, shouting to stop where they were, Kailar grabbed Baenil around his chest, and putting him between her and the enemy, she placed the tip of the dagger right against the bulge in his throat. "That's far enough!" she shouted right next to Baenil's ear, making him wince.

Her command was heeded – the Darksteel troops stopped cold. Their weapons were trained on her, including several ghosts' gauntlets, but as long as she threatened Baenil, maybe she had a chance.

Of course, she also knew if she killed him, there'd be nothing stopping the Darksteel troops from slaughtering her. She needed out. *Can I summon a portal? Maybe I have just enough left in me.* Portals had come easily to her before, easier than summoning drakes or controlling the thoughts and feelings of others. So if there was one more power she could pull off...

"My dear dark one," a smug, arrogant voice called out, and Kailar stopped cold in her thoughts, stunned.

"No," she whispered. "It can't be..."

The Darksteel troops nearest the stairs stepped aside with military precision, allowing Xavien to ascend, very much alive, and not even a bruised throat to show for it.

"How can you...?"

And beside him strode an old man, dressed in forest-green robes with gold trim, holding a stark white staff with a blood red gem embedded in the top of it.

"*You!*" she spat out, her blood boiling.

Wizard King Sal'fe smiled. "How very astute," he said with a sigh. "You have such a way with words, Kailar."

"And you can die a miserable death," she growled back.

"Oh I have," he replied, a dark smile drawing across his face. "But it seems that even death cannot keep me down."

She frowned at that, but shook her head and turned back to

Xavien. "I take it he brought you back with the staff."

"Well what is the point of an alliance if it does not come with certain perks, yes?" Xavien clasped his hands together. "Now, release our prisoner, and surrender. Your army has been defeated, so you have no chance of surviving if you do not capitulate."

"I don't surrender," she intoned. "Not to you, not to anyone."

"That much is true," Sal'fe narrowed his eyes at her, venom in his voice. "She is quite the treacherous minx. If she did surrender, I would suspect a trap."

"Then we find ourselves at an impasse," Xavien said, arching an eyebrow. Kailar remembered thinking such a thing not a moment ago, and realized how true it was. Baenil wouldn't tell her what she needed, but if she killed him, she was as good as dead. Same with Dillarn, who hovered beside her.

For that matter, they could outright kill her and Baenil right now, and then Sal'fe could simply resurrect the elf to continue interrogation. She maybe had only moments before they came to the same conclusion, if they hadn't already.

So what were her options? If Devor was already conquered, what could she do, where could she go?

The answer came to her like a sledgehammer – she could go back home. To the safest possible city on Halarite. If anywhere still stood vigilant against the Darksteel Army, it was the First City.

Archanon.

Where the Keeper of the Sword was. Baenil could tell him the secret, then, and then they would know what the Darksteel Empire wanted. Maybe they could stop them.

It all depended upon her summoning one last portal.

Sighing impatiently, Xavien promised, "If you surrender, I promise to allow you to live." A grin stretched up the right side of his face. "I happen to know someone who is *very* interested in your powers."

She didn't know, nor want to know, who that could be. But she didn't care.

Turning inwards, Kailar focused her will. It was hard. Between the pain of her ankle, her fatigue, and her need to sleep for a week or more, she didn't think she could do it. But she had to.

She would.

So Kailar did it. Focusing her powers as much as possible, she glanced at Dillarn and said, "We move fast."

No one else could probably quite sense what she was doing, but Xavien's smirk shifted down into a scowl.

An ethereal wind gathered, and slower than she ever had, Kailar pulsed her gathered power through the dagger, and she pointed the tip away from Baenil and unleashed it. Shields went up everywhere, but they were expecting a last-ditch, fatal attack. Instead, a portal winked into existence directly before her, unstable at first, but she managed to inject just enough will into it as the room began to spin.

"Go!" she yelled, and then didn't wait for Dillarn. She shoved Baenil through the portal, and then stumbled forward. Firm hands grasped her, and then Dillarn pulled her through the portal.

Straight onto Main Street in the Archanon Market District. This far east, the sun was just rising behind the Ilari Mountains, and the warmth of summer caressed her face.

She collapsed then, her head spinning, her dagger clattering out of her hand.

And then darkness.

Chapter 43

KAILAR'S RETURN

The tower tunnel under the mountain was too narrow to easily open a portal for Cardin, Sira, Elaria and Reis to pass through, so Cardin allowed General Vellar to precede them out into the main tunnel.

This is going to work, he thought, remembering Tana's words. *'The answers you seek so desperately are already before you. Or rather, beneath you.'* The Cronal was the answer. To a lot more, as it turned out, but at least to Cardin's father.

When they spilled out into the main tunnel, the General turned to head off, only to stop as running footsteps echoed down the corridor, and by the light of everlasting torches, they saw Amaya running towards them. During times of a siege, he expected her to be wearing full steel armor, but instead she wore only leather.

"Your Majesty!" she called out urgently, and stopped, waving them to follow. "Come quickly! A portal has opened in the city!"

Cardin's eyes widened. "A...what?!"

"Three people from Devor have come through, including Kailar!"

While that didn't fully settle him, Cardin breathed a little easier — only dark magic could craft a portal within the city's protective barrier, though he wasn't sure before now if it would work through an active shield.

Without waiting for them, Amaya started running back for the Western Gate. Cardin followed, with the others beside or behind him, and all the while, he cursed his fortunes. He needed to get to his father *now*, before it was too late, and get down to the Cronal. There wasn't time for more distractions!

But this wasn't something that could be put on hold, either. What was Kailar doing here? And who had she brought from Devor? Were they under attack as well? The orcs *had* said that the Darksteel invasion had been across their entire world.

They came to the end of the tunnel, and Cardin's heart leapt into his throat – the predawn glow was already present, growing brighter by the moment. The sun was probably already rising behind the Ilari Mountains, which meant they had even less time than he realized.

Amaya led them down the very same stairs they had climbed only minutes ago to meet with Aezara, and then she led them to Main Street towards the Castle District. As soon as they turned onto the street, Cardin saw a crowd of soldiers, weapons drawn, encircling another group on the streets.

With Cardin's troupe slowing to a brisk pace, Amaya commanded, "Make way for the Prince!"

The scene was not what Cardin expected – Kailar lay on the cobblestone road while another man knelt next to her, checking her chest to ensure she breathed. Standing over them was a wholly unexpected sight.

"Beanil!" Elaria exclaimed and rushed forward.

"Elaria?!" he was equally surprised, and clutched her in his arms.

Could this week provide any more surprises?

"Stand down," Cardin ordered the surrounding soldiers. "Attend to your duties, we'll handle this."

As Elaria pulled away, she asked, "What's going on? How did you escape from Darea?"

"Thank the seas, I was afraid I'd not see a friendly face again," Baenil said, shaking his head. Then, in answer to Elaria's question, he motioned at Kailar's unconscious form and explained, "As surprising as it may sound, I have this one to thank for my rescue." Cardin's eyes widened, but Baenil hastily added, "But not from Darea. The Darksteel Empire brought me to Halarite from there. It is a long story, but…"

"They needed him to find an ancient ruin," the other man said, standing up and facing Cardin. "They called it the Conduit."

"So that's what she was hiding," Cardin mused. The thing Aezara couldn't tell him about. But… "What is it?"

"A pyramid-like structure," Baenil explained. "D-do you, um, know what a pyramid is?" Cardin nodded. Relief melted Baenil's expression, "Ah, good, good. I think it is meant to somehow convey power to the Darksteel army, though beyond that I cannot say how or what it is exactly."

"And…you know where it is?" Cardin asked.

"Yes. Well, not precisely," the elf hastily amended. "But I believe I have an idea where to look."

"Which means the Darksteel Army can't get their hands on him," the older man said. "That's why we came here, Kailar hoped he would be safe here."

With a grimace, Cardin looked to Sira, Reis, and Amaya, and then shook his head. "I'm afraid not. He…"

"Bwahszat?" Kailar suddenly blurted, sitting up quickly and pointing a suspiciously dark-colored dagger at nothing. She winced a moment later and pressed her palm to her head. "Oh gods, my head…" And then she looked around, looked up at Cardin.

Fury flickered between them both, and Cardin remembered arriving at the Wizards' Guild to a field of bodies three months ago. His hands twitched, aching to draw the Sword. Her eyes shifted from him to the hilt of the Sword sticking over his shoulder, and he knew that she longed for it.

Last time they saw each other, they'd worked together to defeat the wraith Degrin. What about now? Was the invasion enough to keep her in line and willing to cooperate?

Was it enough to make everyone else cooperate with her?

"Um, Cardin?" Sira's soothing voice broke his deathstare with Kailar. "You're summoning a lot of magic all of a sudden. It's, um, scaring Raida." Her face contorted for a moment into various expressions, and then she sighed. "Okay, fine, it's scaring *me*."

Startled, he realized she was right – he had unconsciously gathered star magic into himself and channeled it into the Sword, even without drawing it. It hummed noisily in its enchanted sheath, as if begging to be let out and unleashed.

Gritting his teeth, Cardin closed his eyes and dispelled some of that magic, allowing the flow through him to normalize into a steady stream.

Then he felt Kailar's presence through the darkness. Her void powerful, if unsteady.

The only other human to wield dark magic. This time, the balance he had worked to establish within himself allowed him to sense her, unlike three months ago when it had still been an either/or matter for the different magics within him.

Huh. When did I figure out how to feel both?

Sighing, Cardin nodded, and looked to the surrounding soldiers. "I know we all have personal grudges against Kailar, but for now, we have more important matters to attend to. General Vellar."

"Sire?" Cardin hadn't noticed that he'd drawn his weapon.

"You have your orders. Deploy the troops."

He looked at Cardin, then back at Kailar, before sighing. Sliding his weapon into its sheath, he shouted, "Alright, show's over ladies and gents! Fall in and follow me!" He led the surrounding soldiers towards the Western Gate's guard house, and added, "I need every captain and commander in the city to report to me at once!"

The older man from Devor helped Kailar up onto her feet, and Cardin noticed that she winced when she put weight on her right foot. How had she injured it? What were the circumstances of her arrival? All good questions, but none of which he had time for right now.

"Alright, Baenil," Cardin started, "We have a lot to do and not a lot of time before Archanon falls."

Kailar's face blanched. "What?!"

"There's no time to explain," he shook his head. "But it sounds like we need to keep you," he pointed at Baenil, "out of the hands of the Darksteel Army."

Nodding his agreement, Baenil said, "I would never willingly divulge what I know to them, but I would prefer *not* to be a prisoner *again.*"

Cardin sympathized with him. "Right. So here's the deal. We *also* need to stop the Darksteel Army from getting their hands on the Cronal, which they can use to find this Conduit. But I need to use the Cronal to save my father first. Kailar, can you portal them down into the Cronal chamber?"

She raised her eyebrows at his commanding tone and looked ready to rebuke him. But then she stopped and looked at her companions before she shook her head. "No. I'm too weak. I think opening a portal to here nearly killed me."

So that's why her powers feel so unsteady, Cardin thought. "Alright, then." Drawing upon dark magic, Cardin looked towards the Upper City and summoned forth a dark portal, a wall of violet light with harmless bolts of blackened lightning lancing out randomly. "That'll take you to the antechamber above it," he said. "Baenil, I need to either dismantle or safely destroy it. Get me a solution, but don't enact it until I arrive."

Eyebrows arching skyward, Baenil nodded, and then looked at Elaria. "Would you accompany me, my friend?"

Elaria hesitated, and then looked at Cardin. Her enthusiastic reply from moments ago in the tunnel was not lost on Cardin, and he realized that she must still have feelings for him.

"No," she shook her head. "I promised to help Cardin."

"If you went with him," Cardin nodded, "it would help."

"I know," she smiled sweetly at him, "but that's not what I meant. I'm sticking by your side, if you'll allow it."

He looked at Sira uncomfortably, wondering if she'd display her usual jealousy…only to find that she looked completely unperturbed by Elaria's insistence. That was curious.

Knowing there was no time to argue, he nodded and assented, "Alright."

Elaria gave Baenil one last hug, and then rejoined Cardin, Sira, and Reis. Baenil proceeded through the portal after that, disappearing into the wall of dark magic. Cardin looked at Kailar and the other man, and he hesitated. What if he just left Kailar in Archanon, for the Darksteel Army to take care of?

She must have thought the same thing, and she stared at him, her expression blank, but her dark magic stirred ever so subtly. And that was when Cardin knew that, much as he despised her, now was the time to put aside old hatreds.

Halarite should have been much more prepared than it was. If only the Allied Council had listened to reason. Maybe it would have been too late any way, but instead of presenting a united front against the Darksteel, they were all separate, alone.

Queen Leian and the Wizards had refused to work with the orcs. Could Cardin turn away help from Kailar?

So, feeling the pain behind every word he said, Cardin said,

"You're welcome to join him, and then leave with us after we finish with the Cronal."

"You're leaving Archanon to them?" Kailar gaped. "Are you kidding? I thought you'd been made Prince, how can you abandon-"

"I DON'T HAVE A CHOICE!" he snapped, rage roiling into him, and his dark portal almost destabilized. He reaffirmed his focus on it and forced himself to breathe slowly. "I can't let them have the Sword of Dragons, I can't risk capture. So either come with us, or stay here, I don't care, but choose *now*."

She snapped her mouth shut and glanced again at the black hilt over his shoulder. Nodding once, she looked at her companion, and he helped Kailar limp through the portal. Cardin immediately let it dispel after that, and he turned to his friends. His hands were shaking, and he wanted to take his anger out on something, *anything*. Instead, he looked into Sira's violet eyes, and she stared back, her face emotionless in the face of his rage.

Sira said nothing, nor did the others. Maybe they were smarter for it.

And then he felt the surges of magic that preluded massive, off-world portals.

The closest was to the west, and the four magic-wielders turned that way, with Reis cluing in and following their gazes.

Almost as big as the portals that had brought the enemy forces against Archanon, walls of blue-white were opening all around the city, including just above the cliffs of the Western Gate. Only the portal didn't face the shield, it faced south. When the first airship passed through, lumbering slowly and noisily with its back-facing whirling blades thrumming, it flew parallel to the shield.

It was a strange sight to see, to say the least. A giant, blackened oval bladder suspended what looked like a black-hulled sailing ship, and on the deck of that ship, creatures from probably a dozen different worlds worked the ship's rigging feverishly, while several lined up on the ship's port side and drew weapons.

All around the city, the same scene played out, though Cardin could only see a couple more such ships from their vantage. They all had come at once, all were orbiting the city in the same direction, and all readied their crew for battle. Expert, precision military discipline.

As one, their battle crew unleashed attacks upon the city's shield, which lit up brighter than ever, though their attacks were nearly noiseless compared to the siege weapon assaults. Cardin frowned at their tactics at first, but then the ships began to ascend, higher and higher, while their assault upon the shield continued.

They meant to find the upper edge of the shield.

"We're out of time," Cardin murmured. Drawing dark power into himself, he prepared to open another dark portal, and hoped that it would work through the Wizards' Guild shield the same way it worked through Archanon's. He felt the connection establish, and then the portal winked into existence right where the previous one had been.

"Go ahead," he told the others, and then looked at Amaya, while Sira, Elaria and Reis marched past him, disappearing through the portal. "You're welcome to join us."

The Guardian smiled at him, and he saw in her something unexpected – a rebellious look. "With all due respect, Your Majesty, if you don't mind...I think I can do more for the crown here." Nodding towards the Sword's hilt, she said, "I don't think you need me to protect you."

He grinned, but then said, "You can't stop them from taking the city. None of us can."

"No," she agreed, and her mischievous look turned to a roguish grin. "But I can give them hell after they occupy it. And I've found a few more Guardians to help me do it."

"Aaah," he nodded understanding. "Well, if anyone was qualified to run the resistance, it's you."

"Exactly," she nodded. Then, her grin faltered, and she looked up at the rising airships before looking again at Cardin.

He knew what she wanted to ask. So he nodded. "We'll come back for you. For all of you," he motioned his hands to encompass all of Archanon. "This isn't over, Amaya."

She looked reassured by that, and then, surprising him, she drew closer and placed a hand on his shoulder. Cardin might not be used to being royalty yet, but he knew just how strange it was for a soldier to do that.

"You know, for what it's worth," Amaya drew in a deep breath, and finished, "King Beredis would have been proud of you. And I don't care what that harlot Kailar thinks." Cardin's eyes rose up at her words. "You're doing the right thing."

It was strange to be reassured by a subordinate, but it was

welcome, and Cardin clasped her hand. "Thank you. Now go, with the full authority of the throne, and make them pay for every inch of this city."

"Oh, and then some," she nodded, and then she turned and ran off. Not towards the gates, but into the city. Not to face the enemy head on, but to undermine them once they were settled.

Cardin almost pitied the Darksteel Army.

Drawing in a deep breath, Cardin walked over to his portal, only to pause one last time. He looked up at the airships, towering above now, and then he looked around at the city. The city he was abandoning. The city that had stood for ten thousand years as a testament to humanity's ability to withstand any storm thrown at it.

Now the city would fall, and it would do so under his watch. His chest ached like it never had before. His fury grew. They had taken so much from them all, and now they would take Halarite's last vestige of hope.

But Cardin vowed that it wouldn't last. This city had withstood occupation once before.

He would be back.

The First City would be theirs again.

And then he walked through the portal to save his father.

Chapter 44

BLINDSIDED

Passing through a dark portal wasn't so different to Kailar as passing through a star portal, but when she and Dillarn arrived at the other end of Cardin's, she was shocked — not by how it felt, but by the scene she found.

Chaos and threat.

The antechamber, the very same one in which Kailar had stabbed the possessed Prince Beredis and then was flung away by a surge of power, was full of men and women scrambling in a panic, and before her stood Baenil and a woman in leather armor wielding a curved, long sword.

In fact, the armored woman held it menacingly at Baenil.

Kailar tensed, and realized she still held a dark dagger in her hand. In that same moment, the woman saw the new arrivals, and her eyes widened. *"You!"*

"Really?" Kailar scowled. "Is that the only reaction people have towards me?"

Letan would have had something laughable to say right then. Maybe. *Gods, I hope he's alright.*

Turning towards Kailar and Dillarn, but keeping Baenil in her peripheral, the woman took up a more aggressive posture, no longer defensive but one that conveyed to Kailar her intention to attack.

"I told you, the Keeper sent us!" Baenil pleaded. "The Darksteel Army..."

"Is already here," the woman remarked coldly, eyes set on Kailar in a deadly gaze. "They're in the tunnel marching towards the dwarven city as we speak."

Kailar's stomach dropped along with her jaw. That was when she realized that the chaos around her wasn't because of their arrival, but rather the men and women were grabbing various tools and personal items spread around the antechamber and streaming out the door, heedless of the new arrivals other than a few worried glances.

"Convenient that you arrive when they do," the woman said. *Anila!* That was her name – Kailar finally remembered her from the last time she had come down to the dwarven city.

"We came because the Darksteel Army is about to breach Archanon," Kailar rebuked. "And your precious Prince Kataar wants to destroy the Cronal."

Anila started at that, her jaw tightening more than it already had, though how that was possible, Kailar couldn't guess.

Baenil corrected, "Destroy or dismantle."

Eyes darting towards the spiral stairs descending into the substructure, Anila shook her head. "He...can't."

Kailar glanced that way as well and noticed that the golem or whatever it was, the giant humanoid, armored statue had been pushed off of the stairs and away from its pedestal. Still a dead husk, though.

"He must," Kailar stated, and glanced at Dillarn, whom still helped her remain upright. "He must or the Darksteel Army will be able to find *exactly* what they came looking for. Or worse..." She looked down, the possibility registering on her in a sudden rush. "They could use the Cronal itself to affect the Universe, to conquer it all in one fell swoop, if they so desired to."

"If they're idiotic enough to risk bringing another wraith or ten through, yes," Anila nodded. "But...find what they're looking for?"

By now, the rest of the men and women had streamed out, all but one of them. A man in dirt-soiled clothes stood back, watching the exchange with a mix of fear and fascination. Kailar eyed him curiously, but then replied to Anila, "Some building or structure on Halarite that's important to them. It doesn't matter, your Prince, the

Keeper of the Sword," she scowled at using that term to describe him, "ordered us to be here. Are you going to defy him?"

Anila's sword had started to dip, but now it rose up again, her eyes turning ice-cold. "And how do I know you speak the truth."

"Do my words carry any weight with you?" Baenil asked. Anila glanced ever-so-briefly at him. "After what has been said and done in the past, I would hope that you and I have come to an understanding, Guardian of the Covenant."

Anila's jaw tightened again. "The Covenant is…no more." She shook her head. "All I have left of what I believed in, what I guarded with my *everything* is down here. In that library."

Arching an eyebrow, Kailar glanced through the exit door, into the square and the dwarven city beyond. "If I understand what I just saw and heard, you're about to lose it anyway."

Sword tip drooping again, Anila heaved a slow, lingering sigh. "I suppose that is true."

"Good," Kailar said, earning a scorching glare from the strange woman. "Then you know what has to be done, to protect it from our common enemy." When Anila frowned, Kailar clarified, "The Darksteel have invaded my new home on Devor, and they've already occupied our elven friend's world," she nodded to Baenil, and Anila's eyes widened in surprise. "And Archanon is about to fall. So help us."

Chin rising up, either defiantly or pridefully, Anila seemed to make up her mind then, and she carefully slid her weapon into its sheath on her hip. "Very well."

"Anila," the errant man hesitantly started. "We need to go now."

Looking to the man, Anila shook her head. "I'm staying. You evacuate with everyone else."

"But…"

"Go!" Anila pointed towards the doors. "Before they cut you off from the catacomb exit."

Glancing at the new arrivals only briefly, the man nodded, and took off at a full run, leaving Kailar, Dillarn, Baenil, and Anila to defend the antechamber from an army.

"How long until they get here?" Kailar asked.

"Depends on how fast they progress through the city," Anila shrugged. "I've no way of knowing."

Baenil pointed up. "Perhaps you should visit the roof to see."

Anila looked up, and nodded, "Good thinking."

"You," Kailar pointed at the elf, "Need to get down there and figure out how to destroy that thing." Baenil lifted a pretentious finger at her, and she quickly amended, "Or dismantle, *whatever!* Just figure out how to do it without killing us all."

"Um, right," Baenil nodded.

"Dillarn," she looked to her last Devorian companion. "Maybe you should stick with him."

Gracing her with a doubtful look, he asked, "What about your ankle?"

Kailar eased weight onto it, and it felt a little sturdier. A little. "I'll be fine. You stay safe. Besides," she added with a grin, "I think you might like what you find down there."

Easing away from her, he narrowed his eyes at her, but either he knew how stubborn she was, or he was too curious about what was down there. He joined Baenil, and together they headed down the stairs.

Regarding her apprehensively, Anila asked, "Your ankle?"

Wincing as she added more weight to it, Kailar shook her head. "It disagreed with a Darksteel soldier."

Giving her a brief smirk, Anila replied, "Nice. Keep up, if you can."

Kailar glared at the woman as she headed out, and then she went after her, limping heavily but managing to catch up. Then came the hard part – they entered a stairwell just off the antechamber and began the arduous climb up. Arduous for Kailar, anyway.

Thankfully there was a railing, and that helped Kailar immensely.

Four stories later, they spilled out onto a flat rooftop, marred only by the capitol building's stone crenellation and a tower that reached higher, a pulsing light atop it. She wondered what that was about, but for now gave it little attention.

Anila led her to the edge of the building, and they stared out towards where Kailar guessed the main tunnel once existed. Multiple wide support pillars stretched up to the ceiling all around them, but there was a distinct line of them leading from the capital building's encircled square to a far wall. Leftover, dusty webs from the city's previous tenants marred their view, but she could see a wide-open tunnel, and a whole lot of trouble coming their way.

Columns of Darksteel soldiers marched dutifully down the city's main avenue, eliciting a flashback to a similar sight in Tieran.

Except there were fewer of them this time. It wasn't a whole battalion, she wagered, but a detachment, maybe to find out if the rumors about the tunnel were true.

Which baffled her. "I thought the main tunnel had collapsed," Kailar remarked.

"Aye, it had," Anila nodded. "By Prince Kataar's orders, we began clearing it, in hopes of one day finding where it opened up to the surface and making it easier for scholars to explore the city."

Eyes wide, Kailar shook her head. "Kind of a stupid call, given what's down here."

"Perhaps," Anila agreed. "However, Prince Kataar also thought that if we could keep the entrance a relative secret at first, it might also provide an alternate means for citizens of Archanon to escape, should the Darksteel Army breach the city."

"Huh," Kailar mused. "Actually not a bad idea. Too bad there wasn't time to finish." Then she frowned, and wondered, "How did the Darksteel Army find out about it?"

At first, Anila didn't reply. When she did, her voice was somewhat hushed. "Some within the Covenant, and the Alliance, suspected insiders from the Darksteel Army had already infiltrated our world. It was how they sowed so much chaos and destruction."

"Some?" Kailar arched an eyebrow. "Like who?"

"Prince Kataar was chief among them," Anila replied, and glanced behind them. "Will he be arriving soon?"

Kailar glanced back as well, angry at herself for wishing he had already arrived. The army was already halfway up the avenue. They'd be here in minutes. "He's just retrieving his father." She glanced at Anila, and then looked out at the approaching army again. "I expect he'll be here in minutes, but I don't know if it will be in time."

Another moment of silence passed.

Something jabbed Kailar's lower back through her armor, a pin-prick that was immediately followed by a burning sensation.

She whirled towards Anila, her dagger still in-hand and ready to slice at the woman, but the woman had already deftly backed far away from Kailar. She held in her hand a slender silvery dagger, the tip dropping with Kailar's blood intermixed with some toxin.

The burning sensation suddenly turned cold, and spread *fast*.

Anila regarded her with cool contempt. "Well, then," she said to Kailar, whose legs began to shake. "That doesn't leave me much time, does it?"

The pain in her ankle faded, but so too did all other feeling. She collapsed, first to her knees, and then to her side.

Anila? The gods damned Covenant Guardian?! *NO!*

But she couldn't scream. The numbness had spread everywhere.

For the second time that day, Kailar blacked out.

Chapter 45

CONJUNCTION

"Well, this is awkward," Raida remarked. They had just passed through Cardin's portal to the receiving courtyard of the Wizards' Guild, and now she, Elaria and Reis stood face-to-face with a handful of Wizards, staves pointed in their faces.

Inwardly, she remarked, *I see your sense of humor is back.* Outwardly, she said, "You'd think by now you all would know us. Or me, anyway."

Granted, Sira didn't recognize any of the Wizards before her. Judging by the runes embroidered into their robes, none of them were masters.

"Who are you?" the eldest, a woman with striking brown hair with distinct streaks of white, asked.

"Sira Reinar," she stated, old habits taking charge. "Adviser to Prince Kataar, Keeper of the Sword."

"Reis Kalind," Reis added, "Captain of the Tal Guardians."

"Elaria of the College of Serelik," Elaria added.

The Wizards arrayed before them hesitated and looked to one another. Then they looked over Sira's shoulders at the violet-colored portal, still open. Sira followed their gaze, hoping Cardin had come through, but he hadn't yet. Her stomach did summersaults, as she immediately thought the worst – what was taking him so long?

But, just as she looked away, Cardin stepped through, the portal closing behind him.

Even if they didn't recognize Sira and her distinctive violet eyes, everyone knew Cardin, and the staves returned to their vertical, planted positions on the marble foundation.

"Prince Kataar," the woman nodded. "I apologize, we…did not think anyone could get through our shield."

That was when Sira really took in their surroundings. They had emerged from the portal in the receiving courtyard, the skeletons of permanent portal arrays running along either side in rows, meant to one day provide a hub of transportation throughout Halarite, but now unlikely to ever fulfill their original design.

Ahead was the Grand Wizard Hall, a polished marble, granite, and stone structure that towered high, high enough for a Star Dragon to enter the massive golden and white doors, currently closed.

Above and around them was a blue-white, domed shield, encompassing the large Wizards' Guild campus. Domed to ensure they never fell victim to a meteor shower. Domed to ensure they didn't have the same weakness that their enemy now exploited at Archanon.

Sira's jaw set, frustration boiling within her, and she felt Raida cue into that and grow angry as well.

It didn't help when a familiar, body-shaking sound greeted them – *BOOM!* The Wizards were under siege, same as Archanon had been.

"Dark magic portals appear to circumvent star magic," Cardin explained, impatience giving his voice an edge. "I'm here for my father."

The Wizards exchanged confused glances. Perhaps they wondered why Cardin would be so focused on that during what seemed like the end of the world.

"Of course…" she replied in a calculated, careful tone. "I can escort-"

"That won't be necessary," Cardin walked around them and headed to the left, towards the building with the Recovery Ward. "I know you have your hands full already." Sira and Reis exchanged glances, and then they and Elaria rushed to catch up with Cardin.

The Wizards didn't follow, but Sira knew they would summon a Master Wizard, if not the Grand Master, to meet Cardin at the ward.

The grounds were relatively empty, the day-to-day bustle of the Wizards abandoned in their attempt to defend against the Darksteel Army.

BOOM!

She cringed, wishing she'd heard the last of that. The blue-white shield flared, but it held.

Towards the outer edges, she saw multiple towers, the defense towers she'd seen during various stages of construction when she'd come to the complex with Cardin. Several Wizards congregated around them, and she could see at least one touching each pillar, though she couldn't fathom what they were doing.

Sira could feel the power, however. Or rather, Raida did, and conveyed it to Sira. Throughout the wars and conflicts, but especially when they first fought Falind and Kailar at the beginning of all of this, Sira had seen what the Wizards were capable of when they worked together.

The shield surrounding them practically blinded her and Raida with the power fueling it. It was power beyond anything she had yet felt, even from Cardin, and she wondered if the siege assault upon it was a futile effort. Would the Wizards be the last holdout? The last free civilization on Halarite, long after Archanon and Tal, Asirin and Devor were conquered and enslaved?

"That's a rather cheerful thought," Raida remarked. *"Do not give up, Sira. I am here with you, and we will face this darkness together."*

Darkness. So much darkness. The word 'dark' was becoming something she felt sick about. Dark magic, Dark Dragons, Darksteel. Darkness was something she occasionally used to find peace in, she *loved* starry nights when the moons weren't visible. Gazing up into those endless heavens, especially back when she and Cardin were still together, had been a source of comfort and wonder.

"I thought you still were together with Cardin?"

Guilt ground away at the edges of her rage and frustration, and she looked at Cardin, whose expression was one of determination, not fear, not hopeless.

Sira still loved him. But did that still mean they could be together? Especially since the world was ending?

BOOM!

They finally came upon the Recovery Ward, contained within a relatively modest structure compared to the rest of the Guild complex, and they entered hastily. That was when Sira found her thoughts turning to shock – there were countless Wizards occupying the beds!

The Ward was bustling, with caretakers moving from bed to bed, magic flaring as they aided the wounded. Even Cardin paused to take in the scene.

And then Master Wizard Sana, her grey robes disorderly, her hair a frazzled mess, approached. "Keeper," she breathed. "I did not expect to see you here, now."

Cardin's eyes drifted towards his father, and Sira followed, seeing Draegus Kataar still unconscious beneath an enchanted blanket halfway into the ward. "Is my father still okay?"

Sana glanced back and exhaled. "For now, yes."

Cardin nodded, and then looked around before asking, "What happened? I thought the shield protected you all."

"It did, once we erected it," Sana replied, rubbing her face. "They appeared out of nowhere, but still on the perimeter. Thank goodness the Grand Master thought to conjure a protection spell to keep unwanted portals out of our complex. Even still…"

"Several opening salvos wounded many of our people," Grand Master Syrn's curt voice spoke from behind. The trio turned to her as she entered. She looked almost as bad as Sana, though her robes were in a little better condition. "Beyond that, the strain of keeping our shield empowered against such a constant barrage has exhausted the limits of some of our younger Wizards, despite regular rotations upon the perimeter."

Surprised, Sira asked, "So you mean you cannot hold the shield indefinitely?"

Syrn arched a curious eyebrow at her, but then replied to Cardin, "We can hold the shield. My people are stronger than you might imagine." Sira narrowed her eyes, spurned by the Grand Master's attitude towards her. Towards all Mages, for that matter.

"Good," Cardin nodded.

An uncomfortable silence fell between them, then, and Sira remembered the last Allied Council meeting. There was definite tension between Cardin and Syrn, and she wondered if they could look past it. Magic stirred in the room, kicking up a slight breeze…

"Grand Master!" Sana's sharp voice cut through the tension, breaking the moment. "I must protest, this is a place of healing."

Sira arched an eyebrow, and exchanged a rebellious, amused look with Reis. It wasn't often they heard a younger Wizard rebuke an elder, and as far as Sira was concerned, Syrn deserved it.

Magic settled, and both the Grand Master and Cardin shifted anxiously. "Of course," Syrn nodded. "I apologize." She looked at Cardin, and said, "Keeper, I…I must…apologize. You… You were right."

"Well, now, this is a surprise, isn't it?" Raida chuckled inwardly, spreading warmth through Sira's core.

Hush, you, Sira rebuked. *This isn't the time.* She paused for a second, but added, *But yes it is. And a pleasant one, at that.*

Cardin regarded the Grand Master for a moment, his hardened eyes softening just a little. Sira knew him. Knew he didn't usually hold grudges. Yet she also knew how frustrated he'd felt over all of the politics, all of the maneuvering. "There isn't time to get into that right now," he finally said. "Archanon is falling as we speak, the Darksteel Army are using airships to circumvent the shield. They're goal is the Cronal."

Syrn's eyes widened. "How could they possibly know about it?"

"I don't know," Cardin shook his head, "But I need to get my father to it before they do. I've learned that it can reunite his soul with his body. And then I need to dismantle or disable it before the Darksteel Army can use it. They could make their way down there in a matter of hours, and I might need every second to save my father."

Sira noted that Cardin neglected to tell the Grand Master how he found out how to save Draegus, but that was probably for the best. Syrn likely still wasn't ready to accept the orcs as allies. Not that it would matter for much longer.

"Very well," Syrn nodded, and glanced towards Draegus's bed. "Do you require assistance?"

Looking around at the busy ward, at Master Sana and her impatient expression, he shook his head. "I think you probably can't spare anyone just now. But I'll come back," he looked to Syrn. "I have a lot to tell you, and we have a lot to talk about."

"Indeed we do," Syrn acknowledged. "Very well, Keeper. As it seems you can come and go as you please…"

Cardin's eyes widened, and he quickly said, "Be ready to defend yourselves against Dark Dragons. I don't know what happened to them, but they are working with the Darksteel Army. They could breach your shields just like I can."

Syrn's expression darkened, her head drooping. "I...I do not know if we can defend against such darkness."

Sira hadn't considered that fact, either. If Cardin and Kailar could create portals through shields and anti-portal fields, then so could the Dark Dragons. For now, they were probably too wounded to fight, thanks to Endri, but even that was a total guess. For all they knew, the Dark Dragons could be coming even now.

"It would be best if you made haste and returned as soon as possible," Syrn said.

"Agreed," Cardin nodded, and turned. "Master Sana, may I-"

BOOM!

"Please," she turned and motioned them on. "Hurry."

Without further hesitation, the trio passed the ward Master and hurried over to Draegus Kataar's side. He looked the same, ghostly-pale faced, white wispy hair – his body was not taking the loss of its soul well at all.

But he still breathed, slow and steady. He still lived.

Sira rushed to the other side of the bed, and then helped lift him into Cardin's arms. Magic surged in him, and she knew that he enhanced his strength to be able to carry his father alone.

Then, they headed out, weaving in between healing Wizards and cots. Sana had already moved on to help others, and Syrn was gone, no doubt to go help defend the city.

Once they were out of the ward, Cardin wasted no time and summoned another dark portal, wide enough for three. Without hesitation, she, Elaria and Reis passed through together.

On the other side, they found only silence.

Sira wasn't sure what to expect, but she knew that there were a lot of workers that were supposed to be living down in the antechamber of the dwarven capitol building. Instead, they found what looked like abandoned sleeping bags, along with digging and mining gear. But no people.

Cardin followed them a second later, and then paused, taking in the sight as well.

"Where is everyone?" Sira asked.

"Anila?" Reis called out, walking further into the room and looking around, his voice full of hope. When was the last time they had seen each other?

"Baenil," Elaria added, spreading out in the other direction.

But no answers came.

"Come on," Cardin said, "Maybe she's down in the library with…"

He jerked to a stop, and Sira felt something then, too. A steady pulse of magic, similar to what she'd just felt at the Wizards' Guild, but a thousand times smaller – a shield.

Raida, where is that coming from?

Cardin already knew, and he slowly edged towards the descending stairwell. A second later, Raida replied, *"I believe it is from the library itself."*

She hurried over to Cardin's side, and they stopped at the edge of the stairs, with Elaria joining them a second later. The buzzing feeling was stronger here, and she knew Raida was right. Sira pulled her white-dyed longsword from its sheath, imbued it with a little bit of protective magic, and then lowered the tip towards the stairs.

"Be careful!" Elaria cautioned.

Sira narrowed her eyes at the elf, and resisted saying something snarky, before she lowered her weapon a little more – a blue-white shield flared, long enough for them to see that the entire stairwell was protected below the floor of the antechamber. Her sword bounced up from the discharge of power, and she yelped at the sting it jolted through her arm.

Gods, if I hadn't imbued my sword with magic, or if Reis had tried to go down there…

"It would have hurt a lot more," Raida agreed. *"Maybe even killed you or Reis."*

"What the hell?" Cardin frowned.

Reis scowled, wide-eyed. "Kailar…"

"No," Cardin shook his head. "She didn't do this, it's star magic. And powerful. It's-"

Elaria's head jerked towards the double-doors leading out to the terrace and courtyard outside. Everyone else followed suit, staring towards the sound of…*something*…

"What is it?" Sira asked, while Raida stretched out their sense of magic.

Then she felt it. And heard it a second later.

There were a lot of people outside. A *lot*.

Dread swelled inside of her, and she exchanged a look with

Cardin. While he set his father's limp form down next to the shielded stairwell, Sira and Elaria ran towards the doors, while Reis hurried to meet them.

Even Reis heard it by now, and he drew his bronze-dyed longsword.

Cardin made it to the doors at the same time as the rest of them, and her worst fears were confirmed. Streaming in from three different entrances through the wall surrounding the wealthy district was the all-too-familiar sight of darkened steel armor and weapons, and men and women of varying species.

The Darksteel Army was already here!

They had only just made it into the wealthy district, however, and that gave them a few minutes.

"Dammit," Cardin grit his teeth. "Come on, let's close this door."

If they could. Sira and Reis took one of the double-doors, while Cardin and Elaria took the other. They pushed upon the ancient steel doors as hard as they could, but hers and Reis's barely budged. Cardin's screeched loudly, and then broke free and closed with a loud *k-thlunk!*

Then he came over and helped them, while Elaria stood back, unable to fit in behind the door to push. Shouted orders came through from the Darksteel Army, but it was in a language that Sira couldn't understand, and Raida wasn't translating just then.

They got the second door closed, and then looked around for a bar or something for the door. Surely the dwarves would have a way to protect their capital building, right?

Elaria knew where to look, and she shoved past them, slapping her palm on a hand-shaped symbol next to the doors that Sira hadn't noticed before. From a long, thin recess in the archway above the doors, something clacked, and then a metallic-looking bar, with glowing blue runes etched into it, slammed down from the ceiling, halting midway down the door with a deafening bang. The runes surged, and then previously unseen runes in the door flared brightly. She felt as much as saw magic gather into the door, and knew then that it would hold a long while.

They were safe.

"The other doors," Reis's panicked voice cut through her relief.

She saw him and Elaria race towards the opposite end of the hexagonal antechamber. She couldn't see another door, but the hulking mass of the defeated statue possibly blocked it from view. While they raced around the statue, Sira and Cardin chased after.

Reis reached the entrance first, two steps ahead of Elaria. It looked like the doorway led further into the capital building, and he started to close it, but Elaria skidded to a stop and drew her daggers.

A pulse of magic blasted into Reis, sending him sprawling across the marble floor, his armor screeching and his sword clattering away.

And Anila Kovin stepped inside, her curved sword held tightly, vibrating with power, just as she unleashed another blast at Elaria, who dove out of the way.

Sira and Cardin slid to a stop and gaped. "Anila?!" Cardin asked.

The Covenant guardian stepped further inside to allow two more figures to follow. The first was about as tall as Sira, lithe, clothed in black and dark grey cloth and chainmail, though her gauntlets looked like Darksteel, and Sira could *feel* the power radiating from the new woman. Her skin was pale blue, her eyes the color of ice. The other person was one of the large, eight-foot-tall brutes covered in Darksteel plate armor, and she recognized his species – she had fought several in the village on Stella.

Her mind made the connection all at once, even though she didn't want to believe.

"You?!" She gaped at Anila. "You're with *them?!*"

Quirking an eyebrow up, Anila asked, "You really never suspected?"

She and Cardin exchanged looks, but it was Reis who replied, "You...lied..." His voice shook, and he looked unsteady while trying to get up onto his feet, but somehow she suspected that had nothing to do with the blast he had just endured.

"Yes I did," Anila nodded at him. "I do that often, if you had not noticed."

"I don't understand," Cardin shook his head. "You're the most trusted guardian of the Covenant, a hybrid child of a Wizard and a-"

"A Mage?" she asked. "You really believed that story, didn't you, Keeper?" Her companions spread apart, stalking the room and preparing to flank them. Sira kept a close eye on them, while Elaria eased back to join her and Cardin.

Be ready, Raida...

"*I will destroy them,*" Raida growled within. Sira shared her companion's rage, and they both focused in on the larger brute, who held a double-sided axe that reminded Sira of the one Arkad of the orcs wielded. Would it be enchanted with fire elemental magic as well, or something different?

Either way, he was their number one target – Sira and Raida knew how to deal with the brutes, and they had a score to settle with the Darksteel Army.

"That was what made you easier than most to manipulate, Cardin Kataar," Anila shook her head. "You wanted to believe in the good in everyone. You wanted to believe that even amongst so much hatred in your culture, so much bigotry and favoritism, someone somewhere could overcome it, and that love would prevail above all. The Universe is not so pretty as it is in your delusional head."

"Then," Reis shook his head, "how? Why?"

"Why?" Anila frowned. "Surely you must see it by now, the why. We have invaded so many worlds, and one of the surest ways to sow dissent amongst the people, to weaken them from within, is to start with religion. And yours provided so *much* fuel for us to use. All the lies. To be honest, spending so much time with your people has made me hate you more than the others I've helped conquer."

Sira's grip on her sword tightened, her leather gloves groaning against the leather of the handle. Cardin reached back and took hold of the Sword of Dragons, bringing it forward. And Reis edged towards his dropped weapon.

"You cannot defeat me," Cardin stated. "The three of you against just me could not hope to prevail, let alone with my friends."

"Perhaps not," Anila stated, and brought her sword up parallel to the ground. "But I am prepared to die for my cause. Are you?"

And she turned on Reis first.

Sira screamed when a blast of lightning arched out from Anila's sword. A dark shield saved Reis, no doubt Cardin's handiwork, but Sira immediately turned her attention to the brute, who came charging at her with reckless abandon.

But Elaria wasn't going to let him. She dove at the brute, rolling low under the swing of his axe, and she swiped at his feet. The Darksteel armor proved too much, and even charged with magic, her weapons bounced off.

The brute kept coming and swung his axe, unleashing a wave pattern of icy shards at Sira. Thanks to Raida's attuned instincts, Sira rolled beneath the shards, came up, and pointed her sword at the brute, unleashing a powerful arcane blast at him from inches away.

The brute wasn't so easy to take down as his companions on Stella – he batted the blast away with his axe, something Sira didn't even think was possible, and then barreled over her, sending her sprawling across the smooth floor.

Sounds of magic and battle raged around Sira, but the brute had her on the defensive, so as she scrambled onto her feet and dodged a top-down swing from her nemesis, she could spare no time to pay attention to what happened with Anila or the other Darksteel troop.

Elaria clambered up the brute's back suddenly, and stabbed her vibrating daggers into the base of his skull. He howled in pain, but her daggers hadn't penetrated as much as they should have, and he threw her off, smashing her into the husk of the statue.

Sira spun around, charging her sword with as much magic as Raida could spare, and tried to connect to the brute. He was fast, too fast to be believed, and the haft of his weapon intercepted Sira's weapon. Despite the magic powering her sword, she failed to cut through it, and then he shoved again. Sira kept her balance, dodged, ducked, and the brute kept on coming.

Anila hadn't just brought a couple of disposable grunts, Sira realized – she intended to keep that back door open long enough for the full force of the Darksteel army to come to her aid.

But Raida had other plans.

The brute knocked Sira onto her back again with a well-placed punch, the plate gauntlets cutting her face and knocking her senseless for a second.

Literally knocking her unconscious, except she felt Raida's spirit surge within her. Healing magic whirled into her body at the same time that she saw a violet haze cover her vision, and she was no longer at the helm of her own body.

The axe came down on her – and hit a solid shield, stopped cold, all of the magic gathered in it discharging and deflecting, destroying random sections of the antechamber around them and bouncing off of Elaria's hastily erected shield. Raida pulsed their own shield forward, a trick Sira had seen Kailar do once before, and it shoved the brute back. His arms splayed out in a vain attempt to keep his balance, and then he crashed onto his back.

Raida/Sira were on their feet a second later, and the dragonsoul flared its power. Though Sira couldn't see, she *felt* the imprint on her back shift and move, and it expanded off of her body. Ethereal wings unfurled behind her, and the energy that flowed out of Raida and into her sword was too much for the blade to handle, and the pulsating magic extended *past* the sword's length, becoming a glowing extension, deadlier than any physical blade.

The vision must have terrified the brute. Beneath his helmet, Raida/Sira saw his eyes open wide, and he scrambled back, abandoning his axe in his fervor to escape.

Then he was on his feet and bolting for the door.

Turning their attention to the others, Raida/Sira saw similar terror upon Anila and the ghostly woman's faces. They glanced at one another, and then abandoned their fight with Cardin and ran after the brute.

"Anila!" Reis shouted, but she paid him little heed.

"So much for willingness to die for one's cause," Raida spoke, loud enough that Reis and Cardin heard her much as they would a Star Dragon.

The others gaped at Raida/Sira then, and Cardin, his voice full of fright, asked, "S-sira?"

Raida/Sira nodded. *"She is here, but unconscious. I control our body for the moment."*

"Raida?" Cardin frowned. "I didn't know you could do this."

"I can."

And then a thunderous, deafening boom slammed into the barred double-doors, the runes upon it flaring brightly. Raida/Sira felt incredible power behind that attack, and knew that the doors would hold, but only for so long.

"You must go," Raida/Sira said to Cardin. *"Go now. Save your father. We will hold them off."*

Another *BOOM!* resonated throughout the chamber, and Cardin, Elaria and Reis glanced nervously at the door.

Raida/Sira looked to the backdoor, the sound of rushing footsteps in the corridor beyond coming closer. With a wave of their hand and a flare of power, they shoved the door closed, and activated a similar enchantment over it as that which protected the main doors.

"There isn't much time, and I am no more all-powerful than you are, Keeper of the Sword," Raida/Sira stated. *"Go."* When Cardin didn't move, Raida/Sira's eyes flared brightly, and they shouted into his thoughts, *"NOW!"*

Cardin staggered back, but then shook his head, and nodded. "Alright. Alright, but promise me you won't recklessly endanger her!"

"We will protect each other," Raida/Sira assured him. *"We promise you."*

Though still obviously uncertain, Cardin sheathed the Sword of Dragons, and then he and Reis, who picked up his own weapon along the way, rushed back to the stairs. Elaria stared at Raida/Sira, open-mouthed and speechless, but then she, too hurried after Cardin.

Raida/Sira lifted from the ground and floated over the corpse of the statue, and hovered above the center platform, turning their full attention to the doors, and began to gather magic into themselves.

"Let them come and taste our wrath," they said to each other. *"Let them taste our vengeance!"*

Chapter 46

TEMPTATION

At the foot of the stairs, Cardin stooped beside his father's lifeless, pale body, and reached out with magic, searching for a clue as to how to dismantle the protective barrier that lay evenly with the floor.

It was powerful magic, and it could have taken a long time to figure out how to disenchant it, had anyone else tried. Thankfully, Cardin was the Keeper of the Sword. Closing his eyes, he pushed star magic out of his body, creating a void that filled with a negating power.

After that, it was a simple process of projecting the equivalent of an arcane stream of dark energy at the shield. It was powerful indeed, and it took far more effort and time than he would have liked, impatience growing stronger within him.

BOOM!

Another surge against the double-doors, and the runes flared brightly. It would hold, but for how long?

He streamed more dark magic out onto the shield, the point of impact strangely muted by the intersecting opposites. Until, finally, when he felt fatigued and his mind bleary, the barrier fell. The way to the Cronal was open.

Switching to star magic, Cardin sheathed the Sword and imbued extra strength into his muscles to scoop up his father, standing upright. Reis and Elaria preceded him down the stairs, their boots clacking on the stone. Cardin looked up at Sira, his jaw clenched, and he watched as the ethereal wings stretched out around her, holding her aloft above the pedestal that the statue had once stood upon, her glowing violet eyes fixed upon the double doors.

Assuming Sira was still in there. Was he going to get his father back, only to lose her?

One problem at a time, Cardin, he reminded himself.

Gritting his teeth, Cardin followed the others down. The shallow stairs were a little awkward to descend at first, but they must have been built that way to account for dwarves, and it was easy enough to adjust his gait.

Descending through the open doors, he found the room much as he remembered it before. Half-expecting to find the bodies of Kailar, Baenil, and the older man, he was surprised to find it void of life. *Great, all that effort to protect Baenil, and he ends up in their hands after all.*

There was nothing he could do for them now, he didn't even know where they were, or if they were even still in the dwarven city.

The room holding the Cronal apparatus was a cylindrical library, the walls lined with bookshelves chronicling the creation of the Cronal or relating to the research leading to its construction. The newest books were at the foot of the stairs, and grew older the further around the room one walked.

In the center was a podium-like apparatus sticking up on a pedestal, with the top opened to the inner workings, where several 'gears,' as he had learned they were called, were placed. Four gears had once been absent, removed possibly by the original builder when he came back to guard it from further use, or removed by Zairel, the sixth god of the Order, when he had first found it. Degrin had restored the apparatus only a few months ago, possessing Cardin's father to do it.

Back then, dark magic had saved them all, and destroyed the Degrin wraith in both realms. But if Draegus hadn't reunited with his body then, and his spirit was still tethered to this place, how would Cardin reunite the two?

Coming to the bottom of the stairs and running up to the pedestal, Cardin knew the answer almost immediately, as he watched the gears turn and rotate in smooth fashion. He would have to use the Cronal.

He would have to journey to the Great Library himself, and hopefully find his father's soul.

"Great, it's still working, now what?" Reis asked, glancing nervously up at the stairs when another *BOOM!* echoed from above.

"Now you two watch my back," Cardin set his father's body down next to the apparatus, and then pushed one of Draegus's cold, pale hands against it. He looked at Reis and Elaria, and waited for his friends to look back at him. When they did, he said, "If anything happens to Sira, you're the last line of defense we'll have." Standing back up, Cardin looked inside of the device, and knew immediately what would be required. "If you can't stop them, then shove a weapon into the gears."

"Uh," Elaria stammered. "You're kidding, right? You know what that'll do."

"It should destroy it," Cardin nodded, and then swallowed down his fears. "And probably the entire dwarven city. Maybe even Archanon."

"Um," Reis started and stopped. "Uh, o-okay."

He reached over to Reis and clasped him tightly on the shoulder, looking hard into his eyes. "You need to do it," and he looked at Elaria. "They *cannot* have this, it's too great a risk for *everyone.*"

"Sure," Reis shrugged. "I mean, yeah, I always wanted to go out in a blaze of glory." He glanced nervously at Elaria, his characteristic grin reappearing for the briefest moment, but then turned to something else. Something darker. "And at least it'll take out Anila in the process."

Cardin remembered images of a vengeful Reis, seen in a prophetic vision on Stella. Was this how it started?

One problem at a time, he reminded himself, and then turned his full attention back to the Cronal.

He had closed himself to it almost automatically before, but now Cardin opened up his senses to the device before him, to the greater device beneath the ground, running deep into the planet, its magic stretching miles in any direction, beyond any power he had known before.

Not sure what would happen to him, Cardin knelt down and sat on his heels, and then he touched the apparatus with one hand, connecting the flow of star magic through him to it, while he touched his other hand to his father.

Vertigo overcame him, and a bright light consumed his vision. He felt his body tilt, and then he felt like he floated, endlessly upon a void. There was no heat or cold, no pain or pleasure, nothing but a persistent *nothingness*.

Until it became *something*. Pressure on his feet and legs. He stood. Breath in his lungs. Light beyond his eyelids.

Opening his eyes, he saw before him the great library. Endless bookshelves. He stood in an intersection of stacks, and could look in four directions…six…eight…*endless* directions. Infinite paths to choose from. Infinite knowledge.

It was down one path in particular that he found his focus. His hand automatically reached towards it and pulled him along, as if tethered to something or someone. Below him was nothing, no visible floor, just endless stacks beneath, yet he walked upon a solid-enough surface. Above, the stacks stretched forever into a white haze.

And ahead was a powerful man, sat upon the invisible floor, books piled all around him, his nose buried in one tome whose cover was as big as Cardin's chest.

Draegus Kataar.

"Father," Cardin breathed.

His father blinked, frowned, and looked up. Then his face slackened and his eyes widened. "Cardin!"

Bursting with joy, Cardin rushed forward and knelt next to his father, pinning the book between them as he embraced the man he feared he would never see alive again. "Oh gods, I'm so glad you're okay!"

Joyfully laughing, Draegus returned the embrace. "Of course I am, son! I've been here all along. I never left your side."

Shaking his head, Cardin pulled away and frowned, "But you did. I thought I'd lost you."

"No," Draegus replied, smiling plaintively. "You never lost me. There is just…so *much* here," he waved out, and set the open book aside. Suddenly he stood, no transition, no act of getting up, he simply stood, as did Cardin beside him. "I have learned much, my son, but not enough. Not nearly enough to save Halarite."

"Father, Halarite is under attack right now," Cardin spoke

earnestly. "The Darksteel Army has invaded, they are breaching Archanon's walls as we speak."

"I know," Draegus waved towards the piles of books. "I know why they are here, why they have invaded. I know they invaded earlier than planned, by a matter of years. I know that Anila Kovin betrayed us. I've read much of what has happened, but...I can't find anything beyond this moment. I knew you would come for me, but I can't find..." He looked around at the stacks, and huffed. "It must be here."

With a deep frown, Cardin asked, "You knew?"

"What?" Draegus asked distractedly. "Oh, yes, I knew. But I must find out more. The answer to how to save us all *must* be here." He moved away from Cardin, scanning the bindings of the bookshelves as he went. "It must be."

Cardin stared, dumbfounded at first, but then followed along. "Father, we're out of time. I have to get you out of here, the Darksteel Army is about to breach the chambers to the Cronal."

"I know they are," he murmured, never looking back at Cardin, his attention focused on the bindings. "Go, leave me here. I will find the answer..."

"You don't understand," Cardin shook his head impatiently, "you have to come with *now*. After I return to Halarite, I must dismantle or destroy the Cronal, though I don't know how-"

"Take off the gears," Draegus absently said. "Remove the four gears again, they will come off without protest or consequence, except to disable the larger apparatus. Take the gears away, and they will be unable to use the Cronal."

"But then you'll be trapped here!" Cardin stepped closer.

"I'll find out how to come back on my own," he murmured again.

"Your body is barely hanging on!"

"I'll find the answer to that too," Draegus muttered, pulling a tome out of the shelves and opening it, scanning the first page quickly. "It's all here, I just need time."

Looking at the endless stacks around them, Cardin shouted, "And what if it's too late by the time you find the answers? What if Halarite is no more, destroyed by the Dark Dragons?"

"There's an answer for that too," Draegus shrugged, still not looking up at Cardin. "I am certain I can find a way to journey back-"

"And bring what with you?" Cardin asked. When Draegus muttered too quiet to hear, Cardin slammed the book out of his father's grip and seized his shoulders, forcing him to look at Cardin. "Stop! Stop and think, Father! How did Degrin come back? How did he ride Pevrin's soul back to our realm?" Draegus frowned, and Cardin realized that he had never had the chance to tell his father about his visit with Zairel in this very Library. "Pevrin looked back in time to when Degrin died, and then Degrin's soul followed him back from the past to the present. You could unwittingly bring another wraith with you, or bring something *worse*! It's not worth it."

Staring incredulously at Cardin, Draegus laughed. "N-not worth it?" Waving and looking around, he said, "It's all here, Cardin, *all* of it! Every bit of knowledge in all of the Universe, we just have to find it!"

"But what if time is endless?" Cardin asked. "What if knowledge is endless? Dalin and Endri both said it, the Universe is infinite. You could spend millions of lifetimes here and *never find the answer,* all the while being stalked by who knows how many wraiths or other unfathomable monsters."

Draegus shook his head and tried to break free from Cardin's grip, but he held firmly. "No, stop! Stop this."

"But I *have to!*" Draegus glared at him, fire raging in his eyes. Cardin swore something further away suddenly cued into that – something sensed his father's rage, his frustration.

Something was coming.

"I have to find the answers, Cardin, you don't understand. I have to save everyone! I have to!" He sounded desperate, and Cardin frowned. "I have to save anyone and *everyone!* The King, I can bring him back. Grand Master Valkere. I can save every life lost, ever, I can save us all!" He broke from Cardin's grip then and stumbled along, glaring at the bookshelves.

"I can save the King," he murmured. "I can save your mother." Cardin's breath caught. "I can undo every mistake I ever made."

Every mistake. Cardin understood then.

As Captain of the Guardians, Draegus's greatest mission was to protect the throne. Protect King Beredis. When the Prince and Degrin killed King Beredis, he had failed.

And even though it was disease, not war or bandits that had killed his mother, Draegus still blamed himself for not having been at her side when it happened. He'd felt it, that much he had admitted to Cardin once – he'd felt her pass away, and was already rushing back to Daruun when a messenger found him and delivered the news that he already knew.

Draegus Kataar wanted to change history and bring back the people he had sworn to protect.

"Dad," Cardin said. Draegus's eyes slackened. "They're in the past. They're gone, but I'm *here*. Right now. And you're the King now. Your kingdom needs you, *now*." He gently touched his father's shoulder this time, and drew his eyes up to Cardin's. "Don't fail them *now*." He waited, held his breath, and then added quietly, "Don't fail *me* now."

Draegus drew up his chin, staring into Cardin's eyes, a plethora of emotions passing across his expression – anger, realization, guilt, sorrow, and then, finally, the most important one, determination.

He clasped Cardin's hand, and sighed. "You're right. You're right…"

The something he'd felt before was coming closer. He felt it like it was breathing down his neck, and Cardin shivered. "We have to go. Right now."

Draegus nodded. "Then let's go."

Cardin frowned. "How?"

Grinning, Draegus replied, "That's the easy part." He looked down. Cardin followed his gaze.

And the invisible floor suddenly wasn't there. They fell, and he felt his father's powers flex.

Stifling air. A sudden temperature change. Cardin sucked air into his lungs and sat up.

So, too, did Draegus.

Were they back?

BOOM!

"We're back," he whispered.

"Hey!" Reis called. "Draegus!" The new Captain of the Guardians raced around the Cronal and clasped the hand of the old Captain, pulling him up onto his feet while Cardin was left to help himself up.

"It sounds bad up there," Reis said, looking towards the stairs, where Elaria stood halfway up, prepared to be the first line of defense. "I think they got in the back door, and Sira, or *Raida* is fighting them off."

Cardin looked up and heard it as well – the sound of explosions from magic, clashing steel on steel, shouts of battle. *Screams* from falling soldiers.

Sira was holding off an army single-handedly, but he doubted even Raida could keep her safe if that main door was breached. It was time to go.

He rushed up to the apparatus again and looked inside. The gears turned slowly, steadily, unaware of their power to change the Universe. Holding his breath and hoping Draegus was right, he reached his hand in and pulled the first gear.

The others stopped turning, and the immense power throbbing beneath the city faded away. No other sign that something changed, no flash of light or explosion of power, just a simple fade to nothing.

Knowing how dangerous even one of those four gears were, Cardin pulled the other three out, and then stuffed them into a pouch on his belt, which they fit in neatly, being the size of gold coins, but infinitely more valuable.

"Alright," he looked at the others, "Let's get Sira and get out of here."

Leading the way, Cardin rushed back up circling stairs, past Elaria, and came out on top to find an incredible scene – Sira had turned to the back door and was moving faster than he could have imagined. She flew in the blink of an eye from one side of the room to another, beheading a brute with the edge of the blazing magic surrounding her sword, and then blinked to the other side and split one of the ghostly-like magic warriors in two, before cutting down four regular, elven-looking soldiers. Their Darksteel armor did little to blunt her magic, and he felt so much pouring out of her.

Out of Raida.

Their eyes flashed towards Cardin, then at Draegus, and a grin totally uncharacteristic for Sira stretched across her face. Her violet eyes flashed, a magic shield intersecting another blast of magic…

…but not the bolt of lightning that lanced in from the door, catching Sira's shoulder and sending her spinning through the air. Raida's ethereal encapsulation vanished, and Sira crashed hard, her sword clattering away from her.

"SIRA!" Cardin roared, magic gathering within him instantly. The Sword was in hand, and he leapt the distance to her before he unleashed a terrible wave that destroyed the ground, ceiling, and walls near where it passed, as well as the remaining Darksteel soldiers.

The building shook, the whole *city* must have shook as Cardin's burst of uncontrolled power shook the foundations and obliterated a massive section of the dwarven capital building.

And it started to collapse all around them.

He realized his mistake in an instant, the rage not cooling, but redirecting.

A dark portal opened, beckoning him. Cardin stowed the Sword back in its scabbard and stooped down, gently picking up Sira just as a chunk of marble or granite smashed down from above. Then the massive crystal above the statue's platform gave way and fell, shattering with a deafening sound, shards of crystal flying everywhere.

"Come on!" he shouted at the others. They ran as fast as they could, another chunk of debris falling, and they were saved only by a shield that Cardin had hastily erected above them.

They rushed past Cardin, and then he followed, only a step behind them when they passed through the portal.

Instantly, stifling heat and intense humidity greeted them, and the stench of the Wastelands assaulted Cardin. His portal closed behind him.

They were safe. The orc village lay ahead, untouched, and no sign of the Darksteel Army nearby.

Sira stirred in his arms, and she opened her eyes ever so briefly. They no longer glowed – it was her, not Raida. She smiled, and then her head lolled back limply. The burn on her shoulder was bad, but he felt life in her still, and healing magic flowed from the dragonsoul and into her wound.

She was going to be okay.

They all were.

Looking out at the orc village again, he wondered how long it would last.

Chapter 47

BENEATH RED SKIES

Kailar's first brush with consciousness was fleeting, a blurred image of being surrounded by troops carrying her upon something, possibly a bier. Panic tried to take hold, fearful that she would be buried or burned alive.

Then she was on the surface. Early dawn judging by the color of the sky. A dark shadow watched over her. No, not a shadow, a person. They were armored in entirely plate-steel armor, eyes glowing orange through the slits.

That moment was just as fleeting as the previous, and the next could have easily been dreams. It was only when she awoke to the sensation of utter cold and darkness in her heart that she truly felt *awake*.

Because something pierced her soul, something *latched on*. A sensation she had felt once before, and only once. A sensation that had awoken within her the power she had come to rely upon ever since.

A sensation she hoped never to feel again.

When she opened her eyes, it was to the sight of a red sky. Not red like a setting sun, intermixed with other shades, pleasing to the eye and relaxing at the end of a long day. No, this was a mute sky of pure red.

A low growl nearby seized her heart.

She knew the soul of the being who touched her heart now. Kailar would never forget it.

Lying on her back, Kailar stole a deep breath, and had to hold back a cough, fearful of drawing the attention of the nearby dark soul. It growled again, or...no, not growled. *Groaned.* As if it hurt for it to breathe.

The air was dry, dusty. She wanted to breathe more, to draw in reassuring breaths, but she couldn't. She was afraid. Kailar Adanna, wielder of dark magic, adviser to the Empress of Devor, willing to face down kings and armies and Wizards, was afraid.

But she turned her head, looked left.

Lying a hundred yards away from her amidst a black, sandy-like soil lay the massive, hulking form of a Dark Dragon. *The* Dark Dragon.

Nuuldan.

Even lying so far away, he towered over her, his front paws crossed over one another and his head rested upon them. Even in such a peaceful repose, he looked terrifying, wicked, and the light from the reddened sun did little to pierce his contours or features. He was a shadow.

Black, sandy soil. Red sky. Where the hellfire was she?

There was no red, glowing eyes visible, so she hoped the Dark Dragon slumbered, and she carefully sat up. Kailar's head spun, but she held herself together and held her last meal down. *Wait, how long ago was my last meal?*

Then she took in her surroundings. Black, sandy soil, but behind her, *around* her and the Dark Dragon was a god-like structure, a massive burgundy half-circle building with columns and towers and crenellations, architecture that was both familiar and alien all at once. The burgundy of the stone comprising the tower was in stark contrast to the black soil and even the lighter red of the sky, and made for the most surreal vision she had ever seen.

Turning around in a circle, she took in the building, and then saw that a burgundy-stone road lead away from the courtyard she had woken up in, towards...

Towards an arch. A portal apparatus.

Wait...I know this. I've seen this before.

But where?

The colors, the building, the portal, it all struck her as familiar, yet she *knew* she had never stepped foot on another world. The only time Kailar had left Halarite was in pursuit of the Sword of Dragons, when the portal vials taken from the great scorpion of the Desert of Ca'aluun sent her to a realm outside of her reality.

The Orrery. The Vrol who kept the way, speaking in puzzles, barely sane after three thousand years alone.

His maps.

The maps! So many strewn about his table, the Vrol flinging them about while looking for the map of Halarite that would lead her to the violet dragon beneath the Ilari Mountains. One map in particular had fallen at her feet. She had picked it up, looked down upon what she had thought was a small fortress, and then the Vrol had snatched it from her.

The name…he had said the name. She remembered it.

Kalas.

Only, this wasn't a small fortress. It was a *city*. And the archway, which she had thought to be a gateway for a portal or some similar passage, was taller than Nuuldan.

'Kalas will find itself in your future.' That's what the Vrol had said.

He knew then. He *knew* she would end up here.

Next to the Dark Dragon, whose eyes were open now, a single, glowing red iris gazing across the distance. Not enough distance. Not enough space.

She was alone with the Dark Dragon on a strange world.

Fear gripped her ever tighter.

Lifting his gargantuan head up, the dragon gazed upon her, and Kailar was certain she would die.

And then Nuuldan winced and groaned, his breathing accompanied by a wheeze.

He was wounded. She could not tell how or where, not in the shadows of his dark scales, but he barely seemed to live. Someone or something had hurt him, badly.

Maybe she would live. Except…could she create a portal back to Halarite?

"You've…finally awakened," Nuuldan's voice spoke in her head. He sounded weak. Forming the words sounded difficult.

Her mouth opened, and a wind blew blackened sand into it, and she coughed and spat. A gruff, weak chuckle escaped the dragon, echoed by his thought-speech. *"Yes, this place is rather arid, is it not?"*

She frowned up at him. *What the hell?* Was Nuuldan…making small-talk?

Screwing up her courage, she managed to shout up to the dragon, "What do you want?"

Narrowing his glowing eyes, the dark dragon lowered his head, not quite touching the ground, but low enough that she didn't have to strain so much to look up at him. *"I want your secrets."*

Blinking in surprise, Kailar shook her head in bewilderment. "My secrets? What secrets could I possibly have that you want?"

A wave of cold dread passed over her, the dragon's mood passed on to her through magic, and he growled. She noted that if he decided he was hungry, he wouldn't even have to chew her, he could just swallow her whole. What would… *No,* she mentally shook her head, *I don't even want to think about what that experience would be like.*

"I want…" Nuuldan paused, closing his eyes and groaning, his breathing still coming as a wheeze. *"I want to know…how you live…with dark magic."* The glow pierced the air again, a fresh gust of wind blowing black dirt around them, creating a haze around his eyes. *"How you live with it…without torment."*

Her mouth fell open ever so slightly, almost enough to let the strange-tasting, coarse sand blow in.

"I want. My. Sanity BACK!"

The Dark Dragon roared in frustration, his pain forgotten for just a moment as he bellowed his fury and frustration to the red skies above.

Kailar despaired.

She had no answers for him. And if the dark magic had driven him insane…

Oh gods. I'm in trouble.

Chapter 48

BRIEF REPRIEVE

When Sira awoke, her heart was filled with light. The light of her companion, the light of a dragonsoul.

But she awoke in a strange place. A yurt or some similar structure, made of animal skins and bone, and yet...yet it looked cozy, well-made. The smell of burning wood and some kind of scented leaf in the fire caressed her senses, and she smiled.

The orc town.

They were safe.

Raida?

"I am here, dear heart."

Warmth radiated, the sense of a smile from her passenger. The one who had kept her safe when she could no longer function. The one who kept making her smile.

The one who was becoming more and more a part of her.

Looking about the yurt, she saw Carding sitting upon a chair built from the bones of some great creature, finely-crafted. A throne for the Prince who watched over her. He tended to the fire idly, poking at the burning leaves and ashen logs with an iron poker, but then he noticed she was awake. A smile blossomed across his face, and then it faltered.

Frowning, she asked, "What's wrong?" Her voice was hoarse, but her words came out clear enough.

"Your…your eyes," he said. "They're still glowing. So…who am I talking to? Raida?"

Quirking an eyebrow up, Sira shook her head. "No, it's me. It's Sira." *Raida? What's going on?*

A flurry of emotions passed through the dragonsoul – guilt, excitement, apprehension. *"I do not know. But he is right, I can feel it."*

"But," Cardin shook his head, setting the poker down and reaching for her. She took his hand, and he drew in a shuddering breath. "It is. I sense it, but I feel Raida as well, *strongly*."

Before, when Raida had exerted control of any kind, she had seen a purple haze around her vision, but this time, there was no such vision. Instead, she simply…saw. She *saw* more than she normally could. *What's going on?*

"You are seeing with my eyes," the dragonsoul said. *"I believe you are seeing what dragons see. More than just your limited visible light. You are seeing more."*

"I…don't know what's happening," she admitted, but smiled reassuringly at Cardin. "But I'm okay. *We're* okay." He looked doubtful, so she squeezed his hand and insisted, "I promise."

He nodded, and then stood up, tugging on her arm. She stood up with him, and then he wrapped his arms around her tightly. "Gods, I thought I might lose you in that fight. When that bolt of lightning struck you…"

Smiling at his words, Sira caressed his back, realizing for the first time that he wore simple, loose clothing, a tunic and trousers. Not armor, nor anything formal. The Sword was the only thing that felt awkward, safe in its enchanted sheath.

And yet…

Raida…I can feel his connection to the Sword.

"Yes," the dragonsoul acknowledge. *"Of course you can. It is, after all, called the Sword of Dragons, and I am the soul of a dragon."*

Narrowing her eyes, she admonished, *Don't get cheeky.*

The rumbling warmth of laughter echoed from the dragon.

Pulling away from Cardin, Sira asked, "How long since…?"

"Two days," he sighed, and his smile faded to sadness. "Two days since Archanon fell."

"And…the Cronal?"

"Dismantled," he assured her. "And it looks like I, um…well, when I thought you…I mean," he sighed and shook his head. "I may or may not have accidentally destroyed the capital building when I thought you might have been killed."

Eyebrows rising skyward, she grinned. "Well, now, temper temper."

"That's what Kemila said," Cardin said hesitantly.

Hope surged within Sira. "Kemila? She's okay?"

"Aye, love, she is," the *Starfire* captain's voice greeted, and the captain opened the flap of the yurt and walked in. "And she's damn glad to see you awake, Pretty Eyes!"

Happiness exploded within, and Sira rushed over to her newest friend and crushed her in a relieved hug. "Oh thank the gods!"

"Oh, *my*," Kemila replied, and lithely slid her arms around Sira.

Suddenly blushing, Sira extracted herself awkwardly, and then saw Elaria and Dalin duck in a second later. She greeted them enthusiastically too, but not so much as she had Kemila.

Raida…

"What?? It wasn't me this time."

Sira's face burned warmer, and she glanced hesitantly at Cardin. He looked…distant.

And then Reis came in. He wasn't quite so cheerful, but he hugged Sira none-the-less. "I'm so glad you're okay," he said, his voice dreary.

She wanted to joke, or rather *Raida* wanted to joke that he didn't sound happy, but she knew what he was going through. His relationship with Anila had always been a bit of a wild ride, but her betrayal…

"I'm so sorry," she whispered to him.

Shrugging the remark off and looking away, she was heartbroken that his characteristic grin was nowhere to be found. All the women, all the flings he'd had, but for the first time in his life, Reis was heartbroken.

"We'll get her for him," Raida growled. *"No one messes with our family, right?"*

Sira tried not to grin, knowing Reis would misinterpret it, but she inwardly nodded enthusiastically. *You better believe it.*

"So, what happened?" Sira asked. "How did you find the orc town?"

"A lot of luck," Dalin remarked.

"And a dash of dashing on my part," Kemila added with a grin.

Smiling, Sira looked at everyone, and thought, *You're right, Raida.*

"I am? Oh good, I love it when I'm right!" She paused, and asked, *"What am I right about?"*

This is my family. Cardin, Dalin, Reis. Elaria and even Kemila. And...and you. You're part of this family now, too.

You're part of me. And I don't think I would want it any other way.

Chapter 49

A NEW ALLIANCE

There was tension in the orc longhouse. Cardin looked as those in attendance sat in morbid silence, now that everyone had caught one another up on all that had transpired. The orc shaman, Tana, sat at the head of the long table, the very same long table they had negotiated at only a few days ago. Behind her stood the indomitable General Arkad, towering over everyone present, his arms folded, his tailored tan clothes a stark contrast against his pale, mottled skin.

Cardin likewise stood behind his father at the other end of the table, Draegus naturally taking up such a position as King of Tal. It was such a relief for him to be back that Cardin felt as if at least one giant weight were lifted from him.

But Tal had fallen to the enemy under his watch.

Filling in the rest of the seats were Cardin's companions, the people he had come to know over the past year and a half, faces old and new alike. Sira and Reis, his two oldest friends, still by his side. Dalin, true to his word in staying with Cardin, fulfilling the vow he made in Archanon and the promise he had made to Grand Master Valkere. Kemila and Elaria, refugees from their home worlds, lost to the same army that had now conquered Edilas and Devor.

So many miles behind them.

So many more ahead.

"It isn't over yet," Cardin said. He hadn't meant to say it out loud, but as the others looked up, their despondent looks turning to curiosity, he capitalized on it. "This isn't over," he said louder, and began to walk around the table, thinking carefully about his words, choosing them ever so carefully. "We have all of us lost so much. Human," he looked at Kemila, "orc," he looked at Tana and Arkad, "and elf," he looked at Elaria. "But with all of us here, today, we have already won our first victory."

"How do you assess that?" Arkad asked, squinting with his one good eye. "We've all lost so much, and the Darksteel Army stands victorious in your most fortified city."

"But we stand *here* free," he stated. "And united against a common enemy. What's more, the Wizards Guild remains a safe haven, and with my powers, we can work together with them. It's a beginning."

As he circled around behind Tana and Arkad, his father asked, "The beginning of what?"

It was so strange to see his father as he was – color had returned to his skin, but not his hair, still pure white and wispy, a sign of the trauma his physical body had endured.

Smiling, *forcing* himself to smile against the weight of hopelessness that wanted to crawl into his heart and nestle there stubbornly, Cardin said, "An alliance."

His words were met with silence at first, but he let them sink in. He let the others consider it, and anticipated the first objection to it before it happened. "That didn't work out so well for the Four Kingdoms," Reis remarked grimly.

"Didn't it?" he asked, still pacing back towards where he had started. "What would this invasion have looked like if we had not allied ourselves? Could we have held against Klaralin long enough? Could we have defeated the necromancers?"

As he came full circle, he stopped beside his father's chair, resting a hand on Draegus's shoulder. This wasn't a new revelation for him, he had thought of this moment, this speech, days ago. Now, to a far different audience than he had thought he would face, he knew what was needed. He knew what to say.

"But the Four Kingdoms aren't enough," he continued. "And wouldn't have been even if we were still unified. Tana, you said that you once had a vision of humans and orcs standing side by side in the field of battle." She nodded. "Is it still your intention to follow through with that vision?"

Straightening up, she nodded confidently. "Absolutely."

"Good," Cardin nodded. "That's the beginning. I see here people from four different worlds all victims of the Darksteel Army, and from what I have gathered, they have invaded countless other worlds, spending time isolating each world, dividing their people to ease their invasion. Well, that stops now. It's time we stand up to them *together.*"

"And what exactly might you have in mind, handsome?" Kemila asked, one eyebrow arched in doubtful curiosity. "An orc village and my ship, as advanced as she may be and as talented as her captain is, is hardly a force to stand up against the Darksteel Army."

"No, it isn't," Cardin agreed. "As I said, it's just the beginning. On Halarite alone, we have other allies we might turn to."

Looking down at his father, he saw Draegus's face draw down into a grimace. "Cardin," he looked at his son, shaking his head slowly. "Surely you do not mean the necromancers."

"As a start," he nodded. "Assuming they haven't been captured by the Darksteel Army, they would make a powerful ally. And they'll follow my orders."

"Maybe," Reis remarked. "Assuming they aren't still mad that they've been virtually ignored since the skies burned."

"It won't be easy," Cardin nodded. "But that's just one ally." He looked to Sira then. "There's also another species living here, possibly with a powerful army all their own."

At first she frowned, the violet starlight in her eyes burning steady. Then realization softened her features. "Ligeia," Sira said. When everyone else stared dumbly at her, she shook her head, and added, "The people who live under the ocean. Ligeia was the one we met on that derelict ship between Edilas and Trinil before the necromancer invasion."

"Exactly," Cardin nodded. "Halarite is their home too. But...well," he felt his face warm a little, and said, "they probably won't negotiate with myself or you, Father," he glanced at Draegus.

"Right," Elaria piped in, "I remember they were a matriarchal society and treated males as slaves."

A strange grin stretched across Tana's face, and she glanced briefly at Arkad. He remained absolutely stoic through the entire exchange.

Kemila, on the other hand, remarked, "Kinky."

Ignoring her remark, Cardin continued, "Beyond that, maybe we can find allies elsewhere, from other worlds."

"There may be pockets of resistance still on Darea," Elaria suggested. "If we could coordinate with them, maybe we can help each other out."

Cardin nodded. "Plus you've explored a lot of other worlds," he said. "Any chance we could find allies out there?"

The elf looked to Kemila, and she in turn look back to Elaria. After a moment of staring at one another, and who knew what kind of history passed between them, it was Kemila who answered. "Aye, there may be. But it won't be easy to convince them to step up."

"Nothing about our future will be easy," Cardin stated, and addressed the table at large again. "But I won't back down. I won't let them just walk right over us. It stops here. Halarite is the line we draw, the line we hold. We have the advantage that they need something here, and we know that at least one of the Darksteel generals is willing to work with us, as much as she can."

Sira scoffed. "You don't actually trust her, do you?"

"Not really, no," Cardin shook his head. "But I'll take whatever help I can get, and we'll just take anything she says with a grain of salt."

"A wise precaution," Arkad grumbled. "Trust will be difficult to come by in the coming days."

"Particularly because the Darksteel Empire works so hard to foment distrust," Tana agreed.

"Yes, and that's why they've always won," Cardin replied, planting his hands on his hips. "So the best thing we can do to counter them is to look past the distrust." He looked at Arkad, stared straight into the General's good eye. "Learn to put our hatred and prejudices behind us, and stand together against a much more dangerous nemesis."

Arkad's jaw flexed. But he nodded. "Agreed," he murmured.

Looking to the others, Cardin asked the question without speaking it aloud.

Kemila flippantly saluted. "Aye, I'm in."

Sira looked surprised. "You are?"

Winking, Kemila replied, "What can I say, Pretty Eyes – I'm

invested."

Cardin suppressed a flash of jealousy, and looked to Elaria. She smiled warmly at him. "You know me – I'll follow you to the ends of the Universe."

He nodded, and then looked to his father. In the absence of the Allied Council, he was the next best thing. What Cardin didn't expect was the beaming look of pride Draegus gave him. He stood up and clasped Cardin on the shoulder. "Of course, my son. We will stand united."

Cardin grasped his father's hand, and then looked at the others.

"We can do this," he said, forcing the most confident smile he could muster onto his face. "I believe in us all."

EPILOGUE

Aezara had failed.

Just as she had hoped to.

Any delay, any setback would give her time, would give the *Keeper of the Sword* time. Time enough to find a way to end this all, to stop Sageth. Maybe time enough to allow her to take her rightful place upon the Vrol throne.

Time enough to ensure the death of her world was not repeated upon Halarite.

Archanon was theirs, to be sure, and reports from Devor were positive – thanks to the help of the Wizard, Sal'fe, their ambassador yet lived, and the new Devor Imperium was under their thumb. Asirin had fallen faster than any landmass the Darksteel Empire had ever invaded.

But the Cronal was buried in rubble, and if Aezara's senses were right, it was no longer functional. A team of magic-powered soldiers cleared the rubble of the dwarven capitol away, and Aezara watched carefully.

Her armor felt stifling down in the deep caverns beneath Archanon, but a part of her felt cut off without the ability to open portals. They had hoped that dismantling the shield wall around Archanon would have restored portal capabilities, but it seemed as though something else blocked such magic.

Something older and more powerful. Perhaps the Cronal itself?

A presence approached, and Aezara watched the traitor human approaching. "Anila Kovin," Aezara narrowed her eyes. "So you were the spy Sageth sent."

With a distasteful smirk, Anila came up next to Aezara, though she kept a good ten feet between them, and watched the engineers work at clearing the rubble. "Yes, well, the Emperor wanted results, and I am known for my subtlety."

Aezara narrowed her eyes, peering at the human through the slits of her armored helmet. "Indeed," she remarked coldly, and then looked upon the ruined capitol. "And yet it would seem your failure is complete."

She expected a sneer from their spy, but somehow Anila remained calm, outwardly unmoved by Aezara's remark. Perhaps she had played her role too long, and her time amongst the Covenant of Halarite had tamed her.

One of Aezara's subordinates, a ghostly-white woman whose bracers surged with energy, approached. "General," she bowed before Aezara, "we have found the Cronal apparatus."

Aezara nodded, and followed the subordinate, Anila only one step behind her. They carefully crawled across the remaining rubble, and then down into the ruined library beneath the capitol. Surprisingly, the apparatus was completely undamaged, aside from dust from crumbled stone covering every inch of it.

She and Anila stopped next to the apparatus, and Aezara, being so much taller and still standing atop rubble, had to kneel next to it to more easily peer inside of its inner workings. Dozens of tiny, interlocking gears sat unmoving within, and even though Aezara was not an engineer, she knew something was wrong, or rather very *right,* before Anila pointed out, "Four pieces are missing. The four Cronal pieces," she shook her head.

Aezara looked at the spy, and was ever-so-grateful that her armor hid her expression of relief. With her voice, she conveyed contempt. "The Emperor will not be pleased with you."

There should have been banter. Anila was nearly a millennium old, and their feud had run for as long as she had known the human.

Instead, Anila stared plainly at her. "Perhaps not."

Aezara's confidence and relief stopped cold, and an unsettling taste drew up the back of her throat. "No?" she cautiously asked the spy.

The spy's stoic façade disappeared, briefly replaced by a confident grin. "Come with me. *General.*"

There was worry in her heart, but Aezara followed, hoping she conveyed genuine interest as she followed.

The subordinate from earlier caught up and asked, "Orders, General?"

"Continue to clear the debris away," Aezara replied. "I want easier access so that we may study the Cronal in detail. Recover any books that you can from the library."

"By your command," the subordinate clasped a fist to his chest, and then turned away to attend his duties.

Anila carefully, patiently led Aezara through the dwarven city, towards what she knew to be the back entrance. The battalion had spread out through the city, and every column of glow panels was alight, casting the entire city in a bright, white light.

They came across the secret back entrance, and Anila led them up the stairs and through the tunnel, short enough that Aezara had to stoop low to follow. Long-disenchanted power remained within the walls, remnants of a powerful spell left behind at some point, now dispelled. But what concerned Aezara more were the remnants of spider-like webs.

The kiklar.

"You should know," Anila remarked upon seeing Aezara's focus on the webs, "the device the dwarves used to protect their city from the kiklar was atop the capitol building." Aezara felt her eyebrows rise. The kiklar were not to be taken lightly, even the lesser-intelligent forms that lived upon Halarite. "They will no doubt return to the city."

"Then we will need additional troops to hold them at bay," she replied.

"Indeed," Anila nodded. Good, she didn't sound suspicious of Aezara's motives. The more troops she could commit to guarding the cities of Halarite, the less there would be to search for the Conduit, and they still had an entire world to search.

They traversed an endless series of tunnels, following a line of everlasting torches as they went, while ignoring countless side tunnels. Aezara felt that they ascended, closer towards the surface. Growing impatient, she asked, "Is there a point to all of this? Or do you mean to assassinate me in quiet?"

Still completely nonplussed outwardly, Anila replied, "The thought had crossed my mind, but I would never dare incur the wrath of the Emperor that way."

Aezara narrowed her eyes, not sure if she should be insulted or not. "Then why are you wasting my time in this endless maze of tunnels?"

"Because we still cannot create portals here," Anila explained plaintively. "Otherwise we would already be at our destination. Settle your impatience, dear *General*. Our destination lies just ahead."

Finally, they came to a fork in the tunnel, built at such an extreme angle, and the rockface so repetitive and appearing so alike that Aezara knew it was meant to be a hidden branch tunnel. Anila led her down the left branch, which curved sharply to help hide it. And then they came out to a much taller room, and for the first time in nearly an hour, Aezara was able to stand up straight again.

Several everlasting torches illuminated the room, and on either side of them were two halves of a large boulder, flattened unnaturally by tools that no human of Halarite could have ever possessed. On one wall was inscribed text, in a language that Aezara recognized from ages long ago, but could not read.

On the other wall was a map of Halarite. She recognized the four great landmasses, having studied maps of the world for months before the invasion. It was a complete map, though some of the features were not quite accurate to today. Aezara drew closer and noticed that the lands where Sharenth, the now-lost capitol of Saran in the south, looked nothing like they did now. The human affect upon that area had been distinct, even before the meteorites had fallen and Nuuldan had wiped the city from the face of the world. Additionally, the Crystalline Forest and Peaks of Devor were absent, and in its place was a depiction of what appeared to be a fertile forest.

But it was the landmass now known as Trinil in which Aezara's gaze wandered, and then her heart seized in her chest.

Trinil was actually four large landmasses near one another, with wide channels of water separating them, though they were still close enough that massive land-bridges had been artificially grown between them, a result of powerful, patient magic, and done long enough ago that this map portrayed them.

But in the southeastern landmass of Trinil was an all-too-familiar shape – a great pyramid, with slits carved into the top opening the pyramid within to the sky above.

A Conduit.

"I believe this is what we were searching for?"

Swallowing hard, and hoping that she kept her voice neutral, Aezara nodded and said, "Indeed it is." She studied the map further, and realized that the location depicted was non-specific. As large as Trinil was, and if that part of Trinil was covered in the jungle depicted upon the map… "It will still take us time to locate this."

"I agree," Anila said. "But perhaps the Emperor will not be so quick to punish me. I have now brought us closer to finding our solution."

"Yes," Aezara said quietly, and then turned to Anila. Did anyone else know about this? What if Aezara were to just impale the young spy now, leave her body here to rot? If she doused the everlasting torches in here, it was unlikely that anyone would find the room again for a long, long time. Especially if she diverted attention away from it.

Aezara was tempted, oh so *very* tempted. It would incur incredible pain, she knew that – the armor was already making her uncomfortable, the enchantments sensing her desire to disobey. She could feign ignorance then, at the risk of even more pain from the armor.

It would be too much. The risks were too great.

So she decided to follow a different course. "You are familiar with Trinil?"

"Only somewhat, yes," Anila nodded.

"Then take a detachment and search that jungle," Aezara pointed to the map. "Find the Conduit, and report back to me."

Anila started at that command. "Excuse me, General? A single detachment…to search all of *that?*"

Few in the Darksteel Army knew of how well their invasion had gone on Halarite, so Aezara bet on Anila's ignorance and said, "Yes. We still have much work to do here, and on Devor and Asirin. I cannot spare much of our military at this time, but I will send reinforcements whenever the situation allows."

Eyes narrowing suspiciously, Anila said, "That is not what I meant. You wish for me to report the Conduit's location to you, not our Emperor?"

Pausing only a moment to collect her thoughts, Aezara asked, "Is there a problem with that?"

"Yes," she stated bluntly. "You wish to take the credit when I will be the one performing the work."

Relief washed through Aezara. *If that is her concern, then...*

"I swear to you now, if – *when* you find the Conduit, we will present our findings to the Emperor together, and I will credit you. But I am the commander of this invasion, and you will follow the chain of command. Do I make myself clear?"

Eyebrows rising up in surprise, Anila hesitated. Almost long enough that Aezara would have been within her rights to severely punish Anila for insubordination, which would have made this all a *lot* easier.

But the human traitor nodded and assented. "By your command. *General.*"

"Good. Carry on."

Still with the glint of suspicion in her eyes, Anila turned and left Aezara to the map room. She looked upon the map then, and sighed. This wasn't what she wanted. She had hoped it would take years to find the Conduit. Now she expected only months. Maybe less.

There was never enough time.

But she wouldn't give up. She wouldn't watch Halarite's sun die, its world crumble, life turned to ash. She wouldn't let the house of Zelnir continue.

She would find a way.

The Vrol empire would return to her family, and the Darksteel Army would finally end its endless war against the Universe.

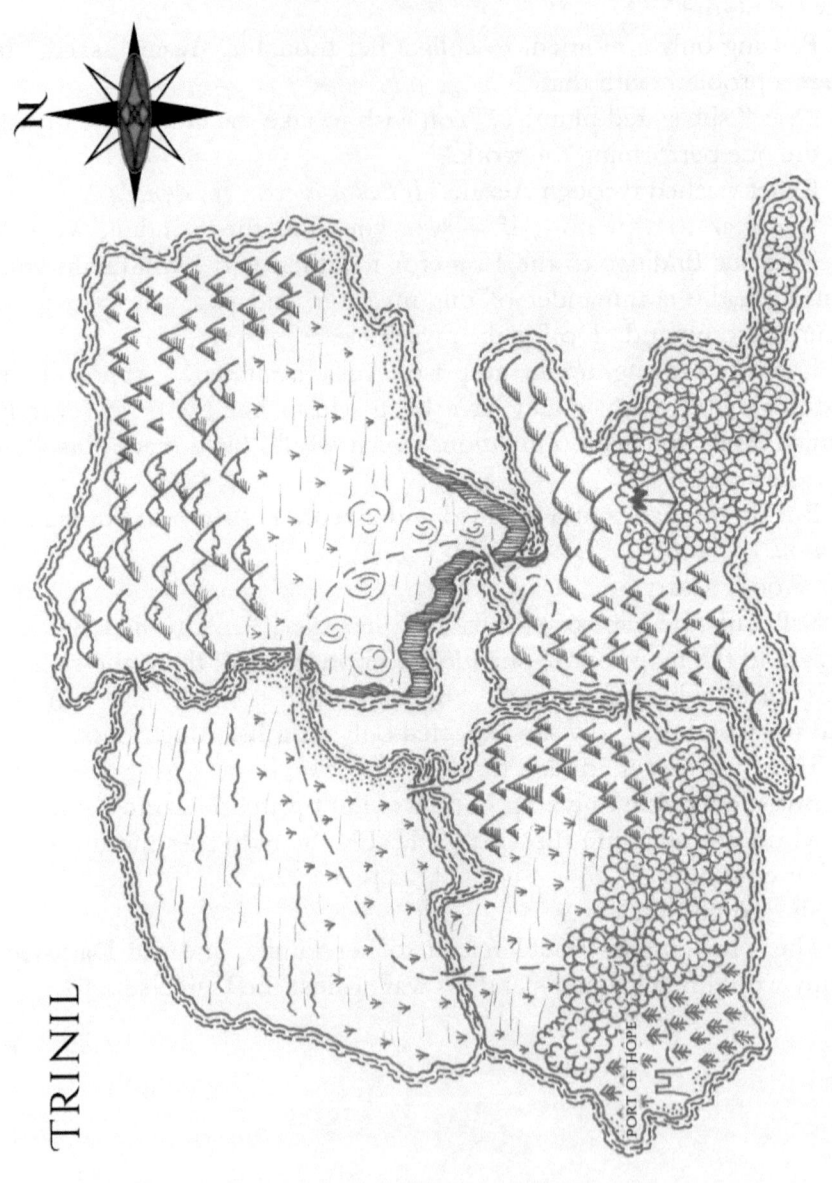

TRINIL

N

PORT OF HOPE

DID YOU LIKE THIS BOOK?

Reader reviews play an important role in a book's success by helping other readers discover stories they might enjoy. Please consider taking a moment to leave a review for *Advent Darkness* on Amazon! You'll be making this author's day :D

ABOUT THE AUTHOR

Jon Wasik has been telling stories since he was a little boy, usually with a cookie and milk at his Great Grandma's kitchen table. It wasn't until 5th grade that he finally put pen to paper, and from that moment on, writing has been his greatest passion.

When he isn't writing, Jon likes to read, play video games, and watch insanely geeky movies with his wife. His Gollum voice impressions are eerie, he quotes Doctor Who like others quote the bible, and he can leap terabytes of data in a single bound!

You can find out more about him by visiting his blog, http://kataar.wordpress.com/

Want to keep up on the latest news about Jon's books? Subscribe to his mailing list! Just go to the Sword of Dragons website and click "Join Mailing List" at the top!

http://www.theswordofdragons.com/
https://jonwasik.com

www.ingramcontent.com/pod-product-compliance
Lightning Source LLC
Chambersburg PA
CBHW050846210726
48290CB00004B/1100